About the author

With ten novels to her name, Maria Galina is one of the most interesting authors among those who made their names in the turbulent 1990s. She is the leading exponent of "hyper-fiction," a popular new genre that blends fantasy and reality. She is also a prize-winning poet, a thoughtful critic, and a translator of English and American science fiction. After graduating from Odessa University in marine biology, Galina took part in several sea expeditions before taking up writing professionally in 1995. She has won numerous prizes for her prose, poetry and critical essays. She has been nominated for the Russian Booker and short-listed for the Russian Critics Academy Award. *Iramifications* was awarded the International Portal Prize.

GLAS NEW RUSSIAN WRITING

contemporary Russian literature

in English translation

VOLUME 43

Maria Galina

iramifications

a novel

with an afterword by the author

Translated by
Amanda Love Darragh

Edited by Natasha Perova and Joanne Turnbull
Camera-ready copy by Tatiana Shaposhnikova
Cover picture by Maria Galina

GLAS PUBLISHERS
tel./fax: +7(495)441-9157
perova@glas.msk.su
www.russianpress.com/glas

DISTRIBUTION

in North America
NORTHWESTERN UNIVERSITY PRESS
Chicago Distribution Center
tel: 1-800-621-2736 or (773) 702-7000
fax: 1-800-621-8476 or (773) 702-7212
pubnet@202-5280
www.nupress.northwestern.edu

in the UK
INPRESS LIMITED
tel: 020 8832 7464; fax: 020 8832 7465
mail1@inpressbooks.co.uk
www.inpressbooks.co.uk

Within Russia
JUPITER-IMPEX
www.jupiters.ru
shop@jupiters.ru

**The translator gratefully acknowledges
the support of Arts Council England**

ISBN 978-5-7172-0082-0

"Remember, upon the conduct of each depends the fate of all."
Alexander the Great

Pshh-shh whispered the wave.

Givi screwed up his toes, carefully crossing the fragments of broken shells on his tender feet, which were generally used to a little more protection. The shells were sharp, and the water was cold.

Givi had been in a bad mood all day. The damp sand was annoying him, the sea was annoying him, but most of all he – Givi Mesopotamishvili – was annoying himself. Viewed from above, his legs looked rather short and bowed – a commonly observed optical effect already identified, in relation to other things, by Hemingway. But Givi wasn't a big fan of Hemingway and was unaware of the optical effect, and therefore his legs were a constant source of disappointment to him. He only had to look down at himself to feel his spirits sink.

And how the hell had he managed to end up on this nudist beach anyway?

Well, for a start, he had scrambled down the not inconsiderable precipice onto this specific sliver of beach because he had suddenly felt the urge to go for a swim but he didn't have his swimming trunks with him and didn't want to be seen in his baggy underwear. Plus he had hoped to feast his eyes upon a few naked, tanned blondes. But there wasn't a single blonde around – maybe that breed is particularly sensitive to the cold or something. To be honest, there weren't any women at all, apart from an aging brunette with a moustache, picturesquely draped in her towel. There were a couple of naked individuals of the male variety, their dark bodies sprawled like starfish on the sand, playing cards. Another wave hissed, like an angry cat. It obviously had something against Givi.

Givi screwed up his toes again and stepped back.

Everyone seemed to be looking at him.

The wave caught up with him and bit him on the heel. It was wet. And cold.

Givi rubbed the sole of one foot on the opposite ankle and nonchalantly tried to give the impression that he hadn't wanted to go for a swim anyway, that he had just come down to admire the view. A slight haze shimmered lazily over the sea, and in the distance a white ferry hovered, somewhere between heaven and earth. A stripe of thick violet fog drifted behind it, gradually dissolving into its surroundings.

Givi sighed. He wished he were on the deck of that ferry. He would give anything to be reclining on one of its sun-loungers. Preferably in trousers, rather than shorts, because he didn't look that great in shorts. And the trousers would have to be white, and loose-fitting... And he would be sipping a cold beer. Givi spent some time torn between the idea of a heavy glass tankard, frosted with ice, and a cocktail glass with a straw, but eventually decided in favour of the former. And there would be a couple of tanned blondes sitting next to him. Well, one, at least, who would look just like Alka Kucherenko, whom Givi had attempted to seduce at a drunken party back home in St. Petersburg. Her feet were small and she had skinny ankles, everything else was pretty much perfect. He liked her, though the feeling was unfortunately not mutual.

"There he is!" a woman's voice rang out.

Givi didn't turn round. He wasn't from the area and didn't know anyone.

You scoundrel!" the voice said tenderly. "Oh, you dirty, n scoundrel!"

The voice, previously softened by the distance, now sounded very close indeed. Right in his ear, in fact.

"I've been looking for him all along the beach, and here he is, hanging out with the gay boys," the voice continued reproachfully. "Get dressed, you wastrel!"

Givi hunched his shoulders up around his ears. He was too embarrassed to turn around, because...well, he was just too embarrassed.

"Misha's ready to go... Come on, get a move on! Misha! Shenderovich! I found him! A poor excuse for a man if ever there was one...."

Givi felt his ears turning red. He turned round. The woman looked like Alka Kucherenko, although she was fully clothed. In a very low-cut top and an ankle-length skirt. Her ankles were a bit skinny, but everything else was pretty much perfect. Givi tried to work out how she could have got from the ship to the shore so quickly, but then gave up. He waved, or would have done, were both his hands not occupied in holding the new towel that he had instinctively wrapped around his scrawny legs. It was emblazoned with the garish slogan 'I ♥ Odessa.' Givi had bought it on the way to the beach.

"Shit!" said Not-Alka.

"Sorry!" said Givi.

Not-Alka looked at him, then at the broad-shouldered hunk in shorts striding handsomely down the path.

"Misha! Retreat!" cried Not-Alka. "Slow down! You'll break your neck rushing like that, and all for nothing... It's not him!"

But the hunk had already stepped onto the sand and was now approaching Givi, shaking his head reproachfully.

Great, he doesn't like me either, thought Givi.

"You're not Stavrakis," the broad-shouldered hunk said sulkily.

"No," Givi humbly agreed.

"So where is he, then?" asked the hunk, still sulky. He was looking at Givi as if Givi had literally just buried Stavrakis in the sand with his own hands.

"I have no idea," Givi answered truthfully.

"I knew that Yannis would be trouble," said Not-Alka sternly. "It was obvious right from the start!"

Givi, who had just started hunching his shoulders up around his ears, carefully began to emerge again as he realized it was nothing to do with him after all.

"He's lying low," Not-Alka went on, in her gentle, pearly voice. "With that red-headed snake of a woman that you picked up in The Pearl. And where are we supposed to start looking for him now?"

"You've got his passport, haven't you?" the hunk inquired phlegmatically. "Yes, you have! Well, he's not going to get very far without his passport, now is he…"

"You don't think?" asked Not-Alka in surprise. "What's stopping him? What does he need a passport for right now? He's not planning on taking her to the Registry Office, I assume. You shouldn't have had so much to drink, then we wouldn't be in this mess!"

"And who was it that dragged us into The Pearl in the first place? You did. And who invited that silly cow to join us? You did."

"But that was yesterday!"

"Well he obviously felt she would do for today as well," Shenderovich concluded gloomily. Then he turned to Givi, who was hopping about on one leg trying to get his trousers back on. "Sorry, my friend. We thought you were somebody else. You really are the spitting image of Yannis, you know…."

"I see," said Givi, nodding politely, then losing his balance and missing his trouser leg. "This Yannakis chap has disappeared, then…"

"Stavrakis," Shenderovich corrected him.

He took two steps backwards, his hands on his hips and his head on one side, and looked at Givi intently, as if he were about to paint his portrait. Givi started to feel a bit uncomfortable.

"Anyway," Shenderovich suddenly concluded, "what the hell. Let's go, my friend. Do you fancy a beer?"

"Misha!" Not-Alka sounded worried. "Don't be silly! The ferry…"

"Ah!" Shenderovich brushed aside her objections. "We've jumped ship!"

He turned round and headed off in the direction of a little beer stall, despondently finding himself a place to sit in the long grass. Givi watched him with envy – Shenderovich's legs were long, muscular and tanned.

"Well, I'm coming too!" Not-Alka shouted after him.

"What a disaster!" Shenderovich opened a bottle with a flick of his thumb and started to drink greedily from it, spilling beer all over his muscular chest. "A total disaster! We'll never get our money back on those tickets. And they were return tickets too! Everything's ruined… everything! I ask you, is this any way to do business?"

"No!" Givi blurted. "That's no way to do business."

He was very eager to please Shenderovich.

"God knows what it is," agreed Shenderovich. He neatly launched his empty bottle into the long grass and sighed. "He's bad news, that Yannis. We should never have got involved with him. But no, he forced himself upon us… Making out he was such a big shot… I'm this, I'm that… I know all the right people, I can sort customs out for you… Contacts in Istanbul…"

"Yeah, that's no good… A man should keep his word…" Givi felt guilty, as though he were somehow directly responsible for the misdemeanours of the mysterious Yannis. "I would never have…" He wanted to be absolutely indispensable to someone. He wanted Shenderovich to come running down steep precipices looking for him and to be delighted when he found him. But then he wouldn't have had to go running around looking for him, because he – Givi – was someone you could rely on… He looked shyly at Shenderovich, as if he were awaiting praise for such exemplary behaviour. But Shenderovich was gloomy and thoughtful.

"You – what's your name?"

"Givi," said Givi.

"Yes… Maybe you're more dependable, but you're not the one we need. We need Stavrakis…"

"And you can't do without him?" Givi asked timidly. "At all?"

"No, not at all…" sighed Shenderovich. "But, on the other hand…"

He narrowed his eyes and looked at Givi very carefully, and then his mood suddenly lightened.

"Hey, my friend… How about another beer?"

The world was swaying from side to side. Givi groaned and half-opened his eyes. And closed them again. The world continued to sway. The bed he was lying on was strangely hard and narrow. Givi tried to move his toes but couldn't. It took him a while to figure out that it was because he still had his shoes on. He tried to move his whole body and fell onto the floor. The floor was cold and the ceiling, for some reason, hung very low. The window was round, and he could see waves through the glass. Givi cried out.

"Hey, what's all that noise for?" reproached a plump woman, raising herself up on her elbow in the opposite bunk. Her cheek was all crumpled, and her magnificent shoulder bore marks where her bra strap had cut into it, alongside the impressions left by her pillow. "Why are you shouting, my heartache?"

"I'm not your heartache," muttered Givi through clenched teeth.

"Don't worry about him, he's always like that," explained

Shenderovich. He leaned over from the top bunk and patted Givi on the shoulder with his powerful hand and an open, friendly smile. "He's terrible when he's got a hangover, like a wild animal. And why? Can't take his drink. I've lost count of the number of times I've said to him 'Yannis, don't mix vodka and beer,' but he ignores me and carries on…"

"Yannis?" the woman seemed surprised. Nothing surprised Givi any more.

"He's Greek," said Shenderovich with pride, as if having a Greek friend were a great achievement. "They're not used to our vodka. They drink wine, mainly. Red wine, and usually diluted too. But we went out last night, had a little celebration before our trip, and he's paying the price today."

"Yes, my love," agreed the woman, "It's not like your Rtsikateli, or whatever it is you lot drink over there in Greece."

"No, he's from over here," corrected Shenderovich, "He's a Russian Greek. Born here. Not many of them left now." He examined Givi again benevolently, admiring his ethnographical rarity. "They've all left," he sighed.

"Why, what was their problem?" the woman asked indignantly.

"It was the call of their ancestors. The historical mother-land. They all went: the Panaiotis family went, the Satyros family went… They all went. Only the Stavrakis lot hung on. He's got a family here, he's put down roots."

Jesus, thought Givi, what family is he talking about? Where did he get that from?

"I'm not Stavrakis," he cried out and started shaking his head, but the bunk started to revolve around him and he thought better of it.

"Sorry, of course, I meant Yannis," Shenderovich mollified him. "Yannis Stavrakis."

Givi looked around him in horror. He saw only sympathetic faces looking back at him – the gloomy, good-looking face of Shenderovich and the homely, chubby face of the woman. I've obviously gone mad, thought Givi. Or maybe I'm dreaming? I'm just going to close my eyes now...

He closed his eyes. The bunk started revolving again, whereas previously it had just been rocking smoothly. As if that hadn't been enough!

The ferry company, he decided, seizing upon a vague thought – he must be in the company hotel. He always had strange dreams the first night in a new place... If only it could be something a little more erotic, but no, he was stuck with this nonsense dream... Givi always liked it on the rare occasions when he dreamed something a bit erotic. He tried to swap the dream for a new one, a better one, more erotic, and without the fat woman – he didn't like her much. But all he could see was coloured spots... He felt sick again.

He opened his eyes.

Shenderovich and the woman were both looking at him.

"I'm not Yannis," he repeated mournfully.

"You're Yannis, Yannis," agreed Shenderovich, for some reason kicking him on the ankle with the tip of his boot. It hurt, the bastard.

"I'm not Yannis!" yelled Givi, grabbing his ankle. "I'm Givi!"

"Ahhh," drawled Shenderovich. "Here we go again..."

The woman gathered herself together and moved away slightly.

"He's always like this when he drinks vodka," explained Shenderovich. "You see, this is what happened... He had a good friend called Givi. But he – Givi I mean – drowned last year, right in front of his – Yannis' – eyes... And ever since then Yannis has been... His conscience bothers him, you know, because he didn't save his best buddy. He dived and dived till he was literally blue in the face..."

"Who, Givi?" the woman asked in a whisper.

"No, they never found Givi. He was a goner. But the rescue divers pulled my Yannis out. Barely alive, he was... And since then, when he drinks, you know... He calls for his friend Givi. Really howls his name – it's quite scary. And sometimes he thinks," Shenderovich also lowered his voice at this point to an intimate whisper, "that he, Yannis, was the one that drowned. And that Givi's still alive, drinking vodka somewhere... And he calls his name, really howls it, it's quite disturbing: 'I'm Givi, I'm Givi!'"

The woman moved again, this time quite radically.

"My brother-in-law's like that," she said sadly. "He drank too much, the fool... Now he's locked up in a loony bin."

Givi rubbed his eyes with his fist.

"Who am I?"

"You're Yannis," Shenderovich gave him a friendly pat on the shoulder. "Yannis Stavrakis."

Givi stood up. His shoes were hurting. They probably weren't too keen on having been left on all night and were now expressing their indignation in the only way they knew. Givi winced and took them off.

"Stavrakis?" he straightened up with dignity, at least as far as the snug cabin would allow. "I'm not sure about that."

There was another bunk above his, which was empty.

"You don't have to be sure about it," said Shenderovich soothingly. "You just need to remember it. Ya-nnis Stav-rak-is... Learn it off by heart."

The friendly hand patting Givi on the shoulder clenched into a powerful hairy fist, which hovered under Givi's nose. "And don't forget it."

And then to the woman: "Really madam, there's no need to worry. He's not the violent sort... In any case, I can handle him..."

The woman stood up hastily with a sigh, which caused her ample bosom to heave enormously (Givi bashfully averted his eyes), and made for the exit.

"I'm going," she said, to no one in particular. "You lot are all..."

Whereupon she exited sideways through the door, which

was really a door in name only because it slid along grooved runners rather than opening like a door is supposed to.

Shenderovich thoughtfully watched her go.

"Well, well!" Shenderovich sounded strangely satisfied. He looked around the empty cabin pensively and then also let out a sigh.

Givi looked at him morosely.

"What am I doing on this boat?" he asked coldly.

"Sailing," answered Shenderovich, stating the obvious.

"Where to?" Givi was starting to panic.

"Turkey."

"Why Turkey? What do you mean, Turkey?"

"We're shuttle traders, you and me," Shenderovich explained. "A couple of days on the boat, twenty-four hours in Istanbul, and a couple of days back. No big deal. It's practically a pleasure trip. Oh, don't look so worried – honestly, look at your face! Come on, let's go and get some breakfast… We'll have a drop of mineral water, sit on deck, watch the girls. Doesn't that sound good?"

"Can we sit on the sun-lougers?" Givi perked up.

"Where else?"

Givi continued looking at him with a measure of distrust.

"Listen," he eventually asked in a whisper, "I'm really Stavrakis, then, am I?"

Shenderovich shrugged.

"Just for a little while," he said. "Until we get through customs back in Odessa. We get the goods through, and you're Givi again. Givi… what's your surname?"

"Mesopotamishvili," said Givi, self-consciously.

"Yes. You'll be Givi Mespopotami…shvili… Honestly, it's only for a couple of days… That bastard Stavrakis has gone AWOL, disappeared off the face of the earth, and the ferry was already sounding its horn… No chance of a refund on the tickets – I would have lost at least fifty percent, probably more like seventy percent. There's the interest on the credit too. And they'll fleece me for excess baggage, the bastards, more than the cost of the goods. They've got their quotas to fill… But with three of us, we'll be able to spread the load… How much would Alka and I have managed to bring back, just the two of us? Fifteen hundred dollars' worth of goods. But with you we'll manage five thousand easily. I mean, with Stavrakis…"

He looked despondently at his impressive fists.

"I tell you, that Yannis is a real bastard. How could he have let us down like that? If you hadn't turned up, I don't know what we'd have done… Good job I took his passport when he was prancing about like a drunken fool in the restaurant fountain, and Alka was looking after the tickets."

"What?" Givi was horrified. "You mean I'm traveling on somebody else's passport?!"

"Ah, they don't really look at them anyway," Shenderovich reassured him. "And in any case, you're the spitting image of that bastard Yannis."

He leaned towards Givi.

"Look, what's the problem? You're getting a free trip to Turkey. Twenty-four hours in Istanbul with a fake identity… you could get up to anything! Get yourself a couple of girls, drink yourself stupid – I'll pay for it all! Within reason, of course. Or not – I'll give you the cash, you can do what you want with it! I'll give you a hundred dollars – in Turkey you could spend a week cavorting in a sultan's harem for that… Plus ten percent of whatever we make."

"Ten?"

"OK, OK," Shenderovich quickly agreed, "fifteen…"

"Plus traveling expenses…"

"Plus traveling expenses," said Shenderovich with an expansive gesture. "No problem."

Givi sighed. He wanted to wring Shenderovich's powerful neck. If only he (Shenderovich) had gone about it in a gentlemanly fashion and said something along the lines of "Givi, my friend, I desperately need your help, I'll be eternally grateful…" then there's no way he could have refused. But instead they got him drunk and bundled him onto the ferry like a sack of potatoes. It wasn't so much the element of force or even the sheer randomness of it, more the deception. You should never cheat a friend, a drinking buddy, someone you've just thrown your arms around and to whom you've just declared "You're a good bloke, Givi my brother!" It was all coming back to Givi now. He couldn't remember it before, but now he could. It wasn't right… That's not how men should behave. Not how friends should behave, frankly.

Givi wanted to say all this to Shenderovich, to just go up to him and tell him what he, Givi, thought of him, Shenderovich. But just then the cabin door slid open and Not-Alka appeared in the doorway, all fresh and creamy-pink, with her fair hair pinned up in a plastic butterfly clip.

"Boys!" she said, with a flash of her white teeth and an affectionate nod at Givi. "Boys, come on! Let's eat."

"Let's go, Yannis my friend!" Shenderovich laid his heavy hand on Givi's shoulder. "Let's go and grab some food… It'll make you feel better. Just put something on your feet."

"Eh?" asked Givi, absentmindedly.

"Put your shoes on, will you… You look like a peasant."

"Uh-huh…" said Givi.

"Let me pour you some mineral water!" fussed Shenderovich.

Givi nodded distractedly.

It was nice in the restaurant… peaceful… A team of young waitresses were bustling about the room, and the pearly sea light was flowing through the panoramic windows. Seagulls were wheeling above the waves and making a racket in insolent expectation of food scraps…

He was sitting next to Not-Alka, who was getting stuck into her salad. His neighbour on the other side turned out to be that same woman, their cabin-mate. She kept surreptitiously glancing at Givi and was clearly trying to move her chair as far away as possible, at least as far as the round table would allow. Not-Alka on the other hand was sitting right up close to him, and a couple of times her thigh brushed against his. Compensation, thought Givi cynically: he wasn't stupid. He wasn't usually much of a cynic either. But they had treated him with such abominable cynicism, Shenderovich and that Not-Alka... If they could behave like that, why shouldn't he?

"Hey," he turned to Not-Alka, who looked brazenly back at him. "What's your name?"

"You don't remember us drinking toasts together last night?" she kept her clear, open gaze fixed on him.

"I don't remember," said Givi brusquely.

"Alla," Not-Alka introduced herself. "But you can call me Alka."

"Kucherenko?" Givi repeated, horrified, as once again the world started to lose all sense of reality.

"Kucherenko? No, Kolesnichenko."

"Well," Givi conceded magnanimously, "that's fine, then."

"Let me introduce you!" Shenderovich stretched out his long arms, embracing Alka and grabbing Givi at the same time, and pressed them close to one another. "This, Yannis my friend, is our translator and guide... She's writing her dissertation, would you believe it! On Trickology..."

"Turkology," Alka corrected him, shamelessly snuggling up to both Givi and Shenderovich at the same time. "But actually, to be honest, I specialize in comparative linguistics. Turkology's just a hobby."

"What are you shuttle trading for, then?" Givi asked reproachfully.

"Well, Misha asked me!"

"Come on, eat, Yannis my friend!" Shenderovich resumed his solicitousness. "Would you like a beer?"

"God, no!"

"Well, I'm having one! Excuse me, miss..."

"Is he feeling better?" the plump woman was looking from

Shenderovich to Givi and back again with a mixture of hope and fear.

"Absolutely!" said Shenderovich, piling multicoloured salad onto his plate. "I told you, he's fine. He's not great when he mixes vodka with beer, but otherwise he's absolutely fine…"

"No one's great when they mix vodka and beer," the woman observed mournfully. "It shouldn't be allowed. Take my brother-in-law…He drank himself crazy…"

"That's men for you," Alka concluded. She sounded as though she were talking about a species of unruly but magnificent wild animals. Givi felt himself swell with pride.

"Indeed," agreed the plump woman, somewhat less enthusiastically.

"You're not going to be carrying on again tonight are you, eh, sweetheart?" she threw Givi a look of silent supplication.

"No," Givi muttered. He liked the look of the salad, but his body clearly wasn't going to allow him to ingest anything more substantial than mineral water just yet. What a bastard this Shenderovich was! He had drunk the same amount the day before, yet he was shoveling food in like there was no tomorrow…

"So, you're heading to Turkey, then?" The plump woman was obviously bored and in the mood for a chat.

"It would appear so," Shenderovich answered vaguely, helping himself to even more salad.

"Me too," the woman informed them.

"You mean," Givi panicked, "the ferry's going on somewhere else?"

"No," Shenderovich placated him. "Don't worry! Only as far as Istanbul."

"Well, so they say," the woman sounded rather less sure. "But who knows? Ah, it's nothing to worry about, sweetheart. Just look at me: I'm scared too, but I'm still here!"

"What are you carrying?" asked Shenderovich, out of professional interest.

"I've got a nylon robe, a cotton dress... They reckon it gets pretty hot over there..."

"No..." Shenderovich frowned at the woman's stupidity. "I mean, what goods are you taking back?"

"I won't be taking anything back, my dear. I'm staying in Turkey. I'm going to be a nanny... A babysetter..."

"Babysitter, you mean."

"Whatever, sweetheart."

"Why do you need to go to Turkey to do that?" Shenderovich was surprised. "There are hundreds of New Russians looking for nannies. I had a friend who spent ages looking for one, three hundred dollars a month he was offering, too..."

"I had to leave home," the woman said sadly. "There was no way I could stay."

Givi tensed up. She seemed completely harmless, but who knew what her story was? Maybe the mafia were after her? Or the police? Or both? Best not to get any more involved – she could even be a seasoned drug smuggler, hiding it in her stockings, or wherever women hide smuggled drugs.

"What's the matter with you?" asked Shenderovich lazily.

How come nothing ever fazes him, Givi wondered. He wished that nothing fazed him either, but he just wasn't made that way.

"What's your name?"

"Mikhail Abramovich."

"Well, listen, Abramovich... And you too, sweetheart – Yannis, or whatever your name is. Back home... I'm better off anywhere but home... And the more water there is between us the better. They can't get you over the water, apparently..."

"Who can't?" Shenderovich was interested all of a sudden.

"Whoever wants to," replied the woman darkly. "They can't get you..."

She's obviously paranoid, Givi thought bitterly. And she had the cheek to move her chair away from me!

"I bet you think I'm crazy," the woman correctly observed. "Well, I'm not. Let me tell you what happened to me and then you'll say, she was right, that Varvara Timofeevna, oh, how right she was! That's me, by the way. So, this is what happened…"

What Happened to Varvara Timofeevna, or
The Reason for Varvara Timofeevna's Trip to Turkey

My Dad died early, God rest his soul, and my Mum was a teacher. She taught Russian. She was a good mother, if a little strict. Even the other teachers were a bit afraid of her. And she certainly ruled us with a firm hand – she had to be both Mum and Dad to us, you see. My mission in life, she said, is to raise you, to teach you, to get each of you a career. And to be fair, she did a good job with us. She got Nina, the eldest, onto a business course. She got Vanya, the middle one, studying construction. And she got me, the youngest, training to be an accountant. So, we studied, then we went our separate ways… Vanya stayed in Salekhard after his national service, building roads. He met Lilya there. Mum wasn't too happy about that, I can tell you! She didn't like Lilya, not one little bit. She didn't even invite them back for the summer. You've made your choice, now get on with it, sort of thing. But she loved Nina, and Nina's husband… And Mum loved her because Nina was the best looking of all of us. She had a beautiful voice, too… She used to sing, and Mum would sit propping her chin up with her hand, listening, and just gazing at Nina. She really did love her. She used to say, Vanya can stand on his own two feet, but my daughter will always be a part of me… And Nina loved her too. She used to write her letters and send parcels… And then one day, a letter arrived some time around Easter. Nina, it said, I've taken to my bed. She wrote this to Nina, I mean, not to me. Come quickly, my darling daughter, she wrote, I'm in a bad way, I no longer have the use of my legs… come and brighten up my dying days, because you're the only light in my life… Nina, bless her, immediately took unpaid leave, stocked up on imported medicines – for leg ailments, headaches, the works – and went. She called me, from the post office in Sychavka. Mum's bad, she said, but don't worry just yet, I'll sit with her for a bit and if she gets worse, I'll send a telegram to let you know... Well, I had enough on my plate at the time with the financial year end, no time to breathe, so I said fine Ninochka, just keep me informed, if anything happens, make sure you let me know... It's fine for now, she said.... So anyway, I carried on tallying my credits and debits, and Nina called me from Sychavka with weekly progress reports, to let me know what was happening... Mum's feeling a bit better now, she said, the foreign medicines seem to have worked... She's up and about a bit and is itching to get out in the garden with her spade, there's no stopping her! Nina said to her, don't worry about it Mum, I'll do it, you should stay in bed until you're fully recovered... Spring was early that year, it was hot, and the earthworms were all coming out. They were coming out in their hundreds, it looked like the earth itself was moving! Anyway, one day I came home, and the neighbour said to me, you had a phone call, from Sychavka. I asked if it was Nina. Had Mum taken a turn for the worse? No, she said, it was Praskovya herself. But if Mum was calling herself, I thought, what did that mean? She must be on her feet again, if she's made it all the way to the post office. She must have called to tell her youngest daughter not to worry. Although she never had much time for me – she was always quite stern with me, never really hugged me... But she had brought me up, taught me well, given me a good education... And it can't have been easy raising three of us on her own.

That night there was another long-distance phone call. For some reason my heart began to thump in my chest, and I had a bad feeling about it... I picked up the receiver, and it was Mum. Come quickly, she said, my darling daughter, Ninochka is dead! Oh such sorrow, such pain! Mum was crying. I said, what? Nina? But she was strong, Nina was, still young, healthy, beautiful... Our dear mother, may God preserve her, wasn't much to look at, but Nina was a beauty. She took after our father.

And then she died, sobbed Mum, suddenly, and the doctor has already been and gone. Our Ninochka is lying in her coffin, so beautiful... She's telling me all this, and crying her eyes out. She loved Nina, she really did. To be honest, she was never that keen on me, Nina was always her favourite. She felt sorry for me, she said, our golden Ninochka, she had the soul of an angel... I was so worried about the garden, and she said to me, don't worry Mum, I'll do it... And she started digging... She spent all day in the garden, in the sun, and then no sooner had she put the spade down than she put her hands to her head, groaned, and collapsed. Mum ran to her, and her eyes were already rolling back in her head... She was lying there, saying, why has it all gone dark? Mum poured water over her, fanned her with a damp sheet, but all in vain... The ambulance came, but Nina had already stopped breathing... More tears. Come quickly, she said, and call Nina's husband for me, and Vanechka too, I don't have the strength any more... I got up from my death-bed, she said, to wash and dress her, so that she could have a decent burial...

So, what could I do? I called my brother-in-law, who started crying. I called Vanya, who started crying. I'm leaving right now, he said. The next morning, I went straight to our benefit fund for a loan, then packed one suitcase full of imported medicines for Mum and another full of food, so that we had enough to put on a decent spread after the funeral and at the ninth-day and forty-day wakes. No expense spared: salami, sprats, the works... I almost burst a blood vessel trying to lift my bags. And so to Sychavka.

When we arrived, Mum was crying her eyes out, although she did seem a bit better in herself, thank God. Nina's medicines had helped, and now I'd brought fresh supplies... When tragedy strikes, what else can you do? You have to pull yourself together. Mum was hanging in there. Wheezing and moaning a bit, but hanging in there. My brother-in-law chose to drown his sorrows, and is still drowning them to this day, but Mum held it together. She always was strong like that... Such sorrow, she said, but you have to stay strong... Well, someone had to sort the funeral out, and the ninth-day and forty-day wakes, otherwise what would people say? But she was still crying... The neighbours tried in vain to comfort her, but she was inconsolable. Such a tragedy, she said, it's us old folk that should be departing for the next world, not my favourite daughter, in her prime... The doctor said she'd had a stroke: she'd forgotten what country life was like, she'd turned soft... and then she suddenly went and overdid it. Everyone knows city life is easier, and Nina's job was office-based, and furthermore her loving husband did everything for her and wouldn't let her lift a finger at home... And, like the doctor said, it was hot enough to bring down a bull...

We buried Nina.

Vanya and Mum seemed to be getting on OK, though he still couldn't quite bring himself to forgive her for not welcoming Lilya into the family. But he was softening towards her, he felt sorry for her. And Mum seemed to be softening towards Lilya too. It's true what they say, if you put up with each other for long enough, love will grow. She started saying, Vanechka, Lilechka, you should come and stay more often, and bring my grandson to see me, let him come and eat some berries in the garden. We're family, after all! When Vanya came to leave, Mum loaded him up with jars of home-made jam and all sorts of preserves... he could barely lift the suitcase. He left, and so did I. Well, the year-end accounts were calling. Mum was alone again. Never mind, said Vanya, I'll take Lilya there this summer, let them spend a bit of time together, get used to each other... we'll probably end up moving down there! He was as good as his word, too – he and Lilya went to Mum's on Midsummer's Day, and everything seemed to be working out well. Mum took Stepka in hand – once a schoolteacher, always a schoolteacher, I guess: wash your hands, sit up straight, don't speak with your mouth full, etcetera... Lilya very probably had her own views on the matter but held her tongue and put up with it: yes Mum, no Mum, three bags full Mum... And she wasn't so flighty after all – she actually turned out to be a hard worker, spending all summer digging in the garden... Mum couldn't have been happier. Vanya was still rushing around looking for work. He found a good job somewhere nearby and a room to go with it. It was in Kotovsk – a depressing little town, but still, a town. So he came to pick up Lilya and took her to one side and asked her, why don't you stay on here a little while, my love? At that point Lilya dug her heels in and said, no way. We're all staying together, she said. So what if it's a bit of a mess there? That's nothing new, we can handle it...

Despite Mum's best efforts to get her to change her mind, Lilya wasn't having any of it: no, she said, and she stuck to her guns. Vanya kept popping over to Mum's, putting up fences, fixing the roof... bit of a DIY expert, our Vanya. But Lilya stayed away. Mum sent him home laden with jam and pickled cucumbers and cabbage, and Lilya for her part sent him back again with cheese, sausage, sprats... so your mother doesn't think we're not grateful, she said. And Mum invited her neighbours over, fed them city sweets, and praised Lilya to the skies, such a caring daughter-in-law...

Next summer, the same thing happened. Lilya refused point blank to go. We're fine here, she said. Mum seemed to be doing OK, she was hanging in there. She was missing Nina. One year passed, then a second, and a third... Then Stepka started school, and that winter Mum took a turn for the worse. She wasn't so bad... just not so good. Her back was hurting, her legs were aching... The neighbours were helping a little, but not that much... They'd fallen out over something silly like a fence being moved, or a shed being pulled down... I don't even remember. Anyway, she needed some firewood, and the roof was leaking again. So Vanya went, and as usual Lilya stayed. When he arrived, Mum was in bed. Oh my darling son, she said, you're my only hope... You couldn't just chop me some firewood, could you? Just a little, enough to see me through the winter… So Vanya took the axe and went off to chop. But that evening he came over all peculiar – his heart, I think it was. He felt dizzy, his chest was tight… Call a doctor, Mum, he said, I feel terrible… But that would have meant asking the neighbours to use their phone, and they weren't on speaking terms. Come on son, she said, you're young and strong – lie down, rest a little, you'll feel better in the morning. My poor legs are too weak, she said, to run to the post office, and the doctor will be cross with me for wearing myself out… No Mum, seriously, he said, I've got a problem with my heart, it was playing up in Salekhard before I came here. What are you talking about, she said, you're as strong as an ox. So the ox just lay there, and he was dead by morning. So, yet another tearful phone call from Mum: our Vanechka, my only joy… Yet another benefit fund loan, unpaid leave, and off I went. Lilya came too, though she left Stepka and didn't stay long herself – she didn't even wait for the ninth-day wake. As soon as she arrived in Kotovsk, she grabbed Stepka and headed back to Salekhard, to her parents' house. Fair enough, really: who can look after you better than your own mother? She needed a hand with her half-orphaned son, too. She'll have no problem finding herself another husband there either, she's still young…

Mum was crying her eyes out, but she did seem a little better in herself. Hanging in there. She was up on her feet and getting about a bit… The ninth-day wake came and went, and the forty-day wake… I had my year-end accounts to worry about again, so I stayed for a little while then left. Mum was alone again. I sent her parcels of medicine and visited from time to time. I'm all she's got left now, and she seems to be warming to me. She calls me in tears – oh, my darling daughter, come and see me, come and spend a little time with your old Mum… Old? There isn't a single grey hair on her head! I've got a few myself but it's as if she's actually turned back time and is growing younger, or something. Anyway, around the time of the third anniversary of Vanya's death, she took another turn for the worse. By May Day she'd taken to her bed, so I thought I might as well go down there for the long weekend. I packed my bag, jumped on the train, and arrived in Sychavka. Mum couldn't get out of bed. The garden needed watering, so off I went, and while I was out there I planted onions and some baby squashes... Suddenly I seized up a bit – my back was killing me... I'd never had a problem with my back before, but all of a sudden it was playing up. I went into the house to have a little lie-down, and I saw Mum coming over to me. Darling daughter, you shouldn't be lying down in the middle of the day... My darling mother had got herself out of bed to tell me this. And she seemed strangely full of life, her eyes were shining. She laid out a feast for me, her last beloved daughter – a home-made pie, new potatoes sprinkled with dill. I ate while she watched me, resting her chin on her hand. We sat like that until the evening. She was smiling, her eyes were shining, and I was feeling worse and worse... Will you be staying long, my darling daughter? Just for the long weekend, I said. Oh, but stay a little longer, won't you, she said, let me look at you and be happy for a while... OK Mum, I said, I'll stay, it's so nice here... And it's true, it was really nice...

In the evening, I wandered out onto the porch – you could see the stars so clearly, there was a nightingale singing, the sky was deep blue, with a touch of green at the edges, and you got a real sense of Nature's bounty... I went back into the house. Mum was watching me, and smiling. Sit down, my darling daughter, she said, have some supper. In a minute, Mum, I said, in a minute. I just need some fresh air.

I didn't even stop to take my bag. I left the house and headed for the central square, where the buses stop. A bus had just pulled up, so I got on. It was going straight to Odessa, so I never went home. I sent a letter to work, handing in my notice, and went to see Valya – we had studied accountancy together. I was lucky to catch her in Odessa. Things had turned out pretty well for her – her husband works in Antalya as a trade representative, and he had a Turkish friend there, the director of some company. Why don't you come and live with us, she said. We need someone to look after the children and do a bit of cooking. And I thought, why not? I don't care where I go, I said, I just need to get out of here. And I'm not going back to Yuzhnyi. Go on then, I said, what's the address… Why not? I'm a good cook. I might even find myself a husband over there… They say that Turkish men like a bit of something to grab hold of… I'll never set foot in Sychavka again… No, I'm never going back there. And I won't go home. What if Mum wants to come and stay with me? No way, she's not going to get me!

She looked at Shenderovich sadly.

"I called Lilya, once I got to Odessa. Asked her about Stepka, etcetera… We're fine, she said, thank God. But you just watch out next time your Mum 'takes a turn for the worse'… As soon as she does, the best thing you can do is run as far away as you possibly can in the opposite direction."

"Forgive me," Shenderovich looked thoughtful, "but did you think of using holy water on her?"

"Well, that would have been a bit awkward," the woman sighed. "How could I have just started sprinkling holy water on her?"

She pursed her lips.

"I wanted to take her to church. Come on Mum, I said, let's go to church. We can light candles for Nina and Vanya. No, said Mum, you go – I don't feel comfortable going to church, as a teacher and a party member. As soon as I step inside a church, she said, I start to feel bad. Her eyes grew dark and clouded over… And it was true, I asked the neighbours – she never set foot inside a church. She gave money, but never went herself…"

She sighed, pushed her chair back, and gathered the crusts of bread into her napkin.

"I'm going to go and feed the gulls," she explained, to no one in particular. "They're so hungry, the poor little things..."

"You see, Yannis my friend, how things can turn out," Shenderovich was deeply moved. "And you're letting yourself get so wound up over nothing... Here you are, out on the open waves, the forces of evil will never get you out here, and you're still not happy."

"What have the 'forces of evil' got to do with it?" replied Givi, defensively. "You're the only force of evil around here..."

"If I were you," said Alka, thoughtfully, "I wouldn't be so sure. Maybe you've been living your entire life in darkness and now you're coming out into the light..."

"Can't you feel it?" continued Shenderovich. "This sense of freedom, the open space, casting off the burden of your everyday responsibilities... What do you do for a living, by the way?"

"I'm an accountant for a ferry company," said Givi, staring fixedly into space. "Based in St. Petersburg."

"So, you'll have something amazing to reminisce about, once you're back in boring, shabby old St. Pete... Right, let's go up on deck, get a breath of sea air, check out the girls..."

Givi sighed and obediently followed him. Shenderovich had charisma, whereas Givi had nothing. Not even a pair of white trousers. Or the faintest clue what was going on.

The sea air was making him feel a bit better. The deck was rolling, but comfortably so. A solitary cloud was dragging itself along after the sun. The air was full of salt and the smell of rotting fish...

Alka had already installed herself on a sun-lounger, all got up in a fancy swimsuit – she really was perfect! Givi blushed and averted his eyes. There were two young men hanging around her sun-lounger, with gym-toned legs and muscular necks.

"Have you two lost something here?" asked Shenderovich

coldly, sitting down next to Alka. The young men said no, they hadn't lost anything, that's not why they were there…

Alka tittered shamelessly.

Givi wondered whether there would be a fight, and if so, what should he do…

But it all blew over. The young men called a waitress over and ordered a couple of beers, and Shenderovich also ordered a beer and sprawled back on his sun-lounger like a sheikh… Alka, on the other hand, got up and went off with one of the new arrivals, to 'feed the seagulls,' apparently.

"What exactly is your relationship with Alka?" Givi was tormented with the awkwardness of it all. "Are you two, um, together?"

"Oh, Alka," Shenderovich waved his hand dismissively, "you know… She's just an old friend, and actually not even a very reliable one… So, I won't stand in your way, Yannis my friend! Though others might…"

Givi sighed. He couldn't work it out. The most annoying thing was that Alka was the only blonde around. Had they all died out or something? There were a couple of buxom though very middle-aged brunettes. One was even fluttering her eyelashes at Givi, who was pretending he hadn't noticed.

"Anyway," he asked, trying to shake off his lecherous thoughts, "why are we going to Turkey? What are we buying?"

"That," answered Shenderovich, lowering his voice, "is top secret. The competition have got their spies out… I had a bit of a brainwave… nobody else has thought of it, it was my very own idea… top quality merchandise…"

"What kind of merchandise?" asked Givi also whispering. Shenderovich was obviously up to something.

"Balloons," said Shenderovich, barely audibly. "Blow-up balloons."

Givi blushed.

"Is that some sort of metaphor?" he asked. "Do you mean…"

"Condoms?" Shenderovich exclaimed loudly. "No, of course not!"

His voice dropped again, like a flag in the wind.

"Just normal blow-up balloons. All different colours… The whole of Odessa has gone mad for them. You can fill them with helium, and you can get all kinds – hearts, stars, moons… They sell like hot cakes…"

"So you think it'll be a bit of a money-spinner?" asked Givi, in as professional a tone as he could muster.

Shenderovich started counting on his fingers.

"One, they don't take up much space… And before you blow them up they don't take any space at all. Two, they don't weigh much. Three, you can buy them in bulk for peanuts. Four, you can stick a huge mark-up on them… Igor, the idiot, brought a load of plastic graters back, can you imagine? We'd never seen anything like it – they were beautiful, bright and shiny, great design. They didn't weigh much but took up a ridiculous amount of space, and then people started asking for their money back – the graters didn't grate! Well, they were made out of plastic, weren't they. But people will always want balloons – they drag them along for a bit, then let go of them, and buy another one the following day. And you can charge the same as for a grater. Me and you, Yannis my friend, and that irresponsible Alka… where is she, by the way? Shit, has she really gone off with that bloke? Anyway, the three of us are going to fill the skies of Odessa with balloons…"

"I can't help thinking," Givi pursed his lips, "that the whole thing sounds a bit risky."

"Life is a 'bit risky.' And you'll get your share of the profits… Yannis my friend, you seem troubled. Is it because of Alka? I wouldn't lose any sleep over it. You know, it's all about the trousers… You'll never sweep Alka off her feet in those trousers, they're not really the most attractive, are they… There's a clothes shop on board, but their prices are ridiculous… As soon as we get to Istanbul, I'll buy you some new ones.

White ones, nice and tight. You'll come back dressed like a king... Then you'll be able to tell all your friends in St. Pete how you went to Turkey on business... Don't keep looking over there, there's no point, she's not coming back... Let's have another beer instead, a nice cold one."

Givi sighed again.

"What the hell," he said. "Go on then."

Givi's head was spinning like crazy – the hustle of the streets and the blinding sunlight combined to give the distinct impression that he had fallen into a beehive. This impression was further compounded by the sweet smell of honey-soaked pastries that enveloped him – hawkers danced on every corner, surrounded by clouds of delirious wasps. He had instinctively tightened his grip on the bottle of Pepsi that Shenderovich had bought him, which was growing warmer by the minute.

A mirage hung over the city.

I am in Istanbul, Givi reminded himself. This is me, and this is Istanbul. Now, what am I doing here?

"Hey!" someone grabbed his sleeve. "You Russian, yes? Look here, Russian!"

Givi struggled to free his sleeve. But his captor – a skinny Turk dressed in a red waistcoat – had dived back behind his counter, without relinquishing his hold...

"You take carpet, yes?"

"No," Givi answered firmly.

"Khali, bring kilim! Look, how beautiful! You give to girlfriend! You give to girlfriend mother!"

"No, thanks," Givi tried again to free himself.

"You give to that girl!" the seller nodded at Alka, who was holding strings of coral up against her neck a couple of stalls away. "Beautiful girl. She will love you!"

Givi finally managed to disengage himself.

"What are you talking about?" he asked angrily. "Where am I going to put a carpet, in my pocket?"

"Ah!" the seller nodded, understanding. "Then look here! Something for real man!"

He drew back a multicoloured curtain and gestured to the wall behind it, which was covered top to bottom with the most curious array of curved daggers. Givi was rooted to the spot. He had a real weakness for weapons, especially side-arms. They boosted his self-confidence.

They must be yataghans, Givi decided.

He reached into his pocket indecisively and then grimaced.

That bastard Shenderovich.

The seller, obviously experienced in reading faces, immediately lost interest in him.

"Givi!" yelled Shenderovich, emerging from the neighbouring stall. "Shit! Yannis! What are you loitering over there for? Come here!"

"Don't shout at me" Givi muttered through clenched teeth, reasserting his battered dignity.

Shenderovich smoothly changed his tone.

"What are you up to?" he said, approaching Givi and giving him a friendly slap on the shoulder. "They're all fakes! Everything's fake here. But they still try to fleece you as if they were museum exhibits or something. They've got no shame, I tell you... You wouldn't even be able to peel an apple with one of those daggers... But if you hang on, we'll go to the flea market, you'll get a good one there..."

Givi threw one last sorrowful glance at the daggers gleaming menacingly in the sun. They did look just like fakes are supposed to, better than the real thing...

"Let's go, Yannis my brother," Shenderovich cajoled him. "Let's go, we've got a meeting."

"I'm not going!" Givi suddenly declared.

Shenderovich was taken aback.

"What do you mean? What else are you going to do?"

"I'm going to the Russian consulate. There is one here, I assume?"

"Yes," Shenderovich reluctantly agreed. "There's an embassy. And what are you going to tell them, exactly? That you got drunk and entered Turkey on someone else's passport? They'll think you're a spy... an illegal alien."

"We'll work something out," Givi said sulkily. "I'll repent, tell them I never meant to do it. I'll tell them how you tricked me, how you trapped me in your web of lies. I don't want any of this. I don't want to be your slave, begging for every little crumb..."

"Ah!" Shenderovich understood. "So, Yannis my brother, that's what this is all about... I'll see you alright, you don't need to worry about that. Just be careful, that's all I ask. You're like an innocent child here, you'll fall for all their nonsense..."

"But I want..."

Shenderovich shrugged.

"You want to show off in front of Alka, I know," he noted, shrewdly. "You want to impress her, to buy it all and lay it at her feet! She was particularly interested in the coral necklaces, I noticed..."

"That's none of your business... Listen, which is it to be, either I am an equal partner, or a victim of your scam..."

"You're an equal partner, of course... Here you go," Shenderovich pressed a crumpled wad into his hand. "Splash a bit of cash! Buy whatever you want. Just don't come crying to me when they rip you off..."

"I told you I can look after myself..."

"Boys!" Alka cried impatiently, throwing yet another necklace onto the counter, this time a turquoise one. "Are you going to be long? Misha! I thought our meeting was at two?"

"We're coming, we're coming," Shenderovich fished a dog-eared map of Istanbul out of his pocket. "Aha, here we are... Right, so we need to go left here... Don't worry, it's only a couple of minutes from here. If I were you, Yannis, I'd put that money away. You can spend it later, we've got plenty of time."

He took Givi's arm and swept him down the street, brushing off the increasingly persistent hawkers as they went.

"Just remember," he coached Givi as they walked, "you're Yannis. And you've got everything under control. You go in, you see Ali, you say 'Hi, Ali!' straight away."

"In Turkish?!" Givi was horrified.

"D'you think that moron Stavrakis was fluent in Turkish? No, in Russian, of course, you idiot…"

He thought for a moment, then magnanimously conceded:

"You can say 'Hello!' in English – 'Hello, Ali!'…"

"And how will I know which one's Ali?"

"Well that moron only saw him a couple of times at most. When you go in, shout 'Ali!' straight away. Then you'll know. Then you introduce me, like 'This is Misha, our boss.' Got it?"

"Got it."

"I'll let Alka work her magic on him. He won't even be looking at you. They love blondes. So, nothing to worry about, we'll be fine. I'll take it from there… You just sit there, don't say anything."

"Fine. And what if they ask me something?"

"What are they going to ask you?"

"You know, 'How's it going, Yannis?' sort of thing…"

"Say 'Fine.' Alka! How do you say 'fine' in Turkish?"

" 'OK'," answered Alka, without turning round.

"See how easy it is? Here we are."

Shenderovich dived through an open door. Givi, hurrying after him, was immediately swallowed up by the murky gloom, and the smell of coffee was so strong that Givi felt as though he were swimming in it. Figures moved about indistinctly behind the tables.

"What's this?" he asked in a whisper. "His office?"

"His office?" Shenderovich repeated irritably. "It's a coffee house. You really think they do business in an office?"

Several male faces with black moustaches slowly turned towards the new arrivals.

Alka whispered something into Shenderovich's ear.

"Merhaba," he said, politely. "Nerede Ali?"

Then he elbowed Givi in the ribs.

"Ali!" yelped Givi.

A waiter wearing a fez, and looking just like a character from a musical comedy, came running up and looked at them closely.

"Rus musunuz?" he asked, and then, shouting back into the room in Russian, "Ali! Hey, Ali! Someone to see you."

"Eh?" Givi muttered weakly.

"Don't worry!" said Shenderovich, giving him another friendly slap on the shoulder. "You see, our own people here too…"

Ali appeared from out of the gloom, completely indistinguishable from the others. A thick gold chain nestled on his hairy chest.

"Salaam aleikum," said Shenderovich, politely, and elbowed Givi again in the ribs.

"Salaam aleikum," Givi repeated obediently.

"Greetings," nodded Ali. "Please, sit down. Hi, Yannis. It's been a long time. How's tricks?" Givi opened his mouth to reply, but Ali had already turned away. He looked at Alka, smoothed his moustache with his finger, then shot a dark look in the direction of Shenderovich.

"Misha?" he asked.

"This is Misha," Givi repeated mechanically. "He's our boss."

"What's a boss? Sometimes on the ball, sometimes at a loss," commented Ali.

And, leaning towards Givi across the table, he asked in a theatrical whisper:

"Can I trust him? He looks a bit sneaky."

Shenderovich kicked Givi under the table. Givi jumped, and the table scraped across the floor.

"As I would trust myself," Givi quickly replied.

Ali glanced at him suspiciously.

"You seem nervous," he noted.

"He's not used to this," Shenderovich explained.

Ali nodded sympathetically.

Hang on a minute, balloons? The thought suddenly flashed into Givi's mind. Oh God! What have I got mixed up in? They're probably trafficking drugs. Or weapons... Why did I trust this charlatan? Any minute now the... whatever they're called... the carabinieri... will burst in and arrest us... And I'm carrying a forged passport. Oh, woe is me!

He looked around nervously. The coffee house was full of good-looking men sitting at the tables, slowly sipping their coffee.

"Have you got the goods?" asked Shenderovich sternly, playing with a spoon.

"Yes," answered Ali, equally curtly, as he sipped his coffee.

"Where?"

"At the warehouse," Ali shrugged. "Where else? You can pick them up this evening, like we agreed."

"I want to sample the goods before they're loaded. Which number warehouse is it?"

Ali silently handed him a business card. Shenderovich squinted briefly at it, then pulled a fat envelope out of his breast pocket and handed it to Ali in return.

"Here's your advance."

The envelope disappeared into the corresponding pocket on Ali's powerful chest. Ali gave a cordial nod, cast one more sidelong look at Alka, and straightened his shoulders.

"Pretty girl, isn't she?"

Alka burst into a long, incomprehensible sentence – obviously Turkish, thought Givi.

Ali stared at her in astonishment for what seemed like a long time, then carefully said:

"Indeed, indeed..."

Shenderovich turned round nervously.

"Yannis…"

Givi was deep in thought. It was a big city, full of people, literally crowds of them, and everyone was going about their business. Everyone had some business to go about, everyone knew their place and who they were. Only he, Givi, had no idea who he was. He was nothing but an empty space, surrounded by air.

"Yannis, shit! Get up, we're going…"

Givi stood up, grinning politely, and shook the steely hand that Ali held out to him over the table.

"You look rough, man," said Ali, sympathetically. "Like you've lost weight…"

Givi made a vague guttural noise.

"Let's go, let's go…" Shenderovich took his arm and dragged him between the tables. "Say goodbye."

Shamelessly wiggling her backside, Alka was already halfway up the steps, followed by the appreciative smacking of lips and the clattering of teaspoons.

"Well, James Bond would have nothing on you, would he, eh?" said Shenderovich, reproachfully, as they walked. "A real master of disguise. You almost ruined everything! You keep forgetting your damn name! OK, we pick up the goods today, and that's it. Game over. Then we get out of here while the going is good."

Givi recoiled as the sunlight smacked him in the face. Somewhere far in the distance, above the bay of the Golden Horn, swam a blindingly intense heat, breaking the water up into a thousand silver mirrors.

He stopped so suddenly that Shenderovich, who was still dragging him along by the arm and dodging passers-by, lost his balance.

"Misha," said Givi, quietly but furiously. "Shenderovich! Do you love your mother?"

"What has that got to do with anything?" Shenderovich asked gloomily.

"Swear on your mother's life to tell me the truth. Why the big secret? What's the hurry? Why did you just look over your shoulder? You were checking to see if we were being followed, weren't you, Misha? You were checking, weren't you? What are we buying? What are we taking back? There's something very dodgy about all this, Misha."

"So, it's a bit dodgy," muttered Shenderovich darkly, looking away and fiddling with his cigarette. "I tricked you, Givi my brother…"

"I knew it," Givi felt his legs give way beneath him.

"I'm afraid I've got you involved in something dangerous, my friend."

"Drugs, you mean," said Givi, as his heart sank. "You bastard…"

"Drugs?" exclaimed Shenderovich. "What do you take me for? I told you, it's balloons! I'll open one of the containers for you! I'll open it right in front of you, so you can see for yourself!"

Givi couldn't imagine what could possibly be so dangerous about a load of balloons.

"What, is it raw materials for making explosives, or something?" he managed to squeeze out of his dry throat.

"You have a weird imagination, Givi my brother," Shenderovich looked around nervously again, grabbed Givi's elbow, and pulled him into one of the alleys. "What are you on about, 'raw materials'? Plastic is plastic. You fill them with helium, take a load of them out onto Seaside Boulevard, and stand there above the port with them sparkling in the sun, all the hearts, the elephants… People love them."

"Then why?"

Shenderovich looked around again. There was no one about apart from Alka, who was leaning against a sun-bleached wall and tapping her foot impatiently.

"Lysyuk!" whispered Shenderovich, right into Givi's ear.

"What?" Givi jumped back out of shock. "What's a 'lysyuk'?"

"Not so loud!" Shenderovich exclaimed nervously.

"Well, what is it?"

"It's not a thing, it's a person!" Shenderovich looked from side to side. "It's… he's… You wouldn't have come across anyone like him in St. Pete, that's for sure! Lysyuk, he's an out-and-out rogue, in a league of his own. And the worst of it is that he's forever on my tail. Now I'm worried that the jackal's picked up my scent again… He circles above me like a vulture."

He sighed and flicked his cigarette away.

"That's why we are working under conditions of utmost secrecy. Otherwise, Lysyuk would pick up my fresh tracks at the office then he'd intercept the goods, buy up my suppliers, and poach my clientele. Or scare them away."

"Hang on," Givi furrowed his brow, "you mean Ali is the only contact in the whole of Turkey trading in balloons?"

"No, there are loads of them!" Shenderovich waved his hand. "That's not the problem! Lysyuk doesn't need the balloons. It's me he's out to get, do you understand? He and I are bound by the mysterious threads of fate. It's like the Law of Conservation of Happiness in a closed system. When things are going badly for him, things go well for me. When things are going badly for me, things go well for him. And of course he prefers the latter version. And that, Givi my brother, is the way it is. That's why I want to pick up the goods in person – that Lysyuk is capable of all manner of dirty tricks. He could easily replace them with inferior goods, or even pierce holes in them with his own filthy hands…"

"Ah, I see," Givi relaxed.

He wasn't too worried about the mysterious threads binding Shenderovich to the invisible Lysyuk. But he still asked:

"So what, is he in Turkey too, then?"

"Who knows, Givi my brother," Shenderovich answered vaguely. "Who knows…"

He made a sweeping gesture with his powerful hand.

"OK, let's go! Look, Alka's already champing at the bit.

She doesn't like to stay in one place too long. Let's go and sit inside somewhere where it's nice and cool, get something to eat... Some protein, some carbs, that's what we need... Some fried fish, a kebab... What do you fancy? Let's go for a walk, have a Turkish bath, go and check out the Galata district... There's a great little restaurant in Galata – the food is delicious, and they've got belly dancers and everything. Have you ever seen belly dancing?"

"No," Givi answered weakly.

Beautiful, dusky maidens appeared to him in a swirling mist, their arms swaying like willowy branches in the wind, their tender faces concealed behind gauzy veils, precious stones glittering in their delicate navels... He swallowed hard and opened his eyes.

The scorching air hung heavily above the alley, and two turtle-doves were fighting lazily over some stray nuts... Alka looked anxiously at her watch.

"What's up with you?" Shenderovich was suddenly interested.

"Um, well..." said Alka, vaguely, "I said I'd meet someone. At six o'clock."

"Hang on a minute," Shenderovich looked worried. "What do you mean, you're meeting someone? Who's going to translate for us?"

"You don't really need a translator, do you?" asked Alka, lazily.

"Well," Shenderovich answered, vaguely, "you never know... What did we bring you for, anyway?"

"Because I can increase your baggage allowance by 150 kilos," answered Alka, dryly. "Which means an extra one and a half grand. Plus my business contacts. And what do you think this meeting's about anyway? I'm looking after our image. Call it a public relations exercise."

"Yes, I can imagine what kind of relations you'll be exercising," Shenderovich waved dismissively.

"Whatever," said Alka in a conciliatory tone. "First of all, he might be useful. And secondly, you'll save yourself the cost of my ticket to the belly dancing show. I've seen it all before – a load of shuttle traders just like you two, tourists with their tongues hanging out! He knows some amazing places…"

"I bet he's all mouth and no trousers," said Shenderovich, gloomily.

"No trousers? Fine by me… OK boys, see you later… I've got to go and freshen up a bit, get changed, do my hair, you know how it is…"

She turned round and wandered off down the lane. The hawkers turned to watch her go.

"Wait!" Shenderovich pulled himself together. "Where can we find you if we need to?"

"Don't bother looking," Alka advised him over her shoulder with a smile, without slowing down. "I know the way back to the ferry… I'll be fine."

"When should we expect you? In a week?"

"Maybe. Don't worry, the ferry won't go without us."

"And why not?" Shenderovich asked indignantly. "What makes you think you're so special?"

"Not me, him," Alka explained. "I'm meeting the captain, OK? God's right-hand man."

And without further ado, she set off down the winding alley. Her outline shimmered and melted in the scorching dove-coloured mirage of the street braziers.

"Well… There you go, Yannis my friend," said Shenderovich, with exasperation. "She always does this. Mind you, the captain, no less… She'll certainly be doing her bit for public relations…"

"Do you think she's lying?" Givi asked hopefully.

"No chance… Alka's not a liar. That's the problem. Let's go, my Greek friend, let's go. You should at least try some fried fish."

"I don't want any," said Givi, mournfully.

The crumpled wad of money was burning a hole in his pocket. Givi frowned.

He had wanted to buy Alka a coral necklace. The best he could find... The most amazing coral necklace she'd ever have seen... But now he'd changed his mind: let the captain buy it for her.

The crowd was getting denser. Now it wasn't the hawkers moving out of their way, they were having to move out of the way of the hawkers, and the people sitting cross-legged on little carpets. Multicoloured lengths of cloth were displayed over the counters, copper trays shone like little suns... The carpets were a riot of colour, like a swarm of butterflies in a flowerbed. The daggers glittered, like miniature but deadly bolts of lightning.

"Hang on," said Givi.

Alka didn't need his coral necklaces. He wasn't going to be sharing a bottle of chilled wine with her on any vine-covered terrace...

He stuck his hand in his pocket and pulled out the crumpled ball of notes.

He would go back to St. Petersburg, spread his carpet of many colours out in the gloom of his damp room in the communal apartment, and invite his friends over. What friends? He'd find some. His friends would admire his carpet, and he would tell them how one of his close friends had invited him to join him, completely out of the blue, on a trip to Istanbul, because he was so well respected. His reputation had even spread as far as Odessa, and everyone wanted to know Givi from the St. Petersburg ferry company! He would buy that fez for the Finance Director – he always had trouble keeping that bald spot warm.

"That one," he pointed at a carpet, then turned to Shenderovich for help. "How do you say 'How much is it?' in Turkish?"

Shenderovich looked uncomfortable. Without Alka, he was a little less sure of himself.

"Um, bu ne kadar?" he finally came out with.

"How much, this beautiful one?" the seller called from the counter. "Take it, is good quality, I make present to you! I make good price!"

"Good price, how much is that? Misha, ask him, how much?"

"Stop hassling me!" cried Shenderovich. "They speak better Russian than you do!" Then he turned to the seller, who by this point had grabbed Givi's shirt and didn't appear to have any intention of letting go. "Leave him alone! Get your hands off him!"

He grabbed Givi's other arm and tried to drag him away from the stall. A brief tug-of-war ensued, which Shenderovich won.

Givi went off the idea of buying the carpet.

A strange, indifferent world was unfolding and revolving around him, reminding him of the little bits of coloured glass in a kaleidoscope. The calls of the hawkers, the guttural cries of the shoeshine boys, the cooing of the fat doves, the crackle of the braziers, the honking of cars trying to nose their way through the crowd... And for some reason it all seemed somehow intangible, unreal... An illusion, a fairy tale...

He felt himself being grabbed again. This time it was his trouser-leg.

Givi jumped.

"Lütfen beni... misiniz..."

Well, fancy that, he thought. They do speak some Turkish here after all. He carefully tried to drag his leg away, but the dry bird-like claw had him in a tight grip.

He looked down.

An old man was sitting on a shabby little carpet, so threadbare that you could barely make out the pattern. He was looking hopefully up at Givi.

"Misha!" called Givi, helplessly. "Misha! What does he want?"

"He wants you to buy something," Shenderovich shrugged.

"But… what?"

There wasn't anything on the tiny carpet. Apart from a pair of slippers with pointed toes, which were hanging off his calloused brown heels. There were also a pair of thick black shalwar – or whatever they were called, thought Givi – and a faded waistcoat that looked as though it may once have been red, which was mercifully covering the man's skinny chest. An earring in the shape of a half-moon, blackened with age, hung from his wrinkled ear.

"A proper native," Shenderovich observed with respect. "They don't make them like that any more."

With the dexterity of a practised conjurer, the old man produced a shabby felt bag from out of nowhere and proceeded with a flourish to empty its contents onto the floor at Givi's feet.

"Huh?" Givi turned to Shenderovich again.

"It's all rubbish," said Shenderovich, waving his hand dismissively. "Dusty old tat."

Several different daggers materialized on the little carpet. With a smooth, professional hand, the old man unsheathed them one by one and waved them about in the air. The metal gleamed dully in the sun – they had nothing at all in common with the highly polished daggers on the multicoloured stalls. Before the next dagger was safely back in its sheath, Givi managed to notice that they were all suspiciously serrated and covered with patches of equally suspicious-looking rust.

"Do you think he's nicked them from a museum?"

"What museum? Who's going to want that old rubbish?"

"Misiniz…efendi…" repeated the old man.

"Eh?" Givi looked questioningly at Shenderovich.

"He's saying 'Buy something, please,' or something," said Shenderovich, not sounding completely sure about it.

"Are they real?"

"They look pretty real," sighed Shenderovich. "I wonder if he's used them on anyone…"

One dagger stood out from the rest – its sheath was bound in silver, and the blue-white blade was covered in a smoke-coloured pattern. Givi couldn't help falling in love with it. A dagger like that was made for piercing an enemy's cowardly heart, for freeing a beautiful captive from the chains that bound her… and he was sure he could think up a few more uses, too.

"Damascus!" croaked the old man, proudly. "Damascus!"

Ah, the blessed city of Damascus, where at night by the fountain you might happen upon the hunched figure of Haroun al-Rashid, where camel trains shuffle along the scorched stones, cosseting heavy bales of silk and henna… lean your beautiful body against mine, oh Leila, and Zeinab, beautiful as the moon…

"How much?" Givi couldn't help himself. "How much for this? Then he tried again, in English. "How… many?"

The old man must have been a natural linguist, because he instantly held up three fingers.

"What does that mean?" Givi turned to Shenderovich.

"Three," he explained.

"Three what? Dollars? Roubles? What?" He turned to the old man. "Three dollars, yes?"

And for some reason he also held up three fingers.

He and the old man eyed each other silently.

"I don't understand," Givi was at a loss. "What does he want?"

"It's not exactly complicated," Shenderovich retorted. "It's how they do business round here… Now you name a higher price, he names a lower price. That's all there is to it. But you have to haggle, otherwise he won't have any respect for you. Allah likes a bit of haggling."

Givi shrugged and held up one finger.

The old man looked at him with loathing and held up two. His fingers were gnarled and crooked.

"Well?" Givi turned to Shenderovich.

"Well what?" Shenderovich answered impatiently. "Get on with it, for God's sake. I'm starving."

But now Givi was caught up in the excitement of it all. He held up one finger again. There was something rather rude about his erect digit.

The old man gnashed his teeth again and reached for his belt. His crooked hand fell upon the handle of the dagger.

Givi stepped back, just to be on the safe side.

The old man unsheathed the dagger and started to wave it around. The blade glinted as it cut a swift arc through the air.

"Look, batono, at this magnificent dagger!" the old man seemed to say. "Look, genatsvale! What is a man without a dagger? Kill your enemy, rescue your friend! Carry off your woman! Look at this dagger! A man needs a dagger to be a man! Sertskhvile serkhvale!"

"Indeed!" agreed Givi, out loud. And he held his finger up again.

The old man spat on the ground and, with more gnashing of teeth, pulled another item from his bottomless pocket. It was nothing special. Something small, completely shapeless. The old man threw it to the ground next to Givi's feet.

Givi bent down to get a closer look.

The ring appeared to be as old as the dagger, or possibly even older. Centuries' worth of dust had settled on it and turned to a black patina.

"Huh?" Givi looked at Shenderovich in confusion.

"Look, just buy it will you, and get a move on," said Shenderovich. "It's a lovely ring. A perfect souvenir! And customs won't even look at it… You'll be able to clean it up a bit when you get it home, a bit of sandpaper should do the trick."

Givi turned to the old man again, who quickly held up his two fingers again and began waving them under Givi's nose.

Givi groaned and stood up, clutching the ring in his fist.

"Oh," he said, "go on then..."

He rummaged in his pocket, pulled out the crumpled wad of money, and with Shenderovich's help peeled off two thousand lira. The ring looked a bit odd on his finger. As if it were actually part of his finger. It was like a signet ring, with some kind of stamp on it. It was difficult to make out... Givi looked at it more closely, turned it round...

"Hey!" shouted the old man. "Efendi!"

"Damn," Givi exclaimed. "I forgot about the dagger."

He gingerly took the dagger from the unhygienic old hands and carefully fastened the battered old sheath to his belt. It looked ridiculous.

The sun was slowly setting behind the burning cupolas. Crosses and crescents were melting in the thick azure syrup of the skies...In the lengthening shadows, the crooked figure on the carpet looked like a giant and not particularly friendly spider.

Givi gave an involuntary shiver.

"Enough already," Shenderovich could stand it no longer. "Let's get out of here."

Givi followed him obediently. The dagger was banging against his thigh with every step. It wasn't a particularly pleasant feeling and, moreover, it was swinging out of step. It was behaving like a foreign body.

It obviously had something against Givi.

Steel chooses her own master, thought Givi. I wonder how she gets rid of the one before?

They forced their way through the crowd, trampling over the multicoloured cloth, brushing aside the annoying salesmen in unnatural ethnographical fezes and comically fake moustaches and the women in their shiny, figure-hugging blouses, which barely concealed their magnificent, heaving bosoms. For some reason, as if by some process of natural selection, all the women seemed to have auburn hair.

"Just don't get started on the carpets!" begged Shenderovich. He was singling items out from the colourful commotion as he went along, throwing some things back, holding on to others... After a few minutes, he had a handful of silk scarves that fluttered in the evening breeze – red, gold, green...

"Presents," he explained, meeting Givi's curious gaze. "You can choose whichever you like. There must be some girls in that accounts department of yours. Maybe a couple? Take two, then."

He cast another furtive look around. Givi did likewise.

"Misha!" he whispered in astonishment. "Where's he gone?"

"Where?" Shenderovich jumped. "Who? Lysyuk?"

"Not Lysyuk, you idiot. I've never even met him. I mean the old man... the one on the carpet. He's disappeared! He was sitting right there..."

"No wonder," huffed Shenderovich. "He's done a runner, before you realize you've been ripped off and want your money back... Yannis, my brother, you need to keep your guard up, otherwise they'll have you quicker than you can fart. They're all the same, they don't miss a trick. They don't consider it a sin to cheat an infidel. Anyway, let's go and get some fried fish. Over there, under the awning... I'll show you how to live the good life, my freedom-loving little Greek."

"I know how to live the good life," Givi answered brusquely.

In actual fact they paid him peanuts, but in his dreams he lived the good life. At least, he tried to imagine how one might go about it. Shenderovich strode decisively over to a cluster of little tables under a striped awning. The tail of one of the silk scarves poked cheekily out of his pocket.

"Two portions of fried fish, and two rakis," Shenderovich announced in Russian, leaning back on the fragile, warped frame of his plastic chair. Then he repeated himself in heavily accented English. "Two... Two fish, two raki. Understand?"

"Certainly," responded a waiter, coldly.

"A bottle," Givi raised his voice.

"A bottle of raki?" the waiter asked in surprise.

"No. Cognac. Armenian brandy. Ever heard of it?"

"Givi," Shenderovich reproachfully shook his head. "What are you on about, cognac? Il fait chaud, my friend. What kind of weirdo drinks cognac in this kind of heat?"

"I do," said Givi, despondently.

"Wait till this evening," Shenderovich said gently. "I told you, we'll have a proper session tonight. This is just a quick pit-stop."

Oh, fragrant, fair-skinned Alka, carelessly kicking her sandals from her delicate feet in the shadowy recesses of the captain's cabin… Givi threw his pile of crumpled notes to the table with a flourish.

"**I** looked for my sweetheart's gra-a-ave," Givi howled the words of a classic Georgian love-song. "And grief tormented my heart. Without lo-o-ove my heart felt… hic!... heavy…"

"Where are yo-o-ou, my Suliko?" Shenderovich loyally completed the verse. "Seriously, where are we?"

The evening had stolen upon the glorious city of Constantinople undetected, like a thief with a penchant for daylight. Just a few moments ago, the cupolas had been glowing golden in the sun, the minarets darkening against the backdrop of the yellow sky. But now the sun itself was no longer visible and the only trace of the final rays of light was their reflection in a solitary crescent at the top of a tower. And then even the crescent grew dark and was extinguished, transformed into a silhouette cut from black pasteboard.

The cries of the cicadas and the muezzins vied with each other for attention.

There was a rotten smell coming off the water.

Waves bearing all manner of detritus were breaking against the wooden pillars with the faintest of rustles. The tar-coated hulls of the moored tugboats and fishermen's boats with rubber rings strapped to their sides softly bumped against the pier. They were held together by half-hearted ropes, which were obviously thinking, why make the effort?

The warehouses and their gangly stacks of cardboard boxes towered into the sky, the gaping jaws of cranes frozen above them like giant insects.

"Where…" Givi started singing again.

He suddenly realized to his dismay that he didn't know the rest of the words. Either he'd forgotten, or he had never known… In any case, he repeated the last line, counting on Shenderovich to join in.

"Well?" Shenderovich asked encouragingly.

"That's it," confessed Givi.

"Shame," Shenderovich shook his head, momentarily losing his balance, but immediately straightening up his starboard side. "You're a disgrace! How can you forget the ancient culture of your own people?"

"Culture-schmulture," said Givi, sadly. "Ekh!"

The fresh wind from the sea hit him in the face, and he flinched and looked around.

"Misha," he said, almost soberly. "Where are we?"

"At the warehouses, of course," said Shenderovich, slurring as he enunciated each word with care. "We're loading up."

He extracted from his pocket the card that Ali had given him in the café and squinted at it, trying to make out the address, which was not easy in the dark.

"Warehouse number… what number is it? Aha! Twenty-two," he muttered, and to further emphasise this turned to Givi and repeated it carefully in English.

"Arabic numerals," Givi repeated dumbly.

"What else?" Shenderovich asked in surprise.

Screwing up his eyes again, he peered through the gloom, trying to make out the numbers daubed on the walls of the warehouses in black oil paint.

"Eight…" he muttered, "eleven… Ah, this way, Givi my brother…"

He turned decisively into a narrow opening between the containers. Givi trudged after him.

"We just got a bit lost," he continued muttering as they walked. "And it was all your fault, you and your love songs You drink like a Greek. Jesus, you're worse than Yannis…"

A startled seagull gave a dry cough.

Givi began to have a bad feeling.

"Misha," he whispered. "Why is it so quiet?"

"Because it's Friday night," Shenderovich shrugged. "No one works on a Friday night."

"Apart from us," Givi lamented. "Why *are* we working on a Friday night?"

"Because of Lysyuk," answered Shenderovich in a nervous whisper. "Haven't you ever heard the word 'conspiracy'? Ah, here we are…"

Warehouse number twenty-two stood a little apart from the others, with its corner facing the black water. The doors were wide open, revealing the shadowy interior, and a solitary loading truck stood motionless in the doorway. Several dark figures were moving about efficiently inside.

"Oh!" Shenderovich cried excitedly. "They're already loading up!"

Givi shivered. His guardian angel, the one responsible for watching over drunken sinners, breathed tenderly on the back of his neck.

"Misha," Givi whispered uncertainly. "Something's not quite right here… Misha…"

But Shenderovich was already striding cheerfully towards the warehouse and looking inside.

"So," he began, in the bored but simultaneously pushy tone of the successful businessman. "You're already loading the goods? Why didn't you wait for me? I told them… Hey! What are you doing?"

Givi was about to rush to his friend's assistance when he felt with horror something cold and hard pressing between his shoulder-blades. A voice that was equally cold and hard said something, but not in Russian.

"What?" asked Givi, politely.

"Ah, Shaitan!" said the voice. "Ingilizce biliyor? Speak English?"

"Uh-huh," Givi quickly replied, instinctively groping about in the darkest recesses of his mind. "I, uh, yes... a little..."

"Stand still," the voice said, in English. And to underline the point the cold object pressed a littler harder into Givi's spine.

"OK, OK," Givi wasn't about to argue.

There was a strange noise coming from beyond the enormous, greedy jaws of the warehouse, as if several people were grunting heavily as they thrashed something soft...

The cold thing continued pressing into Givi's spine, but the tactile contact did not stop there. Givi felt a hand efficiently patting up and down his sides.

Has he got three hands or something, Givi wondered in disbelief.

The hand fell on the dagger at his waist. Givi felt practised fingers unfastening the sheath.

"Oho!" said the hand.

"Uh-huh," agreed Givi, resignedly.

Givi caught a fleeting glimpse of a hand covered in a black glove. It slid with the smooth touch of a lover into his jacket pocket and pulled out his modestly bulging wallet. The wallet flaunted itself mockingly under Givi's nose then disappeared.

Well, there you go, thought Givi.

A similar trick was performed by the two silk scarves – presents intended for Lila and Ella in the office.

The hands swiftly patted his remaining jacket pockets then slipped into his trouser pockets and had a good rummage around. That was the final straw for Givi. He gritted his teeth and prepared to respond to the insult like a man. What the hell did he think he was doing, fondling him like that?

He jerked his elbow out.

It met with something hard, like a wooden plank. No reaction. Just to check, Givi tried again, this time with his foot. It met the same hard object. A voice behind him groaned, and Givi felt an answering knee meet his backside with such force that he flew up into the warm air and was temporarily suspended there.

"Why, you…!" Givi cried indignantly and turned around in mid-air to look his unknown assailant in the eye. And then he gasped – through his gritted teeth – in horror. Looking back at him was a terrifying black figure with a smooth black head, no nose or mouth, and hollows for eyes.

"Oh my god, it's an alien!" was the first thought that rushed into Givi's mind.

Hostile Martians, or whatever they were, must have secretly landed on earth in their UFOs.

Givi even felt himself swelling with pride – his heart missed a beat in anticipation of something wonderful and terrible that had chosen him, Givi, to happen to. However, disappointment was swift to follow.

"Son of bitch!" said the creature, grabbing its crotch. The voice sounded muffled, and Givi's heart sank as he realized that it was simply because of the black nylon stocking that was stretched tightly over a very ordinary human head.

The strong grip relaxed, and Givi slipped away, darting between the hangars like a wild hare, every second expecting to feel a shot in the back and every now and then remembering to call out:

"Help! Misha! I'm being attacked! Somebody, help!"

He added "Misha!" to prove that he hadn't abandoned Shenderovich in his hour of need but on the contrary was really rather worried and wanted to help.

It wasn't clear whether his yelling had succeeded in scaring off the attackers or whether the mysterious people in stockings had simply accomplished what they had set out to achieve, but the whole episode drew abruptly and unceremoniously to a close. An engine started up somewhere behind the hangar, and Givi's anxious ear detected several pairs of heavy boots running hurriedly past him. The engine spluttered to life, a door slammed, the engine roared and the car flashed past Givi and sped away, covering him in a mixture of hot southern air and exhaust fumes and spreading the puddle of oil further across the asphalt.

Crouching down in confusion, Givi watched the rear lights as they moved off into the distance. They winked mockingly at him before disappearing out of sight around a bend.

"Ekh!" said Givi.

A sticky pool of shame was nestling in the pit of his stomach. Givi knew that once more he had failed to measure up. That was no way for a man with a dagger at his waist to behave. No way for a man without a dagger to behave, even. A real man would have seized the opportunity presented to him by his adversary's momentary confusion not to run off, leaving his friend to his fate, but rather to turn round and deliver a powerful kick to his adversary's jaw... Or, alternatively, a quick blow to the windpipe with the edge of his hand: sorted! With his opponent writhing on the floor in agony, Givi throws himself into the terrifying black jaws of the hangar. A series of precise, professional blows are heard then the camera pans back to reveal Givi standing in the midst of a sea of lifeless bodies, reaching a strong hand out to Shenderovich. Shenderovich stands up, worried and grateful. Givi asks if he's OK, then says, "Right, let's see who we've got here..." as he bends to pull the black mask from one of the villains...

But seriously, who were they?

And what on earth had happened to Shenderovich?

Hanging his head, Givi plodded towards the hangar. Maybe they had killed him, he reflected as he walked. Maybe his dead body would just be lying there… Poor, poor Misha… And what would he, Givi, tell the Turkish police? And what was he going to do now, alone in Turkey? OK, he could always head back to the ferry. He wondered whether the Ukrainian authorities would hand a foreign citizen over to the Turkish authorities, even if he came in on a Ukrainian ferry. And come to think of it, why was he so sure the ferry was Ukrainian…?

He felt another flush of shame – what was he doing worrying about his own fate at such a tragic time!

Poor, poor Misha…

The hangar was dark and empty. Well, there was a solitary light-bulb hanging from the ceiling, naked and lonely, like an abandoned film star, but unsurprisingly it wasn't serving much purpose. Givi paced up and down a bit by the entrance, then mustered his courage and peered inside.

"Misha!" he called quietly.

"Sh-sha," answered the hangar.

Then something moved behind an empty, overturned container. A disheveled head appeared from around one of the sides. Even in the dull light of the lonely film star it was clear that one of Shenderovich's eyes was swollen and blue, and his shirt collar was half ripped off and hanging shamelessly from his muscular shoulder.

"Misha!" Givi almost cried with relief. "You're alive!"

"Sort of," answered Shenderovich, gloomily.

Grimacing and groaning theatrically, he finally emerged from behind the container, carefully feeling himself up and down to make sure he was still in one piece.

"Are you OK?" Givi asked mechanically.

"Of course," answered Shenderovich.

"Who were they, Misha?"

"A bunch of bastards," snapped Shenderovich. Then he cheered up. "But I showed them!"

Somewhere deep in his soul Givi had his doubts, but he opted not to share them with Shenderovich.

"They robbed me," he informed Shenderovich. "They took my wallet, ekh! And my documents. They even took those silk scarves... And they took my dagger. What did they have to take that for? What use is it to them?"

"Your dagger?!" snorted Shenderovich. He was gradually coming back to life. "You paid two poxy dollars for that dagger. Who cares about your stupid dagger? I had five thousand dollars on me! Five thousand! That's what they took from me! And the goods? What goods? There aren't any! Where are the balloons? Have they floated away? What has he done with the goods?"

"Who?" Givi was surprised. "Ali?"

"What's Ali got to do with anything? Ali's just a pawn in the game. He sold his goods and is sitting happily in the coffee house with all that mess around him... No, it's that filthy scumbag. The snake! He got me, after all. It's him, I tell you!"

"Lysyuk?" Givi took a wild guess.

"Of course it was Lysyuk," answered Shenderovich, matter-of-factly. "He set his bandits on me. He followed me, hired a few hitmen and set them on me. I'll get him for this! I'll show him! Just wait till I get back..."

He stumbled, blinked and fell against the hangar wall with his head in his hands.

"Jesus! How am I going to go back now? I'm never going to be able to pay them back, with all the interest and everything... I'm a dead man!"

"That five thousand..." the cogs in Givi's brain were working overtime. "You mean it wasn't yours?"

"Of course not!" Shenderovich mournfully confirmed. "Where am I going to get five thousand dollars from? I went to a loan shark... I would have made back three times that amount! Do you know what sort of returns you get on balloons? Do you know how fast they sell?"

"Well, they certainly 'disappear' all right," said Givi, despondently. "Anyway, what are you worrying about? We're not going home. They won't let us in. Passports please, they'll say, where are your passports? What do you mean you haven't got any passports?"

"Christ almighty," Shenderovich breathed out. "What's the big deal about the passports? We're not the first to lose them, and we won't be the last. We'll go to the embassy, tell them what happened… show them our bruises."

"We need to go to the police, Misha," Givi said firmly. "That's the only way. They'll give us a form to fill in, then we take that to the embassy, where they'll give us another form to fill in…"

"Bugger the forms," Shenderovich cut him off. He was slowly returning to an upright position, leaning on the hangar wall again.

"Well, you can do what you like," said Givi, firmly. "But I'm going to the police. Let them get to the bottom of it. I've had enough of all this nonsense, Misha. Everything's fine, you said, don't worry, we'll sort it out. Well, is this 'sorted' enough for you?"

"Fine, go on then," sighed Shenderovich, brushing off his knees. "Go to the police. Tell them all about Greece, about your historic motherland…"

"Fine, I will."

"Go on then. You know how much the Turks love the Greeks? To death!"

Givi paused for thought.

"Hang on, Misha," he said finally. "Did you give Ali an advance?"

"Yeah, so?" answered Shenderovich, bitterly. "A third of the total, like we agreed."

"Did he deliver the goods, though? Where are they? You should get your money back."

"Ali's got nothing to do with it," sighed Shenderovich. "I told you, it's Lysyuk… He tracked us down and…"

"Ah yes, but Misha, they cleaned the warehouse out before we even got here. And how did they know which warehouse to come to? Who else knew, apart from us? Ali, that's who. Ali put them on to us. So he can give you your money back. That's no way to do business."

Shenderovich thought tensely for a moment.

"You're right," he said eventually. "The weasel, I'll teach him… I'll shake his soul from his body. 'You trust me, you trust me'! Ha, Yannis! Ha, Stavrakis! Ha, the bastard!"

"Do you know where he lives?"

"Italianskaya Street, on the corner of Kanatnaya."

"Not Stavrakis, you idiot. Ali!"

"How should I know? Maybe Stavrakis knows."

"We need to go back to the coffee house. He said so himself, that's where he spends most of his time."

"You're right!" Shenderovich declared delightedly. "Let's go to the coffee house. We'll pin him down, the repulsive little worm. We'll make him give us the money back! All of it! And if he won't, we'll get the police involved. Let's get out of here, my wise brother, before we get into any more trouble."

"Where are we going?" asked Givi, hopefully. "The police station?"

Shenderovich stopped to think.

"Nope… we'll save that for later. They'll want a full description… Did you get a good look at the nutter that attacked you?"

"Sort of," said Givi.

"Well?"

"He was wearing a black stocking, I couldn't really see…"

"That," said Shenderovich tersely, "I could see for myself. What else?"

"He was dressed in black as well…"

"Yes, I noticed."

"I saw a car."

"What colour?" asked Shenderovich, in a business-like tone. "What kind was it? Did you see the registration number?"

"It was massive," said Givi, forlornly.

"And that's it?"

"Uh-huh."

"Great. And you want to go to the police... What are we going to say to them?"

"There are some tyre-marks in the oil."

"Well, that's something, I suppose," agreed Shenderovich. "Right, this is how we're going to play it... We'll go back to the ferry, sort ourselves out, calm down a bit... Then tomorrow morning we'll take Alka and go to the coffee house."

"Right, so we're going to the ferry, then," answered Givi, obediently. "That's an acceptable plan of action. Very sensible. Will they let us on board, do you think?"

"Why not?" shrugged Shenderovich.

The night embraced them, dark and warm as tar. In the distance, the lights of the vessels moored in the harbour were sparkling in the black sea, like precious stones spilt from a broken necklace. Givi suddenly really wanted to be out there, as far as he could possibly get from shore. He sighed and straightened his shoulders as best he could.

"I showed mine a thing or two, as well," he said to Shenderovich.

It was quiet on board the ferry, so quiet that Givi could make out the gentle lapping of the tiny waves. The passengers – carefree tourists and shuttle traders alike – had dissipated throughout Istanbul in search of cheap entertainment and were drinking coffee at white tables on vine-covered terraces, devouring kebabs and pastries, sweating in the hammams, enjoying themselves at the belly-dancing shows... There was all manner of pleasure to be had after nightfall in this blessed city, capital of a blessed country, washed on three sides by three different seas... Givi had started feeling sorry for himself again.

He looked at the lights in the lounge with longing, then bitterly turned away. All the money that Shenderovich had given him for expenses had disappeared into the greedy clutches of the thieves.

To Givi's surprise, their cabin light was on. Varvara Timofeevna, whom Givi had managed to completely forget about, was efficiently arranging some sort of colourful jumble on her bunk. The jumble shimmered and sparkled in the dim light of the cabin's lamp.

She turned and seemed flustered at the sight of Shenderovich's handsome face. But she immediately clasped her hands to her chest and exclaimed, "Oh, sweetheart! What happened to you?"

"Ah, you know…" answered Shenderovich, vaguely. "I thought you would have been in Antalya by now. Babysitting."

"Well, my love, I thought, when will I ever get to see Istanbul again?" answered Varvara Timofeevna, good-naturedly. "So I called Antalya. Please, I said, let me spend a couple of days here. I like it here. The people are so nice and polite. Not like Russians."

Even in the weak cabin light it was obvious that after only one day in the free city of Istanbul Varvara Timofeevna had undergone quite a transformation. Her hair was now curled into ringlets and had acquired a rich Rubenesque shade. Her eyebrows had been shaped, and her comfortable round shoulders protruded cheekily from a sparkly red blouse cut so low it made Givi blush and look away. Varvara Timofeevna's feet bore a stunning pair of expensive but elegant black patent leather shoes with a low heel, and her legs shimmered in silk, proudly displaying their perfect, round knees.

"Well, Istanbul certainly agrees with you," said Shenderovich, registering some surprise. "You look like a Persian rose!"

"I went to the hammam. They're so polite in the hammam. And the girls are so nice. So kind… You, they said, beautiful lady, you are a joy to behold, we just need to change your clothes… Then they sent me off to one of the shops, one of them even came with me to help me choose a blouse…"

"She probably got commission," Shenderovich observed matter-of-factly.

"So what if she did? They're happy, and I'm happy. She took me to a beautician, bought me coffee. Come and see us again, she said, beautiful lady…All the best people come to our hammam… And you are young, interesting…"

And Varvara Timofeevna shyly straightened her skirt, revealing as she did so one perfect, round knee.

"It just goes to show, Yannis my brother," said Shenderovich, sadly. "Some suffer from war while others profit…"

"But why have you left Allochka all alone?" Varvara Timofeevna was curious.

"She was the one who left us," Shenderovich answered curtly. "Allochka is making merry with our esteemed captain."

"The tall one? Good-looking?"

Givi felt depressed.

"Yes," Shenderovich answered impartially. "Tall and good-looking."

"But he's here," Varvara Timofeevna was surprised. "Our captain's on board. He's sitting in the lounge, in a dreadful temper, too! He's sitting there, drumming his fingers on the table."

Shenderovich leapt up.

"Where is he? In the lounge? Let's go, Givi!"

"Now he's Givi again, is he?" Varvara Timofeevna asked in surprise.

Varvara Timofeevna was not wrong – the captain was sitting alone at one of the tables, irritably drumming his fingers on the starched tablecloth. He really was tall, and good-looking, and as Shenderovich burst into the lounge he looked at him so coldly that Shenderovich seemed to instantly deflate and shrivel up.

"What's going on?" Shenderovich was also cold, but polite.

He pulled up a chair with his foot and sank into it. Givi wasn't brave enough to sit down, so he paced shyly up and down behind his friend.

"I should be asking you that," answered the captain, equally coldly. "What happened to your eye? What have you been doing? Where is Alla Sergeevna?"

"I haven't got the faintest idea where Alka is," Shenderovich was affronted. "You're the one who should be telling me. You had a date, didn't you?"

"No," the captain cut him off. "Alla left with you in the morning and didn't come back. You know, I'm not used to…"

"Shit!" Shenderovich looked helplessly from the captain to Givi, and back again. "I don't believe it! Has she gone off with someone else, then? How the hell did she manage that?"

"May I ask you," said the captain, coldly, "not to speak of Alla in that tone."

"He doesn't like my tone!" Shenderovich was gradually becoming more insolent. "Well I'm sorry, but what have you been doing? One, we've been mugged – beaten up and mugged! Two, a girl is missing! Three, our consignment of goods has disappeared into thin air!" He waved the remaining two fingers under the captain's nose. "Janissaries! They're all completely wild! You're the captain, you tell us what we should do now. They took our passports and all our money."

"Hang on," the captain looked helplessly at Givi. "Were you really mugged?"

"Yes," confirmed Givi sadly. "Their police are useless."

"So where's Alla?" the captain was starting to get worried. "What have they done with her?"

He bounded over to Shenderovich and jerked him powerfully into the air. Shenderovich moved his head from side to side, grunted and tried to brush him off.

"Why you, you bastard!" the captain was yelling. "What have you done with Alla, you bastard?"

After some elementary cerebral calculations, the captain had evidently come to the conclusion that Alka had ended her earthly existence at the bottom of the sea. Either the bandits that had attacked Shenderovich had had their fun with her and then thrown her alive into the turbid water off the docks, or else the temperamental Shenderovich and his swarthy friend had violated the poor thing and then disposed of the evidence... Whatever, it was clear that a dark deed had been done. And the worst of it was that the captain now found himself by association mixed up in the whole affair. That Shenderovich and his impudent eyes...

Givi hovered around the captain, timidly pulling at his sleeves. The captain elbowed him away without turning round.

"Good heavens!" Varvara Timofeevna appeared at the doors to the lounge and clasped her hands together. "What are you doing to poor Misha?"

"I'm getting to the bottom of this!" said the captain between gritted teeth. "Now, you worm, tell me! Where is she?"

"Aarghh!" Shenderovich was trying desperately to breathe. He finally managed to twist himself free from the captain's tenacious grip, swung his arm back and punched him neatly in the stomach. The captain merely straightened his jacket with disgust.

"Oh, my darling!" exclaimed the horrified Varvara Timofeevna. "Misha! Yurochka! What's going on? They've got nothing to do with it, Yurochka! Allochka went off all by herself! I saw her! Misha wasn't there at all! Neither was whatsisname!"

"Where did you see her?" The captain had seized hold of Shenderovich again and started to shake him rhythmically and very deliberately. "Who was she with?"

"Not with them, not with them!" Varvara Timofeevna hurriedly intervened. "She was alone. Let him go, Yurochka! Look, he's turning blue..."

The captain reluctantly let go. Shenderovich fell onto a chair, gasping.

"Compared to you," he finally spluttered, "those bandits were a bunch of amateurs."

"They should have finished you off, you swine," answered the captain, adjusting his cuffs. "So, where did you see her, then?"

"In the museum, that's where it was," explained Varvara Timofeevna. "The folk museum…"

"The what? Where?" Givi was stupefied.

In his mind, Alka and museums were fundamentally incompatible.

But Shenderovich and the captain were both nodding, the captain because of his belief in Alka's boundless intelligence and Shenderovich because of his belief in her equally boundless unpredictability.

"What do mean by 'folk museum,' my dear?" the captain asked politely, having finally succeeded in bringing his cuffs into perfect alignment. "There are hundreds of them."

"Now, which one was it…?" Varvara Timofeevna pursed her lips. "Was it the one near the park… Gülhane Park, was it? Oh, I don't remember. There's so much to see here in Istanbul… Bargain clothes shops… Ooh, and you should see their bazaar, Yurochka, you can get anything you want… Aubergines, peppers… You can even get fresh mackerel, can you imagine? You can't get fresh mackerel for love or money in Odessa."

"If we could just stick to the point," Shenderovich reminded her.

Varvara Timofeevna sat at the table and neatly rested her plump, dimpled elbows on the tablecloth.

They all looked at her expectantly. "I wouldn't mind a cup of tea," she said.

The captain, working his muscular wrists free from his cuffs again, clicked his fingers at one of the waitresses.

"One tea," he said curtly. Then, taking pity on the morose Shenderovich and sorrowful Givi, he added, "and two beers… no, make it three!"

"You sit yourself down, my love," urged Varvara Timofeevna, having evidently assigned herself the role of hostess. "Sit down, Yannis… Or whatever your name is… Anyway, sit down."

The waitress silently placed tall glasses, cold and shiny, in front of them, but Shenderovich had already opened a bottle with his teeth and was guzzling directly from it.

"So, which museum was it, ma'am?" asked Shenderovich, managing to drag himself away from his beer.

"I didn't go there straightaway," Varvara Timofeevna was lost in thought. "It was, hang on… Misha, where are the carpets? No… Oh, the carpets, I tell you… No, it was the one with the grave…"

"Which grave, exactly?" Shenderovich pressed her.

"You know, that scarofagus… King Alexander's… They say he had two horns, or some such nonsense… I don't know, there weren't any horns on the lid of his grave, anyway…"

"Iskander the Two-Horned One," the captain elaborated. "Alexander of Macedonia. Alexander the Great to you and me. His sarcophagus is here, in Istanbul… They found it during a dig at Sidon. It was empty, unsurprisingly."

"I thought he died in India," Shenderovich was surprised. "I'm sure I read that somewhere."

"Who knows where he died," answered the captain, vaguely. "So anyway, is that where you saw Alla Sergeevna?"

"I think so," Varvara Timofeevna was doing her best to remember. "Or maybe not…"

"I read that he put on a black crown that erased his memory then died of sorrow…" insisted Shenderovich.

"More beers," the captain clicked his fingers again.

"And what are you having, ma'am?" Shenderovich became solicitous.

"I'd like a glass of wine… sweet, red wine…"

"And some wine…" consented the captain.

"They stole our money," Givi thought he ought to remind him.

"Ah!" the captain waved aside his objection. "It's on the house!"

"In that case, I'll have a cognac," Shenderovich was making himself at home, sprawling in his chair.

"One cognac," the captain obediently repeated.

Givi was full of admiration for Shenderovich's innate impertinence.

"Yes, definitely!" Varvara Timofeevna finally exclaimed. "It was there! I remember, she waved at me."

She gave an embarrassed shrug.

"And I'm sorry Yurochka, but she wasn't alone…"

"What do you mean she wasn't alone?" the captain tensed up. "You said…"

"I said that she wasn't with these two," Varvara Timofeevna explained. "But she was with a man. He was holding her arm, like a proper gentleman…"

The captain's mood darkened.

"Fine," he said through clenched teeth, looking at Shenderovich reproachfully. "I get it."

He started to get up from the table.

"Hang on a minute," Shenderovich panicked. "What do you 'get'? What about us?"

The captain worked his wrists free from his cuffs again and made a show of looking at his watch.

"What about you?" he asked, with the utmost civility.

"We were robbed!" yelled Shenderovich, also leaping up from the table. "Beaten up! Look what they did, here's the proof, on my face! Look!"

In the heat of the moment, he accidentally poked his finger into his black eye and cried out in pain.

"If you were robbed, then go to the police station," the captain interrupted his rant. "What's it got to do with me, for God's sake? Every trip, some idiots get cheated…"

And, proudly straightening his shoulders, he headed for the door. Shenderovich made as if to follow him but thought better of it and, with a bitter wave of his hand, flopped back down at the table.

"What a nightmare," he declared. "It's all Alka's fault, the little viper… She's the reason he's so angry! What was she thinking, the little minx? Swapping a captain like that for some Turk. When she gets back, I'm going to kill her, the wanton hussy. And in the meantime, what are we going to do? What are we going to do, Givi my friend?"

He emptied the remaining cognac into his beer glass.

"Misha," said Givi, timidly. "I'm hungry."

"Well I don't know what you expect me to do about it," Shenderovich answered petulantly. "We haven't got any money! Not a bean!"

"I'll get him something, Misha," Varvara Timofeevna said soothingly. "I'll get him something right now. Valechka! Sweetheart! What have you got left in there?"

"Nothing," answered a girl in a white headdress, who couldn't have been less interested. She was looking at Givi with something approaching disgust.

"Then rustle them up a couple of fried eggs, would you, love? With tomatoes. A slice of ham... Go on, darling, do what you can."

Without a word, the girl turned round, brazenly flicking the hem of her short skirt under Givi's nose, and headed for the galley kitchen.

"Drink up while you're waiting, Yannis. Or whatever your name is..."

"His real name's Givi," admitted Shenderovich.

Varvara Timofeevna put her hand over her mouth and looked at Shenderovich with horror.

"He's gone mad," she concluded sadly.

"Not at all," Shenderovich assured her. "It's all down to twists of fate, ma'am. What's in a name, anyway?"

"It's what's in your passport," Varvara Timofeevna said firmly.

"A passport," Shenderovich declared wisely, "is one of life's great variables."

"Exactly!" thought Givi, who had been growing steadily more depressed. "What have I got? I haven't even got a name.

I was beaten up like a little kid, they stole my money and my dagger, my new toy… They took everything, and Alka's gone. And good for her – she's better off out of all this nonsense."

"To his friends, he's Givi," Shenderovich was busy explaining. "To others, he's Yannis. And to his enemies… to his enemies, he's a force to be reckoned with…"

"Well, I don't know," Varvara Timofeevna shook her head. "You are a complicated bunch! Anyway… Givi, Yannis, what difference does it make? The main thing is that he's one of us! That's why he needs to eat… and it wouldn't hurt him to drink a drop more either – look at him, he's clearly lost weight!"

She looked at Givi's sad puppy-dog eyes.

"Romochka, pour him another."

"Coming right up," the barman sleepily responded, obediently uncorking a new bottle.

"And I'll have a strong cup of tea."

"Coming right up!"

The fresh, cool wind from the Bosphorus, the warm, velvety wind from the Princes' Islands, and the hot, jasmine-scented wind from the sleepy gardens of Istanbul took turns caressing the impressionable curtains in the lounge, causing them to quiver and to tremble and to long to leap from their tracks and fly far, far away to a place where salads and fried eggs were but a distant memory, where nobody spilled beer on the tablecloth, where they could fly on their cloth wings in the coal-black sky like weightless daughters of the air…

"Poor Yurochka," Varvara Timofeevna sighed sympathetically, propping up her cheek with her hand. "He's not a happy bunny! He really has taken quite a shine to Allochka, hasn't he… So tell me what happened, Misha, my love. Who did this to you?"

"Lysyuk," Shenderovich replied, lustfully eying the plate of fried eggs winking its red tomato eyes at him. "I swear it was Lysyuk."

"You're insane," said Givi, as he pulled the plate towards

him, shielding it from Shenderovich with his elbow. "You're completely obsessed... There's even a medical term for it."

"The medical term is 'screwed'," said Shenderovich, taking a knife and furiously hacking off a portion of egg. "To be more precise, it's 'utterly screwed'."

"What's he talking about?" Varvara Timofeevna asked Givi in a whisper, having obviously decided that for the time being Givi was of marginally sounder mind.

"Some rival," shrugged Givi. He really wasn't in the mood for Shenderovich's conspiracy theory. He was concentrating on his food.

"Some rival?" Shenderovich turned on him. "He's not just any rival! I told you."

"Yeah, yeah," agreed Givi. "I remember. You're bound by the mysterious threads of fate."

"If I were you, I wouldn't be so flippant," said Shenderovich reproachfully as he devoured his egg. "The visible world is merely a smokescreen. If you look beyond it, you can see the wheels of fate turning. I don't know whether you realize it, but these wheels of fate have spokes, which are tightly secured by the most basic laws of mechanics, with the result that two points on the rim that seem to be far apart are in actual fact inextricably linked by a stupid spindle. And if you aren't going to drink that cognac, I will."

Mikhail Abramovich Shenderovich's Story, or A Tale Concerning the Personal Application of the Law of Conservation of Universal Happiness in Nature

He joined us in Year Seven. Quite unassuming, he was. The maths teacher brought him in, I seem to remember – she was our form monitor. Her surname was Barenboim, I think, but that's not important. We called her Carrot because she had ginger hair. She brought him in before the lesson started – she was holding his hand and he was letting her, trotting obediently along beside her. She stood him in front of the class. Say hello, she said, this is Marik Lysyuk, he's your new classmate. He stood there in his glasses, with his little schoolbag, his Young Pioneer's tie all skewed to one side. A smart little chap, basically, and he stood there, with only his eyes blinking behind his glasses – blink, blink!

I took an immediate dislike to him.

They sat him next to me, because Zhorka Shmulkin was off sick that day. He sat down, politely said hello, got out his textbooks, his notebooks, etcetera. I elbowed him in the ribs, you know, just being friendly, but he didn't elbow me back or whack me over the head with a book, or anything – just carried on sitting there, blinking at me.

The lesson began, and I was called up to the board. Maths wasn't exactly my favourite subject, but I was pretty good at it, I have to say. At that moment, though, I just had a total mental block. I'd done my homework, I knew the answer, but it just wouldn't come! I was standing in front of the whole class like a complete idiot, blinking in confusion – I must have caught it from him. Carrot said, what's the matter with you, Misha? Didn't you do your homework?

Yes, I said, I've just forgotten. A likely story, I know, but I honestly had done it. I was supposed to be going to football training camp – the coach had arranged for me to be called up sooner rather than later, so they could submit their accounts before the end of term.

I mumbled and bluffed my way through – someone could have whispered me the answer, the little bastards! I could hear someone whispering something from the back of the class but it was too far away to make out. And then I saw the new boy's hand go up. Basically, he got an A, I got a D. And as for football training… no chance. It all kicked off at home – you're neglecting your studies, all you care about is football, blah blah blah… Dad saw to it personally that I spent all summer holiday studying.

Anyway.

The new school year started. Carrot said, I would like you to congratulate Marik Lysyuk, he did a brilliant job representing our school at the maths championships. He came second in the district, third in the city. Attaboy, Marik!

I've hated maths ever since. And Lysyuk. I got him in a corner and beat him up a couple of times, just so that he didn't think life was all a bed of roses. I had a bit of help, I have to say – the other boys hated him too. To be fair, he kept his mouth shut.

Then towards the summer, he broke his leg. This is how it happened... They used to take us down to the estuary in teams to play the war-game "Summer Lightning" – we were supposed to dig ourselves trenches in simulation of combat situations, but we actually spent more time drinking in the bushes. Then one day, Zhorka Shmulkin and I went AWOL for longer than usual. While we were drinking fortified wine in the ravine, pushing the cork in with our thumb, cutting up a piece of sausage to chase it with, our team decided to move in behind the enemy. The bus left without us. They shouted out of the window, head north-west! It was about a mile at most, so we had a bit more to drink and set off. While we were walking, a lorry ran into our bus. And it was some collision – the seat where Shmulkin and I should have been sitting, on the left-hand side, was totally smashed in. They would have had to cut us out of the wreckage with a blow-torch. As it was, Lyusyuk was the only casualty – he broke his leg. It was crushed by the seat. The one in front, where Zhorka and I should have been sitting.

That was the end of "Summer Lightning" game. Our military instructor got an official reprimand, naturally, even though it wasn't his fault, and he was forced to resign. The lorry driver was the one at fault, really, he'd cut the corner. He must've been drinking fortified wine too. Ugh, horrible stuff, it was...

Lysyuk spent the whole summer limping about in his cast. The break didn't heal properly, so they had to break it again. I wouldn't have wished that on him, but personally I had a great summer. Our football team won the city championship... then we went to Yaroslavl for a friendly match, then to Saratov. Then just before school started again, we went to Sochi. I took a couple of days out of September too, so missed the start of the school year and only started back somewhere around the seventh, all tanned and feeling good about life.

I was walking down the corridor, saying hi to the lads, when I saw Lysyuk coming towards me, and he was walking with a stick. Limping, rather. Hi Marik, I said... Hi, he said back, quietly and through clenched teeth, but polite enough. And those eyes – blink, blink! I thought, fair enough, let's forget about last year. Plus he'd had a bad time of it, his whole summer had been ruined.

Everything seemed fine, for a while. Then again, I was supposed to be off to football camp and he was up for the maths championships. By this time I was getting nothing but C's in maths.

The idiots in the education department had just introduced this new system of coursework essays. In the arts subjects – history, literature, etcetera. Our compositions evidently weren't enough for them. They said it helped to develop skills in working independently with the material. Basically, some fool had invented the new system so he'd get official recognition for his services to education. And our school was one of the ones to suffer. We'd just covered the October Revolution before the holidays, so we were sorted for the history assignment – I cut out a picture from *Ogonek*, showing a sailor running, a soldier running, both shooting as they went... job done. I got a C. Nobody was really taking it very seriously at the time, and frankly, it showed.

For literature, I was stuck with Lev Tolstoy and his *War and Peace*. That epic tale of the people's wrath. The essay was supposed to be typed, to get round the problem of our dreadful handwriting, and contain illustrations. We had to pick a topic – the circumstances in which Tolstoy wrote this immortal work of literary genius, how he loved the people, the role of his wife Sofia Andreevna, etcetera… By the way, for your information, she copied the novel out for him by hand at least twenty times, and each time right from the beginning. The historical situation in Yasnaya Polyana at the time he wrote it, you know, stuff like that… And it was the middle of the football season. I wasn't getting home before ten o'clock most nights and was absolutely knackered. Needless to say, I missed all my deadlines. Sonya Golden Hand (we'd nicknamed her after the famous thief) had already complained a couple of times to Carrot, who had her own problems to worry about: her daughter had had a baby girl, and no one knew who the father was, though everyone suspected it was one of the forwards from the Chernomorets football team. She gave me a real bollocking, going on about how football was the root of all evil, including the loss of spirituality in society, and that I was ruining my life because I had the makings of a good engineer but instead of hanging out with Lev Tolstoy I was wasting all my difficult teen years kicking a ball about. Well, she had her own issues with football. So I went home and set to work on that sodding essay. I missed my football training, skipped school, and sat there at the typewriter bashing the bloody thing out with one finger. I nicked a book from the local library, cut out the picture of Tolstoy and stuck it in my essay, along with a picture of Natasha Rostova at her first ball. That one was from the film, but it still looked good. I went in the next day with my essay in a file, all set. Everyone was giving me funny looks. It didn't bother me, though. I ran to the literature office with my file and found Golden Hand. Hello, Sofia Ruvimovna, I said, I've finished my essay."

"I know," she said. She had red blotches all over her face and neck, her eyes were clouded with tears and she was looking at me like I was something she'd scraped off her shoe. She looked like she really hated me. Up to this point, she'd been quite nice to me – called me 'Mishenka' and wasn't too hard on me.

"Here it is," I said, holding the file out to her.

She recoiled from it in disgust.

"That's enough," she said. "Just stop it now."

Whatever, I thought.

"Fine, I'll stop," I said, although I was a bit hurt. "I made a special effort for you though! I did it for you!"

"You certainly did!" she was shouting by this point. "Well, thank you for your 'special effort'! What have I ever done to you, Misha? I've always been kind to you! How could you be so cruel, Misha?"

Hmm, I thought, I always knew teachers had mental health issues.

"I didn't mean to. I know it's a bit late... But I've got it here!"

"You can't possibly have done it by accident," she said, her voice full of loathing.

I really didn't have the faintest idea what she was talking about.

"So, do you want my essay, or not?"

"Another one?" she said and clutched at her throat, as if I was trying to strangle her.

"What do you mean, another one?" It was slowly dawning on me. "Please, Golden... uh, I mean, Sofia Ruvimovna, here's my essay, the only one I've done."

"I've already read it!" she was shaking. "And that was certainly one of a kind! Quite unique! Was that not enough? You've brought another one?"

"May I ask, where the other one is?" I asked.

"With the headmaster," she said. "Where else?"

Something inside me skipped a beat and sank.

"I would like to look at it, please," I said.

"Of course you would," she said coldly, having pulled herself together and looking at me once more as if I were a worm. "The headmaster wanted to look at it too. I completely understand why you can't keep away from it, although frankly it is beyond pathological. Go on then! Admire your handiwork!"

Well, what can I say? I went to see the headmaster. There's no point repeating what he said, but at least I got to see 'my' essay. It was called 'Lev Tolstoy as a Mirror of the Sexual Revolution of the 20th Century.' You don't need to know the details, although I have to say the style and the language were perfectly acceptable. I certainly learnt some interesting stuff about Mr Tolstoy. And a fair amount about Mrs Tolstoy too. I learnt how he overcame his complexes – he was irresistibly drawn to prostitutes and high-society gold-diggers and took vengeance on them by punishing them in his novels. Countess Bezukhova, Anna Karenina, the one from *The Kreutzer Sonata*… they all got what they deserved. He showed a bit of mercy to Katyusha Maslova, to be fair… The essay was, as they say, extensively researched and well executed. But the illustrations! Where the author had got those pictures from, I have no idea. Books like that were not easy to get hold of at the time. In fact, it was virtually impossible! I had the impression that the essay had been thoroughly reviewed by every member of the staff because it was dog-eared and covered in fingerprints, especially the pages with pictures…

It was signed, in black and white: Mikhail Shenderovich, Year 8.

The signature was typewritten, as was the entire essay on the sexual behaviour of the count and his heroes. Otherwise they would have known from the handwriting that it wasn't mine – they weren't completely stupid.

Anyway…

An investigation was launched, but it didn't go any further because they were too embarrassed to take it higher up. It turned out that the essay had just appeared on Golden Hand's desk and nobody knew how it had got there – it had materialized in the staff room as if by magic, on the very same day that I was cutting Tolstoy's bearded face out of the encyclopedia and sticking it in the real essay. If I had known, I wouldn't have bothered mutilating the book… Maybe someone else could have used it. Anyway, I got off quite lightly. They logged some comments about the whole affair, but they were all a bit embarrassed about it. The headmaster took the essay home with him, a bit of bedtime reading. I got a C for my behaviour that term, in the end. That was borderline special measures, but the bastards gave it to me anyway, because they still weren't a hundred percent sure whether or not it was mine. I knew it wasn't! But whose was it? And it was all done so subtly as well – there was no big punishment. If whoever it was had tried something similar with Lenin and his wife and the October Revolution, there would have been no way I'd have got off with a C. But as it was… Nothing really bad came of it. Mum cried a bit, I suppose, because I'd been corrupted by football, and I used to be such a good, studious child. Dad laughed his head off, although he tried to make sure I didn't hear…

Needless to say, there was no football training camp for me that year either.

Everything seemed to be linked – the way football had affected my moral attitude, Lev Tolstoy and the sexual revolution. I went off football a bit after that anyway, lost interest… I mean, I liked kicking a ball about, but as for trying to win… I just didn't care about it any more… But that wasn't Lev Tolstoy's fault, it's just the way it turned out.

And Lysyuk, the son of a bitch, won first place in the next maths championship.

And finally, it dawned on me.

I went up to him after the holidays. He was sitting there, with his head down, just looking up at me – blink, blink!

"Was it you, you little shit?" I asked.

He didn't even try to deny it.

"Yes, it was," he said, as calm as you like. "But you'll never prove it."

"But why? What did I ever do to you?"

I had actually beaten him up a couple of times, but I wasn't the only one, nobody liked him. And if you must know, I had even stood up for him once, when they were planning to jump him. That was back in Year Seven when he was winding everyone up by always being the first to put his hand up in class, the little freak, and not letting anyone copy his homework...

"Nothing, really," he said. "That's why you'll never prove anything. I did it as an experiment. I'd noticed," he said, "that when things are going well for you, then I'm generally having a hard time. And vice versa. And I," he said, "really needed to win first prize at that championships. I want to go to university," he said, " and winning the championship would look good on my application. As it is, the fact that I'm Jewish may be an obstacle."

"Well I'm Jewish too, so why are you taking it out on me, you son of a bitch?" I said. "Why are you ruining my life?"

"But I'm a Jew with a Ukrainian name – they won't like that. So you'll fill their Jewish quota. Basically," he said, "it all comes down to looking after number one. You've got strong legs, they'll earn you a living, but I have to rely on my brain. As long as it's working OK, everything's fine – I'm up on my horse, ready for battle. And I'm afraid that you, my friend, will be the one getting trampled underfoot."

I really wanted to punch him, to turn things back in my favour. But I looked at him, and he really was such a weed, with his lame leg... I just couldn't do it. I hit him over the head with the real essay, the one I'd sweated over, which was no longer any use to anyone, and walked off. A week later, he left – he was transferred to a new school. His conscience was obviously bothering him.

We haven't seen each other since. He went off to university – well, not to university but to an engineering college, but he got in straightaway, the first time he applied... I went too – well, not to an engineering college but to a communications college, but that was pretty good too... And now whenever things start to go wrong for me, I think it's Lysyuk up to his old tricks again. Up until now, he obviously hasn't had any real need for me, at least not until the collapse of the Soviet Union and the battle for independence and the need to make a living. When that happened, I heard he left college and went into business, started wheeling and dealing. I found that out later, after two of my deals fell through for no apparent reason...

Shenderovich fell silent then summed up morosely: "And now this is the third."

"That's quite a story," agreed Givi. "It does sound quite plausible. Similar phenomena have been observed in the natural world."

"You're telling me!" agreed Shenderovich, picking at the empty plate with his fork.

"So, you think he hired those bandits?"

"How should I know? I wouldn't put it past him. Apparently he's loaded, or so I heard. He must have had some really big deal set up or something, so he's come after me, shelled out some cash and got someone to do his dirty work for him. They tracked us down and did what they were paid to... There's no direct material gain for him – on the contrary, I probably cost him a fair amount! But it's the metaphysics that counts, the Law of Conservation of Happiness. Because, Givi my friend, they didn't kill us. He can't kill me – that would be pointless, it would mean losing his source of happiness. He needs me alive, and suffering."

Givi glanced at Varvara Timofeevna, who had been nodding rhythmically throughout the story, her cheek propped on her hand.

"So," he whispered, "tell me more about the pictures..."

It was the morning after the night before.

He had a splitting headache. Furthermore, all the bits of his body that had been damaged the day before were aching too – yesterday, his elbows seemed to have forgotten how they had been twisted by strange hands in sinister black gloves, but this morning it was all coming back to them. And his coccyx ached, right where it had come into contact with the stranger's knee-cap.

And he wanted a hot drink. Preferably coffee. Things were looking up a bit: Shenderovich had found some money. He'd found it in the pocket of Alka's jacket, which she'd left behind. He'd found it and pocketed it. He wouldn't let Givi have a coffee, though… We'll get one at the coffee house, he said. We'll drink it calmly and coolly while we look that shameless Ali right in the eye. Because regardless of Lysyuk's involvement, Ali is the one who betrayed us. I wouldn't mind finding out where he's hidden his grubby little conscience and beating it out of him.

Shenderovich looked very impressive – it gave Givi goosebumps just the sight of him. He was wearing a clean, unripped shirt and looked as wise, as hostile and as cold-blooded as a snake.

"But what will Alka say?" Givi asked, because in theory rifling through someone else's pockets could hardly be considered acceptable behaviour by anyone's standards. "She won't have any money, will she?"

"Let's worry about that when she gets back," Shenderovich brushed aside his objection. "We're only borrowing it. We'll get our advance back off Ali, then we'll pay her back."

He half-closed his eyes and a dreamy look came over his face.

"It would be good to buy something else with that advance… something amazing… Something that would sell even better than balloons!"

"Misha, give it a rest."

"Fur coats, for example," Shenderovich was already making plans. "In Odessa, fur coats don't sell very well – the market's saturated… There are piles of them everywhere, like a cavemen's convention… But maybe we could take some to St. Pete?"

"Maybe we couldn't," Givi replied firmly. "Anyway," he said, turning his head with some discomfort, "shouldn't Alka have been back by now?"

"Maybe," Shenderovich agreed sullenly. "When she does show her face, I'm going to kill her. So anyway, Givi my friend, how are we going to play this? Let's go and see Ali. We'll shake him up a bit, get our advance back and find out who he was working for, the sneaky little rat... We'll get names, find out where they hang out... And we'll use force if we have to!"

"Misha, I don't like the sound of that," Givi objected.

"Well, I don't like the sound of someone's fist hitting my face either. Or the sound of my name being added to someone's hit-list. No, if he wants to live, he can tell us where Lysyuk is hiding. Or else I'll... I'll... I'll make sure word gets round, for starters! The whole of Odessa will know what a scumbag he is. Givi, my friend, I have nothing to lose. I am above the law. Like Zorro! No passport, no family, no ties!"

"No money," Givi added quietly.

"Money," Shenderovich cut him off, "is not a problem."

"Really?" asked Givi, in surprise.

A sleepy, morning Istanbul lay before them. Shutters were banging lazily, bolts were scraping as the stalls awoke... The fierce sunlight had not yet fully vanquished the shadows of the night, and the air over the bridge was clean and cool, like freshly washed glass.

"Aren't we a bit early?" Givi worried.

"We're better off waiting for him inside," Shenderovich answered menacingly.

For some reason, Givi had expected the coffee house to be bolted shut. In the worst-case scenario, in place of the door with its sign full of promise they would find just a blank wall, covered in meandering cracks. The coffee house would have disappeared into thin air. But the door was exactly where it was supposed to be and even slightly ajar. The smell of burning sand and metal and the aroma of freshly roasted coffee beans floated out of the dark opening to meet them...

Shenderovich pushed Givi aside and strode majestically through the soot-blackened archway.

Several men, sleepily whiling away the morning at their tables, looked lazily up and then down again, at their cups and morning papers.

Shenderovich cleared his throat.

"Salaam aleikum," he said, politely. "Um... nerede Ali?"

The barman shrugged in the semi-darkness.

"Very well," Shenderovich graciously agreed, although all was far from well. "We'll wait for him here, OK? Iki Türk kahvesi... yes?"

He sat down at one of the tables and made himself at home, drumming his fingers on the tablecloth in a blatant imitation of the captain.

The barman brought two coffees and placed them in the middle of the table, without smiling, then in direct contravention of the accepted protocol continued to hover in front of Shenderovich until he gave him a crumpled note. Givi noticed how several men at the neighbouring tables got up and moved further away. A clearing gradually formed around them.

"Misha," he whispered. "I don't think they like us."

"Good," said Shenderovich.

"But what if he doesn't show up?"

"He'll be here. He works here. It's like his office."

"Maybe he's got a day off."

"I'll give him a day off alright," Shenderovich hissed. "If he doesn't turn up soon, I'll make sure he never works again! I'll be here every day, waiting for him, like the ghost of Hamlet's father. I won't go home...In any case," he lowered his voice and added, "that wouldn't be advisable without the money."

"So we're going to drink coffee for free, are we?"

"We'll get some money," answered Shenderovich, confidently. "We'll think of something..."

"Misha," Givi said, firmly. "I am not going to rob a bank."

"Who said anything about robbing a bank?" Shenderovich was indignant. "We're smarter than that! We'll just beat it out of Ali. Aha, speak of the devil! Here he is now."

Ali, with his handsome face and black moustache, confidently entered the inner sanctum of the coffee house. Like an experienced paratrooper, Shenderovich slipped softly out from behind his table and laid his hand on Ali's shoulder while his eyes were still adjusting to the lack of light.

Ali jumped.

"What are you playing at?" asked Shenderovich reprovingly. "You son of a wayward mother…Why did you go and set us up like that?"

Ali shrugged Shenderovich's hand off with a jerk of his shoulder. His face registered surprise and confusion.

"Rusça konusmuyorum[1]…" he said.

"What?" Shenderovich was surprised.

"Rusça konusmuyorum," repeated Ali, quite clearly. "Effendim? Anlamadın.[2]"

"Where's the money, you scumbag?" cried Shenderovich. "Where are the goods?"

"Tekrar sőlyer misiniz?[3]" Ali politely replied.

"Sailor? Messy knees? What are you whittering about?"

"Misha, let's go, this is a waste of time!"

"He's pretending he can't understand Russian, the lying toe-rag! Yesterday he spoke better Russian than either of us! Just you wait, I'll find a way to make you speak like Pushkin!"

"Pushkin!" said Ali, enthusiastically. "Oh, Pushkin! Rus musunuz!"

"Rus, rus!" Shenderovich repeated happily.

"Rusça konusmuyorum," explained Ali, for the third time. Then he politely added:

---

[1] I don't speak Russian

[2] I'm sorry? I didn't understand.

[3] Could you repeat that please?

"Hoşçakalın[4]…"

"Hang on a minute, hoşçakalın?" Shenderovich leapt up. "I don't think so…"

"Güle güle[5]," explained Ali.

"I'll kill him," croaked Shenderovich. "Givi, did you hear what he just said?"

Ali batted his magnificent black eyelashes and thought for a second. Then he joyfully declared, in English:

"Bye-bye!"

"Bye-bye?" Shenderovich lost it. "I'll give you bye-bye!"

Givi noticed out of the corner of his eye that several of the café's patrons, who up to this point had been idly meditating and sipping their coffee, had pushed aside their cups and were slowly getting up from their tables.

"Misha," he whispered, "let's get out of here."

"No way!" retorted Shenderovich indignantly.

He grabbed Ali by his shirt-front, jumped up and kneed him in the stomach. "You lying snake!" he shouted. "You pointless waste of space!"

Ali flew towards the wall, appealing plaintively to the assembled spectators in pure Turkish.

The patrons of the coffee house drew closer, forming a neat semicircle behind Givi and Shenderovich.

"Misha!" yelled Givi at the top of his voice.

"I would advise you to leave, gentlemen," suggested the barman in equally pure Russian, coming out from behind his counter.

"Bastards!" yelled Shenderovich, retreating in the direction of the door. "They're all in on it! It's a conspiracy!"

The semicircle of coffee-lovers moved one step closer.

Givi turned round in despair.

"Param çalındı[6]!" he yelled.

---

[4] Goodbye

[5] Bye-bye

[6] I've been robbed

"I haven't taken a penny more than you owed," the barman retorted. "And as for your tips…"

He extracted a handful of coins from his pocket and threw them for some reason at Shenderovich.

"Here they are: I hope you choke on them! Cheapskates!"

"No!" Givi elaborated. "Hier! Shit, bunun türkçesi ne[7]… dün akşam[8]!"

"What has that got to do with us?" the barman asked in surprise.

"You're all accomplices!" yelled Shenderovich. "Gangsters, the lot of you!"

"Well, it takes one to know one," the barman lazily replied.

"OK!" said Givi. "That's enough! En yakın polis karakolu nerede[9]?"

"Sure," said the barman indifferently. "It's just round the corner."

He moved towards them with obvious reluctance, suddenly revealing himself to be a whole head taller than Shenderovich, not to mention Givi.

"Blackmailers!" he said, shoving both of them towards the door with his powerful chest. "Get out of here, you idiots!"

Shenderovich was desperately craning his neck and trying to catch sight of Ali, but he had disappeared behind his comrades-in-arms. The semi-circle closed up, putting forward the barman as a particularly effective warhead. Much to his own astonishment, Givi suddenly found himself out on the street.

The light that fell on him from the scorching skies was so bright that he involuntarily narrowed his eyes.

"You shouldn't have wound them up like that," Shende-rovich reproached him.

---

[7] What's the Turkish for…

[8] Yesterday evening

[9] Is there a police station near here?

He was getting up from his knees and brushing off the rust-coloured dust. His shirt collar for some reason was once again half torn off and hanging from his neck like a tie.

"Don't be silly, Misha!" Givi bashfully objected. "I didn't do anything! They wound themselves up. I only got involved at the end. After you…"

"How did they wind themselves up? They were after you like jackals! Why did you have to go and open your big mouth?"

"I honestly don't know," Givi was genuinely surprised at himself. "I just wanted to sort it out."

"And why didn't you tell me you could speak Turkish? You sounded like a native in there."

"I don't know, Misha," answered Givi, somewhat unconvincingly. "It just came out!"

He tried hard to summon another flash of linguistic aptitude, but his newfound language skills seemed to have disappeared as quickly as they had appeared in the first place. He hunched his shoulders up a bit, fully expecting another burst of rage, but Shenderovich was looking at him with something approaching respect.

"You said something about the police, didn't you?" he said.

"I don't remember, Misha."

"Yes, you did, I heard you. You called their bluff. Blah blah blah, police, you said… But there's no point even thinking about it, Givi my brother. They'll never betray their own."

"I think it was them, Misha," Givi said firmly. "They were the ones who robbed us. Lysyuk's got nothing to do with it. It was all a big scam. There never were any goods."

"You think so?" Shenderovich shook his head in disbelief.

"Well, think about it. Who else knew about the deal?"

"You're right!" Shenderovich breathed out. "They did! They were all in on it, like you said. So, they were the ones who set me up… Well, Yannis! You back-stabber! I'll get you, you see if I don't!"

Givi took a precautionary step back, but Shenderovich was

obviously referring to the real Yannis and only clapped him on the shoulder.

"You're a good friend, Givi my friend!" he said with conviction. "Nothing like that idiot Stavrakis!"

Givi sighed. At long last Shenderovich had recognized that he was a good person and worthy of being his friend. But why is it that the minute you get something you've been longing for, you don't want it any more? Such is the will of kind and merciful Allah, to join and cast asunder. But why has he got such a warped sense of humour?

"What are we going to do, Misha?" he asked.

"What to do…" thought Shenderovich, wrinkling his handsome brow. "Going to the police is not an option, Givi my friend. What's the point? You know what the police are like over here. They'll believe whoever slips them the most cash. And those jackals probably keep their palms well greased. We don't stand a chance. Are we in any position to provide material recompense? No! We'll turn up, tell them what happened. They'll say, prove it… where are your witnesses?"

"I'm a witness," Givi struck his chest with his fist.

"With fake ID," Shenderovich added morosely.

Givi deflated.

"Alka's a witness," he suggested tentatively.

"Well…" Shenderovich reflected. "She could be. She definitely saw us making the arrangements and handing over the advance. And she'd easily lie about seeing us getting beaten up. In fact, she'll be better than a real witness, she's great at making up stories… You know, I wonder who she was meeting… Whoever it was must have been pretty special for her to abandon us to the mercy of callous fate."

"Where is she, the loathsome vixen," Givi joined in. "The evil minx. Kidnapper of hearts, mistress of daydreams, oh where is she, princess of provocation, beautiful as the moon, oh, with firm thighs, lithe body and slender waist, oh, she of silver limbs but heart of stone…"

"Stop it…" ordered Shenderovich. "Great speech, very impressive – quite erotic, too. But that's enough. If she's not back on that ferry…"

"Then… what?" Givi said.

"Then I don't know what I'll do to her!"

Alka wasn't on the ferry. The cabin was empty. In fact, nobody was there – not even Varvara Timofeevna, bless her, or the captain himself. There was not a soul to be seen. The ferry was as deserted as the *Marie Celeste*. They probably all fled the *Marie Celeste* for a night out in Istanbul too, mused Givi idly. Shenderovich sullenly pulled on his last shirt. How long will that one last, wondered Givi… Shenderovich and shirts just did not seem to get on.

There was nobody in the lounge either. A bored waitress at the bar livened up a bit at the sight of guests and wordlessly placed two plastic plates of Russian salad and two bottles of beer in front of them.

"Uh…" Shenderovich was embarrassed. "We, um…"

"You haven't got any money," shrewdly observed the girl. "I know. Don't worry about it. It'll only go to waste. There's not a living soul on board, they're all off gallivanting. And I'll just say I dropped the beer bottles."

"Oh my houri, generous as a honeycomb," Givi was delighted. "Oh, source of comfort, bringing bliss to weary souls…"

"Yeah, whatever," the girl was embarrassed and bashfully straightened her headdress.

"You wouldn't happen to have another couple of beers, would you, sweetheart?" Shenderovich wondered.

"No," the girl snapped. She obviously wasn't quite so keen on Shenderovich and his overly familiar tone. She went back to the bar and turned on the television, which started jabbering away.

"Misha?" Givi suddenly became agitated. "Did you hear that?"

"Hear what?" asked Shenderovich, coldly.

"They're saying something about the museum. Something's happened there, you know… There's been a theft."

"What, are they talking Russian?" Shenderovich pricked up his ears.

"English, I think," answered Givi, uncertainly.

"It's CNN," the girl explained from her bar stool.

"And when did you suddenly start speaking English?" Shenderovich asked suspiciously.

"It's pretty easy to work it out, Misha… Just before closing, when everyone had already left, thieves broke in wearing black masks… no, black stockings over their heads… Tied up the security guards… ah, no, they didn't tie them up… they knocked them out with sleeping gas… cut the wiring and made off with… what did they make off with… aha! The tablet! The star exhibit, the pride of the museum."

"Wearing stockings?" Shenderovich perked up. "Black ones? Like our attackers. What, is it the fashion round here, or something? Who needs the Moulin Rouge!"

"Uh-huh. The tablet is… worthless? No, invaluable… Basically this tablet is worth a fortune, and there is a… reward… for anyone with information… leading to its safe recovery…"

"What else are they saying?"

"It's supposedly from the Temple of Jerusalem… Dating from… wow! This thing is ancient, Misha. Which was the first temple?"

"Well," Shenderovich was struggling. "They built them like this, like steps. The first one, then the second one…"

"Don't be ridiculous," the girl on the bar stool bristled with indignation. "God, you're an idiot! They're not numbered according to their relative position, but the order they were built in… The first temple, that's Solomon's. The second was built under the Persians. And the third – well, no one knows for sure whether it even exists."

Shenderovich was already on his feet.

"Where are you off to?" worried Givi.

"Alka," Shenderovich explained. "Our Alka is missing… 'Bye-bye'… It's… They're after some ransom money! They took her, my Mesopotamian friend. She must have been on to them in the museum, so they decided to shut her up."

"Forget it, Misha," Givi replied uncertainly. "How could she have been on to them? She doesn't know anything about tablets. She just went into the museum, you know, to look at some old stuff…"

"Alka?" Shenderovich was surprised. "Are you kidding? She's the favourite post-graduate student of Professor Zebbov the Elder himself, and she even outwitted him once in a scholarly debate. Which he admitted publicly, too. Alka rattled them, I tell you. She was about to blow their cover. They probably grabbed her, tied her up…"

"No!" Givi was horrified and also leapt to his feet.

So Alka hadn't betrayed anyone, neither the gallant captain nor his friend and partner Misha Shenderovich. Alka had disappeared: she'd been kidnapped by a villainous gang. Oh, she was probably lying right at that very moment on the seabed, sewn into a sack with an anvil tied to her slender ankles… She was lying on the seabed, with her blonde hair undulating lazily in the water. Silvery little fish were swimming through her golden tresses, diving into them as if they were seaweed… Or maybe not… Alka was probably lying in some dingy cellar, with her hands and her slender ankles crudely tied… and someone was approaching her, some Ahmed was walking up to her, fondling his curved dagger and smirking ominously into his black moustache…

Givi groaned and gnashed his teeth.

"I'll rip them to shreds…" he choked.

"Ooh, you animal!" Shenderovich commented admiringly, hurrying after Givi down the steep gangway.

But Givi had already taken off and was running through

the port to the square, completely oblivious to Shenderovich, who was struggling to keep up.

"Hey," Shenderovich cried after him in desperation. "Hang on! Where are you going?"

"Where's the bloody bus station?" yelled Givi, shoving passersby out of his way.

"Hey, watch it," Shenderovich wheezed threateningly. "That sort of language could get you into trouble!"

Givi just shook his head.

"Where's the bloody bus station?" he cried again, causing a burly stevedore, who was wheeling a trolley laden with mysterious packages, to take fright and jump out of his way. "Nerede the bloody bus?"

The stevedore timidly waved his hand in the direction of the square.

"Come on!" cried Givi, looking over his shoulder as he ran to check that Shenderovich was with him.

"Jesus!" muttered Shenderovich in disbelief, increasing his pace. "Straight out of the Caucasus! That's hot Georgian blood for you! Look at it go!"

The bus crawled lazily up to meet them on the scorching tarmac, trailing a stream of dove-coloured smoke....

They managed to get away without paying for the ride.

They also saved on tickets for the museum, but that was unintentional.

They had rushed across the park, scaring away the turtle-doves and ruthlessly trampling the delicate lace shadows of the acacias that decorated the cobbled paths, only to find their mission thwarted. The museum was closed.

A sign in three languages blatantly lied about the museum being closed for cleaning. Obviously quite a specific kind of cleaning, because the interior was a hive of activity, with people in suits ducking under the velvet cords and looking very busy. Some of them had gun-shaped bulges under their arms.

"Wow, look what a fuss they're making!" whispered Shenderovich admiringly.

Givi gnashed his teeth.

"Whoa, cowboy!" muttered Shenderovich, absentmindedly checking out their surroundings. "First things first. We need to get the lay of the land. Ekh, I need an old woman!"

"Pervert," commented Givi.

"For business, not pleasure, you idiot. We need to interrogate a few of the old biddies that hang out here, maybe someone saw her. We need witnesses! But this lot have driven them all away. Where are the guards? Where are the ticket-collectors? Where are the museum staff?"

Givi sank more deeply into despair. His hopes had been cruelly dashed. Now they had no chance of finding any trace of the white-skinned, fair-faced, golden-haired houri, with thighs like sheaves of wheat, lips like honeycombs, eyes like cool mountain lakes... Oh, princess of seduction, queen of voluptuousness, mistress of mine, who has disappeared into darkness...

"Misha," he asked shyly, studiously ignoring a couple of turtle-doves in the throes of passion. "What's the deal here with harems?"

"Forget it," Shenderovich replied despondently. "We haven't got enough money to visit a harem. We haven't even got enough for a spot of polyandry... I mean, frankly we haven't even got enough to go halves..."

"That's not what I meant! Listen, maybe they didn't abduct Alka because she rattled them... Maybe they took her because of her beauty? Whisked her off to a harem?"

"Alka?" Shenderovich was surprised. "Any fool who tried to whisk Alka off somewhere like that would only be making trouble for himself. He would certainly live to regret it – she'd raze it to the ground!"

He cast a melancholy glance at the wide-open doors where two hefty security guys were lazily killing time. Givi sighed. Ekh, he thought, frowning, she'd probably be better off in a harem…

"Mishenka!" a voice rang out right in his ear.

He opened his eyes.

Crossing the square towards them, her plump feet advancing over the cobbles in their shiny black shoes, was Varvara Timofeevna.

"Mishenka!" she tried again to attract Shenderovich's attention (Givi suspected that she still couldn't work out his real name, which was destined to remain a mystery to her). "Are you looking for Allochka too?"

"Why else would we be here?" Shenderovich confirmed morosely.

"Well, so are we. Yurochka was worried."

At this point the captain, who had been hiding in the flickering shadows of the acacia bushes, stepped out into the light. He cast a hostile sidelong glance at Shenderovich but greeted him quite politely.

"Have you heard?" he asked, nodding in the direction of the detectives, who were busily scurrying about by the doors. "The tablet has been stolen."

"We heard," replied Shenderovich, failing to conceal the hostility in his voice. For some reason, the appearance of the captain had irked him. "It was that lot… with their black stockings."

"I heard, albeit from a somewhat less than reliable source, that it was the Kurdish Workers' Party," the captain contradicted him. "It was their way of highlighting the plight of ethnic minorities here. And of topping up the Party coffers at the same time. Apparently, they carried out several similar thefts across the city yesterday, which helped to divert attention from the museum."

His anger suddenly turned to sympathy.

"It was probably the Kurds that attacked you too. It's got all the hallmarks."

"The Kurds, you reckon?" repeated Shenderovich coldly. "What makes you think that it was them and not the Grey Wolves?"

"Well, it's like that Ockham fellow said," explained the captain. "Entities should not be multiplied beyond necessity. The Grey Wolves are still biding their time."

He sighed.

"This is what I think. Alla Sergeevna was probably an unwitting witness to the theft. Therefore they eliminated her. I've already been to the police about it."

"Really?" Shenderovich pricked up his ears.

"Naturally. Although I'm not sure there was much point. There's no body, no witnesses to the kidnapping. They're saying she went off drinking with someone, got a bit carried away… we've all been there."

"You and her…" Shenderovich interjected.

"Me?" the captain was astonished. "Never! Alla? Sergeevna? No, Mikhail… What's your surname, Aronovich?"

"Abramovich."

"No, Mikhail Aronovich, she's not like that. Alla's not that kind of girl. She's highly educated, completely respectable, that's immediately obvious. No, no, I'm telling you. Describe it again, how it was, Varvara Timofeevna… He went up to her… What did he look like? Was he a local, would you say?"

"I would have said so," Varvara Timofeevna was thoughtful. "He was dark-complexioned, with a hooked nose and fire in his eyes."

"And how was he dressed, ma'am?" asked Shenderovich. "Was he quite smart?"

"I should say so! A white jacket, a bit like yours, Yurochka, and a red scarf around his neck. And he had a very peculiar voice…"

That caught the captain's attention. "Ah, so you heard him speak, then? What did he say, exactly?"

"Well, I can't remember exactly. They were standing by

that scaro-thingy... by the tombstone, and he was saying something like, I'm so happy that I bumped into you like this, out of the blue... You see how Allah brings people together, and keeps them apart... He mentioned some professor, Moscow, some seminar or other... He was talking, and smiling. Then they left. Together."

"Obviously the ringleader," surmised the captain. "He was probably masquerading as a professor. That was his cover story. His intentions were obviously to undermine us. Let's go, Varvara Timofeevna, my dear. You'll be able to assist the police with their enquiries. They'll need an eyewitness account."

And he strode decisively towards the heavily-guarded entrance, dragging the confused Varvara Timofeevna behind him. The captain cut a striking figure, and the guards immediately stepped aside, allowing them to enter the building. Without halting, he turned and instructed Givi and Shenderovich to wait, then was promptly swallowed up by the museum.

"They're probably pouring him a whisky and soda in there," said Shenderovich enviously. "With ice."

"Oh, just drop it, Misha," Givi gave an exhausted sigh. "I'm not in the mood."

Then he nearly jumped as he felt a dark, dry hand on his shoulder.

"Effendim!" said a quiet voice.

Givi turned round.

The man standing behind him could easily have passed for an extremely suntanned European. And he was dressed in a very European style, in a smart, black suit with a narrow tie. The outfit's only nod to exoticism was a red fez with a jaunty tassel.

"Effendim," the man said again. "Messieurs... Eh..."

He looked the partners up and down once more and then began to speak hesitantly in Russian.

"Gentlemen?"

"Yeah," confirmed Shenderovich morosely. "I suppose so."

"Oh, how lucky I am," their new acquaintance continued in Russian, though with an obvious accent.

Givi remembered Varvara Timofeevna's comment about a 'peculiar voice.'

He looked down, suspiciously checking out the stranger's footwear, but he was wearing shiny black boots with pointed toes – new ones.

Ekh, so it wasn't him, thought Givi.

"Gentlemen," repeated the man, a little more sure of himself. "Pardonnez-moi… I would like to speak with you… très important… a very important matter. Very serious."

"Well, make it quick," Shenderovich urged.

"Oh no," the stranger shook his head, causing the tassel on his fez to jump into the air. "It's a very serious matter. Il faut… What's the Russian… it requires… un long… a long conversation, yes? Discussion. That's it! A proper discussion. Would you be so kind as to… go avec moi… just here, not far."

Shenderovich straightened himself up.

"With whom do I have the honour?" he asked, adopting a formal manner.

The man slapped his thighs.

"Ah, je ne me suis pas presenté … I didn't introduce myself. Un moment!"

He slapped himself again, this time on the chest, and fished out of his pocket a small shiny rectangle.

"Lenoir, Doctor of Archeology," he explained, handing Givi the card.

"Corresponding Member… of the International Assassin… Asso… Association of Archaeologists," decoded Givi, blinking in the bright light.

"There you go," the stranger nodded cordially. "My business is… anciens rarités… It is very… très intéressant… fascinating, no? Rarities. Antiquities, in Russian. Ma mère… my mother was Russian. My grandmother was a refugee… she fled to

France – la Révolution Rouge, yes? First Istanbul, then Paris…
I have roots everywhere… Marchez, gentlemen, marchez!"

He tapped his shiny boot impatiently.

"Mon appartement is here! Not far!"

"Hold on," Shenderovich said menacingly. "Wait a minute!
We've got some very important business of our own to attend
to…"

"Business! Travail! Oh, but I also have a big travail for
you! Grand travail!"

He looked around furtively again then leant towards
Shenderovich's ear and said in a low voice:

"I'm talking money, gentlemen! Grand argent! Très grand
argent."

"Go on," Shenderovich encouraged him, with feigned
indifference.

"How would you like," Lenoir looked around nervously
again, "to find the tablet?"

The air quivered, dry and burning hot, as if they were in a
blacksmith's forge, and this impression was further strengthened
by the banging of millions of tiny little hammers. There were
grasshoppers everywhere, chattering, scraping and scratching
themselves right up to the overgrown, dry grass of the precipice,
beyond which the shimmering sea was turning the colour of a
dove's breast. A bird was singing in a prickly bush at the top of
the precipice.

"Hey, Givi my friend, are you asleep?"

Givi rubbed his eyes, which were temporarily blinded by
the glare from innumerable iridescent mirrors.

"Well, I…." he began cautiously.

"Don't fall asleep," worried Shenderovich. "You'll freeze
to death…"

A wave broke coquettishly and cast a bright beam of light,
which fell directly into Givi's eye.

"Ekh!" said Givi.

"And may I remind you," said Shenderovich with dignity, "that we are supposed to be carrying out a surveillance operation."

The villa was sheltering in the deep violet shadows of the valley. From where they were stationed all they could see was the blank wall wrapped around the perimeter of the house and its tiled roof. The twisted tentacles of a rosebush were reaching up and over the wall.

"Who are we spying on?" Givi asked miserably. "The goats?"

Dirty white-grey balls of goat-hair lazily roamed the ravines and were the only visible sign of life.

"I wish. If the ancient Greeks had kept a closer eye on their own goats," said Shenderovich with menace, "they would still have been running marathons here. But they took their eye off the ball, and the goats devoured Hellas!"

"They devoured Hellas? How?" Givi was horrified.

"Silently, of course," Shenderovich answered laconically. "How else? They destroyed an ancient culture. Did you understand everything he said?"

"I think so, Misha…"

"Tell me again. The bit about the dogs. And the security. Otherwise I can see us getting set upon by a couple of Alsatians. Maybe three! And a couple of thugs with guns."

"He said, Misha, that the professor is scared of dogs. He should know, he's spent the night there. And he can't afford thugs, Misha. That Maurice said he'd sold his entire collection of antiquities just to pay those Kurds, or whoever they are. Who's he going to get for security? Those mercenaries? He's frightened of them himself – that thing is worth a fortune! He's hiding from them anyway, only Maurice knows about the villa. They only loaded it into the lorry in the museum courtyard and he took it from there, making sure to cover his tracks."

"But what if they 'eliminate' him?"

"Then that's it, Misha. Game over. That Maurice said vite,

vite… in other words, get a move on… Or the valuable antiquity could fall into even darker hands."

Shenderovich's brow darkened for a second, but his natural insouciance soon got the upper hand and he casually dismissed Givi's objection.

"Don't worry," he said. "We'll find a way in. And by the way, how come you can speak French all of a sudden?"

"Actually," said Givi morosely, "I have no idea. We had German at school and English at college, and I didn't learn much of either."

"Maybe some of your chakras have opened up… Due to the favourable geomagnetic conditions or something?"

"Maybe, Misha…"

The banging and sawing of the grasshoppers gradually subsided, giving way to the wailing of the cicadas, as doleful as muezzins. In the east, the first green star trembled into view.

Givi sighed quietly, so as not to bother Shenderovich. He was thinking about Alka, wondering mournfully where she could be. Maybe someone was hurting her, maybe she was struggling in a stranger's arms, calling "Givi! Givi!"

But Givi wouldn't be coming to her rescue, because he'd sold his soul.

It was getting dark.

The cicadas were wailing dementedly. The green star above the sea was joined by one friend, then another… Their fine, sharp rays of light reached out to touch the dark water. The thin leaves of the olive trees rustled, revealing their silvery underbellies, and a hot wind brought with it the heavy scent of roses and stifling pollen from the grasses of the plains. Givi sneezed.

"Isn't it time yet, Misha?"

Shenderovich turned the idea over in his mind then waved his hand, displacing a certain volume of air.

"OK! Let's go, my criminal friend! Time to make a move…"

He stood up purposefully, groaning and rubbing the small of his back, and headed for the prickly bush. Givi heard him rummaging about on the ground with his hands, whispering and swearing.

"Aha, there it is!" he said finally. "Shit! Bloody hell! There's broken glass everywhere…"

"Did you cut yourself, Misha?" asked Givi, although he already knew the answer.

"Yeah, just a bit," Shenderovich confirmed forlornly. "What's the matter with people, eh? There's broken glass everywhere these days… I bet even Antarctica is covered with it."

"What is the world coming to?" commiserated Givi.

"Shh!" Shenderovich was already standing in front of him, rising up out of the gloom like the tower of Lebanon, which looketh toward Damascus.

He took a sack that had been waiting patiently under the prickly bush and emptied its contents out onto the ground at Givi's feet. All the necessary tools for the job in hand lay before them: a grappling hook with a strong rope attached to it, a pocket knife with a sharpened blade of illegal length, a laser pointer, a normal torch, glass-cutting equipment, a crowbar, two pairs of gloves and a mobile phone.

Shenderovich, stepping softly and doing his best James Bond impression, moved towards the wall engirdling the villa, carrying the grappling hook easily in his strong hand.

Givi tiptoed after him.

All manner of night creatures flew out from under their feet, catapulting in all directions before returning to their hiding places in the dry grass.

Shenderovich crept stealthily right up to the wall and flattened himself against it, pressing his ear to the warm stone.

"Well?" asked Givi in a whisper.

Shenderovich shrugged.

"I can't hear anything…"

Taking a couple of steps back, he spun the grappling hook

round until it whistled – Givi barely managed to get out of the way in time – and flung it over the fence. He pulled gingerly on the rope. There was a horrible scraping sound. Shenderovich moved backwards holding the rope until it pulled taut, forcing him to stop.

"Sorted!" he muttered, with satisfaction.

A kind of path had been cleared from the entrance door through the house and the blisters on the old paintwork bore scratch marks, as if something heavy, and with hard edges, had been dragged across the floor.

"It's in there!" whispered Shenderovich reverentially, staring straight ahead like a dog scenting the quarry.

"Careful, Misha!"

But Shenderovich had adopted a crouching position and was already stealthily approaching the far wall. Through an archway in this wall lay another room, as empty and abandoned as the first. The trail stretched across the second room until it stopped abruptly by a neat little door. The door was ajar, and its frame was chipped and scratched, as if someone had tried to drag at least three chests of drawers through it all at once.

The light from the torch slipped through the doorway and dissolved in the darkness. Shenderovich slipped after it.

"It really is here!" he said, incredulously. "Look, Givi my friend."

A round, uneven patch of light lay on the surface of the stone, which bore the ravages of wind and rain. The tablet was leaning at an angle, like a very tired sentry, and for some reason it seemed to Givi as though it was looking back at them… and not altogether approvingly.

It had been washed by the damp flow of sea air for hundreds, even thousands of years and by the dry, scorching wind from distant deserts. Sand had been scattered over its surface, gnawing away at the smooth stone, and water had trickled down the intricate writings that covered its surface in lines until the symbols carved into the stone had been smoothed out to such an extent that they resembled nothing more than the strange interplay of fissures on an uncut stone. In the tremulous light from the torch quivering in Shenderovich's fearless hand, Givi suddenly detected a faint, but menacing, movement.

"Misha, can you see that?" he breathed.

"I can," confirmed Shenderovich. "Big stone... big money!"

"No! The... symbols... they're moving!"

Without looking, Shenderovich silently clapped him on the shoulder. Then he switched off the torch and moved out of the storeroom.

"Where is it?" he muttered, looking at the illuminated panel of the phone. "Got it! He showed me how to get in touch! The number's already programmed in somewhere... Ah, found it... the address book! Now press 'yes'... now that one. Hello?" he said into the phone.

"Police station!" Givi could just about make out a far-away, almost microscopic voice.

"We are... concerned citizens..." Shenderovich breathed into the phone. "We have found... the missing exhibit... It's at... Yep, that's it... Kadiköy, and the villa's called 'Rems.' Will you be long? Excellent."

He finished the call and turned to Givi.

"Well that's that," he said, with obvious relief. "Let's go, Givi my friend. We're all done here. We can wait for the police outside. We'll tell them what we saw, how they brought it here... they can draw up their report, take notes, all that stuff... And I need to call that French bloke so he can corroborate our story. Otherwise I know what the police here are like – we'll have to prove that we were the ones who found it."

"What's he going to corroborate, exactly?" Givi was dubious.

"Well, you know, that we are the ones who deserve the reward. Money... Beaucoup d'argent!"

"There won't be any argent, Misha..." Givi replied despondently. "You might as well forget about the reward."

"And why's that?"

"Because... What language did you speak to them in?"

Shenderovich stopped dead, his body at an angle, in apparent imitation of the tablet in the storeroom.

"No!"

"Since when do the Turkish police answer the phone in Russian?"

"So, it wasn't really the police, then?" Shenderovich was catching on. "So, who's the archeologist? Not really an archeologist either?"

"You got it," Givi concluded morosely. "He's probably not even French."

Shenderovich dropped the torch, which projected an arc of light onto the block of stone from top to bottom, causing the writings to start moving again in a menacing way.

"We need to get the hell out of here..." he muttered, rubbing his hands together nervously... "Come on, get a move on... marchez... Shit, the car! I punctured the tyres with my own bare hands... Ekh, we'll never make it!"

"We wouldn't have made it anyway. They're probably outside now, Misha," Givi pointed out. "They've been sitting right here all this time, waiting for us to make a move."

"But why us?"

"Because we're nobodies. No documents, no money... No rights. We don't exist!"

"That's us alright," Shenderovich confirmed sorrowfully.

"So we were just instruments of execution. Like that crowbar..."

Shenderovich looked up.

"Did you hear that?"

There were heavy footsteps on the porch. Hunching his

shoulders up around his ears, Givi listened as the steps and their echoes slowly merged to fill the empty house.

Shenderovich slammed the door.

"The tablet, Misha! Lean on it."

Putting all his weight behind it, Shenderovich leant his shoulder against the heavy stone and desperately pushed. The stone clearly had no intention of giving way.

"Bloody thing!"

Shenderovich took a run up and slammed into the tablet with both hands. The tablet groaned and tilted further over.

"Come on! Push!"

The tablet crashed to the ground, stirring up a cloud of dust and smashing into the door on its way down.

"Sorted!"

They heard a muffled blow from the other side of the door. The tablet shook but stayed in place.

The door creaked, then a splinter shot out of it, scratching Shenderovich's cheek.

"They're breaking it down!"

"What shall we do?" muttered Shenderovich, feverishly looking round. "What shall we do?"

And suddenly he froze, his mouth hanging open. There was a thin shaft of light coming from somewhere at the back of the room.

"Look!"

"Barukh ata Adonai" breathed Givi. "There's another door! Did you notice that earlier?"

"No, did you?"

"No! But who cares?!"

Impudently trampling the tablet underfoot, they clambered over it to get to the far end of the storeroom. There they found a solid door made of sheet iron, like an underground bunker.

The door opened slightly. All by itself.

Givi was bathed in a dazzling light. He screwed up his eyes and took a step forward.

"What can you see?" shouted Shenderovich behind him. "I can't see anything!"

Givi fell through the door into the light, which completely engulfed him. He didn't see so much as feel Shenderovich fall out behind him, swearing under his breath.

They lay side by side, gulping in the hot air. There was a heavy noise behind them. Givi turned round, but it was just the tablet, which had fallen out after them with a stony crash and then frozen in the same position as before, leaning slightly to one side.

"There he is!" cried a voice.

"It worked!" answered a second voice.

"Greetings, greetings, Prophet of Nu, Prophet of Had, Prophet of Ra-Hoor-Khu! Let us rejoice! Come forth into our splendour and delight! Come forth into our frenzied world and write words fit for a king!"

Givi stood up, brushing his knees. He stood in a burning hot shaft of sunlight. Bizarre steep rock faces showed up white all around him, like bones stripped of flesh. There were numerous black holes in the rock faces. Givi initially presumed them to be the nesting holes of coastal swallows but then, as he began to appreciate their scale, realized that they were easily large enough to accommodate an adult human. Stone steps led up to the openings, although in this world without shadows they were virtually invisible.

Shenderovich stirred and groaned nearby.

He wore a puzzled expression and was looking around blankly at the lifelessness that lay before him, reminiscent of the surface of the moon.

"What's going on?" he asked eventually. "Where are we?"

"I have absolutely no idea," Givi answered sadly.

"Why is it so light? It was the middle of the night a minute ago… I remember."

"Are we still alive, Misha?"

"I think so," answered Shenderovich uncertainly, gingerly feeling his cheekbone with the tips of his fingers. "Otherwise this wouldn't hurt like it does. Jesus, what sort of Ku Klux Klan is this?"

A figure loomed nearby. A massive chain on its chest reflected the unbearable sunlight, and its white robe seemed to glow with its own fierce flame.

"O Master of Silence and Power! We are your prophets – your humble servants!" came a voice from under the hood, and the figure bowed deeply before Shenderovich, who was looking around uncertainly and struggling to his knees.

Noticing the new arrival, he recoiled slightly but then pulled himself together, straightened himself up and politely asked:

"Can I help you?"

Shenderovich was displaying such inhuman composure that Givi could only marvel quietly to himself.

"Rejoice! For he has come among us, Empress and Hierophant, Secret Serpent! Heir to the Great One, Prophesier of the Present and Devourer of the Future!" the new arrival continued, still bowing at a right angle before Shenderovich.

"With whom am I..." began Shenderovich uncertainly.

"O! Unspoken names and nameless beings! In this world we have different names, and the other world has no names for us. A name ties knots and imposes fetters. You can simply call me Master! Master Therion at your service," said the man, modestly but with dignity. "And this," he nodded somewhere off to the side, and Givi saw another figure, shorter and in a pale yellow robe that looked rather like a dressing gown, "is my assistant, Frater Perdurabo."

"Pleased to meet you," Shenderovich said politely. "Allow me to introduce myself – Mikhail Abramovich Shenderovich."

The newcomer (or was he the host?) bowed even lower, this time forming an acute angle with his body.

"Michael! Blessed be this name, chosen in the present incarnation by you yourself, O Great One! For it truly is an angelic name. Was it not the bearer of this very name who stood before the Lord of Spirits? Who triumphed over Kasbeel? Who took the oath Akae in his hands?"

"Well," Shenderovich admitted cautiously, "I suppose so..."

The man in white clasped his hands together then turned to Givi, apparently noticing him for the first time.

"And who is this?" he asked sternly. "This one is surplus to our requirements!"

"He's with me," said Shenderovich, grandly.

"It is not my place to contradict the Mighty One," Master Therion deferred politely, though with obvious reluctance. Then he nervously exclaimed:

"Careful! Don't drop it! There, put it there!"

Givi jumped and turned round. Two men, the backs of their necks red from the effort involved, were dragging the ill-starred tablet.

"These are our Children," their host politely explained. "They are delivering the Tablet of Union to its rightful place.

Givi thought they were the most bandit-like 'children' he'd ever set eyes on. The Children dragged the tablet through, scraping the dry earth, and disappeared into a cave.

After a little while there was a series of muffled blows from inside the cave, as if someone were trying to erect the tablet onto a stone pedestal and meeting considerable resistance.

The Children eventually returned, dragging exotic cushions and enormous fans. The cushions were thrown onto the floor in front of Shenderovich and their two hosts, who immediately sat down on them, crossing their legs. Givi thought for a moment then sat down on the ground. As if by magic, a pitcher suddenly materialised out of nowhere, its sides covered in condensation. It was accompanied by a plate of figs. The Children took up position behind the seated ones and began fanning them indifferently.

Master Therion raised himself slightly from his cushion

and bowed reverentially to Shenderovich once again, pressing his hand to his chest.

"Will you take some refreshment, O Leopard of the Desert?"

"Don't mind if I do," answered Shenderovich, benevolently.

"Please accept our apologies for transferring you so crudely. But the astral paths were becoming warped under the weight of the Tablet of Union, with which you are one…"

"Um… yeah…" agreed Shenderovich. "So, it's the Tablet of Union then, is it? You know, I thought as much."

"Of course! And finally, it is here! And you are here, O One and Only! Such happiness, a celebration of fire and a celebration of light! A celebration of life and a celebration of death!"

"Right…"

"A celebration of the one who understands the secret language! Is it not so, Frater Perdurabo?"

"Indeed it is so," came the gloomy response from the taciturn Frater Perdurabo.

"Yes," Givi perked up a bit. "Actually, I was wondering… speaking of languages… Where did you learn to speak Russian so well?"

Master Therion shrugged expressively as he replied, "What is the language of humans to one who communes with angels?"

Givi stole a glance at Shenderovich. He was nodding politely, maintaining the sympathetic look of an experienced psychiatrist.

"There are so few Chosen Ones," Shenderovich said in awe. "I hadn't dared hope to meet an Initiate in this world! Especially not in such a… um," he looked around, "…so far from the enlightened world! But of course, one could not imagine a more perfect spot for a Hermit's refuge."

"We are few in number," answered Master Therion bleakly. "But we keep the ordinances. The enlightened world to us is nothing, and so-called learned people are no more than frogs croaking in a stagnant pond. Hear my story, O Bridge of Time and Space, and you will understand that the forces weaving the astral carpet of fate brought you to me by rights and that I am truly destined to possess the Tablet of Union. Is it not so, Frater Perdurabo?"

"Indeed it is so," echoed Frater Perdurabo from beneath his hood.

The Story of Master Therion and His Series of Former Incarnations, or On the Difficult Paths of High Magic

"My knowledge in this subject is extensive, for in one of my previous incarnations I was none other than Sir Edward Kelley, travelling companion and medium of John Dee… I will not hear a word said against John Dee – he was a very capable man, but without me as his spirit guide he would have been a complete nonentity. For, despite his continued assertions to the contrary (though he may have been buried beneath a rose bush in Sussex almost four centuries ago, he continues to thrive and prosper to this day, albeit on a higher astral plane) I was the one who guided him along the paths of magic.

I was born into that particular incarnation in the Year of Our Lord fifteen hundred and twenty-seven, and it was noted that whilst yet in the cradle I bore the sign of the Archangel Raziel, keeper of the book of all celestial and earthly knowledge, primogenitor of the Kabbalah and of all magic. The first word I uttered was "Ai!" which in the language of magic means "Our Lady of the Western Gate of Heaven!" and is an appeal from the initiated to Our Lady of Babylon!

Diligently and devotedly I developed my magical abilities, which led to my rejecting all worldly goods and becoming separated from my kin – those benighted people, who were unable to comprehend my true calling and selfishly demanded that I earn my daily bread by the sweat of my brow. I refused likewise to allow myself to be bound by the ties of matrimony, for there is no prospect more terrible to a man of intelligence than to enter into any union with a vulgar and earthbound being... In any case, my bride-to-be soon took comfort in the arms of a local shopkeeper, a man indeed worthy of her, uneducated and greedy, who soon drove her to her grave with his incessant fault-finding and truly beastly outbursts of rage... Meanwhile, I continued diligently perfecting myself in the sciences and was soon able to interpret the will of the stars in fire, in water and in my crystal ball. I made particular progress in my observations of the latter...

John Dee, court astrologer and confidant of Her Majesty Queen Elizabeth I, was an irresponsible and ambitious person, whose desire to fathom the mysteries of fine matter was exceeded by his passion for adventure. My actions were worthy of recording in magic books, for I befriended him nevertheless and taught him to understand the language of the angels, that is to say the Enochian language, and summoned unto my magic crystal the spirit of the Archangel Raziel. Dee, that profit-seeker, became convinced in his arrogance that he was the one chosen by higher forces to interpret the sermons of the angels. However, during the course of our travels around Egypt and Turkey, I understood that the schemer was not actually a faithful interpreter of the angels' words (which, of course, he was only able to grasp at all thanks to my ability to associate with astral entities). He had dedicated his earthly incarnation to vulgar politics, and his main desire was to be well received in the most influential houses of that world, whereas I was hungry for knowledge alone... Having learned through my crystal ball from Raziel himself of the existence of the Tablet of Union, which he had left on earth, I threw all of my spiritual and physical strength into the search for this greatest of treasures. However, Dee, that adventurer, enticed me into visiting barbaric countries and cities. In particular we visited Muscovy, where we were treated with kindness by Tsar Fyodor Ioannovich, who showed me particular favour in asking me to become his personal physician (he was already, thanks to my efforts, strengthened in mind and body, and if he hadn't been burdened by the sins of his former incarnations he would have made a complete recovery – as it was, alas, in spite of my successful healing, he soon died). Dee still maintains that it was he, and not I, who was in favour with the Russian Tsar. However, no one believes him...

We also spent time in Krakow, where we were treated like royalty by Stefan Batory, and in Pressburg, where Maximilian II showed us favour. Finally, we came to Prague, which was ruled at the time by Emperor Rudolf II.

However, treated with affection by Rudolf, the alchemists' king, Dee fell victim to his own fondness for precipitate promises. Three years later, having promised him the world and unable to deliver, he elected to go into hiding and found shelter under the wing of Her Majesty Queen Elizabeth I, whom he outlived, incidentally, by a short time. In the vain hope of finding a quiet haven, I remained at the court of Emperor Rudolf, who was hungry for the power of the Philosopher's Stone and was only too glad to be assisted in his efforts by one so valuable as the former incarnation of your obedient servant. Fortunately I was able to come by a small quantity of magic powder, capable of transmuting base metals into gold..."

"From that Jew," Frater Perdurabo prompted him readily. "The Prague magician, what was his name?"

"The rabbi? I know not how you came by this information, Frater Perdurabo, but whoever related it to you was a filthy and ignoble liar. For a start, I arrived at the precise formula for the power by dint of my own intellect, and furthermore Rabbi Bezalel himself gave it to me on hearing of my power. And in any case I only borrowed the smallest amount... The merest of pinches... And my intentions were always of the most noble kind, for I had no need for gold – knowledge was what I sought. I had more than enough gold already, and not from the Philosopher's Stone but from Emperor Rudolf himself, who was delighted with my work and rewarded me ten times over in relation to that which he obtained by means of my powder. Which infuriated him subsequently, for, alas, once the powder had run out, the magic forces wiped from my memory the recipe for its preparation…"

"Naturally," interjected Frater Perdurabo.

"In short," continued Master Therion, dismissing the comments of his disciple with a wave of his hand, "I had attained an advanced knowledge of magic and my power was great, but vile calumnies drove me beneath the vaults of a Prague dungeon. I ended the century cold and hungry, despised by all worthless individuals and wracked by consumption, within the damp and disgusting walls of that foul dungeon, in the Year of Our Lord fifteen hundred and ninety-seven… But my power was great and my subsequent incarnation in the Year of Our Lord seventeen hundred and forty-three gave the world Cagliostro, of the Knights of Malta…"

"Ah," Shenderovich commented happily, "I've heard of him."

"But you know everything, O Bearer of Light! My father, a mercenary-minded and earthbound individual, was occupied with buying and selling, speculating and accumulating, being as he was a merchant, which was profoundly repellent to me. I felt immediately drawn to foreign lands and finer matters. Forsaking my family home and renouncing my coarse family name, I dedicated myself to the High Art, studying chemistry and alchemy in the monasteries of Sicily. And I attained unprecedented heights and extraordinary power, for I succeeded in mastering the secret of the elixir of eternal youth, which is, in essence, the liquid fraction of the Philosopher's Stone, known to Sir Kelley in the form of the magic powder."

"Known to Ben Bezalel…"
"Be silent, you worthless fool!"

"Thus, I remained young, powerful and brilliant. However, I was persecuted by certain contemptible, envious individuals and forced to flee France, where I had been living under the patronage of King Louis XV. The loneliness of my previous incarnation had been hateful to me, and so I resolved to choose someone with whom to share my life, someone loyal and worthy of my talents. The maiden Lorenza Feliciani, whom I charmed with my virtues, turned down the most eligible bachelors in the whole of Italy and, forsaking her family home, eloped with me to share my exiled fate. Thus, we roamed the lands, enduring indigence and deprivation, until we arrived in Muscovy and visited the city of Saint Peter…"

"I've heard of that too…"

"…where I secretly assisted Her Majesty Catherine the Great, that Northern Cleopatra, in her ascension to the throne. There I was given the power to increase threefold the gold reserves of Her Majesty's favourite, His Highness the Grand Duke Potemkin, whilst at the same time making a little for myself in order to support my scientific research. However, owing to the vile calumnies of slanderers and envious individuals I was expelled from Russia by the will of the monarch (a wild country, what can you do?) and headed for Krakow and Warsaw, and from there to Pressburg, where I suffered further persecution by envious individuals and ill-wishers.

We finally reached Rome, and I decided to settle there for the remainder of that incarnation and to increase my power in peace and quiet, for I had attained a high level of initiation and stood poised on the threshold of unprecedented riches and great fame. However…"

"Owing to the calumnies of slanderers and envious individuals…"

"Exactly… I was arrested and thrown into…"

"A dungeon…" Shenderovich prompted amiably.

"Exactly… where I reached the end of my earthly path in a cold and damp cell of the Castel Sant'Angelo in the Year of Our Lord seventeen hundred and ninety-five, despised by all and alone, for my spouse, Lorenza, had been incarcerated in a nunnery, where she endured innumerable hardships and soon after expired.

However, my astral power was so great that in the tenth year of the nineteenth century I was granted a further earthly incarnation in the form of Alphonse Louis Constant, alias Eliphas Levi Zahed… Already in early infancy I showed an astonishing aptitude for magic, saying "ah-goo," in other words a distortion of "AUGMN" – the Word of Power, by means of which the energies of Gore execute their will in the world of Assiya. It was distorted thus, for the mouth of an infant is not capable of mastering such a mighty Name… Once I had grown a little and realized the Way, I disowned my father, that coarse bootmaker, and began to move swiftly forward along the path of magic. However, soon…"

"Certain contemptible, dark and envious individuals…"

"Precisely… Those vulgar and spiritually blind materialists excluded me from a catholic seminary for practising the occult arts. You can surely guess the rest. For the entire duration of that particular earthly incarnation I suffered the inexplicable yet severe persecution of an indifferent world. My talent was mocked and held in contempt. Alas, how I pined for my beautiful Lorenza, who withered in her prime. It seemed to me that I had succeeded in finding her true likeness. However, in this incarnation troubles tormented not only me but my fellow-traveller as well. Mistress Constant, my wife, was unable to endure the pressure of my astral being, so she drank herself into oblivion and went completely insane. My children died from neglect one after the other, my mother disowned me, my friends abandoned me… However, even under these dreadful conditions I managed to make considerable progress along the path of the Chosen Ones. I finished my great work *The Key to the Great Mysteries*, which provides an interpretation of certain of the finer phenomena of the heavenly world, and I amassed unprecedented power and might. However, utter ruin and failure befell me and I was…"

"Thrown into a dungeon…"

"Oh no, this time I was luckier. I reached the end of my earthly path in damp and cold furnished rooms, in the Year of Our Lord eighteen hundred and sixty-five, languishing in obscurity and destitution…"

"Despised by all…"

"Despised by all. However, my power was so great that I was able to transfer my astral being into the form of Sir Aleister Crowley, who came into the world six months later… Already in early infancy I felt magical abilities within myself, which terrified my poor parents, who were uneducated and, alas, earthbound. They were nevertheless rather well-off, for my father was the successful owner of a brewery and had bought and sold, and speculated and accumulated, until he had acquired a fair share of worldly goods. However, I was drawn not to business operations but rather to Magical

Operations. Suddenly, by a fortuitous confluence of circumstances, my father passed away. I mourned him sincerely until I understood that fate was leading me along the path of the Chosen Ones and that this path now lay open before me.

As soon as I had buried my father and inherited his fortune, I devoted myself entirely to the study of magic. Soon, oh, soon I became a Chosen One and a member of the magical order 'Golden Dawn,' attained Nirvikalpa Samadhi, and became Master of the Order and a secret member of the Masonic lodge... I was well received in the most influential houses of the time – I socialized in Paris with Somerset Maugham and Auguste Rodin and was welcomed by Sir Conan Doyle into his London home... I visited Saint Petersburg and Moscow again, where I was received by Tsar Nicholas II and Her Majesty his wife, and it was there that I completed my Gnostic Mass... To this day I do not know whether the war of 1914 began as an earthly reflection of the Great War of the Magi, which I unleashed in the Year of Our Lord nineteen hundred and ten, or as a result of the appearance in the world of this work, which shook the strings of the World Ether. Ultimately I comprehended (or rather, recalled) Enochian magic and turned my attention to the Tablet of Union! However..."

"Malicious, envious individuals..."

"Exactly... Malicious, envious individuals continued to persecute me even in that incarnation... My friend stole from me, my mother disowned me, the magic order expelled me, I suffered defeat in the Great War of the Magi, I was subjected to vile attacks and a court of law, and I was exiled from France, that wild, corrupt and exceedingly mercantile land. But even in my native England, owing to the death of my pupil and comrade-in-arms Loveday, which those carrion-crows considered 'suspicious,' I was hunted down by a pack of jackal-like journalists and forced to flee to Sicily (from where I was also soon exiled, incidentally) and from there to Germany, where the last of my friends turned his back on me, whilst still affecting to support me… Alas, steadfastness is not a merit of the simple man.

Moreover…

I had long been seeking a companion with whom to share my life, who would remind me of my poor Lucia and my poor Constant, and finally I found her – Rose Kelly appeared to be a worthy partner for a great magus. And I must admit that, with my customary insight, I was not wrong – she did indeed turn out to be a fair medium, and it was through her that the demon Aiwass dictated to me the Book of the Law.

However, finding herself unable to endure the mighty pressure of my astral being, she too, like her predecessor, gave herself over to drink and went out of her mind. By that time I had attained an ineffable might and had fathomed all the secrets of life and death – immortality and glory were in my hands, and my power was incomparable with the might of all magi, past and future. However, I…"

"Owing to the calumnies of slanderers and envious individuals…"

"Was exiled from there and brought to ruin, declared bankrupt and discredited throughout the land. Thus, I reached the end of my earthly path…"

"In a damp and cold… cell? Furnished rooms?"

"Furnished rooms. From an attack of asthma, that affliction of the poor and the ignorant I, master of the secret of immortality and complete and absolute healing! I had to begin all over again. I will spare you an enumeration of all the sufferings that befell me in that incarnation. Suffice it to say that my reward for the manifold trials and tribulations I suffered in my quest for the magical enlightenment of humanity was nought but universal disdain, corporeal suffering, despair and spiritual paralysis!

However, I did succeed in nurturing a narrow circle of followers, naturally far less knowledgeable than myself about the fine matters of magic. Furthermore, having based myself within the eternal light at the very heart of the world in order to perform my experiments without further hindrance, I also succeeded in opening the doors of space and time. And, eventually, I succeeded in summoning the Tablet of Union and rescuing it from the filthy clutches of the servants of darkness, whose name is Chaos... For I learned from the angels, that is to say the spirits of the light, that the treasures of great knowledge inscribed upon the tablet are mine by rights and that I shall rise up... Right, Frater Perdurabo?"

"Indeed it is so," agreed Frater Perdurabo.

"The angels serve me as they served my previous incarnations, with no less fervour and maybe even with more, for in the course of my various reincarnations I have strengthened my astral being to the point where it has attained indescribable might..."

"It must have been great, this power of yours," Shenderovich was nodding importantly although he was also fidgeting slightly on his cushion, "if you're served by the angels themselves, those free children of the air... I hope you don't mind my asking, but how do you talk to them, exactly?"

"The angels," explained Master Therion, "are able to express their thoughts like any intelligent substance. And if you ask them something, they can answer you. Of course, you have to ask them the right way, that is, forcefully. My present-day medium," he nodded towards Frater Perdurabo, "saw them in the crystal ball which I have kept from my previous incarnations. And they said that a man would come, as bright as summer lightning, as formidable as an army marching into battle. He would break through the curtain of time and space bringing with him the Tablet, for he and the Tablet are one and the essence of the Tablet is bound to his essence, like iron to a magnet."

"Or vice versa," nodded Shenderovich distractedly.

"Or vice versa. And if the Destroyer of Destroyers has already recovered his strength and would deign to come through and take a look…"

Shenderovich stood up reluctantly, looking warily up at the fan suspended menacingly overhead. Givi, untroubled by the fan, quickly grabbed a fig from the plate and took his place at the rear of the procession. The Children made way for him and then closed ranks behind him. Ekh, thought Givi, if these two are the caretakers of this madhouse then heaven help us…

"Let us go, O Mighty One, so that you may meet face to face!"

The path stopped suddenly at the next oversized swallow's lair. In the bright sunlight, the dark jaws seemed to lead into pitch blackness. However, once they were inside the cave, propped up by the Children, Givi understood that it was all relative: there were lamps emitting fumes along both sides of the carpeted path, their tongues flickering weakly.

The vaulted arches of the cave suddenly opened up onto a vast underground chamber completely covered with panels of scarlet and crimson fabric, which made it feel like the inside of a giant box of chocolates.

"Here we are!" Master Therion announced cordially, leading his guests in.

At the back of the chamber stood a stone pedestal, which Givi estimated to be approximately two metres tall and one and half wide. It was covered with a raspberry-coloured altar cloth bearing an image of a blazing sun embroidered in golden thread. Three steps led up to the pedestal – they were covered in black and white squares and were lined with giant obelisks, which bore obscure but somehow disturbing symmetrical black and white images. It all combined to give the impression of a chessboard gone mad.

On top of the pedestal, lazily reflecting the flames of two candelabras, lay a crystal ball picturesquely draped in a scarlet cloth.

The Children fell dramatically to their knees behind Givi, the carpet softening the impact.

"Behold, the very heart of the Order," Master Therion whispered reverentially. "Behold, the Vessel of Truth, the Bearer of the Highest Knowledge… This object sought me out in the British Museum and came into my possession of its own volition… All by itself! Despite the filthy lies that those sceptics wrote about me in their nasty newspapers…"

"Of course it found you, Master," interjected Frater Perdurabo, "for it belongs to you alone…"

"Indeed, indeed… it was already mine when I was speaking to the Children of the Light on behalf of Dee… But enough! It is time to begin."

"Begin what?" Shenderovich was visibly taken aback.

"The Deed, of course!"

He adjusted the chain on his chest, which flashed a dull crimson, and nodded to Frater Perdurabo, who extricated from the folds of his pale yellow hood a heavy, battered tome bound in leather. The sides of the binding had evidently provided some sustenance to the local mice.

"By the name of this Book of the Law…"

Jesus, thought Givi, who are these people? Why are they acting out this bizarre pantomime? And why is Misha behaving so weirdly? No, I must be dreaming. Because if I weren't there's no way Misha would be going along with it all. Would he?

He glanced furtively at Shenderovich who gave a majestic nod as he took from Master Therion's hands a weighty silver staff, crowned with an ugly cone.

"Your Staff for all Chalices and your Discus for all Swords, but do not betray your Seed."

"That goes without saying," agreed Shenderovich.

A scarlet robe flowed from his shoulders to the chequered floor. The Children stood behind him, one holding a pitcher and periodically sprinkling Shenderovich's robe with something bearing an uncanny resemblance to plain water, the other swinging a thurible in a gentle arc. At the far point of its arc, the thurible suddenly released a stream of acrid smoke right in Givi's face, causing him to recoil and start coughing.

"Hurry, Frater Perdurabo! Don't just stand there!"

Frater Perdurabo came forward and, leaning over the black pedestal, kissed the Book of the Law three times and placed it on the smooth surface...

"Accept this sacrifice, Most Secret of Secrets, whose name is Chaos!"

Shenderovich became suddenly alert and started to back away.

"What sacrifice?" he asked suspiciously.

"It is there, on the altar, O Bridge of Bridges. Can you really not see it? We are sacrificing a live astral being! This being will dissolve into the ether. I summoned it tonight specifically for our purposes and have swaddled it in fine energies."

"Ah, I see..."

"Forgive me, Father of Fathers! Maybe you are vexed because you require the sacrifice to take the form of crude matter? Well, if you insist..."

Master Therion turned his head beneath his hood. Givi took a precautionary step backwards.

"It... no, no, that's fine," Shenderovich said quickly. "Personally, I don't think that would be a very good idea. Crude matter... has an adverse effect on the astral planes."

"Do not fret, O Primogenitor of Primogenitors, Life, Health, Power... The only crude matter we will be sacrificing will be magic beetles from the Book of the Law, and a snake. However," he added quickly, catching Shenderovich's cold stare, "the snake will not perish in the true sense. It will merely be boiled in the appropriate vessel then released when the time is right, refreshed and altered, but in essence the same…"

"Oh well, that's OK then," nodded Shenderovich.

"Let us begin!" Master Therion nervously rubbed his hands. "Let the negative Child stand to your left, and the positive to your right, while you utter the magic formula."

"Which one of the many?" Shenderovich asked impassively. "For there are an infinite number from which to choose…"

"Just repeat after me, O Luminary of Luminaries who has pushed back the limits of the world!"

The Children rearranged themselves on either side of Shenderovich like escorts. The positive Child waved an incense burner, and the smoke struck Shenderovich in the face.

"O Secret Energy in Three Hypostases! O Matter Divisible by Four and Seven!"

"Four and seven… Ah-choo!"

"O Weavers of the Cover of the Ether! May each of you carry out your will, like a warrior on the path of the Star that blazes eternally in the joyful company of the heavens!"

"Joyful company… Heavens… Ah-choo!"

"The sign, you fool! You forgot the sign…"

"By the sign of the Man and the Brother…"

Shenderovich sneezed again.

"Well, Descendant of Descendants and Ancestor of Ancestors?"

"Well what, exactly?" asked Shenderovich. "I said it all!"

"Make your prophesy!"

"Uh…. Abracadabra… Boom!"

"ABRACADABRA!" cried Master Therion, raising his hands to the roof of the cave. "He uttered the Word. The Mighty Word! Our great Deed is done!"

"And?"

"Now he will say the rest."

Shenderovich cleared his throat but remained silent. He looked helplessly at Givi, who rolled his eyes expressively and shook his head.

"Why do you remain silent, O Fount of Knowledge?"

"I'm not ready!" announced Shenderovich petulantly, like a capricious primadonna.

"He is not ready…" chorused the Children.

"That is odd…" said Master Therion, icily. "He must speak… make his prophesy. The Tablet must speak for him! Frater Perdurabo, was he really the one you saw in the crystal ball?"

"I think so," replied Frater Perdurabo, sounding a little unsure.

"Fine, in that case I shall ask it myself. May I be informed by a more reliable source?"

"Master, perhaps it is better not to?"

"Amateurs, one and all… If you want something done properly… And you, Children, in the meantime you will look after the Bull of the Bulls… If he is the one we believe him to be, then all is well…"

"And if not?" asked Shenderovich.

"Then all is also well," answered Master Therion glancing at the black polished surface of the altar with affectionate distraction.

He scratched his head under his hood, deep in thought, and then turned to Givi. Givi's insides froze.

"As for this one…" he said ruminatively. "Perhaps we should remove him from the world of crude matter? It seems to me that he is provoking a perturbation of the astral links and mundane fields, do you not agree, Frater Perdurabo?"

"Better to arrange everything properly," Frater Perdurabo gave a loud cough, "so as not to waste life force in vain… For the time being, I'll lock him in an energy cocoon."

"Babylon only knows what you produced last time but it certainly wasn't a cocoon."

"A trifling error," confessed Frater Perdurabo. "I was out of practice."

He busily set about passing his hands around Givi and muttering under his breath. Givi convulsed, as if he were being tickled.

"It is done," said Frater Perdurabo finally. "He is isolated on the appropriate level."

"Then let us begin."

"Let us begin."

"From Chesed I control Geburah by means of the path of the Lion... By this inverted pentagram..."

"Master..."

"Do not interfere..."

"Master, you are going clockwise, and you should be going counterclockwise!"

"Ah you, Astarot! From Chesed... The staff, now! Kindly pass the staff, O Guest of Guests! And be quick about it, Children! Thank you... I point with this staff to the heart of the pentacle, exclaiming DEFILER!"

"Who?" Givi asked in a startled whisper.

"Be silent," hissed Frater Perdurabo, who had been nervously tapping his foot throughout proceedings. "You are in a cocoon!"

"O Malkah be Tarshisim ve-ad Ruachoth Schechalim, I invoke you by the letter Kaf meaning Power, by the letter Nun meaning Return, by the letter Mem meaning Death, and by the letter Fe meaning Immortality. Appear!"

Green smoke began to pour from the centre of the invisible pentacle,

"It is he!" cried Master Therion.

"Buer!"

"WHAT DO YOU WANT, LOWLY WORMS?" roared the demon, turning to face the assembled company.

What the bloody hell is going on, thought Givi. He raised his hand, either to make the sign of the cross or to pinch himself, he hadn't quite decided, but received a sharp rap on the knuckles from Frater Perdurabo.

"O Leader of Manifold Legions, O Protector of Destitute Philosophers, we ask you for one word only…"

"BASTARDS," the demon announced readily, enunciating with precision.

"Oh no, Mighty One! You need to answer my question! I invoke by this Staff and the Book of the Law…"

"GET ON WITH IT."

"Is he the one?"

"HE IS!!!!" cried the demon. His face distorted with fear then he emitted a cloud of sulphurous gases and dissolved into thin air…

"Well, what do you know…" muttered the Master. "But wait! That is not all! Now I say unto you: go, and peace be with you in your domains and abodes, and may you be granted the blessing of the Highest in the name of… What name are we using today, Frater Perdurabo?"

"He has already gone, Master…"

"Do not presume to instruct me in the ways of the Deed! And may there be peace between us until I summon you once more… Right, that'll do."

He turned to Shenderovich.

"Forgive me, O Two-Horned One! Your servant dared to doubt you. But it was because you did not make contact with the Tablet of Union! Which, incidentally, was rather strange. What is your view on the matter, Frater Perdurabo?"

"He sneezed while he was speaking… He mixed up the most crucial of connections…"

"That is nonsense," the Master said sternly. "The astral planes do not depend on such trifling matters."

"Oh, but they do…"

"My voice is just a bit off today," said Shenderovich capriciously.

"That is not the problem, O King of Kings! Your voice is

like the roar of an enraged lion… I think that there is a more serious issue afoot… Perhaps it is because of your fellow-traveller? Perhaps his noumenal body is interfering with the fine oscillations of the strings?"

He looked Givi up and down with the experienced eye of a diagnostician.

"This one is no good," he said.

"Why not?" Shenderovich was surprised.

"His eyes… He has bad eyes… If he does have a place in this chamber, then it is atop the altar."

Shenderovich raised his hand majestically.

"Leave my fellow-traveller and servant in peace, O Master! Otherwise you will have a Misdeed, as well as a Deed, to worry about! This is Givi, my good and trustworthy friend…"

"What did you call him, O Bridge of Azure?"

"My name is Givi," said Givi mournfully.

"Givi?" repeated the Master, with a particular tremor in his voice. Behind Givi, the Children gave a simultaneous gasp, and Frater Perdurabo for some reason straightened up his deferentially hunched shoulders.

"Forgive me once again, O Magnanimous One! I was so blinded by your radiance that I could not discern your fellow-traveller! Truly you are great, if you count among your fellow-travellers the descendant of Shemhazai himself!"

"Well, you won't get rid of him that easily," Frater Perdurabo cheerfully concluded, "if he's one of them!"

"So be it," answered Master Therion sternly. "For that is how the threads of Fate are woven. Here he is with you, one of the giants whose names are Hiwa and Hiya, otherwise known as Givi and Giya, descendants of the fallen angel Shemhazai! Great is the power of those that serve you!"

"I will forgive you this time, O Worthless One," said Shenderovich coldly. "Though I might easily have lost my temper, and my temper, when lost, is a fearsome beast indeed."

"But the Deed…"

"And have you looked after us, the Children of the Light, in the appropriate manner? Have you permitted us to rest after our long and arduous journey? Have you clothed us in gowns of brocade? Have you anointed us with balm? Have you shown the appropriate deference, I ask you?"

"Forgive me, O Fount of Knowledge... I was driven by impatience..."

"That's more like it," replied Shenderovich, sternly. "We are not merely dumb instruments in your hands. And until we are treated with the respect we deserve the Deed will not be done in a manner worthy of the unworthy, but rather in a manner unworthy of the worthy."

"You speak the truth, O Source of Happiness... Let us go now together, you and your giant fellow-traveller, the proud descendant of Shemhazai..."

Givi straightened himself up to his full height and tried to look as formidable as he possibly could... Master Therion was really getting on his nerves.

"Sweet water from mountain springs, beneficial figs from trees..."

"You think to feed the descendant of Shemhazai with figs, O Worthless One? Look at him! Take a good look, for the Eagle of the Deserts is becoming angry!"

"On that snake's life, I am," confirmed Givi.

"The flesh of a young lamb, flavoured with ginger and cardamom, the tenderest of meat, wine from the valleys, and sweetmeats fit for a king – that is what awaits you in the cool shade of our relaxation chambers. Alas, we are unsuitably removed from the world for me to be able to arrange for your eyes to be caressed by the aspect of beautiful maidens, but upon completion of the Deed we will attain such might that all the houris from the Garden of Eden shall congregate before us and flowers from the Rose of Sharon shall blossom in our royal beds..."

"Alright," Shenderovich majestically waved his hand.

"That can wait…. But we do require ablutions and sustenance for our bodies… And quickly!"

"I told you, Master…" reproached Frater Perdurabo. "You weren't treating them properly…"

"Be silent, you schemer… Hurry up, Children! Bring supplies from my cell, furnished at dawn by the spirits of the air and the servants of the vines…"

"That's more like it…"

They headed for the exit in reverse order. The Children were at the head of the procession, followed by Frater Perdurabo, who was trudging along and muttering discontentedly under his breath. Master Therion brought up the rear. Shenderovich glided along amongst them, with the edge of his gown thrown over his shoulder. Every now and then his arm emerged from under the scarlet fabric to elbow Givi in the ribs.

The sun was already yielding to the dusk, painting the cliffs gold and crimson. Dark blue shadows lay in the ravines, and the caves showed up black against them, like pools of darkness.

Master Therion, overtaking the procession, ran ahead into one of these caves.

"In here, O Guests of Guests," he announced, bowing obsequiously. "My repast is humble, but by sharing it with me you will bestow upon me an honour greater than any earthly king has ever known."

"Alright, alright," sighed Shenderovich. "My wrath lieth like a stone in my heart, but I am prepared to let you off this time, for my magnanimity is equal to my might. So, we're having lamb, you say?"

Someone touched his shoulder.

Givi leapt up and spent a moment trying to work out where he was. But it was dark and he couldn't see anything. He groped about on either side of him, felt something elastic and jerked his hand back. But it was only a cushion, tightly stuffed with horsehair, which rolled off to one side.

A black figure towered over Givi. He wanted to cry out, but fear had his throat in a vice-like grip.

"It's just a nightmare," he tried to convince himself. He tried to tell himself that in the worst-case scenario he was in his cabin on board the ferry. In a better-case scenario, he was in the ferry company's hotel. And in the best-case scenario of all, he was at home, in his own bed... This option was particularly attractive to him, so he decided that was the one he would believe.

"Honestly, whatever will I dream up next?" he thought bravely.

"Sh-hhh, O Secret One," said the figure.

Shenderovich was snoring mightily beside him. However, at that moment the snoring stopped and Shenderovich muttered sleepily.

"Hey, I told you... the female slaves first..."

"Wake up, O Stallion of all Mares," said the figure in the same whisper. "For our time will run out when day breaks upon us."

"What's running out?" Shenderovich jumped up in alarm.

"Our luck – if we do not take the appropriate measures forthwith," declared the voice from beneath the hood severely. Do not be afraid, O Fearless One, for it is I, Frater Perdurabo!"

"Well, well, what a turn up for the books... And where are the Children?"

"I disconnected them. I isolated them in a cocoon..."

"You did well, Frater," said Shenderovich amiably. "And what about the old man?"

"That schemer? That impostor, who calls himself Master Therion?"

"Yes. Your boss."

"Him?" snorted Frater Perdurabo indignantly. "My boss? Just because I choose to indulge his fantasies it does not mean that he is who he says he is! For whatever that half-educated charlatan may say, the direct descendant of Kelley and his living embodiment stands before you now. And you, Focus of the Light, did you believe him?"

"He did put forward his case quite convincingly," Shenderovich remarked sternly.

"Of course he did! One cannot deny his cunning! He praised himself to the skies, as usual. But in actual fact he was not Kelley but John Dee himself, who was so thirsty for glory and began interfering in earthly matters to such an extent that my incarnation was appointed to look after him, to keep him from causing trouble. And, would you believe it, sensing something wrong, the scoundrel framed me in that business of the Philosopher's Stone while he himself slipped away. So I was left to rot in prison thanks to that fool Rudolf. But no, that wasn't enough for him! He came back again as that rogue Crowley, even going so far as to encourage him to unleash the magical wars! The half-educated charlatan, the impostor! Did you see how he crucified that toad? Very impressive! You take him for an enlightened man? That couldn't be further from the truth! None of the respectable secret societies wanted anything to do with him, so he initiated himself. Just like that, he initiated himself! That's the kind of man we are dealing with. Rose Kelly, my next incarnation, was appointed to try and control him somehow. But he drove me, poor soul, to drown my sorrows, the despot…"

"I see!"

"And now it's happening again! Why me? What have I done to deserve being reduced to trailing around after that petty tyrant for all eternity? Incarnation after incarnation! I said to the brothers, I've had enough, choose someone else to do your dirty work, but no… You know him better than anyone, they said, you've been joined at the hip for so many centuries… Joined at the hip! I drank myself into a blind stupor because of him!"

"I see…"

"But finally, my troubles are over. For by the will of the brothers I have remained with this upstart until the hour of reckoning! Now our patience will be rewarded and the Light shall spill over all the Great East. Arise, distinguished guests, let us go! And forgive me, Good Cousin," he bowed before Givi, "that that astrally blind fool failed to recognize your mighty essence."

"No problem," Givi hurriedly replied.

"And where are we going, exactly?" asked Shenderovich coldly.

"To do the Deed, naturally," Frater Perdurabo expressed surprise. "For that is why the Great Luminaries summoned you here. Now we will get everything ready. The sooner we start the sooner we can finish, eh?"

"Fine by me," Shenderovich was surprisingly complaisant. "I just need the appropriate tools...As a skilled apprentice yourself, you must know that a Stonemason needs his Master Craftsman, a Carpenter needs his Hammer, and a Blacksmith needs his Anvil..."

In the darkness of the cave he elbowed Givi in the solar plexus. Givi gave a sharp intake of breath. It sounded rather impressive.

"Spare a foolish man, O Chosen One!" said Frater Perdurabo hurriedly. "My impatience is excusable but my negligence is not. Of course I should have taken care of you before imposing the sacred duty upon you!"

"As they say where we are from: more haste, less speed," observed Shenderovich.

"Oh, how true! What exactly do you need, O Fathomer of Depths?"

"In the garden of our repose," Shenderovich began his speech in a leisurely manner, "we left some sacred objects. Four in number. A shortened staff, pocket-sized and fashioned from dark metal, with a curved and forked end – the attribute of wisdom; a diamond wheel mounted on a brace – a symbol of the universe and the attribute of fortitude; a self-illuminating flare, portable and water-resistant – the attribute of insight;

and an anchor with three flukes attached to a rope – the attribute of… uh… anchoring… come on, use your wits, descendant of Shemhazai!"

"The attribute of unity," quickly prompted Givi.

"Indeed! The attribute of unity, and retention! And without these objects the Deed will not be done! That will be all! I have spoken!"

Frater Perdurabo thought for a moment.

"Consider it done," he said finally. "Luring these four attributes here will be nothing in comparison with the effort I expended to secure the Tablet of Union… For whatever that worthless good-for-nothing may suggest, it was my doing, not his…"

"Of course…"

"And if the Brother of Brothers and Cousin of Cousins would deign to wait a short while…"

"I will wait," agreed Shenderovich graciously, settling himself back down onto the cushion.

Frater Perdurabo pressed his palms together, bowed and slipped into the darkness. Shenderovich immediately leapt up from the cushions and gave them an irritated kick, causing them to scatter in all directions, then began to dart about the cave like a shadow, colliding with various invisible objects. Givi drew closer to the wall as a precautionary measure – he had just heard something that sounded suspiciously like their chamber pot falling victim to his partner's impetuosity.

"Well, don't just stand there like that bloody Tablet," hissed Shenderovich. "Get a move on! There's a plate of dates over there in the corner. Wrap them up in the tablecloth, and stick that bottle in with them…"

"I can't find the cork… Ah, here it is!"

"Ready?"

"Ready!"

"Let's go…"

They moved towards the exit and ran straight into Frater

Perdurabo, who was breathing heavily and carrying a large bundle reverentially in his outstretched arms.

"Here you are, O Luminary!" he said, panting. "I succeeded in obtaining your attributes and expended no small amount of effort in doing so, I might add. For if you only knew into whose hands they had fallen, you would marvel at my might!"

"You truly are mighty, Frater," Shenderovich praised him, taking the bundle. "Yes... good... everything's here. Right, we're sorted... Lead on!"

Frater Perdurabo turned and went along the path, still panting and every now and then stopping to lean against the stone wall. Shenderovich followed him, stopping dead and waiting expectantly whenever the disciple slowed his pace. Finally, choosing his moment carefully, he swung his arm back and struck Frater Perdurabo neatly on the back of his head with the crowbar, which he had wrapped in a fold of his magnificent gown in the interests of softening the blow. Frater Perdurabo swayed on his feet and fell gently into Shenderovich's arms.

"Sorted," repeated Shenderovich, with satisfaction.

He carefully extricated the crowbar and laid the gown out on the path, placing the unconscious Frater Perdurabo on top of it.

"Right, there we are," he kept repeating in a business-like manner as he pulled the knots of the gown together over the body of the disciple. "Right, that's that... Let's go, O Cousin of Cousins, before he manages to work his way out of that cocoon."

"Ekh, you've done a good job there!" Givi was full of admiration.

"I told you, stick with Shenderovich and you won't go wrong."

He swung the grappling hook and released it, managing with enviable ease to catch it over the stony ledge.

"Sorted," he said for the third time, lowering the rope and tugging on it to make sure it would hold. "You grab the food, Givi my brother, and lower yourself down there. I've checked, it's not too far. And I'll bring the attributes. That Lenoir, whoever he was, knew a thing or two about attributes, at least. They're good attributes, they'll come in handy. Oh come on, what are you scared of?" he shouted, seeing that Givi was hesitating at the edge of the precipice, unable to take the plunge. "I'll make a man of you yet, my mountain eagle."

"Ekh!" Givi answered mournfully, as he gripped the rope a little tighter and carefully began his descent.

The sun was approaching its zenith like a stone launched from a giant slingshot. Deep blue shadows ran from the low stone blocks across the dry earth, stopping short almost as soon as they began. The sun's rays fell directly on them, flaying the tops of their heads and causing a crimson darkness to throb in their eyes. Givi sighed.

"When I used to read about travelling, this isn't exactly how I imagined it. I always fancied the idea of going on an overland adventure, somewhere nice and warm and dry... But this is a bit too hot for my liking."

"We lack the appropriate means to cover our heads from the blazing eye of heaven, that's the problem. And we are therefore exposing ourselves to a serious risk of sunstroke... But I think, O Descendant of Giants, we need to follow the tracks of these proud animals... For they and their guides are far from foolish..."

"Who knows... They're wild animals, you know, Misha."

"What, the camels?"

"No, their guides."

"Wild they may be, but they know what's good for them. Look over there!"

A solitary bird had just flown past them through the burning air and landed on a fragment of the weather-beaten cliff. Insolently refusing to acknowledge the travellers, it kept one beady black eye on them as it preened its multicoloured feathers shot with ochre and azure.

"A bird!" cried Givi, stating the obvious.

"Exactly," agreed Shenderovich. "Though I am by no means an expert in ornithology, my exhausted friend, I would bet on, um... the Tablet of Union... that where there's a bird, there's water. And where there is water, there is life. So go on, shoo it into the air, O Descendant of Giants!"

"Pshht!" said Givi and waved his hands at the bird.

The bird looked him in the eye and stayed exactly where it was. Darkness swam momentarily before Givi's eyes as he bent down to pick up a dry lump of clay, which he then threw clumsily at the messenger of the skies. The missile sailed off at a tangent and fell somewhere on the other side of the cliff. The bird reluctantly flapped its wings and took off. It circled for a while then slowly flew straight ahead, mockingly wiggling its multicoloured tail from side to side.

"After it!" commanded Shenderovich.

"What about the camels?"

"Forget the camels! Useless creatures. The only thing they're good at is surviving a month without water."

"Misha, I can't go any further... Please, let's go back!"

Right at that moment, in the blazing sunlight, the cool cave with its chequered altar and sacrificial stone of questionable hygiene seemed to Givi positively cosy, the sinister Master Therion merely a harmless eccentric, and Frater Perdurabo actually quite a likeable chap. Furthermore they had plenty of water there, enough to wallow in....

"Let's go back. What's the worst they can do? I don't care. If they want to boil that snake, fine by me..."

Shenderovich blinked his sore eyelids and frowned.

"What's the matter with you, faint-hearted hero of mine, have you completely lost your mind? They will cut us into tiny little pieces!"

"Then let them... Just as long as they let us have some water first!"

"We wouldn't make it!" exclaimed Shenderovich. "Even

if we wanted to, we wouldn't make it! We would die trying! No, my suffering friend, it's best foot forward I'm afraid. Look at that bird preening itself!"

"I can't go any further, Misha!" repeated Givi, dropping to the sand. "Seriously."

"Get up, you idiot! They've probably already noticed that we've gone! They'll have sent those Children of theirs after us!"

"So what if they have? I don't care. Either way, I'm happy to die right here."

"Get up," croaked Shenderovich, leaning over Givi and grimacing as the sun took aim and fired directly at the top of his head. "Get up, you bastard!"

"I'm not getting up!" muttered Givi, spitting out dry sand.

"You are getting up!" said Shenderovich, menacingly.

"No!"

"But you're from the south! Georgian, practically Greek! You ought to love this hot weather!"

"From the south of what?" Givi weakly waved his hand without raising his head. "I was born in St. Petersburg, for your information!"

"But what about your genes? Your hot blood? The call of your ancestors? Get up, you son of a bitch!"

"Bugger off," said Givi, slowly and very precisely, thrilling at his own bravery. "You half-baked adventurer."

"Faint-hearted swine," retorted Shenderovich, kicking Givi accurately in the ribs with the toe of his boot. "I didn't exactly drag you here against your will."

"Yes you did, as a matter of fact. Ouch, that hurts!"

"It's meant to," Shenderovich said coldly, drawing his foot back for another blow. "And the next one will hurt even more."

The bird landed again on a nearby dune and watched them with benevolent interest.

"OK, OK…. I'm getting up. Just leave me alone."

"Good man," Shenderovich said softly. "About time."

The bird was still preening itself. It neatly pulled a feather out from under its wing and took off again, looking back expectantly at the travellers.

"That creature is putting you to shame," reproached Shenderovich.

The sun was already scorching, quite unbearably so. The shadows cast by the cliffs were decreasing to a minimum, but the black cross-shaped shadow of the bird oscillated and slid along the low sand dunes, which were rapidly multiplying all around them.

"It's doing it on purpose," croaked Givi in a dry voice.

"Birds, O Mistrustful Fellow-Traveller of Mine, are not capable of such guile. Their brains are no bigger than peanuts..."

The bird landed once more, this time on a stone, and started cleaning its feathers.

"Look," commented Shenderovich. "It can't leave itself alone. Obviously has some sort of personal hygiene obsession..."

He picked up a handful of sand and threw it at the bird. The bird took off again, squawking in Shenderovich's direction in an injured tone.

"Same to you," he retorted indignantly.

"Leave the bird alone, for goodness' sake," said Givi, wearily. "What are you harassing the wildlife for now?"

"I'm trying to make it understand..." Shenderovich attempted to explain his behaviour. "It's supposed to be leading us to water."

He shaded his eyes with his hand and stared into the scorching afternoon. The air quivered and flowed, breaking into glittering little mirrors, so that the desert in the distance appeared to be paved with glass...

"Oh," Shenderovich suddenly stopped abruptly and grabbed Givi's shoulder. "Look over there..."

"Bloody hell," gasped Givi.

A city had risen up from out of nowhere. Gold, green and turquoise cupolas shone brightly in the sun, proud white towers breathed a lunar coolness, and fountains of cold sparkling water shot high up into the sky, showering the magnificent palm trees in a multicoloured rainbow.

"Wow!" Givi whispered reverentially, gawping at the unbearable brilliance of the golden roofs. "Look Misha, it's incredible! Let's head over there!"

"It's a mirage," Shenderovich brought him back down to earth. "A typical mirage… The most ordinary mirage you could ever imagine."

"How can such beauty be considered ordinary? Just look at it!"

"Such apparitions are a widespread phenomenon in this sort of climate. We are in a desert, you know."

"All I know is that I'm about to die of thirst," commented Givi.

"Mirages occur exclusively in conditions of reduced humidity. And by the way, where is that bloody bird?"

"Over there…"

The bird was sitting on the edge of a neighbouring cliff, cleaning its feathers again.

When it spotted Shenderovich it raised its head suspiciously and then lowered it again.

"Stupid chicken," muttered Shenderovich.

The bird shrugged expressively and turned away.

"Misha!" said Givi suddenly, forcing himself to drag his eyes away from the steep white arches slowly melting into the pale-blue haze. "Look what it's sitting on…"

What had at first appeared to be the edge of a cliff revealed itself on closer inspection to be a structure made of weather-beaten bricks. It was covered with sand, but the surrounding ground was noticeably darker and was dotted with dull little shrubs.

"Water!" Givi wanted to cry out, but a hoarse whisper was all that issued from his throat.

"Look!" Shenderovich was equally astonished. "A well!"

The bird was sitting on the edge of a stone trough, periodically plunging its chest into the water and splashing with its wings.

"It may be a dumb animal, but it's not stupid," approved Shenderovich.

He also started shaking his head like a wet dog, spraying water onto the sand.

"Maybe they'll catch up with us?" said Givi, secretly hopeful.

Shenderovich, balancing dangerously, had clambered up onto the stone edge of the well and was shading his eyes with his hand and peering into the distance. The bird looked at him out of the corner of its beady black eye and moved away slightly, though it didn't take off but merely resumed the preening of its brilliant plumage.

"No sign of them," reported Shenderovich, climbing down. "This is all a bit strange, Misha…"

"Well, seeing as your anxiety will not permit you to rest, O Demon of the Desert," said Shenderovich, smiling artfully, "get up, then! Let's go! We will flee our pursuers while our weak legs can still carry us!"

"No!" yelled Givi, pressing himself into the sand.

"Well, stop snivelling then. Come on, I thought you were made of sterner stuff than that…" Shenderovich adopted a more sympathetic tone as he registered the conflicting range of emotions on the face of his fellow-traveller. "They probably only noticed we were gone this morning, those brothers. And no one would be stupid enough to voluntarily set out across the desert in the middle of the afternoon. So we're safe to stay here for a few hours, waiting out the burning heat of that fiery eye until the cool of the dusk falls mercifully upon this parched land. Then we shall fill the blessed vessel – otherwise known as the bottle – with water and set out…"

"I threw it away," said Givi guiltily.

"What did you say?"

"It was heavy, so I threw it away. It was empty anyway…"

"What are you saying, O Incurable Friend of Mine? You, keeper of the water, entrusted with this vital object, took it upon yourself to just throw it away? What kind of idiot…"

Givi blinked guiltily.

Shenderovich thought for a moment, scratching his wet neck.

"OK, forget it… Closer to nightfall we'll wet our clothing in this spring of life and then leg it… Maybe we'll get somewhere by morning…"

"But where?"

Shenderovich shrugged wordlessly. He settled down in the scant shade cast by the well, placed the bag containing the hard and angular attributes under his head and was snoring within seconds. Givi was in agony – his body, not used to such exposure, had been badly scorched by the sun. It didn't seem to bother Misha at all! He was tanned, Misha was. And he worked out. What would I do without Misha, thought Givi. Actually, without Misha I wouldn't be here in the first place.

He made himself more comfortable, trying to keep to the tiny scrap of shade that wasn't being occupied by Shenderovich. Anyway, he tried to convince himself, it's dangerous to fall asleep in such heat. That's what Mother always said. So he blinked his singed eyelashes and peered into the quivering air in the hope of seeing another mirage… But all that the intense heat had to offer was a series of blinding mirrors in the distance, enormous glittering lenses, flung open into the ochre and azure… Next to the snoring Shenderovich, Givi suddenly felt like the last man awake in the whole wide world.

The bird, which had perched right in the centre of an unattractive prickly bush, suddenly sprang to life and lifted its head up from beneath its wing.

"Hey," said Givi. "What's up?"

The bird shook itself and flew off. After circling low over Givi's head, it shot upwards and flew straight ahead before making a sharp turn to the east.

"Well, there you go…" said Givi, sadly.

It may have been a dumb animal but it was still company.

Now Givi was completely alone. He sighed and closed his eyes.

Then he opened them again, because something had changed. It felt like a shadow had fallen over him.

He covered his eyes again, then rubbed them with his hands, then shook his head.

No, it wouldn't go away.

The fragmented line on the horizon suddenly broke up into separate dark patches, which grew rapidly until enormous muzzles full of bared teeth swam out of the quivering mirage. Giant brown hulks bore down on them, rhythmically demolishing the distance with their long shaggy legs. Enormous riders loomed like towers on top of the swaying monsters, the white fabric of their robes fluttering in the wind… The entire scene was unfolding in total silence, which made it seem as though a ghostly cavalcade were swimming through the air.

"Bloody hell!" whispered Givi.

He stood up on legs that were growing weaker by the minute and started shaking Shenderovich frantically.

"Misha! Wake up!"

"Huh?" Shenderovich raised his head slightly, wincing because the attributes had given him a genuine pain in the neck.

"Misha! Over there! Something terrible!"

"Ah," Shenderovich waved him away, yawning widely. "It's just another mirage! Your nerves are shot to pieces, Givi my friend."

"I know, but…"

"B-boom!"

Givi trembled. The ground beneath his feet also trembled. It was being shaken by muffled blows.

"B-boom… B-boom!"

"OK," admitted Shenderovich, scratching his neck. "That's

not a mirage. It looks like we've got ourselves into another fine mess, O Wanderer, Descendant of Wanderers."

The riders surrounded Givi and Shenderovich, blocking out the sun.

Givi examined the new arrivals with a mixture of fear and delight. The shy descendant of Shemhazai stood in awe as he took in the fierce tanned faces, the fierce eyes that gleamed from beneath white turbans, and the fierce yataghans and daggers, which would have been a credit to any dance troupe from the Caucasus. He was even more impressed with the menacing beauty of the mighty battle animals, richly bedecked with little bells and copper plates that glittered in the sunlight.

There was nowhere to run.

Givi sighed and wiped his shaking hands on his trousers.

Shenderovich bestowed upon the assembled company the cordial yet distracted glance of a seasoned explorer.

The camels shifted their weight from one mighty hoof to another as foam dripped from their muzzles. They looked back at Shenderovich with contempt.

One of the riders – the tallest and best-looking, thought Givi – with a dark, fierce face shaded by a particularly splendid turban, jumped down from his camel, causing his impressive selection of weapons to jingle, and swaggered lazily over to the wayfarers.

Givi attempted to straighten his shoulders.

Shenderovich continued to throw condescending glances all around.

The Leader stared back at the defenceless travellers, with his arms crossed over his chest.

Givi was the first to give in.

"B-ismi-llyakhi-ar-rahman, ar-rachim," he cried, feeling a hitherto unknown language sing through his chest. "In the name of Allah the kind and merciful... Grant us relief and not grief, O Master of a Thousand Camels, and may the blessings of Allah be upon you!"

"And Allah be with you also, stranger," the Leader coolly replied. "For he is the protector of all travellers and the guide to all paths."

"What's he saying?" Shenderovich whispered behind him

"Um… basically, hi," explained Givi.

"Tell him that we don't have anything worth stealing. Tell him we're poor travellers."

Givi sighed. In his opinion, that was pretty obvious. But he obediently began:

"Be gracious to us, O Sheikh, for we are straitened by the wishes of the Almighty. And poverty, O Leader of a Thousand Riders, is a worthy halting place – poverty is the cloak of nobility, the clothing of ministers, the shirt of the righteous man…"

"True," agreed the Leader. "But poverty is also the strength of the humble…"

"The reward of the enlightened, the aim of those who seek…"

"The prison of sinners…"

"Givi, what's he saying?"

"Um… basically, he'd worked that out for himself."

Maintaining his thoughtful expression, the Leader walked slowly in a circle around the travellers. Givi and Shenderovich rotated on the spot, not wishing to expose their unprotected backs.

"I believe it is them!" the Leader said finally.

He turned lazily and snapped his fingers. By way of response, several hefty youths jumped down from their camels and rushed towards the prisoners.

"But we truly have nothing but the shirts on our backs, O Sheikh of the Desert," cried Givi. "We have nothing to give you!"

"But I do not require anything from you, O Anxious Traveller," answered the Leader. "Do not fear, I will not lay a finger on you, for I have given my word and I intend to keep it.

And I will tell you this much, when you reach your destination you will be treated like royalty, for the reward offered to me for delivering you alive and well was most handsome."

"Deliver us?" howled Givi, unable to take his eyes off the camels. "Deliver us where?"

"Givi, what is he saying?" yelled Shenderovich. They had already begun to drag him towards one of the camels, albeit without much success.

"That he was promised a reward! He's got to deliver us to someone."

"A reward?" raged Shenderovich. "Why would anyone offer a reward for us? Maybe that Pedro bloke has put a price on our heads... Or his Master. Ask him again!"

"He's getting angry!"

"Well, ask him politely then!"

"I already asked him politely.... Pah! Where do you intend to deliver us, O Master of the Faithful?"

The Leader, with one foot in his stirrup, turned his sombre face towards Givi.

"It does not befit you to ask such questions, for as you yourself correctly observed you are in a state of poverty, and poverty presupposes patience. For, in the words of Ash-Shabli, when he was asked about patience:

> *To you, whose patience surpasses that of Patience itself,*
> *Patience appealed for help, wearily.*
> *Be patient, you ordered Patience, at one with me...*

"Your words are veracious, O Sheikh," agreed Givi. "And the halting place of patience is a worthy halting place indeed, for patience presupposes trust in the Almighty... Which means that the halting place of trust is also a worthy halting place."

"You speak the truth," agreed the sheikh. "But in the words of Zun-nuna, when he was asked about trust: 'Trust means to lay in stores of food for today, without worrying about tomorrow.' Which means stop asking these questions that irritate me, O Traveller, and submit to your fate."

"Well?" cried Shenderovich, struggling to keep from sliding down the steep, moth-eaten flank of his camel. "What did he say?"

The driver of his camel, who had been clicking his tongue and shaking his head, finally lost patience and pulled a glittering yataghan from its sheath. Shenderovich quickly recoiled, but the driver just rapped it sharply across the camel's knees. Groaning reluctantly, the camel slowly folded its front legs and knelt down.

"Get on, you son of a donkey," said the driver, in a sombre voice.

"What did he say?" Shenderovich continued to shout.

"Get on, you son of a donkey," answered Givi, clambering up on to his own camel.

"No, not him... the other one!"

"That we shouldn't worry. And that if we behave ourselves he'll leave us alone, because he's been ordered to treat us like royalty."

"Like royalty," pondered Shenderovich. "Now, I like the sound of that."

He slipped off his camel again, pushing aside the driver, and calmly swaggered up to the Leader. He made a vague gesture with his hand, throwing the edge of an invisible robe over his shoulder.

"Tell him that... the Bridge of the Desert, Master of the Light and the Terror of Demons greets him. Tell him that the demon Buer himself trembled as he beheld my fearsomeness. Tell him that I am travelling incognito, sort of, in order to check whether my subjects are prospering..."

"Misha, are you sure that's a good idea?"

"Translate!" hissed Shenderovich.

Givi sighed and hopelessly launched into an enumeration of Shenderovich's merits, intoning for greater effect. The face of the Leader suddenly registered a certain interest.

"A king?" he repeated.

"Yes, O Leader of a Thousand Imitators. From the halting place of my confidence I confirm that before you now stands none other than a king in disguise. Which is why you would do well to treat him with the appropriate deference."

"Is that so?" The Leader put his foot back on the ground and slowly walked over to Shenderovich. "Be more considerate, for before you stands a king in disguise? Fool! He is a king, therefore I should not lay a finger on him?"

He looked thoughtfully at his fist then suddenly punched Shenderovich in the solar plexus. Shenderovich bent double, gasping for breath.

"I should lay considerably more than a finger on him," the Leader commented. "For whosoever allows himself to be beaten thus cannot possibly be a king in disguise. Now, get on that camel, you son of a jackal!"

And for once, Shenderovich did as he was told.

Little bells were jingling on the camel's saddlecloth and its brass decorations gleamed. Givi was being jolted along, bouncing up and down. He had no alternative as his camel was strapped to the one in front and was thus unwittingly following the collective pace. Sand dunes were simply throwing themselves under the camels' hooves, throwing themselves under then disappearing behind…

"Misha!" Givi cried to Shenderovich, desperately holding on to the high saddle-bow with his handcuffed hands. Shenderovich was swaying from side to side under exactly the same sorry conditions. "Misha! Where are they taking us? Back to the Brothers?"

"No!!!" Shenderovich yelled in response. "The Brothers are that way!"

"What?"

"No, they're not taking us to the Brothers!"

"So where then?"

"I have no idea!!!"

The rider dragging Givi's camel behind him by the nose could stand it no longer and turned his fierce, tanned face towards Givi.

"Be silent, you jackal!" he said.

"What did he say?" cried Shenderovich, his head bobbing forwards.

"He said, stop talking!" Givi cried in response, caught in the crossfire.

"Ahh!" Shenderovich finally understood and complied.

The sun was disappearing over the horizon, throwing its last rays over the desert. The dunes were shot with gold, ochre and deep blue. The camels rushed along, their necks craning purposefully forwards.

Ekh, thought Givi, why don't these brigands show any respect? They could at least explain where they're taking us, and why... But no, they're just dragging us along like dumb cattle.

He raised himself a little on his decorated saddle, peering into the distance. There was a dark patch on the horizon, which was growing steadily larger in a most un-mirage-like fashion and taking on additional colours and forms. Directly ahead of them lay what is known in adventure novels as an oasis. There were a few palm trees with battered leaves, looking rather sorry for themselves, and some square buildings with flat roofs, which could have been hangars and garages. I bet they've got a secret base here, thought Givi. But never mind, he consoled himself, they'll hand us over. Or exchange us, or something. Yuri Nikolaevich would surely not just have let the matter drop... He's a captain, for goodness' sake, an upstanding citizen. Would he really have allowed two of his passengers to disappear without trace? He probably made such a fuss that they sprang into action and this was the result. It would be quite straightforward: they would be exchanged for one of their mukallafs... Jesus, where did I get a word like that from?

"Look at their houses," exclaimed Shenderovich. "An anthropologist would have a field day!"

The houses turned out to be felt tents. Yet another camel was tied to the side of one of them, gloomily chewing the dry grass. The procession came onto a tiny square in the centre of the camp, whereupon the Leader jumped down from his camel, carelessly throwing the reins into the obligingly outstretched hands of a sentry.

There was an open hearth nearby and a few more men sat around it, watching with interest as several lamb carcasses mounted on spits and dripping with fat crackled over the coals.

Givi suddenly felt hungry.

Shenderovich, glancing expressively at his companion, slid from his camel, staggered and fell to his knees, impotently hanging his head. His eyes rolled, and his jaw hung loose.

"O Patron of the Omnipresent," said Givi in as firm a voice as he could muster, looking reproachfully at the mighty satin-covered back of the Leader. "This man is dying of hunger."

"Ah!" exclaimed the Leader, without turning round. "The king in disguise?"

"Yes, O Most Faithful One. He ardently desires to eat. And an ardent desire is a state to admire."

The Leader stopped and folded his arms, clearly anticipating a lengthy exchange.

"I was told by Abdullah," he began, "who heard it from his father, who heard it from Kutaiba Said from the words of Akila from the words of Salima Abdullah from the words of his father, 'Calamities are like salt to true believers, and when the salt runs out, the true believer will rot.'"

"Hope," insisted Givi, "is also a state to admire. And trust, as I said before, is a worthy halting place."

"I was told by Abdullah, who heard it from his father, who heard it from Abd-as-Samad from the words of Abu-Burda, from the words of Abu-Musa: 'A young female camel should be driven to a new camp on an empty stomach'."

"They speak the truth," sighed Givi. "This life is paradise for a sinner but hell for a righteous man."

"The beauty of the day, O Complaining One," the Leader parried the blow, "can be enjoyed only in combination with the darkness of night, and this is why the good of the universe rests in them both."

"So, are you going to feed us, O Indecisive One, or not?" Givi had had enough of this. "Having agreed to accept a ransom for delivering us alive and well you are taking a great risk in failing to take adequate care of our life and health, for it is a sin to sell what is not yours for the selling, according to Abdullah, who heard it from his father, who heard it from Muhammed ab Jaffar from the words of Matar, from the words of Amir... they both told him."

"I am not selling you, O Impure One, but accepting fay', for fay' is what I consider you to be, that is, spoils obtained without violence, as opposed to ghanima, the spoils of war. You obediently failed to put up the slightest resistance, therefore you are spoils obtained without violence. And how I shall manage this fay' is nobody's business but my own."

"You are mistaken, O Trespasser, for the fay' belongs not to you but to the entire community of these noble people. By allowing us to die a hungry death, you are depriving them of the share that is due them."

The worthy people had formed a semicircle around the quarrellers and were listening with interest.

The Leader shrugged.

"Fine... You think I begrudge you a morsel or two?" he said. "I merely wanted to embark upon a journey of refined and learned conversation with you, since you express yourself exceedingly well, you mangy cur."

"What's he saying?" moaned Shenderovich, collapsing into a heap on the sand.

"Um... basically, he'll feed us like he promised."

Shenderovich stopped groaning, straightened himself up

and rolled his eyes back to their correct position. The riders were slipping down from the backs of their camels, relieving them in passing of mysterious bundles, packages and saddle-bags. Givi started to open his mouth then carefully closed it again – behind one of the brigands, like a cloak, trailed a scarlet altar cloth embroidered with a golden sun…

"**S**our milk," said Shenderovich, tearing himself away from the wineskin. "Yuk!"

"It's probably camel's milk," answered Givi sadly, "from a young female camel, and a hungry one at that, driven as she has been from camp to camp."

"Typical brigands," Shenderovich glanced sulkily at the group of warriors sitting round the fire. "The Brothers fed us better."

"The Brothers thought you were a king."

"And that you were a giant," Shenderovich thought for a moment. "Hey! I've got an idea! Have you told them about Shemhazai?"

"I told them about the king…"

"Yeah, well, the king story didn't go down too well, did it. Tell them about Shemhazai."

"But what if he decides to put me to the test as well?"

"Don't worry about that! Do it after we've finished eating, OK?"

"Why do you confer so secretively amongst yourselves, O Stray Ones?" asked the Leader.

"My friend and fellow-traveller, who despite what you may think is in fact a king in disguise, asks me to relate to the esteemed company the story of Shemhazai and his descendants in order to while away the evening and satiate your minds as your lamb, O Blessed Lion of the Desert, has satiated our bellies," Givi dolefully intoned.

"I pay no heed to any request from that man, who is absolutely not a king in disguise, but I, whose word is weightier than gold, stronger than diamond and sharper than steel, I ask you myself, tell us of Shemhazai, O Stranger," nodded the Leader graciously, as he wiped his greasy hands on the loose end of his turban. "For glorious is this name and it sounds both proud and fearsome."

The Story of Shemhazai, or a Tale of Temptation, Sin and Repentance, as Told by Givi Mesopotamishvili to the Leader of the Brigands by the Fire

O Leader of the Brave, pray listen to this tale, told to me by my grandfather, to him by his grandfather, to him by an old Georgian, who had a Jew-friend. Once upon a time, before man walked the earth, the Lord drew a circular line around the face of the abyss and created the seas, the rivers and the lakes, and He filled them with fish…

"Not fish," one of the brigands intervened. "For that which you in your ignorance call fish, is pronounced 'tan-In' in the language of the Jews, which means 'sea monster,' 'snake,' or 'dragon.' For, in speaking of 'big fish,' the creators of the Holy Book clearly and evidently mean the giant reptiles that once roamed the earth…"

…Filled them with fish. And the fish played in the rivers and lakes, and for this they praised the Lord, and the seas and the lakes sang together with them: 'The Lord in Heaven is mightier than the roar of the mighty waters' – this is what they sang. And thus spake the Lord: 'If an element lacking the power of speech can sing my praises so, how sweet the song with which the universe shall be filled by man, whom I shall create.' And so the Lord created man and released him into the world. But man turned his face from God and began to worship idols. And the Lord lamented with great sorrow. And then, seeing the sorrow of the Everlasting, two angels appeared before him, Shemhazai and Azazel. And this is what they said: 'Sovereign of the Universe! Did we not warn Thee on the Day of Creation that Thy sons of the dust would cause Thee great grief? What is man that Thou art mindful of him?' And then the Lord said: 'What, then, will become of the world?' And Shemhazai and Azazel said: 'Give it to us. We shall find another use for it.' And then the Lord said: 'But I know and do not doubt that if the angels lived on earth in place of man, temptation would conquer you more easily and more quickly than so happened with the human race.' And then they said: 'Put us to the test, Lord. Grant us permission to dwell on earth and Thou shalt see how we shall sanctify Thy name.'

And so the angels came down to earth, and they were full of the best intentions, but then they saw the daughters of the sons of men and found them beautiful. And they decided to take them as their wives, each of them choosing his own.

"It's not 'beautiful' in the language of the book of Jews, but 'tov-Ot,' which also means 'good,' and also 'suitable for some specific purpose' – in this case for leading man to the path of evil," interrupted the same brigand. "Because these angels that you call sons of God were fallen angels."

"That which is implied by 'sons of God' is also open to question," interrupted another brigand. "For those known in the Holy Book as 'sons of God' are in other words 'Bnei ElogIm,' for that is how the descendants of Sif, third son of Adam, were known, since they observed God's Word and were loyal to His Behest. The 'daughters of men,' on the other hand, was a name given to the women of the clan of Kabil (Cain in your language), slayer of the devout Habil (Abel in your language), for their debauchery took them to the utmost destruction."

"Permit me to disagree with you, O Yusuf," intervened the Leader. "For the words were that 'the sons of God chose for themselves' not 'daughters of men' but 'daughters of the sons of men,' which is another matter entirely, for one thing, and for another, why should the Lord become angry if the descendants of Sif took the daughters of Kabil as wives and beat all foolishness out of them, as befits loyal and righteous men, in order that these loathsome, foul and lustful cats should forget the very meaning of the word 'sin'? Continue, O Stranger, pay no heed to these believers of false doctrine."

... That they were beautiful. I personally think that this was all because the angels wanted to ensure the survival of their kind, because it is a well-known fact that angels cannot bear the children of angels.

"Of course," intervened the first brigand, "for angels are male in essence, whereas the female essence is represented by demons, which confirms their primordial impurity... I tell you, women were created to bring about the ruin of mankind, which is about to be confirmed by the story-teller, for that is obviously where this story is going."

No it isn't. When the Lord said 'Pru u'Rvu,' which means 'Be Fruitful and Multiply,' he said this not to the angels but to the people who did just that. The daughters of men were not only beautiful and experienced in the pleasures of love but also most fertile, and I think that this is what is meant by 'tov-Ot,' for they were good in every sense... And not only Shemhazai and Azazel but many of the angels turned then their regard to earth and came to Shemhazai and said: 'We have heard, O Leader of the Winged Ones, that you are planning such and such, and this pleases us, for the daughters of men are beautiful and fecund. And we desire greatly to go unto them as do the sons of men.' That is what they said. Only Raziel remained silent. This displeased Shemhazai. So he asked Raziel: 'Why do you remain silent? Are you not with me? Do you not find the daughters of men pleasant?'

'There is nought more pleasant than they on this earth,' answered Raziel. 'However their kind issues from clay, whereas ours is of fire, and from mixing the two only harm will result!'

'If you bake clay in fire then all that is defective will perish but that which is without flaw will only grow stronger,' said Shemhazai.

'True,' agreed Raziel. 'However, only Enoch among them is without defect – the others are but rottenness and emptiness.'

'Then go unto this righteous man,' said Shemhazai then. 'And we will go unto the sinners. However, I see that you are gnawed by doubts, and maybe you are not the only one. I foresee that you will throng around me one and all saying, see, he is guilty, and I do not wish for that. For, oh, I am afraid that you will go back on your word and will not wish to carry out this deed, and I alone will have to atone for this great sin.' In other words, he was afraid that they would turn out to be weak in spirit and would forsake him, so he sought some kind of pledge from them. And they greatly desired to go unto the daughters of men and to live like men, so they said: 'Let us go and swear a binding oath – we shall not abandon this intention but shall see it through.' And they were two hundred in number. They gathered at the summit of the mount of the Oath, or Hermon, which is upon Ardis, and swore a terrible oath that they would all stand together…And Raziel joined them in their oath.

And they descended and went unto the daughters of men. And they shone with such unearthly beauty and boasted of such might that none could refuse them, save the maiden Istahar, whom Shemhazai himself desired. The maiden was clever and god-fearing and promised Shemhazai that she would return his love if he would reveal unto her God's Ineffable Name, in other words 'Shem HaMeforash,' the pronunciation of which allowed him to ascend to heaven whenever he so desired. I have to say, Shemhazai had little experience of the cunning of the daughters of men – he was still an angel after all, albeit a fallen one – and he innocently said unto her 'Shem

HaMeforash,' whereupon she repeated the Holy Name and flew up to heaven without fulfilling her promise to Shemhazai. But this was probably the only exception, and the angels began to, pardon my French, multiply like rabbits, and they conceived and begat giants, three thousand cubits in stature. However, personally I believe that this is an exaggeration, for no earthly woman would be capable of bearing or rearing such a child. In either event, the descendants were quite gluttonous and lazy too – they did nothing themselves but ate all the fruits of the people's labour and then, so they say, began to devour the people themselves, and all creatures of the earth, and one another, and basically anything they could lay their hands on. Shemhazai himself had two sons – Hiwa and Hiya (known to us as Givi and Giya) – and they, by all accounts, ate one thousand camels, one thousand horses and one thousand bulls every day. At this point the angels became anxious. Our children are hungry, they said! And so they turned again to Shemhazai, saying to him: 'This is your fault!' And Shemhazai said: 'Well, what did you expect? Our children are eating everything the people produce, but the people are not producing enough, for apart from their digging-sticks they have held nothing in their hands since the day they were born. We must instruct man in the methods of plentiful production, then our children will be satiated and human riches will multiply. Let us join together and work for the good of our descendants.' The angels conferred and then set to work. Amezyarak taught the people the casting of enchantments and the cutting of roots, Armaros taught them the resolving of enchantments, Baraqel taught them astrology, Kokabiel taught them the constellations, and Astradel taught them the course of the moon. Only Raziel remained silent.

However, they say that he recorded everything that the angels taught man on a stone tablet, for he knew that their time was coming to an end. And he entrusted the tablet to his friend among men, whose name was Enoch, for although Raziel had sinned no less than the others he was yet capable of distinguishing a righteous man from a sinner. And Enoch was a righteous man and would not have thought to use the tablet with evil intent. And Raziel applied to Enoch such an enchantment that only he or his descendants would be able to read the tablet, when such need should arise. However, this was known to Enoch and Raziel alone.

And Shemhazai said: 'Now the people have found power, when will they find strength?' Then Azazel arose and said: 'I will take this sin upon myself, for this sin is greater than all others.' And he went unto the people and taught them how to smelt metals and to make swords and knives, shields, and coats of arms. And he taught them how to see what was behind them, and how to weave the most outstanding cloth, and how to extract metals from the earth. And Shemhazai said then: 'We have given men enough to keep them busy, and they will buy and sell, speculate and accumulate, battle and trade, and what will women do meanwhile? For, as I have learned by my own experience, they are capable of the utmost cunning and from boredom may contrive the inconceivable and become altogether unbearable.'

'Fine,' said Azazel then. 'I will take this sin also upon my soul, for it is more terrible than the others.' And he went to the daughters of men and taught them the arts of seduction, the plucking of brows, and how to make themselves fair and beautiful with cosmetics and to adorn themselves with precious stones and scarves, which men obtained for them willingly.

I believe, O Leader of Leaders of Camels, that all that came to pass was a result of their own stupidity, I mean that of Raziel and the others, for they did not understand human nature and therefore could not foresee the results – in short, the commencement on earth of Babylon only knows what kind of indecent conduct. The womenfolk became completely impudent and got quite out of hand, and the menfolk, hitherto gentle and industrious, took up arms and went into battle with one another, for they had seen that there was little point in overburdening themselves with labour when it was simpler to take whatever they wanted from their neighbours. Fields were abandoned, rivers ran red with blood, and thus began a time of wholesale death, famine and desolation. Factories and mines were smoking all about, and where they fell idle the smoke came instead from burning cities and forests... And what is more, the people ceased fearing God's wrath since they had decided that they were able to resolve enchantments and prepare potions and avert curses and the like... As for the giants, their hunger continued unabated. They pursued the daughters of men, propagated their seed and multiplied. They devoured all the fish in the seas, including those that the esteemed brigand a little while ago termed reptiles, and all the creatures on dry land, and those that they were unable to catch hid and did not give themselves to be caught. On witnessing all this, Shemhazai was horrified and understood that the Lord, in his wisdom, was right. And he prostrated himself before the Lord, imploring him to put matters right. And then the Lord looked upon this wickedness and became incensed with a great wrath.

And thus spake the Lord: 'People have destroyed everything around them and ruined the beautiful home that I gave them for their joy and prosperity. Therefore I shall send water once more unto the earth, where people have ceased to recognize the Lord as Creator and Master of all living things. For they have pillaged the home that I created for them and know not love, only hate, and not praise or songs of joy, but moans and lamentations... This is what I have learned of the devastated earth.'

And then Shemhazai wept.

'Oh, woe is me! What will become of my children?'

And the Lord said then: 'Your children, you fool, are but weeds in the field. They have neither the good heart of the Guardians nor the mournful sagacity of man; therefore, I shall remove them from earth. However, rather than destroying them I shall place them under guard and may they remain there in the darkness, bound by everlasting bonds, until the judgment of the great day.'

And Shemhazai became filled with a great gratitude and did repent. And he submitted willingly to punishment, suspending himself between heaven and earth, where he remains to this day, in the position of a penitent sinner.

And Raziel came again to the Lord, who was with Shemhazai at this time, and said: 'Dost Thou really intend to destroy the beautiful earth, O Lord, further than it has already been destroyed by man together with our foolish children?' Then the Lord said to Raziel: 'I shall heal the earth, which the angels have so corrupted. I shall plant it again with trees and gardens and fill it with vines; I shall fill the trees with birds, the land with creatures and the sea with fish, that they might sanctify the Lord.'

And Raziel answered: 'But what is the point of the earth without man? Will Thy name be sanctified by dumb creatures and water alone for the whole of eternity? My soul aches, O Lord, for I have become attached to Thy creations whilst I lived among them. Wilst Thou destroy them completely, so that no trace of them should remain on the face of the earth? For we too bear a portion of the blame for what has happened.'

'No,' said the Lord. 'I shall destroy only voluptuous souls and the children of the Guardians, for they have acted foolishly among man, but I shall conserve the human race and, when the earth is cleansed of all sin, I shall revive the righteous and on that day I shall open the treasure-houses of my benediction, which are in heaven, in order to bring them down to earth, that they may enhance the labour and production of the sons of men. And all this will be accompanied by a blessing – justice and truth will sow complete joy evermore.'

'But they will become wild once more and foolish, for all their strength will be lost,' objected Raziel.

'Then let them act by their own will for now their strength is in their own hands,' said the Lord. 'For from this day forth

I forbid the Guardians to meddle in human affairs. And now be off, and bring them the news of the healing of the earth and that not all of the sons of men should perish from the mystery of all that the Guardians have said and have taught their sons.'

And Raziel said: 'But what, O Lord, is to become of Azazel the Unrepentant? His power is equal to the power of two hundred leaders of angels.'

'Tell everyone that the earth has become corrupt through the teachings of Azazel alone, attribute all sins to him!'

'But why him alone?' asked Raziel.

'Because it is better that only one of you appear guilty in the eyes of men than that they should doubt you all,' spake the Lord. 'Or else their faith in you will be lost completely and people will doubt your goodness and will lose all respect and fear and will not know which of you is bad and which good. As for Azazel, you have the power to do with him as you will.'

'No,' answered Raziel. 'I shall not do with him as I will, for I myself know not whether I wish him ruin or mercy. Rather I shall do as Thou commandeth.'

And the Lord said that not one of the Guardians should henceforth be permitted to meddle in human affairs or to change the face of the earth whether for good or for ill. And Raziel obeyed every command of the Lord. And the Lord commanded Raziel: 'Bind Azazel hand and foot and cast him into the darkness, and make an opening in the desert, which is in Dudael, and cast him therein. And place upon him rough and jagged rocks, and cover him with darkness, and let him abide there for ever, and cover his face that he may not see the light.' And that is what Raziel did.

However, others say that he took pity on Azazel, his brother-in-arms, who lives to this day on earth, unrepentant, continuing his sinful existence and taking all guises, including those of the sons of Cain. Likewise the descendants of Shemhazai, who live to this day among men, and of whom your faithful servant is one…

Givi fell silent and sat stunned, looking around. The fire had almost burnt out, and enormous stars had spilled across the sky. The sombre men with beards squatting around the fire were nodding rhythmically. What on earth came over me, he wondered in shock, casting a wary glance at the Leader.

"O Storyteller," said the Leader, "you truly have a way with words and sweet are your discourses, and to listen to them – be they true or false – brings only pleasure, so much so that it will be a shame to deliver you into the hands of those to whom you are promised. But I have given my word, and the sons of the desert have yet to be accused of acting against the wishes of a client."

"But to whom are we promised?" asked the proud descendant of Shemhazai in terror, feeling the ground give way beneath him. "Tell us, what will they do to us?"

"That is between us and them," the Leader answered sternly. "Thus, my lips are sealed. However, take my advice – put aside your worries until tomorrow, for then you truly will have cause to worry. Cool is the shelter of the tent, fresh is the night wind of the desert, and abundant is the water from the well that fills the pitcher by your bedside. Vigilant is the guard at the door, though he will not disturb your repose. And this is the least, and the most, that I can do to express my gratitude for your tale. Now, come on, in you go."

"Uh…" said Givi.

"Take them away," said the Leader with a wave of his hand.

Two hefty brigands picked up the recalcitrant Shenderovich and dragged him into the tent. Givi followed under his own steam.

The camels were already standing in front of the tent, throwing contemptuous glances at Shenderovich. One of them was snow-white and was sporting a harness covered with little bells and a scarlet and gold saddlecloth surmounted by a lavishly decorated saddle. This one was clearly earmarked for the Leader. It was being respectfully restrained by a brigand in an enormous turban with a curved dagger in his sash.

"Isn't she a beauty?" asked the Leader, misinterpreting Givi's trembling. "She's the daughter of the daughter of a fighting she-camel whose hooves trampled the earth under the command of my grandfather as he returned with loot from his glorious raids. Her name is Al-Bagum – the one who bellows – for her bellow causes the cliffs to quake, and sparks fly from her hooves…"

"Indeed it is so, O Trampler of the Desert," Givi cautiously agreed, conscious of a renewed ache in his coccyx which had borne the brunt of yesterday's galloping. "And were she of the male sex, she would doubtlessly be called Marid, meaning demon, or Infid, meaning kind one amongst Marids, for I see by her points that this animal is kind but at the same time formidable…"

"And you, I see, know something of fighting camels," nodded the Leader approvingly.

An enormous camel with powerful shaggy legs and an ill-tempered look was obviously the one intended for the unlucky travellers. This time there were considerably fewer escorts, from which Givi concluded that the Leader didn't plan to be away long.

"Get a move on, O Sources of Good!" The Leader, who was supervising preparations, stamped his foot impatiently thereby provoking the jangling of a multitude of armaments. "For in the desert there are no easy paths, and fierce is the noonday sun."

"Consider your options, O Bounty Hunter," Givi undertook one last attempt. "Would it not be better to hand us over to the UN? They'll pay ten times as much for us…"

"I know not of this Yu-En," the Leader impatiently stamped his foot again. "Perhaps he eats from plates of gold and drinks from vessels of silver… but even were he to offer me a hundred times as much my intentions would remain unchanged.

Firstly, my word is strong and inviolable, and secondly, were I to break the terms of the deal those to whom you are promised would hunt me down even beyond the foothills of Mount Kaf!"

"Wait, O Fearsome One," exclaimed Givi. "Tell us, at least, to whom we are promised. What will they do to us?"

"I will say only one thing," the Leader confessed, "I would not like to be in your shoes."

"Ekh!" Givi said sadly and climbed up onto his camel feeling the sour milk sloshing about in his stomach.

Shenderovich scrambled up behind him, throwing his camel contemptuous looks in return.

"I have not encumbered you with fetters," said the Leader, flying up into his saddle, "for Wisdom and Eloquence should not be constrained. However, should Wisdom betray you, do bear in mind that my men shoot with great accuracy."

Indeed, the escorts had quivers bristling with arrows over their shoulders and short bows strapped to their saddles.

"What did he say?" whispered Shenderovich in Givi's ear, rocking slightly out of time with his camel's jog-trot.

"He said he'd shoot us if we tried anything."

"Have you noticed he's only got two with him this time? Probably the ones he trusts the most. Who are they handing us over to?"

"Definitely not the UN," said Givi firmly.

"And there's no chance of making a run for it..." Shenderovich lamented.

"None at all."

"Yaaa-HA!" the Leader gave a piercing cry as he whipped the white camel.

The ground shook beneath Givi and swam away behind him. Their shared camel moved off and picked up speed, scattering sand with its mighty hooves. Sparse tufts of grass rushed towards them, soon giving way to spiky burrs and then to nothing at all. The gently undulating sand bore small chains of tiny tracks at random intervals where it had been crossed by a mouse or maybe a lizard. These contours gave way in turn to high dunes, casting long lilac shadows to the west.

Givi was terrified.

Two sombre riders travelled alongside them, the reins of the central camel stretched between them. All three animals were racing along and craning their necks identically like a single three-headed beast. Givi fidgeted in his saddle as he tried to make himself more comfortable, though without much success. Behind him, tormented by the galloping, Shenderovich kept up a constant grunting and groaning. Weather-beaten stones poked up through the surface of the desert – the wind and the scorching heat had riddled them with holes and caves, and they could hear the nagging sound of the sand washed by the wind from the cracks. A little farther on, the cliffs were higher and lurked behind their lesser neighbours like the grotesque figures of crouching giants. The rider swaying to their right nervously jerked the reins of Givi's camel.

"This is not a good place," he said, turning round. "If there aren't devils living in these parts, I'll eat my turban."

"Then hurry, you sons of lazy fathers!" exclaimed the Leader, whipping his camel and galloping ahead.

Among the stones in front of him Givi caught fleeting glimpses of the backside of the Leader's white camel, which had raised its tail and was nervously relieving itself as it went. Behind him, Shenderovich continued to moan and groan. The furious pace was making Givi feel as though his ribs were being crushed in a vice, and he took desperate and futile gulps of the hot air like a fish out of water. The sun hung in a scorching white ball over their heads and black dots swam before their eyes in the quivering heat haze. He had just opened his mouth intending to explain to the Leader that death from sunstroke would doubtlessly have an adverse effect on his purchase price when the Leader suddenly stopped pulling his camel up short so sharply that the camel dug its four hooves in throwing up mighty fountains of sand.

"A flock of Ankas!" cried the Leader, turning to his fellow-travellers and simultaneously pointing towards the soaring scraps of darkness that were approaching them.

What Givi had at first assumed to be a heat-induced hallucination turned out to be a flock of birds, which began pouring slowly from the burning sky. They looked exactly like flakes of ash whirling around a blazing fire.

"Shoot them!" cried the Leader. "Shoot, O Children of Tortoises!"

One of the brigands pulled out an arrow, but before he had time to draw his bow a swarm of black hornets began to rain down from the sky. Something flew past trailing a sliver of ripped air, pierced the saddle and remained there, quivering and trembling. Givi recoiled in horror: sticking up out of the saddle was a sharp black feather, with a metallic sheen. The brigand threw his bow to the sand in terror and covered his head with his arms. The Leader's camel began grunting and shaking her head. Flecks of foam flew from her contemptuously protruding lips, landing on the decorated reins. The Leader turned his defiant animal around.

"Back!" cried the Leader. "Head back! To the cliffs!"

The birds swooped above them, screeching like rusty door hinges. One of them dived down and ripped open the Leader's turban with its beak – rags streamed from his head, fluttering and quivering with the frenzied galloping.

The ground shook from the camels' thunderous progress. The tiny cavalcade eventually made it back to the eroded cliffs, rushed past the strange stone pillars and came to a halt under something resembling a massive archway – spectral gates, leading from nowhere to nothing at all.

The Leader was the first to jump down from his camel, thereby indicating that the others should hurry up and do likewise.

Caught between two evils – the mysterious terrible client and the equally fearsome birds – he was clearly nervous, kicking the sand with the toe of his decorated leather boot. He might have been hoping that the birds would lose interest and fly off in search of more accessible quarry.

However, after circling a little, looking for all the world like scorched scraps of paper, the birds didn't fly away. They settled themselves instead on the cliffs nearby, taking off and landing again every now and then, and calling to one another in their piercing, metallic voices.

"Vermin," commented Shenderovich, with scant regard for animal classification.

"Hey, Misha, don't say that," objected Givi, rubbing his camel-weary backside. "Those birds could come in ve-e-ry handy."

"Ah yes, I see what you're saying," agreed Shenderovich looking at the worried face of the Leader who was furiously muttering into his moustache.

The two brigands whispered anxiously to one another then one of them, clearly the braver of the two, cautiously tugged at the Leader's sleeve before retreating immediately, his palms placed deferentially together before his bowed face.

"What do you want, you lizard?" inquired the Leader with irritation.

"It seems to me, O Leader of Flocks, that this place is not good," answered the brigand, shivering nervously. "For I was told by my father, who heard it from his father, who heard it from Abu Suleiman abd ar-Rahim, that this place was once inhabited in a time before history by the people of Amalik the Accursed."

"He is right, O Pillar of a Thousand Buttresses," confirmed the other brigand. "For they scorned the speeches of the prophets and turned away from the Almighty, for which He sent down on them these cursed birds. I was told by my father, who heard it from his grandfather, who heard it from Mahmoud al-Hassan at-Tabasi, that they prostrated themselves before the prophet Hanzala, who drove the lethal creatures away with a prayer. But, alas, there are no creatures more lethal than the sons of Kabila-Cain– such was their gratitude that they threw him in a well, the jackals!"

"However, I was told by my father, who heard it from his father, who heard it from Ahmad abu-Hanifa, that the Almighty raised the faithful and trustworthy Hanzala from the well, and Hanzala then cast a terrible curse upon this people and said, since the well pleases you so, from this day forth you shall be known as Ahsab-ar-Rass – The People in the Well – and the well itself as Barhut, for it leads to the underworld and is inhabited by the souls of the faithless. And to this very day, on moonless nights when the mouth of Barhut opens up, you can hear the groans and complaints of restless souls, for whom there is no absolution from their black perfidy."

"This is of no interest to me, O Hassan," said the Leader through clenched teeth, "unless you yourself are Hanzala and are therefore capable of scaring the Anka birds away. And if it is not within your powers to do such a thing, then you would do well to bear in mind that I have erected here the halting place of my patience, and I urgently advise you to settle firmly therein… for your head is also possessed of a base, which is not as strong as my patience."

Givi looked around. What he had initially taken to be the bizarre works of nature in actual fact appeared to be the work of human hands – wind-weathered colonnades, arches, walls bearing the remains of doorways and windows and strange pediments whose carved decorations had been broken up into smaller fragments that now stared monstrously from the walls.

"None other than the city of devils," muttered the first brigand, "has risen in this cursed place."

"Oh no, I tell you, this was built by The People in the Well, in a forgotten time before history," objected the second brigand.

"Be silent, you jackals!" whispered the Leader. "Unless you wish to bring another disaster upon us all."

In spite of the heat, Givi shivered. A protracted, harrowing sound came from somewhere within the ruins, as if a thousand exhausted souls in harmonious concert were heaving their final, trembling sigh. The camels, which up to this point had been standing relatively calmly, chewing their cud and clearly revelling in the fact that the pernicious Anka birds were no longer dive-bombing their hairy backs, simultaneously jerked up their heads and tucked in their outspread legs.

The brigands fell to their knees as one, resting their foreheads in the sand and covering their heads with their arms. They began to howl so plaintively that for a moment they even drowned out the anonymous cries coming from within the cool depths of the ruins.

"Muster your mettle, O Worthless Ones!" exclaimed the Leader, who, to give him his due, was not lacking in bravery. "For both you and I have need of it. That is only the wind howling through the stones – nothing more!"

"That's not the wind," whispered the first brigand, whose dark face had grown pale. "It's The People in the Well! They're climbing out!"

"No," objected the second in a whisper. "It's demons…"

"What's going on now?" asked Shenderovich with wary interest, elbowing Givi in the ribs. "Do you think this was planned?"

"I don't think so," Givi whispered back.

"Ah!" Shenderovich perked up. "An unforeseen factor!"

He looked all around, clearly planning their escape route.

"Ekh!" he muttered under his breath. "If it wasn't for those damn birds…"

The birds had made themselves comfortable on top of the cliffs. They exuded the benevolent calm of an executioner waiting for the condemned man to smoke his final cigarette. Givi had the impression that they'd multiplied.

"Arise, Lions of the Desert," the Leader had evidently decided to appeal to the valour of his fellow-travellers. "Remember, Hassan, how your father – may he be treated with affection in the gardens of paradise by a thousand maidens – killed with a single blow a ghoul who had taken the appearance of a beautiful temptress in order to lure travellers into her tent, promising them food and drink and other delights, only to devour them completely, bones and all! And remember, Ahmad, how your grandfather's grandfather – may he be washed in the tents of paradise by water from the spring of bliss – struck with his sword a ghoul who, by contrast, had assumed the appearance of a she-monster, with her breasts thrown over her shoulders and fangs protruding from her jaws, who lured travellers…"

"Ooo-woo-oooo!"

The melancholy call reverberated off the cliffs, and this time it sounded like it was coming from somewhere nearby. A grey shadow flitted between the stones and hid amongst the ruins.

"A ghooo-oul!" the brigands echoed, for once in complete agreement, and pressed their foreheads back into the sand.

"Well, Givi my friend," said Shenderovich, with genuine academic curiosity, "and what is your view on the matter?"

"There's no such thing as ghouls," asserted Givi, attempting to cling to the tattered shreds of reason. Just to be on the safe side, he pressed his defenceless back up against one of the few stone walls still standing. "It's probably…"

"A hyena?" prompted Shenderovich.

"No, it's…"

"A jackal?"

"No…"

"Ooo-woo-ooAH!"

The camels began to stamp their hooves and, living up to her nickname, the Leader's white camel let out a heart-rending bellow.

The Leader started to hunch his shoulders up around his ears but then straightened himself up and jutted his chin out. Givi even felt a certain respect for him.

"Watch, you cowardly offspring of earthworms," he said to the two cowering backs. "This is how a man and a warrior should behave."

He pulled his sabre out from its decorated leather sheath and headed into the ruins, creeping along the wall with a cat-like tread and then disappearing around a corner. His fellow-travellers obediently looked up and followed him with hopeless eyes then buried their dishevelled turbans once more into the ground.

"Shall we make a run for it?" whispered Shenderovich, turning to Givi.

"What about the birds?" Givi hesitated, eyeing the black rash that had spread over the ruins.

"Um… sod them?" suggested Shenderovich.

They began to move carefully sideways towards a gap between two half-collapsed stone walls. Ahmad and Hassan didn't even turn in their direction but remained submissively prostrate, particularly since the ominous howling could be heard once more, this time a little further away. It rose to an unbearably high pitch and then suddenly stopped.

There was a muffled blow, like the sound of a heavy body falling onto sand.

Ahmad and Hassan lifted their heads again.

"Hey, where do you think you're going?" cried Hassan, noticing the prisoners' attempted manoeuvre.

"Oh, you know," answered Givi casually brushing sand from his trousers. "Just off for a little stroll…"

"I'll give you a little stroll, you son of a shrew!" exclaimed Hassan furiously, recovering his lost dignity and simultaneously drawing his dagger. "Ahmad, get them!"

"Be reasonable, O Valiant One," Givi flattered him. "We'd have to be crazy to risk absconding in such a dangerous place, where ghouls roam at every step."

Hassan, whom they had succeeded in bringing back to relative reality, backed off slightly, looking round nervously as he did so.

"The ghoul," came a voice behind him, "is no more."

Ahmad and Hassan jumped slightly and turned round simultaneously.

The Leader was carelessly cleaning his sabre on a scrap of his turban, which was covered in sand.

"Only the cowardice displayed by you, O Women in Men's Robes," he said in a voice full of sorrowful dignity, reproachfully shaking his head, "permitted me to show my valour. For this very sabre cut the ghoul in two, from its crown to its privates, if it had any."

Ahmad and Hassan gave a short, simultaneous howl, this time of delight.

"What's he saying?" whispered Shenderovich, elbowing Givi in the ribs, which thanks to previous such manipulations were already sporting a handsome bruise.

"That he killed the ghoul," sighed Givi.

"So it really was a ghoul then?" asked Shenderovich in a whisper.

"No idea."

"Well, ask him! Don't just stand there!"

"I do not wish to arouse your anger, O Source of Patience," said Givi timidly, "but I would like to see this creature with my own eyes and to show it to my fellow-traveller, for in our lands such creatures are not to be found."

"If you do not have ghouls, what then do you have in their place?" asked the Leader in surprise.

"Um… wolves, and bears… and, what do you call them… yetis! Yes! Wild people that live in the hills, enormous and covered in fur."

"They sound like ghouls to me," nodded the Leader. "However, I cannot grant you your wish, O Son of a Curious Mother, for it is customary for ghouls to disappear in a puff of grey smoke as soon as their insides are exposed to the air."

"Ahh," drawled Givi, in acceptance of this explanation. Turning to Shenderovich, he explained: "No chance, Misha. The body of the deceased has disappeared in a puff of grey smoke."

"A likely story," Shenderovich shook his head. "I tell you, he's up to something."

"Look lively, O Loyal Comrades!" the Leader turned to his men. "Cast aside your fears, for evil has been vanquished by this very hand. It is now a matter of the most pressing urgency to gather anything that burns and to make a hot flame, for the night is drawing in and the creatures of the desert that dwell in the darkness fear fire."

"You are sending us to search for dried dung to burn, O Courageous One?" Hassan inquired timidly. "But how do we know that this ghoul was alone?"

"We just do," answered the Leader coldly, playing with his sabre.

"Should we not move further from this place, O First amongst Equals? It would not do to anger those that might become angered!"

"So, now you are qualified to advise me on our plan of action, are you, Hassan?" asked the Leader, his voice as cold as ice. "I answer you thus: if you find a way to raise these birds into the air and send them to Mount Kaf, and then order them to drown themselves in Bahr Lut – the Sea of Lot – then we will gladly follow you."

"I... forgive me, O Support of a Thousand Supports."

"I will forgive a foolish man," nodded the Leader, resheathing his sabre. "However, I will add that if you were the one giving orders and I were the one obeying, then you would be the Leader, and I would be Hassan. Get a move on, you fatty-tailed sheep, before I relieve you of your fatty tails!"

"And what about us, O Exemplar of Valour?" Givi inquired

hopefully. "Should we not add our dried dung to the collective fire? Although we did not personally smite the enemy in an honest fight, I assure you that we are no less courageous than your valiant fellow-travellers!"

He looked around carefully. The Anka birds had clearly settled down for the night. They had stopped flitting about and sat motionlessly with their heads tucked under their wings. Hmm, he thought, maybe they don't fly at night?

"What did you say to him?" Shenderovich was starting to worry again.

"I want to get out of here," explained Givi through clenched teeth. "I suggested that we could help gather fuel for the fire."

"Ah!"

"Stay right where you are, O Industrious Ones," said the Leader curtly. "We will manage without your assistance."

Givi was about to start up the barrel-organ and launch into a discourse on the halting place of zeal but thought better of it – the Leader was expressively slapping the top of the hilt of his sword and clearly had no intention of letting the prisoners out of his sight. The twilight was thickening like a supersaturated solution, and the wind was whistling through the ruins... The camels had calmed down and were phlegmatically chewing their cud. Hassan and Ahmad were evidently reluctant to stray too far and dashed about within sight collecting fuel for the fire in the skirts of their clothes. Wow, thought Givi, that's a lot of dried dung!

"Rubbish," sighed the Leader, looking at the stooped figures of the brigands. "I brought with me a couple of worthless good-for-nothings, for in much wisdom, as one quite intelligent infidel put it, is much grief. So, what do you think, should I put an end to their earthly grief in order that wisdom should not be wasted in vain?"

"What are you saying, O Conqueror of Ghouls?" Givi asked cautiously. "If it is thus, then surely you are in less danger?"

"Oh!" said the Leader, with a casual wave of his hand. "If I were in your shoes, O Curious One, I would not worry ahead of time… For he who worries ahead of time concludes a risky deal, in exchanging an unknown future for disquiet in the here and now."

"Well, if that's the case…" shrugged Givi, his fatigue and his aching coccyx rendering him disinclined to spin the yarn of refined discussion. Moreover, something cold and slippery was doing somersaults in his stomach, as if he had accidentally swallowed a frog.

Eventually, a fairly large pile of shapeless brown fuel stood in the square between the stones, elegantly decorated with dry branches of flowering weeds. Ahmad struck a spark and fanned the tiny flame, the pale tongues of which danced in the hostile air like little desert spirits.

"May the life-giving, warming flame of this fire be blessed!" cried the Leader, stretching his hand out towards the fire. "You, Hassan, and you, Ahmad, prepare dinner, for it will give us strength and satisfy our hunger. In the saddlebags, there is a necessary and sufficient quantity of dried meat and also some bread…"

"Would we not do better to leave this place, O Bounty Hunter?" Hassan asked timidly.

"I told you, no," the Leader cut him off. "And do as I tell you, before I have a talk with your tongue without your participation!"

The brigands went to the camels and started digging around in the bags. The Leader watched them thoughtfully, continuing to slap his hand on the hilt of his sabre. The shadows from the ruins dissolved into the surrounding dusk – the only illumination came from the square, where a weak ring of light shivered around the burning fire…

Suddenly, as if by command, the camels threw back their heads and began to bellow again, immediately forcing the brigands to jump away from them and take up their weapons.

Hassan pulled the last remaining intact bow from his saddle, placed an arrow on the bowstring, dropped to his haunches and froze.

"Bloody hell," Givi muttered indistinctly, as he struggled to regain control of his dropped jaw.

"Bloody HELL!" answered Shenderovich.

A human figure, barely visible in the darkness, had emerged from the ruins. It was moving uncertainly, staggering and bumping into the protruding stone ledges, but Givi recognized in its outlines something strangely familiar. When the man (if indeed it was a man) was close enough for the weak reflections from the fire to fall on his face Givi recognized the Leader of the brigands.

He turned back to the fire.

The Leader was sitting with his legs crossed chewing a piece of dried meat wrapped in a piece of flat bread.

Givi turned his head again.

The Leader of the brigands was approaching the little group and had already crossed the indeterminate boundary separating the surrounding darkness from the light of the fire.

The white camel was bellowing over by the wall and straining at its tether. Ahmad and Hassan started howling.

The Leaders looked identical, apart from the fact that one was standing and one was sitting by the fire.

"It's a werewolf!" they cried simultaneously and stretched out their hands, pointing at one another.

"A werewolf!" howled Ahmad and Hassan, turning their heads from side to side. "A dji-inn! An ifri-i-it!"

"Don't just stand there, you jackals!" cried the Leader who was standing. "Shoot it! It's sitting right there!"

"Sly creature," said the Leader who was sitting in a cold voice. He threw aside his bread and leapt up swiftly reaching for the sabre at his belt. "It's trying to confuse you!"

"What, you jackals, do you not recognise your Leader?" exclaimed the one that had emerged from the darkness, placing his hand too on the hilt of his sabre. "You are sitting with a werewolf!"

Givi and Shenderovich exchanged glances and began to move carefully away from the fire towards the cliffs. Neither Ahmad, Hassan nor their night guest paid the slightest attention to them, but Leader Number One, who apparently had eyes in the back of his head, pointed a sharp, thin finger at them and cried, "Stop right there!"

The friends froze as if they were playing a game of musical statues and the music had just stopped.

"And what are you looking at, you sheep's entrails," yelled Leader Number One, turning to Ahmad and Hassan. "Do your eyes really not see what stands before you? A delusion, a hallucination! Cold steel – that's what we should have welcomed him with!"

"Ooo-ooh!" Ahmad and Hassan began to howl even more than before.

"He beckoned me in the form of a beautiful ghoul and then struck me over the head," their night visitor continued, sticking to his story. "It wasn't until nightfall that I began to come round. Ah, you worthless good-for-nothings, can you honestly not tell real from fake? With whom do you think you have been sharing your bread and meat, O Empty-Headed Ones? With an evil spirit! Just look at his ears!"

Givi cast a sidelong glance at Leader Number One. His ears were covered by his turban.

"No, look at *his* ears!" exclaimed his double.

Givi cast a sidelong glance at the ears of their night guest. They were also covered by his turban.

"What's he saying?" called Shenderovich desperately from behind.

"Christ knows. They're arguing over who's the real one..."

"And which one is it?"

"Misha, you know, I haven't a clue."

"His boots are concealing sharp-clawed paws, I tell you."

"Pull *his* boots off! He's got hooves!"

Neither Hassan nor Ahmad showed the slightest inclination to pull the boots off either of the Leaders. They were frozen as before, crouching down and looking wildly all around.

The new Leader tutted in exasperation and pulled out his sabre, which flashed briefly in the light of the fire. That decided things.

Hassan, whose bow was shaking in his hands, froze for a split second then released his bowstring. The arrow gave a short whistle, ripped open the night air and pierced their night guest in the neck. He lifted his hand in surprise, as if to brush off a troublesome bee, found the short shaft sticking from his neck and gave an indistinct groan. Then his knees bent under him and he began to keel slowly over into the sand. Blood trickled down his neck, looking black in the semi-darkness.

"Ooo-ohhh!" Hassan began to howl, as stunned as the others by what he had just done.

The Leader fell. Each of his feet in their leather boots gave a violent jerk, drawing deep furrows in the sand, and in this contorted position he froze.

Ahmad and Hassan fell to their knees looking around wildly.

"Come now," graciously said the one sitting at the fire. "It's not so bad…"

"M-master!" Hassan stammered, forcing the word out.

"I'm not your master, you fool," the Leader smirked, revealing sharp teeth.

"Eh-h," Hassan seemed to have lost the capacity for articulate expression.

"You just shot your master, didn't you?" asked the Leader, turning to the brigands. "For the one sitting with you at the fire was not your master, 'twas I…"

He had such a look on his face that Ahmad and Hassan set up a simultaneous howl once more and ran off, forgetting about the camels and the Anka birds, which had reacted to unfolding events by raising their heads from their wings and sleepily calling to one another. Two figures, stooped in fear, flitted amongst the ruins… an eerie, almost inhuman wailing rang out in the distance, faded and was gone.

"Well, there you go," said the werewolf with satisfaction, settling himself back down more comfortably. "It didn't turn out so badly after all, did it? To be honest, murder sickens me but those cowardly scoundrels did the dirty work for me."

Givi exchanged looks with Shenderovich once more and started backing slowly away.

"Where are you going, you idiots?" shouted the werewolf. "Do you really wish to exchange deliverance for captivity?"

To emphasise the point, he picked the bow thrown by Hassan up from the ground and laid it across his knees.

"Shit!" said Shenderovich, scratching the back of his head and trying not to look at the body lying nearby. "What's going on? Usurpation? An illegitimate twin brother? Plastic surgery?"

"Just a standard werewolf," explained Givi.

"Ahh," drawled Shenderovich. "I should have known!"

"There is no such thing as a standard werewolf," said the werewolf, who, unlike the real Leader, was multilingual. "I assumed this appearance in order to deliver you from the clutches of those brigands. And if truth be told little ingenuity was required as your captor was both avaricious and cruel. If he had been wise and noble the task would have been immeasurably harder. However," he added, "then I would not have needed to use my wits at all. For a wise and good man would not have thought to barter lives for worldly goods, which, to be honest, are all rubbish anyway… Incidentally, O Wise Givi, why do you always act as interpreter for your friend and fellow-traveller? Did he not inherit like you from his great ancestor the ability to understand all existing languages?"

"Which great ancestor?" asked Givi.

"That's not important. Watch me, O Descendant of Abraham! Though I am not the angel Surush, perhaps I may repeat what has already been done."

He waved his open palm in front of Shenderovich's face. Shenderovich obediently followed his hand as if attached to it by an invisible thread. Givi cast a sidelong glance at the werewolf and recoiled as he saw red flames burning in his eyes. Eventually, the werewolf gave another abrupt wave of his hand, breaking the thread, and Shenderovich jumped backwards and started shaking his head.

"Well?" he asked sceptically.

"Well what?" asked their enigmatic guest in return. "Perhaps my words are too obscure for your ears?"

"I don't think so," answered an astonished Shenderovich, wiping his hand on the back of his head and looking quite perplexed.

"In that case," the stranger said calmly, "I would strongly advise you and your friend to take this unfortunate leader of freelance marksmen and bury him in the proper way. He was not a good man, as I already said, but even he deserves a decent burial. And may he be dealt with thereafter by He who knows us better than we know ourselves, O Travellers Lost in the Expanses of the Universe!"

"And what about the… ghouls?" Shenderovich wondered aloud, exhausted by the effort of holding his tongue. "The monstrous fruits of the desert, or whatever they are… Will they leave us alone?"

"Pardon me, my brave friend," retorted the stranger, "but did you, an educated man, really believe those childish fairy stories?"

"Well," answered Shenderovich uncertainly, scrutinizing the stranger warily, "how can I put this…"

"The truth of the matter is that ghouls exist for those who believe in them and don't exist for those who don't. So, take that cloth from that camel over there and may it serve as the final resting-place for that scoundrel. It's not such a bad resting-place for a man whose nose turned black long ago from his sins. I saw a hole over there, behind that collapsed caravanserai – just about his size, I would say."

Shenderovich gazed around casually then cast a significant sidelong look in Givi's direction.

"And if you intend to take advantage of the situation to flee," said the stranger, reading his mind, "then forget it, for the Anka birds are with me."

He gave a peculiar whistle. A tiny dot broke away from the black flock and gradually increased in size as it came closer, its wings quivering, and settled down on the stranger's shoulder. Putting its head on one side it considered the travellers with a mocking, beady eye.

"Oh!" exclaimed Shenderovich. "We've already met."

The bird raised its crest and played with it for a moment, then lowered it again.

"We call her Hudhud," explained the stranger. "This bird is a most useful messenger for spirits and the inhabitants of the heavens. There is no more illustrious and revered bird in the whole of the East, so please be good enough to treat her with the respect she deserves. She will ensure that you do everything in the correct manner."

The bird took off again and settled on a fragment of the cliff eyeing Shenderovich expectantly.

"Stool pigeon," muttered Shenderovich, reluctantly getting to his feet.

"And when you return," remarked the stranger benevolently, "and have washed yourselves from this water-skin, then I think that it will be appropriate for us to dine together. This meal will serve as a funeral feast, for the soul of your captor slain by his cowardly comrades desires to rest in peace."

"Fine, whatever you say," agreed Shenderovich, dragging the decorated cloth from the camel and with the same reluctance heading towards the body lying nearby on the ground. Givi sighed and followed him.

A sharp-horned moon had risen and the camels were sighing noisily in her cold light and shifting from one foot to the other.

A long, modulating howl rang out from the depths of the ruins then rose in pitch and suddenly stopped. Givi flinched.

"It's just a jackal," the stranger pacified him.

"Ah," said Givi gnawing a piece of tough meat wrapped in bread. "That's alright then…"

"And you a descendant of Shemhazai as well," Shenderovich reproached him.

"Forgive me, O Restless Friend," the stranger was surprised. "But how can he be a descendant of Shemhazai? Og, king of Bashan, the last giant on earth, did not leave any descendants as far as I am aware. Which is not surprising – where would he have found a mate to suit his stature? However, since every living creature on earth is surely someone's descendant, then your friend has reason to be proud."

"But the Brothers, they said…"

"Ah!" said the stranger. "The magi? Their lies are cheap! To be honest, there is not a grain of truth in anything they say – they do not even know how to be truthful."

"Maybe so," agreed Shenderovich, growing bolder by the minute. "But at least they introduced themselves!"

"The names they gave were merely nicknames, for greater show. And if you, O Son of Abraham, are alluding to the fact that I have not yet revealed to you my true name, I have my reasons for not doing so. You may call me Sheikh, for that corresponds at least partially to the truth. I will also add that I wish you no harm."

"I'll take your word for it," said Shenderovich gloomily.

"Wait, Misha," Givi said hurriedly as Shenderovich, oppressed by the compulsory silence and the general humiliation of their position, was clearly rebelling against authority. "If everything is really as you say it is, O Sheikh, then will you not enlighten us as to where we are and who has need of us? We have been followed for several days now by unknown pursuers."

"Who needs you and why I cannot say since it is not my place to do so. All will be revealed in good time," said the

Sheikh. "I can tell you only that your ordeals are not yet over, and for what lies ahead you will need courage and insight in equal measure. However," he bowed slightly to the travellers, "you have shown evidence of both these qualities, so I have no doubt that, having chosen you, He who holds the whole world like a precious stone in His hand will show you His characteristic love and mercy once more."

"Uh…" Shenderovich scratched the back of his head. "I'm flattered. But all the same, where are we? I mean, geographically speaking. We arrived in Istanbul, aka Constantinople, aka Byzantium, aka Tsargrad, and then we suddenly found ourselves who knows where, who knows how…"

"Where?" the Sheikh repeated sternly. "You are at the heart of the world. For the heart of the world is what we call that which exists everywhere – and nowhere. Always – and never. And whatever happens here happens sooner or later in all worlds, like concentric rings spreading from a pebble dropped in water… and not only on earth in all its manifestations but also in the realms of heaven, for all that happens on high results from human actions."

"From a geographical point of view that is somewhat open to question," remarked Shenderovich, sceptically pursing his lips.

"Who said anything about geography?" the Sheikh exclaimed and the red flames burned once again in his eyes. "Geography is the delight of the simple man, instinctively imposing rigid limits on all that exists. For those who look deeper there are no limits at all. For such 'limits' are merely curtains, walls, separating one world from another, but penetrable to the initiated…"

"Sure, whatever you say," Shenderovich concurred wearily. He was getting used to dealing with delusions of grandeur. "We're at the heart of the world, of course we are. And what is geography anyway? A pseudo-science! The corrupt… uh… consort of materialism."

"I sense mockery in your words," remarked the Sheikh. "So tell me, O Secret Scribe, if you set such store by geography, where do you think we are?"

"How should I know?" this was the final straw for Shenderovich. "I'm asking you! And anyway, where are your local government representatives? I want to turn myself over to the authorities!"

"At this moment in time," said the Sheikh with restraint, "and at this point in space, the only authority is me!"

Shenderovich looked at him sulkily and opened his mouth, clearly preparing to tell him exactly what he thought of authority in general and his authority in particular.

"Speaking of the ill-starred magi, O Sheikh," Givi intervened, "and I say 'ill-starred' as despite all their obvious power they were unable to protect themselves from the sons of the desert, you said that we should not believe them, for they speak not a word of truth. However, how can we be sure that you are telling us the truth now, O Sheikh?"

"It is not about what is said," explained the Sheikh. "Rather, it is about why it is said. I do not need anything from you, whereas with your help the magi hoped to obtain immeasurable power, which is why they sweet-talked you to the best of their abilities. However, in their eyes you were merely instruments, nothing more. I think that once they had got what they wanted they would have destroyed you, for such is their accursed nature."

"O Sheikh," sighed Givi. "Your words sound veracious and reliable but my unfortunate friend and I are finding it hard to tell which of you is more truthful, for the Brothers swore too that they wished us only good!"

"In actual fact," the Sheikh pacified him, thoughtfully stroking Hudhud's back as she pecked crumbs from his knees, "working out who is right could not be simpler. Anyone who sacrifices other people's lives for the sake of achieving his goals cannot knowingly, or by definition, as they say in your world, be right. The sacrifice that the aforementioned magi intended for the higher powers was in no way connected to them personally."

"Exactly. They boiled a snake!" Shenderovich suddenly became animated.

"The snake is irrelevant," said the Sheikh with a dismissive wave of his hand. "Although, having said that, the snake was also one of God's creations, so it has my sympathies. But even from what they managed to tell you it was clear that they had sacrificed their nearest and dearest in the quest for dubious power and strength. And, if you believe their stories about reincarnation, on more than one occasion. Which is why failure befell them time after time, for the only sacrifice that pleases the heavens is self-sacrifice. However, he who sacrifices himself does not strive for power, or glory, or riches, for these things are useless and meaningless to him."

Givi lifted his head and saw that the darkness around the fire had faded, the fire had almost burnt out, and the camels were dozing peacefully, chewing their cud. Hudhud, still sitting on the Sheikh's shoulder, raised her head slightly, her crest bristling. On the cliffs nearby, the Anka birds were calling to one another and cleaning their feathers, shaking off their night's sleep.

"A new wind is blowing, bringing with it a change of fate," the Sheikh listened to the quiet chirping of Hudhud, who was attracting his attention by gently nibbling his ear. "I must leave you now, for where you are heading you will have other protectors."

"Not such powerful ones, I hope," said Shenderovich, sourly.

"Their power is great, however it is within the realms of that attainable by mere mortals," the Sheikh placated him.

"Ah," Shenderovich was delighted. "The local authorities?"

"Well," mused the Sheikh, "in a way, yes. As for me, I have done what I was sent to do, so now I must retire. And I do not advise you to run off," he remarked, correctly interpreting Shenderovich's suddenly vacant expression, "because without protection you will be exposing yourselves to serious danger."

He brought his lips together in his peculiar way and whistled melodically. Hudhud listened, with her head on one side, then broke away and flew off to the east. The Anka birds took off and fell into single file behind her. The black ribbon fluttered briefly in the sky and dissolved into smoke on the horizon. The Sheikh watched them go.

"Well, it's time I was going," he said amicably. "I'll see myself off."

"Hey!" Shenderovich cried out. "Wait... I wanted to ask..."

But the Sheikh had risen and disappeared behind the cliffs, with a friendly wave of his hand. Givi listened, his mouth agape with the effort, but amongst the ruins there was silence. Their night visitor had disappeared.

"Ekh!" said Givi sadly. "He was a nice chap..."

"Yes," agreed Shenderovich, thoughtfully scratching the back of his head. "He behaved quite courteously, on the whole. And that is why I say to you again, O Master of Infiltration, grab that wineskin over there, as there's still a bit of that stinking sour milk left in it, and let's go...!"

"But the Sheikh told us not to run off..." objected Givi, who was not very comfortable amongst the ruins but didn't particularly want to end up wandering about under the scorching sun either.

"Well, don't run off then. Just get a move on."

"He said the local authorities are on their way."

"Where are they then?" snapped Shenderovich. "Can you see them? How did he know?"

"They're on their way," Givi stubbornly repeated.

Shenderovich threw him a dark look, shook his head and clambered up to the top of a pile of stones, which in a former life had served as the remains of a city wall.

"On their way," he muttered bad-temperedly. "As if! Dream on… Who did you believe? That wandering conjurer? That performance artist? Local authorities, local authorities… Bandits, you mean…"

"Actually, he got rid of the bandits, Misha," clarified Givi from below.

"He got rid of the competition, alright?" hissed Shenderovich from above. "And that…"

He suddenly fell silent and Givi distinctly heard him gasp. Shenderovich's face, burned by the desert sun, quickly turned pale and his eyes opened wide. He slipped down and shook his head in stupefaction.

"What did you see, Misha?" Givi was terrified.

Shenderovich gave a deep sigh.

"The local authorities, at last," he exhaled.

Givi stood on tiptoes, craning his neck, but couldn't see anything. Shenderovich gestured vaguely towards the top of the pile of rubble.

Givi sighed too and clambered up. Dunes stretched as far as the horizon, covered in sandy ripples, but in the distance there was a dark stripe, which was moving, growing closer. Mettlesome horses in red silk saddlecloths were dancing under their riders, followed by a train of camels. Narrow banners were unfurling in the morning breeze. Their white robes were dazzling, and the sun danced on the points of their spears.

"Wow," murmured Givi.

"The local authorities," explained Shenderovich once again from below.

Givi climbed carefully down.

"Well?" Shenderovich asked coolly, having regained his composure. "Did you see? It looks like they're coming for us!"

"It… yes… Misha, but there's a whole army of them!"

"Looks like it…" Shenderovich thought for a second, distractedly sizing up their dismal surroundings with a glance.

"Right! Come on! Get yourself up onto that stinking ruminant. Hurry up!"

"Why, Misha?"

"We," proclaimed Shenderovich, dusting himself off and vainly attempting to make himself look more presentable, "are going to ride out and meet them like brave men, like sons of the desert. We are not going to lurk amongst the ruins like a couple of Shemhazais! We will go and meet them! On these magnificent beasts! Stand still, you bugger!"

He punched the white camel efficiently in the ribs, and to Givi's amazement she knelt down on her knobbly forelegs.

"That's the way to do it," said Shenderovich settling himself into the saddle. "And now, hup. Ah, you sack of grass fit for a wolf's dinner! Come on, Givi, shift yourself. What are you standing there like a pillar of salt for? Give him a kick! Go on, kick him!"

"Are you sure that's appropriate, Misha?" Givi, who was attempting to master the powerful humps, doubted it. His camel, looking back at him with contempt, smacked his huge, worn hoof into the ground. "It's a bit rude, isn't it?"

"On the contrary, it's what they expect," answered Shenderovich from his summit. The camel beneath him sucked in air with her long upper lip and suddenly gave a joyful bellow opening wide her enormous yellow-teethed mouth. "There you go! Look at this one, how she's trembling! She wants to get out there, as they say... Ah, my Natasha Rostova, you shall go to the ball!"

Somewhere beyond the dunes came the clear, precise answering sound of a horn.

"Ekh-h!" sighed Givi.

Somewhere within the forgotten expanses of his soul, trumpets sounded their response... He straightened his shoulders, as far as circumstances would allow, and trotted behind Shenderovich who was sitting proud in the decorated saddle of the late Leader.

The army drew closer. The orderly chain wavered and then disintegrated – three riders broke away from it on spirited horses with fine legs and swans' necks, wearing rich harnesses and saddlecloths embroidered with silver. The riders were a dazzling sight in their lavishly decorated kaftans and shirts of the finest linen, and the iridescent fabric of their shalwars was ample enough to have made a splendid sail for a racing yacht.

"How are we going to introduce ourselves?" cried Givi, addressing Shenderovich's back resolutely hastening towards the encounter.

I'm not a spy, he kept telling himself blinking from the dust thrown up by the approaching army. I'm an accountant. Maybe this is how they greet accountants? Foreign ones, at least…?

"As kings, naturally," cried Shenderovich, turning round with a menacing glint in his eyes.

"Forget it, Misha. They'll never believe us!"

"So what will they believe?" yelled Shenderovich, whipping his camel. "Inflatable balloons?"

Givi had almost managed to forget about the balloons. Over the last couple of days he hadn't encountered any rubber goods whatsoever. No, they won't believe the balloons story, he thought miserably as he jolted along on his camel. They probably wouldn't believe the accountant story either. I wonder if they'll believe the kings-in-disguise one?

A fearsome, dark-complexioned, good-looking man at the head of the detachment reined in his jet-black stallion, threw the reins to one of his fellow-travellers and jumped down onto the sand. Givi was shocked to see him fall to his knees bowing his proud head in its snow-white turban.

"Greetings to you, O King of Time!" he said. "Finally, the seeker has found what he sought!"

"Greetings to you also, O Leader of a Thousand Spears," replied Shenderovich with dignity.

"Tell me, O Mighty One," the emir delicately took a pinch of burning, saffron-yellow pilaf, fragrant with ginger and garnished with pomegranate seeds. "We were waiting for you but how did you, King of Kings, come to be travelling alone in the desert with but one companion, who is… who is he, by the way, O Mighty One?"

"My great good vizier, of course," Shenderovich nodded benevolently, washing his pilaf down with some cool sherbet, "who is as fierce as a mountain lion and generous as a summer storm. Do not be taken aback by our appearance, O Warrior, or by our humble position – it is our custom to travel in secret so that we might determine at first hand whether everything is in order in my kingdom. And, as is often the case, we were set upon by a gang of savage brigands. Not knowing of our true identity, which we concealed from them, they decided somewhat rashly to sell us into slavery. However, as you can see, we were able to free ourselves with strength and cunning, seizing spoils in the form of these noble creatures."

"Ah!" nodded the emir. "You have taken possession of the finest pearl of the desert, O Great One, for this is the legendary Al-Bagum – the bellowing one – about whom astonishing rumours abound. Furthermore, I might add, she was taken in spoils by the fearsome Reihan, also known as Sharr al-Tarik, which means 'Evil of the Way' – he seized her during a violent raid on the herds of Iram. I might also add that we grieved greatly on that occasion, for there is no better she-camel under the moon."

"And, for my part, I will add," said Shenderovich, coolly wiping his hand on his shirt, "that the famous Reihan, also known as Sharr al-Tarik, is no more."

"You are truly great," said the emir in admiration, "for not one of us had the power to deal with Black Reihan!"

"Well," nodded Shenderovich graciously, "it wasn't easy. However, it was possible by the favour of the Almighty."

"Your power is great, O Bridge of the Desert," nodded the emir.

Filtered through the walls of the tent the fierce desert sun took on an inoffensive honeyed hue. Reflections roamed lazily over the embroidered cushions, the patterned rugs and the narrow-necked pitchers. The pilaf was radiant with a scattering of yellow pearls, the barberries shone with a crimson laquer, and the sultanas – the joy of the east – glowed amber. Ekh, thought Givi comfortably, so this is the famous eastern hospitality. At least until they slit our throats. Rinsing his fingers in water strewn with rose petals he wiped them on the finest linen.

"Forgive me for this meagre repast, O Fearless One," remarked the emir. "You will be received five, nay, ten times more richly in the palace, and you will be served not by my young sword-bearer but by beautiful maidens, to delight the eyes and tempt the flesh. Passionate maidens…"

"With jewels in their navels," Givi prompted readily.

"If you so desire, master," said the emir, slightly puzzled.

"Pay no heed," Shenderovich waved his hand. "My vizier was born under the sky of a far-off land with rather odd customs."

"But… melodic ankle bracelets, and falling curtains, and little bells on slender fingers, and…"

"Alright," Shenderovich nodded grandly, "this will do. Food and shelter are always blessed, no matter how modest, particularly since we have suffered many great discomforts in the course of our travels. But tell me, O Oncoming One, how did you know to find us precisely here? The desert is vast, and it would not be difficult to mislay a couple of travellers."

"It was all thanks to our astronomer and astrologer Duban, O Great One," explained the emir. "He read in the celestial signs that the empty throne would soon be empty no more. True, he expressed himself in rather a vague manner, as is the habit of these astrologers… but he did indicate very precisely where to look for you. So I set out with my army, thinking to offer you timely help and support, should you have need of them."

Shenderovich thought for a moment.

"Really, we are just passing through," he said eventually. "My kingdom, which I abandoned purely out of impulsiveness and folly in the search for adventure, requires dominion and scrutiny no less than yours, and, as you have already noted, O Venerable One, we were able to cast our adversary into the earth by our own hand without recourse to outside assistance. But I will consent to settle your state problems to mutual satisfaction."

The emir also thought for a moment.

"Iram was and will be your kingdom forever, O Boundless One. However, it is not surprising that your travels may have led you to foreign thrones and bestowed upon you new crowns!"

"Indeed," agreed Shenderovich.

Givi sighed quietly. There was no escape. The desert beyond the canvas walls burgeoned with field tents as profuse as spring tulips and bristled with hundreds of spears. Strictly speaking, they were lucky not to have been dragged along behind the horses like foreign spies. So, it seems that Misha's a king again! Well, well…

"So, where will our journey take us?" continued Shenderovich graciously.

"What do you mean, where?" the emir was surprised. "To Iramzat al-Imal, of course! To Iram the many-columned, the great city, the heart of the world!"

Givi recalled the white towers rising to the sky, shaking with the illusory breath of the desert. Shenderovich must have been thinking along exactly the same lines.

"Ahh!" he drawled. "So that's where we're going!"

"I thought it was just a trick played by the light and the air on our heat-addled brains!" Givi couldn't help bursting out. "It doesn't really exist!"

"Maybe you will say that I do not really exist either, O Great Vizier of the Great One?" inquired the emir quietly but with great dignity.

"Uh…" mumbled Givi. "I do not doubt the fact of your existence. You think, O Emir, therefore you are!"

The emir relaxed a little and nodded graciously.

"This vizier of yours truly is a wise man," he said courteously to Shenderovich. "It is no surprise that you should have chosen him to accompany you on your journey under the moon!"

"He is of great use to me," agreed Shenderovich. "And what else did this astrologer tell you relating to our affairs, O Leader of the Army?"

"I think," said the emir evasively, "that you should speak with him personally, O Support of Supports. However, if you, O Eastern Sun Arriving from the West, are sufficiently refreshed, then your servant humbly beseeches you to proceed, for your subjects await you."

He pressed his hands to his forehead and froze in a deferential pose. Shenderovich glanced at the indistinct silhouettes of the guards at the entrance and sighed, then rose smoothly from his cushions and, folding back the curtain, stuck his head outside. A wave swept along the orderly rows of the army. Thousands of men simultaneously shook their spears and began to cheer, harmoniously but incomprehensibly. Shenderovich greeted them with a wave of his hand and dived back into the tent.

"I think that you are right, O Support of the Throne," he agreed. "We really do need to set out now in order to proceed to the, um… hospitable shelter of your palace…"

"*Your* palace, O Keeper of the Earth," the emir politely reminded him.

"The hospitable shelter of my palace," agreed Shenderovich. "Let's go, Givi…"

"You mean I have to get back on that camel?" Givi groaned quietly.

"The camel does not suit your vizier? Perhaps he would prefer a stallion, with strong pasterns – black as the night, fierce as a lion, hot as the desert wind…?"

"No," Givi resigned himself to the inevitable. "I'd rather have the camel. Don't you have any of those... sedan chair things?"

"Sedan chairs are for women and the elderly," answered the emir dryly. "Or the injured. Are you injured, O Fount of Wisdom?"

"Erm... no," Givi was embarrassed.

"Don't try and make them feel sorry for you," hissed Shenderovich through clenched teeth. "Be a man! Order our animals to be brought to us, O Emir!"

The emir clapped his hands and a minute or two later several men dragged Al-Bagum, baring her teeth and digging her heels in, over to the tent. Givi's monster trotted reluctantly behind her.

"You will ride at the head of the army," said the emir with a bow as his warriors restrained the angry Al-Bagum, one of them holding a stirrup and two more hanging on to her reins. "You will enter the white walls of Iram at the head of the army!"

"Good, good," Shenderovich waved distractedly, giving Al-Bagum a hefty whack on the jaw. The camel immediately quiesced and knelt down. Whatever his reputation, at least as far as camel-training was concerned the late Sharr-al-Tarik had no equal.

"Look, look," a whisper spread through the ranks.

The emir threw the troops a proud look and flew like a bird into his saddle.

Iram really did rise up from the desert like a vision. The white city walls seemed to tremble slightly in the scorching white air and the blue of the sky was reflected in the blue tiles of the cupolas. Half of the city was surrounded by mountains, giving it the appearance of a bowl cupped in a stone palm. Sheep grazed on the green slopes as clamorous shepherds and lazy dogs wandered amongst them. The hills were dotted with the colourful tents of shepherds and warriors, and the valleys were rich with splendid gardens whose heavy fragrance carried to where they stood. Warm, turbid water splashed in the irrigation canals. Water-carriers and snow-merchants rushed down from the mountains and cotton pickers bowed as they saw the approaching army – they did not appear to be afraid but on the contrary smiled in welcome, showing sparkling white teeth. I can't believe how friendly they are here, thought Givi, rubbing his camel-weary backside.

A white road ran from the city gates away over the horizon. In the east, where a semi-transparent crescent moon was rising in the thick blue sky, the road dissolved into the heat haze that cloaked the distant mountains. Their lilac peaks rose up to meet the vault of heaven, and thence a cold wind blew. The road was empty.

"What mountains are those, O Emir?" asked Givi.

"The Mountains of Kaf, O Great Traveller," the emir answered uneasily. "Otherwise known as the Mountains of Darkness."

"And where does this road lead?" Givi's curiosity continued.

"To the world outside," replied the warrior. "For Iram lies in a valley and there is only one way out."

Then how the hell did we get here, Givi wondered in amazement. This was definitely the first time he'd ever set eyes on the Mountains of Darkness.

"Your appearance here is miraculous," the emir clearly shared his thoughts. "However, one should expect no less from the Sovereign of Worlds! Even locked doors are no deterrent to him."

"Naturally," Givi cautiously concurred.

"Ifrits have been known to bodily transfer certain chosen ones, in their sleep, from their nocturnal dwellings to faraway lands. Was that, perchance, what happened to you?"

"You've hit the nail on the head there, O Emir!" agreed Givi with relief. "That's exactly what happened!"

He glanced furtively at Shenderovich. Shenderovich was prancing about on Al-Bagum, with his neck straight and his head raised high, as if an invisible crown gleamed upon it.

He became aware of a steady noise. Givi looked around – the water carriers had abandoned their pitchers, the peasants had put down their hoes, the traders had forgotten their stalls, the shepherds had left their flocks... they were all gradually coming together to form a variegated, jubilant crowd, which was following the army like a multicoloured tail.

Within the white walls of Iram a similar animated and joyful hum was eagerly awaiting their arrival. Were the gates to open, it seemed a great tide would flood out, wave upon wave, engulfing everyone and everything in a noisy maelstrom.

"Your subjects, O Master," explained the emir.

"Ah!" nodded Shenderovich benevolently. "Jolly good!"

"Word of your approach reached the ears of even the lowliest beggar, and what the lowliest beggar knows everyone knows! And everyone, young and old, is possessed of a sincere desire to greet you!"

"Uh-huh..."

"It's a big city," observed Givi politely, looking at the gilded azure cupolas rising from behind the city walls.

"City? Oh no, Iram is not a city – Iram is a whole world!"

The bronze binding of the gates flashed in the sun as they swung open and the army rode through the white arches to cries of joy.

Givi looked left and right. Low houses of baked clay alternated with towers of pale stone, roofs met over cool alleys forming arches and graceful vaults, and the cast-iron trellises were so interlaced with vines that at times it was difficult to tell them apart. And there were people absolutely everywhere. They were standing on the balconies, leaning out of the windows, hanging from the flat roofs... The air erupted with joyful cries.

And all this – the noise and the joy and the rapturous

welcome – was for them. Well, primarily for Shenderovich, but partly for Givi, too.

Givi wrestled with the desire to jump down from his camel and seek refuge – he felt like a complete fraud. Unlike Shenderovich, who continued to nod benevolently as he eyed his domains.

White and gold columns rose up into the sky along both sides of the street, and roses were scattered under the feet of Al-Bagum. The emir, spurring his stallion on a little, rode up alongside Shenderovich.

"And here is your palace, O Crescent of the Moon!" he said, stretching his arm out in the direction of a cupola that towered above the roofs.

"Uh…" Shenderovich's astonished gaze followed his arm, then he graciously nodded once more. "Not bad."

"Not bad, O Joy of the World? It is the finest palace ever to exist! Designed by the most skilled architects! Have you ever seen such a cupola? Just look at that design! It is woven from stars made from tiles of blue, turquoise, white and black – each star is unique but at the same time they are linked to one another in a quite indescribable way. And the summit of the cupola is open so that the pool in the centre of the madrasah reflects the sky in the day and the stars at night. And do you see that slender tower over there? It is from there that the astrologer follows the path of the luminaries of the night!"

"Like I said, not bad," Shenderovich stubbornly repeated. "Right, Givi?"

"To the truly wise man," Givi affirmed gloomily, feeling somewhat apprehensive, "even a modest hut is a palace if he is welcomed therein with an open heart."

"Your vizier is none other than King Solomon himself!" exclaimed the emir in admiration.

One more wall appeared before them, white as sugar and sparkling in the sun – this time the entrance gates were bound in silver and the sentries could be heard calling to one another from the towers.

The palace gates swung open to the harmonious roar of trumpets, the guards inclined their spears and the cavalcade entered the palace square, which was paved with the same sugar-white stone. Givi screwed up his eyes involuntarily, then could bear it no longer and opened them again. The palace rose up before them like a precious casket, and courtiers flew out of it like brightly coloured confetti...

Youths dressed in white descended upon them and got hold of the reigns of their tired animals.

Givi had already swung his leg over the saddle, desperate for the feel of solid ground as his buttocks were aching unbearably from the camel's harsh treatment of them. But then he met Shenderovich's steely glare.

"Don't move," hissed Shenderovich.

He himself continued to tower up on Al-Bagum, as motionless as a stone statue.

The emir cast a sidelong glance at him then made a slight movement with his hand. A few more men ran forward and covered the neat cobbles of the palace square with carpets. The palace staircases blossomed with cochineal and indigo, and the carpets shimmered like butterflies in the sun.

"Right, now we can go in," Shenderovich proudly lifted his head, casually threw his reins into unseen hands and proceeded into the palace to the piercing sounds of the trumpets. The shouts of the rapturous crowds outside continued unabated.

Givi followed him through the white and gold reflections that danced on the multicoloured woven carpets. The depths of the palace exuded coolness, and he could hear the gentle sound of water splashing. The guards, standing stiffly on either side of the door, could not suppress their enthusiastic smiles. It was only now, at close proximity, that he noticed the fine black cracks snaking up the porcelain lustre of the palace wall...

As he reached the portico, he looked around. The joyous

bustle in the courtyard continued – sword-bearers and servants were leading the horses away, commanders were refreshing themselves from pitchers, laughing and washing their hands under the sparkling flow of water, and Al-Bagum was backing away reluctantly, coaxed by an impatient hand. Another detachment entered the palace gates. The horses were tired, their belly-bands dark with sweat, though their riders held themselves proudly, shouting to one another in high-pitched voices.

Several camels came after them, richly adorned, their harnesses sparkling with bronze decorations and their humped backs piled high with parcels and packages. Suddenly, Givi's mouth fell open as he caught sight of the massive, angular object that four strong warriors were in the process of unloading. The object was wrapped up in a scarlet cloth, which was embroidered with a golden sun…

"Get a move on, will you…" Shenderovich hissed through his teeth. Givi sighed, closed his mouth, and followed the newly revealed king.

Within the palace walls the sounds faded away. A large room with narrow arched windows breathed coolness. Carpets muffled their steps, and a fountain murmured somewhere nearby.

The walls were lined with the rounded backs of bowing courtiers, the sea shells of their twisted turbans facing the new arrivals, and two rows of Mamelukes stretched from the entrance door, forming an aisle. On seeing Shenderovich they all raised their spears as one, bringing them down again with a synchronous thud.

Shenderovich continued to look graciously all around. At the far end of the enormous hall rose an empty throne, so high that it looked more like a monument to itself, like the idea of a throne embodied in ivory and silver, so majestic that the idea of actually lowering one's backside onto the shiny, polished seat would seem to be an inconceivable blasphemy. Green, white and red gems blazed in the flames of the lamps, the gold was shot with an oily sheen, and the carved ebony blossomed with black petals.

Six steps led up to the throne, and golden animal sculptures stood at both sides of each one, like guards.

Jesus, thought Givi, trembling as he eyed the enormous construction. Misha's going to have to sit on that!

"Very nice," said Shenderovich politely.

"We have kept it exactly as you left it," remarked the emir. "And, naturally, no one else has even attempted to sit upon it."

As if, thought Givi.

"Who would have risked it? After Nebuchadnezzar and the Egyptian pharaoh both failed so dismally…"

"Certainly not me," muttered Givi to himself.

"And certainly not Darius, King of Persia, either." The owner of the quiet, cawing voice had excellent hearing. Givi blinked.

The base of the throne was flanked by two motionless figures, which Givi had initially mistaken for statues. The voice was coming from one of them.

Shenderovich slowed down, turning his glance to the source of the noise.

On a decorated bench to the right of the throne sat a plump little man in an enormous turban, with the face of a convivial fellow partial to a good joke and hard little eyes. Meeting Shenderovich's casually curious gaze he leapt up and bowed, pressing his palms to his forehead.

"Vizier Jamal at your service, O Great One," he said in a voice dripping with honey. "Who has humbly attempted in your absence to steer the vessel of Iram among the sandbanks of fate."

Aha, thought Givi. So, somewhat less than delighted by the arrival of the king then… Jamal clearly possessed the cruelty, cunning, insidiousness and other qualities of a typical vizier, which allowed him to remain afloat in the turbid waters of eastern intrigue.

"I hope," asked Shenderovich, "that you did not find this navigation too burdensome a task?"

"Well…" Jamal thought for a second, pursing his lips and scrutinising Shenderovich. "You know as well as I, O Master, at what a decisive moment you have arrived, as you always do when you are needed most."

"Indeed!" said Shenderovich authoritatively.

"The burden of my troubles grew with every second that passed, and I am happy to place it on shoulders stronger than my own. I dreamed often of retiring, and now, O Source of Strength, I shall hand Iram over to you and go with peace in my heart to tend to my roses…"

Shenderovich also thought for a second.

"It is hard for the faithful to be without devotees," he said finally. "Your wish to withdraw from affairs, O Jamal, constricts my chest and troubles my heart. For without wise advice even the most powerful ruler is nothing. Therefore, I humbly and graciously ask you to serve me with the same zeal and selflessness with which you have served Iram."

The vizier feigned sorrowful obedience, though his needle-sharp eyes remained fixed on the wary Givi.

"But you, O Hope of the World, have brought your own vizier," he remarked softly.

"My adviser and friend is known to be pure of heart, loyal, reliable and an expert with numbers and credits and debits," explained Shenderovich, throwing Givi an indulgent glance. "However, he is ignorant of the subtleties of governing Iram."

"Well, that being the case," Jamal said with resignation, "I shall put aside my concerns about my rose-garden to serve for a while as the base of your great throne."

"Right then," Shenderovich turned expectantly to the sombre figure on the left, who looked for all the world like an old crow roosting on an uncomfortable perch.

The stars and moons embroidered on his black robe and the top of a conical astrologer's cap sticking out from his turban left not the slightest doubt as to his identity. The astronomer, tall and thin, with a dark, bony face, fixed the new arrivals with a piercing stare. Givi shivered.

"Ah," Shenderovich concluded astutely. "My scientific adviser!"

"Astrologer Duban at your service," he bowed with dignity.

Givi noticed that he had not added 'O Master.'

Shenderovich had also noticed and his face darkened.

"The same Duban who predicted my appearance?" he inquired softly.

"I predicted the appearance of the true king," Duban reluctantly confirmed, continuing to appraise Shenderovich with a cold eye.

"Well, he stands before you," said Shenderovich, his voice still soft.

Duban hesitated.

"If we are to be guided by the celestial signs," he said, "then there is no doubt that they predicted your arrival. I waited for your star in the constellation Leo and it appeared. Since then, I have spent every night observing its ascendance in the sky of Iram. However, your star is unstable, O Newcomer – one moon ago it gave birth to a twin. Which shows that its influence on the motion of the celestial sphere is complex…"

"Your point being…?" Shenderovich asked tersely.

"Patience is a virtue," replied the astronomer, equally tersely. "You did indeed come when you were expected, yet I am confused." He pressed his hands to his sunken chest. "Forgive me, O Newcomer! I am only doing my job."

"Anyone can make a mistake," Shenderovich nodded graciously.

Duban stood with his head bowed, but Givi saw his eyes gleam darkly under his knitted brow.

This one's not so keen on us either, he thought.

Duban bowed even lower, though his voice had a hard edge to it.

"Yes, but not everyone, O Veneration of the Almighty, has a reliable means for distinguishing real from fake. The throne has not yet spoken."

"Ah, yes," nodded Shenderovich, visibly perplexed, "the throne... that construction..."

Givi shivered again. The throne struck fear into his heart. The animal figures that towered up the staircase, executed with clear disregard for their actual size – a lion and an ox, a wolf and a lamb, a leopard and a kid, a bear and a deer, an eagle and a dove, a hawk and a sparrow – stared sombrely at the new arrivals... More than anything the throne resembled the work of a mad animal-sculptor, an impression that was indirectly confirmed by the figure of a turtle-dove adorning the back of the chair, which was clutching a hawk in the tiny claws of its outstretched wing.

"Well, let it speak then," Shenderovich said impatiently, inspecting the throne with suspicion.

"It will speak," Duban answered meaningfully.

Suddenly, the floor lurched beneath their feet. Overhead, the pendants of the candelabras tinkled thinly in a silvery voice. Givi froze, looking around in fear.

He didn't like earthquakes. To be honest, who does? News reporters working in the world's hotspots, maybe, but that's about it. If everyone else rushes to the doors now in terror, then I think I might join them, thought Givi, striving to hang on to his dignity.

He glanced cautiously at Shenderovich.

Shenderovich was looking at the throne.

A guarded whisper rolled along the colourful rows of courtiers. Nobody moved a muscle. Givi noticed that for some reason they were all looking at Shenderovich.

"And how do we, uh... find out what it thinks?" asked Shenderovich. It took Givi a couple of seconds to realize that he was still talking to the astrologer. He didn't even appear to have noticed the earthquake.

"Just ascend it, O Crown of Creation," sighed the vizier.

After the underground shock, he seemed to have somehow wilted.

"Right now?" Shenderovich was taken aback.

"Why wait any longer, O Father of the People? Let the knots of fate be untied and tied anew in the interests of general prosperity."

In some confusion, Shenderovich turned to look back at the emir.

The emir's impassive face gave nothing away. It seemed to Givi, though, that the spears of the guard of honour were angled in a rather threatening way.

"Well, what are we waiting for?" asked Shenderovich coldly before making his way majestically over to the intricate animalistic chef d'oeuvre.

"I advise you to think very carefully before proceeding, O One Who Knows Not Fear," warned Duban solicitously. "The Pharaoh, master of Egypt, also decided like Nebuchadnezzar before him to test fate. However, he broke his leg when the lion cut short his path."

It tripped him up, thought Givi. Evil thing. Just look at the way it's watching us.

The lion flashed a dark look in his direction with its ruby eyes. Shenderovich stopped and calmly regarded the short figure of the vizier and Duban's sombre contours.

"No lion," he said, enunciating very precisely, "would dare to cut short *my* path."

"Misha…" Givi cautioned him in a whisper.

Shenderovich flashed a dark, leonine look in his direction.

"Just watch your step…"

Vizier Jamal turned to Duban, who was standing tensely erect and craning his neck forward with a stern look on his face, trying to hypnotise Shenderovich.

"If, by chance, you are mistaken in your calculations of the paths and the knots, O Astrologer…" he said in a velvety voice. "If the throne does not accept him…"

"Then what?" Duban answered vaguely, shrugging his sharp shoulders.

Something somersaulted in the pit of Givi's stomach.

Shenderovich continued at a leisurely pace along the scarlet and gold path to the throne. The silent guards beat the shafts of their spears on the ground as he passed them, generating a soundtrack of muffled tapping to accompany his journey.

Reaching the base of the throne, Shenderovich stopped and turned round, silently, significantly. Then he smiled affectionately at the vizier and lifted his head. Givi sensed a metaphysical cloak flowing from Shenderovich's mighty shoulders. Shenderovich stood there for a second then raised his foot and placed it on the first step…

The throne sprang to life.

The animals started to move, making a scraping sound like a rarely used machine. The birds flapped their wings and twisted their heads, and the lion and the ox guarding the base stood on their hind legs and let out threatening and completely identical roars. Behind Shenderovich, two rows of Mamelukes fell to their knees, striking their foreheads on the floor. The carpet softened the blow.

Only the emir remained standing, his fingers toying affectionately with the handle of his dagger protruding from its sheath. Jamal and Duban had also frozen in their positions at either side of the base of the throne, like bits of broken machinery.

Shenderovich looked calmly at the rearing animals. Then, leaning on the paws that stuck out from left and right like a handrail – one with a hoof, the other with claws – he went up another stair.

Nothing happened.

Shenderovich stood there for about a minute then experimentally raised his foot once more. The second pair of animals became agitated and reached their paws out towards him.

Repeating this procedure Shenderovich gradually reached the highest step, where he froze. Then, before the eyes of a stupefied Givi, he suddenly started to grow. It took Givi a while to realize that his friend was standing on the interwoven wings of two enormous metal eagles, which slowly rose and placed him on the throne. The silvery voices of trumpets rang out, and another eagle flew down from a canopy above and placed a glittering crown on Shenderovich's proud head.

At the sides of the throne, Jamal and Duban exchanged cold glances.

Then Duban slowly stood up before the base of the throne and flung his arms wide, causing the capacious sleeves of his black robe to spread out like the wings of a gigantic bat.

"Ahhhh!" spread around the room.

"Welcome back, O Iskander!" the astronomer intoned sonorously, as he fell to his knees.

Shenderovich waved his hand imperiously from the summit of the Throne, and the high-ranking officials raised themselves from their knees and began to take their seats. Givi thought for a moment and then sat down next to Jamal, who was graciously nodding his head and smiling warmly. Givi didn't like his smile – Jamal had strong, sharp teeth.

"So, O Gathering of People!" Shenderovich nodded majestically. "Tell me frankly of your misfortunes and difficulties! For if everything is going well, what use is a leader?"

Next to Givi, Jamal sprang animatedly to life.

"If a leader does not already know about the misfortunes of his people, what use is that leader?" he queried.

Oh no, thought Givi in alarm, he shouldn't be winding him up like that... He doesn't know Misha!

"That which is not named does not exist," Shenderovich

said sternly and ground his teeth demonstratively, thus conveying his suppressed rage.

Jamal and Duban looked at each other again.

Then Duban stood up and bowed.

"It has come to my attention, O Great King…" he began.

"Yes, yes, get to the point," Shenderovich interrupted him.

"As you, O Sublime One, have yourself remarked," continued Duban in a wounded tone, "Iram appears not to stand on solid ground but rather to undulate, as though on waves… And it has been known since the time of the predecessor of my predecessor, who learnt from his predecessor, that these oscillations will continue to grow until the earth splits open and Iram crashes down into the fiery abyss…"

I knew this place was unstable, thought Givi with horror.

"Upon learning this, the people fell into a great sorrow. The prophesied downfall of Iram presages innumerable misfortunes for the entire world and is indeed a tragedy in its own right, for who would seek to amass riches and extend their family line when faced with a future holding nothing but death and destruction? However, by means of complicated and very difficult calculations the predecessor of my predecessor learned that Iram quakes as it does because there is no true king, for this earth began to shake from the moment you left us, O One Who Has Returned. From that moment, the inhabitants of Iram have been living in expectation and hope. And now this hope has bloomed with realization!"

"Yes," Shenderovich nodded majestically. "I'm here now!"

"So I see," said Duban, slightly uncertainly.

"I'm here now, and everything will be fine," Shenderovich reassured him. "Tell me, O Astrologer, what must I do to prevent this calamity?"

Duban clearly had no idea.

"I do not know, O Deliverer," he said with embarrassment. "I carry out my observations by night and my calculations by day, but the evidence of the celestial sphere is ambiguous. Furthermore, the king's star and its star-twin are confusing all the readings of my astrolabe… However, the stars say quite clearly that the solution to all the problems of Iram lies in the hands of the true king. I presume that you yourself know what must be done!"

"OK," Shenderovich slapped the arm of the chair. "Let's sort this out!"

"If only I had just a little more time I would surely be able to make sense of it all," mused Duban. "The charts are almost ready…"

"Well you get on with that, then," ordered Shenderovich. "And then report back to me with the results."

"Yes, O Two-Horned One," Duban gave a short bow. Shenderovich frowned as he glanced suspiciously at the astrologer, but Duban's face expressed only respect.

"Will that be all for today?" Shenderovich asked grandly.

"Would that it were," sighed Duban. "It would certainly suffice. However, I think Jamal also has some troubles to share."

"Jamal?" asked Shenderovich from above.

"A mere triviality, O Master," Jamal said sweetly. "Indeed a matter so trivial that I am embarrassed to draw your royal attention to it."

"Well don't, then," said Shenderovich sourly.

Givi knew where he was coming from: he was also desperate for something to eat and drink, preferably without an audience.

"But…" Jamal gulped silently for a moment. A quiet whisper ran along the rows. Oops, thought Givi, Misha slipped out of role there. But the quick-thinking Shenderovich made a swift recovery.

"However," he said, fidgeting as he tried to make himself more comfortable, "nothing is too trivial for the King. What's the matter? Tell me."

"The merchants' doyen wishes to tell you of this trifling matter," said Jamal, with evident satisfaction. "I will correct him if he makes a mistake."

A silver-bearded man in a splendid farji stood up from his place and bowed.

"However trivial it may be, O Jamal, it is a source of great misfortune. And it is not your place to deem it a triviality, for it is not within your powers to eliminate this vexation."

"It is not within anyone's power," remarked Jamal in the same sweet voice as before.

They're up to something, thought Givi. It's obviously pretty serious.

"Perhaps," Shenderovich said cautiously, obviously thinking exactly the same, "I can help solve this misfortune?"

"It is indeed a misfortune," sighed the merchants' doyen. "And indeed you have been sent by heaven itself so opportunely, O King of Time! I, the merchants' doyen, have been sent here by my people to inform you that Iram is no longer frequented by caravans carrying gold-threaded brocades, scarlet silks and indigo-dyed fur; nor by caravans laden with aloe and musk; nor by caravans of Chinese cubeb, cinnamon and cloves, cardamom, ginger and white pepper. Deprived of their adornments and fabrics, their ointments and stimulating spices, the women of Iram will soon lose their beauty and the men their power. To be honest, O Luminary of the World, Iram is no longer frequented by any caravans at all."

"What is happening with Iram is unpleasant and sorrowful indeed," confirmed Jamal, who had been nodding his head approvingly throughout this speech, like one of those little toy dogs with springs in its neck.

"So what's the problem, O Most Venerable One?" inquired Shenderovich, displaying a certain weary patience. "Are the export duties on the aforementioned goods too high? Have the suppliers inflated their prices? Has Iram defaulted on payments for earlier consignments?"

"Of course not, O King of Kings!" the merchants' doyen was genuinely taken aback. "Such matters are easily settled with the help of gifts and favours, persuasion and bribes, and wise conversations over a shared bowl of pilaf, for the business of the merchants and traders of neighbouring lands is also to buy and sell, to speculate and accumulate… Would they really have stopped bringing goods to Iram if it were still within their power to do so?"

"Then," Shenderovich tried another tack, "have brigands begun to attack the trading routes, taking the lives of the caravan drivers and destroying the goods?"

"No, O Light of the Universe," sighed the merchants' doyen. "That misfortune would be only slightly more terrible, for it is always possible to meet violence with violence… Our emir is experienced in battle and his warriors truly are lions of the desert."

"So, what's the problem then?" Shenderovich was starting to lose patience.

"Do not be angry, O Source of Aloe and Myrrh!" the merchants' doyen bowed even lower. "Although our army has the power to deal with creatures made of flesh and blood it is powerless before those of fire and air. These creatures can be vanquished by the power of the blessed one alone – the rightful occupant of the Throne of Iram, sovereign of sovereigns and master of worlds…"

"Uh…" Givi noted with a certain internal satisfaction Shenderovich's obvious confusion. "You mean… Duban, what does he mean?"

"Djinns have recently appeared between Iram and the cities concerned," the astrologer explained matter-of-factly. "Moreover, djinns of the most pernicious variety. I do not know of their ignoble intentions, but whatever they may be they are ruinous for Iram, for these creatures have chosen to settle in a passageway between the Mountains of Kaf, precisely where the trade route passes."

"Ghouls, are they?" inquired Shenderovich in the business-like tone of a visiting expert.

"Oh no," Duban shrugged his bony shoulders. "I think they are ifrits. If they were ghouls we would be able to deal with them, O Sovereign."

"What are you saying?" asked Shenderovich carefully. "That they, uh… eat travellers?"

"I do not know for certain, O Occupant of the Throne," answered Duban. "However, I think so, yes, because not one of the caravans has reached us and the sand is strewn with the bones of people and animals… Having said that, there have always been plenty of bones – this place has had a reputation for being dangerous from time immemorial. But you yourself know this already!"

"Of course, of course…" nodded Shenderovich. "And those who found the bones, what, are they… alive?" he continued his interrogation.

"The most courageous Masroor," Duban turned to the emir who gave a short bow in return, "went there personally with a detachment of his bravest men."

"But," remarked Shenderovich shrewdly, "they didn't eat you, did they, Masroor?"

Givi looked at the emir – his face was pale and he kept licking his lips. He had a hunted look. Hello, something's up with him, thought Givi. Maybe he chickened out or something and now he's embarrassed to admit it.

"I went there at noon, O Master, and left also at noon," said Masroor in a hoarse voice.

"So?" Shenderovich was perplexed.

"Because they are afraid of sunlight, these creatures of the night," explained Duban.

"So why don't the merchants also travel by day?"

"But Master," said Duban in amazement, "they do! But in the Mountains of Kaf there are places where sunlight does not reach, which is why they are also known as the Mountains of

Darkness! That is where they have settled and where the caravans are being attacked, for the trade route passes right by these places…"

"Yes, yes, so you keep saying," said Shenderovich peevishly. "But has anyone actually seen them?"

"I have," Duban explained patiently. "In my crystal ball."

"Ah, in your crystal ball!" Shenderovich slapped the arms of the chair once again causing the animals on the staircase to turn their heads. "Right, let's sort this out. Masroor!"

"Yes, Master," Masroor's dark face had turned grey. Is it possible, thought Givi, that he is genuinely afraid? Great: if he's afraid too, then we really are in trouble.

"We're leaving tomorrow morning! Rally the troops!"

"To… in the morning?" repeated Duban in astonishment. "But you will arrive at sunset, O Master!"

"Good," nodded Shenderovich graciously. "We'll lure them out, those ifrits!"

"But they grow stronger at nightfall!"

"No problem! Let them grow stronger. Put your trust in your King. Do as I say, O Masroor!"

"Your wish is my command, O Master," said Masroor, somewhat uncertainly. He pressed his hand to his heart as a sign of respect then suddenly gave a lurch, screwed up his eyes and fell to the floor.

"What's the matter?" inquired Shenderovich reproachfully from his seat. "Come, come…"

"He's frightened!" whispered Givi, feeling a swarm of sticky ants crawling unpleasantly up his back.

"Fear is a stranger to Masroor," Duban replied sharply.

Pushing aside the warriors who had rushed to their commander, he bent over the fallen man and started to feel his wrist, shaking his head sadly. Then he turned to Shenderovich.

"It is necessary to let his blood, O Great One," he said. "Your unworthy servant, if you will allow me, will perform this operation without delay." He shook his head again, this time ominously. "I see evil signs…"

"Fine," said Shenderovich impatiently. "Then report back to me on his condition. Is that all?"

He's starving, thought Givi as he watched four hefty warriors lay Masroor on a stretcher improvised from spears.

"Not yet, O Joy of the People!" Jamal said softly.

"What else, then?" sighed Shenderovich, like a weary film star.

"What about legal matters? Unresolved court cases? Who else but you can undo the knots that no one else is capable of undoing?"

"Such 'knots' are usually undone most effectively with the aid of a sword," said Shenderovich dryly.

"Not in a court of law, they are not," objected Jamal. "However, this case is rather trivial and that is precisely why it is so difficult to resolve. But if you would rather put it off because you are weary and wish to dine…"

The courtiers started looking at one another nervously again. Masroor's bizarre fainting fit had evidently made an inauspicious impression on them. Maybe, thought Givi, they think it's a bad omen? That's how I'd see it, anyway…

"And who would dare to judge me for that?" Shenderovich roared. "You have all become soft as women, incapable of doing anything for yourselves! Yes, I am weary of your complaints!"

"Forgive us, O Moon-Like One!"

"Your court case is not worth one second of my time!"

"Such a triviality," prompted Jamal.

"A triviality indeed! Now I will show you the way to deal with unresolved issues. Give me the details!"

Poor Misha, thought Givi sympathetically, I wouldn't like to be in his shoes! They're not letting him eat, or relax… But he doesn't seem to mind… Or maybe he's just pretending – with Misha, who knows?

"I present to you the venerable qadi, who will set forth for you the essence of this complicated affair."

The qadi leapt up, bowed and pressed his hands to his chest, then awkwardly, still bowing, unfurled a scroll.

"The matter is simple, O Support of Justice," he said falteringly. "However, a resolution has not yet been found. Three hawkers were on their way to trade in the streets when they met in a caravanserai, became friends and decided to continue on their way together. Fate smiled upon them, O Joy of the World, and they made a large sum of money. However, they felt it was not enough and so decided to take their goods further. Keen to safeguard their assets, they hid the money in a place known only to the three of them, intending to dig it up on the way back and share it out. However, when they returned, they discovered that their hiding-place was empty and that the money had disappeared. One of them had obviously been overcome with greed and, while his friends and fellow-travellers slept, had gone and dug up their collective wealth. And now they are pointing the finger at one another and shouting, and blaming one another, and are ready to tear one another's eyes out. None of them has confessed to the theft, and no one knows how to manage this complaint, for they are all complaining about the same thing, each of them distracting suspicion from himself by blaming the others.

A stunned Shenderovich scratched the back of his neck.

"Is that it?" he asked.

"It is, O Judge of Conscience," answered the qadi.

"Um… maybe someone else borrowed the money? Watched them bury it, then dug it up after they'd left?"

"They are adamant that that is not possible, O Righteous One! And that is the only point on which their testimonies agree!"

"And have you carried out a full investigation?"

"A what, Master?" asked the puzzled qadi.

"Well, at the scene of the crime, there must be fingerprints and maybe, I don't know… traces of dirt under their finger-nails… Someone must have dug it up and reburied it somewhere else, right?"

"As for dirt under their fingernails, they've all got plenty of that," sighed the qadi. "The individuals in question are base and slovenly to a man. And as for fingerprints, well I'm not quite sure what you mean by that. They were all scrabbling around while they were uncovering the empty hiding-place, both in the ground and at each other. They were grabbing each other by the sleeves and robes and even the fronts of their shirts, crying, 'It was you!' 'No, it was you!' 'Thief!' 'Brigand!' and other such insults."

"And have the men been interrogated?" inquired Shen-derovich, his voice as soft as Jamal's.

"Well, they've been interrogated a bit, I suppose you could say," sighed the qadi. "One minute they're admitting it, when they can't take it any more, then the next minute they're suddenly remembering something, retracting their statements and blaming one another again."

"So, find them all guilty!" said the hungry Shenderovich, impatiently.

Givi shuddered inwardly. The qadi shuddered outwardly.

"How can we do that?" he exclaimed, forgetting to add 'master.' "True, they're all criminals in one way or another, but only one of them is guilty of this crime!"

Jamal gave a loud, long-drawn-out sigh, obviously for effect. A deep disappointment gradually began to creep over the honest face of the qadi, like that of a child who'd been cheated out of his sweets. Givi was embarrassed.

Poor Misha, he thought, it's even worse for him! He's in the public eye! How's he going to get out of this one? The poor devil…

Shenderovich stood still for a second, with his hand over his eyes.

The qadi stood still at the base of the throne.

The floor gave a lurch.

The courtier started whispering amongst themselves again. Shenderovich opened his eyes.

"This case is quite trivial, O Qadi!" he said sonorously. "Quite insignificant!"

"Eh?" the qadi stirred from his reverie and hope began to burn once again in his eyes.

"So insignificant that it is not worthy of my time. So my vizier will deal with it, right here and right now," Shenderovich nodded majestically in Givi's direction. "For his wisdom is great and superior to yours, though naturally inferior to mine, as you are about to see for yourselves."

Givi screwed up his eyes in abject panic as he felt the floor give way beneath him. Or was it another earthquake?

He cautiously opened one eye.

Everyone was looking at him.

Misha, what a bastard, he thought.

He opened the other eye.

Shenderovich was nodding graciously from on high.

"Eh?" said Givi.

"Yes!" Shenderovich nodded significantly. "Now! He will tell you! Listen! Listen, people of Iram!"

I'm going to kill him, thought Givi.

He opened his mouth, whereupon the qadi peered into it with curiosity, and said, "Eh..."

"Eh?" repeated the qadi.

Givi sighed.

"Bring them before me," he said. "And fortify me with apples."

They brought the suspects before him. All three were dressed in completely identical robes, which were identically ragged. Identical scratches were turning purple on their faces, and they looked at Givi with three pairs of identical black, impenetrable eyes.

Well, that's the East for you, thought Givi. He sighed.

"I will judge your case," he began, spasmodically turning the ring on his finger. "But first, you will judge mine. OK? That's a fair exchange, isn't it, one service in return for another... We're all businessmen, after all."

All three suspects nodded simultaneously, revealing the tops of their dirty turbans.

"I was approached one day," began Givi, "by a... um... a king. Yes, a king! And one day, something quite incredible happened in his country..."

The Tale of the Unresolved Case, as Told by Givi in the Divan on The First Day of Shenderovich's Reign

I heard, O Wise Merchants, that in a certain country there once lived a boy and a girl, who grew up as neighbours. And it so happened that where they lived there were no other boys and no other girls, and no one else for them to look at but each other. And as they looked at each other they fell in love, as young people do, and the boy said to the girl:

"Give me your word that you will not marry another without my consent."

And the girl gave her word, for she liked the youth, as there was no one else for her to look at but him.

However, soon her parents, seeing that she was of marriageable age, promised her hand to a rich man from the neighbouring village. And when they showed her this man, she understood that he was the one she loved and that she had loved the youth because there had been no one else for her to look at but him. And her heart turned away from the youth and towards this man – her suitor – as is the custom with women, for their hearts are as fickle as... um... the summer breeze. And so she promised herself to this man.

However, there was more honour in her heart than in the hearts of other women – ekh! – and so, when she found herself alone with the man, she said:

"Oh, my beloved! Happy would I be to call you my husband, however I cannot be truly yours until I have kept my promise. I gave my word to a youth living nearby that I would not marry without his consent. And now you may judge for yourself, should I break my promise?"

"You should not!" said her young man, who was himself honest and worthy. He loaded a donkey with gold and silver, sat the girl upon it, and led her to the village of her birth in order that she might keep her promise to the youth.

And so they set off, and by nightfall they arrived in the village and knocked at the door of the youth. And when he opened the door, he was quite amazed, for whom should he see but his former love standing there, and with another man. He asked what brought them to his house at such a late hour.

"My friend!" said the girl. "We grew up as neighbours, and you liked me and I liked you, for I knew no one but you and you knew no one but me. And I gave you my word that I would not marry another without your consent. However, my parents promised my hand in marriage, and I looked upon my betrothed and understood that I love him more than anything in the world and I have no life without him. And so let me buy back my word – in gold, or in silver, whatever you wish – that I may be free, and my conscience clear."

The youth looked into her eyes and understood that her love for him was no more.

My heart cannot continue to love if this love is unrequited, he thought, and so he said:

"Oh, my former beloved! It is no more possible to retain a woman's love by force than it is to ensnare the wind! Therefore, I shall release you from your promise, and since you have remained true to your word, my heart bears neither malice nor injury! And I require nothing from you in return, for you have already bought your word back by showing me that even a woman is capable if not of remaining faithful at least of remaining true to her word, and you have thus preserved my heart and my hope for new love!"

And to her young man he said:

"Take your gold and silver and rejoice in your lot, for you have been granted a treasure more valuable than all the gold and silver you possess! For many may love but few are so honest and true!"

And thus he bade them farewell, and they began their homeward journey with gladness in their hearts.

And so eager were they to fall into one another's arms that they chose not to pass the night at the youth's house, nor at a caravanserai, but to travel through the night, when suddenly...

Givi paused dramatically and opened his eyes wide.

... they were set upon by brigands!

Terrible, merciless brigands, with daggers and yataghans, as fierce as desert lions. They seized all their gold and silver and other valuables, even the donkey, and were about to let their victims go in peace – robbed of their worldly goods but alive and unharmed – when the chief of the brigands, a savage, bloodthirsty, dishonourable and unscrupulous villain by the name of Sharr al-Tarik, decided that he wished to rob them of one more treasure – the innocence of the young girl. And by 'innocence' I mean that she had not yet even been alone with her young husband!

"Ah!" said one of the three defendants. "I know someone like him!"

We all know someone like him! So, seeing where it was heading, the girl broke down and sobbed and beseeched the brigand:

"Allow me first," she said, "to tell you my story! For you are no doubt wondering why the two of us are on the road, in the middle of the night, and laden with such riches..."

"I have all the time in the world," said the leader of the

brigands, Sharr al-Tarik, savage and merciless. "So tell away!"

And so the girl told him the story of her first courtship and about how both of her suitors had acted.

And the brigand listened and marvelled at her story, so touching and instructive was it.

"Just think," she added in conclusion, "my husband, to whom I was betrothed, laid not a finger upon me until I had kept my word. And the youth, to whom I belonged by rights, overcame his passion and refrained from touching me, and even rejected gold and silver and allowed me to go in peace! Would you whose power is greater than theirs, who has incalculable riches at your disposal, really act differently? It does not become a strong man to behave worse than the weak! And thus, take our gold and our silver, only spare my husband and me!"

And just imagine, the brigand was so touched by her words that he raised his eyes to the heavens and, repenting of his evil intentions (for he did not wish to be the worst of the worst but rather the best of the worst, as far as such a thing is possible), not only gave the young pair their freedom but also returned their valuables and all their money, down to the very last penny!

"Pah!" chorused the listeners.

"So," Givi nodded gravely, "there you go. What was my point? Ah yes, the king of this land who told me this astonishing story was in a bit of a quandary. For, when he learned of what had happened, he argued with his courtiers over which of the protagonists had behaved most admirably. Some said the girl, some said her first suitor, and some said her young husband! So they argued and they squabbled, so much so that they completely forgot to attend to their state affairs, and all their court cases remained unresolved, and all their laws remained unfulfilled, and so the king of this land asked me to pass judgment on this case, thereby putting an end to this matter once and for all! However, now I find that the burden of this quandary is mine. So, I wish to ask you, O Squabblers, in exchange for a fair trial will you not pass judgment on my case: of all the people mixed up in this story, who most deserves praise?"

The disputants looked at one another. Then one of them stepped forward.

"I think it's the girl," he said, a little hesitantly. "Because she stayed true to her word and preserved her honour. And not many women would."

"I think, O Burdened One," said the second, "that her husband deserves the most praise. For he did not lay a finger on her while she was still bound by her promise to the young man! And her first suitor turned out to be equally magnanimous, which is causing me to waver between these two, and I can't decide which to choose… And even the brigand, if you think about it, refrained from touching the girl. That king gave you a difficult riddle to solve, no doubt about it!"

"Why are you making such a big deal of it?" the third man came forward, shoving the second out of the way with his shoulder. "I'm most impressed by the brigand! It's easy enough to see how the youth was able to turn down the gold and silver, but the fact that the brigand not only released his captive but also gave all the money back? That really is the miracle to end all miracles!"

"Thank you," Givi nodded importantly and closed his eyes. The qadi watched him hopefully for a while, then cautiously leaned forward and said:

"Well?"

"Ekh!" said Givi. "Well, now hear my decision, people of Iram, and you, O Qadi! The first to answer me today has suffered in the past from a woman's perfidy and bears in his heart a deep grudge against the daughters of Eve, which is why he is delighted by a woman who is able to keep her word! As for the second, he clearly has an eye for the ladies and is unable to restrain himself in the presence of female charms. So he is naturally full of admiration for those who were able to keep their lust in check, for he himself would not have been capable of this! As for the third, well... lock him up, kind qadi. The third and last man speaks with such ecstasy of money that he has not even seen, let alone held in his hands, that I wonder what he is capable of doing with the money that is there for the taking. He is the one who took it. Tie him up and torture him, until he confesses where he hid this money!"

The defendant began to tremble and fell to his knees.

"No!" he wailed, crawling towards Givi and trying to embrace his legs. "I'll tell you!"

"You will indeed," the qadi said darkly while people from his retinue attempted to retain the two furious fellow-travellers of the accused, who were violently waving their fists about and letting forth a stream of oaths.

"There you go," said Givi with satisfaction. "You judged my case and I have judged yours, as I promised. I hope you are all satisfied?"

"Well?!" Shenderovich proclaimed triumphantly from his throne casting a proud look around the room.

"Pah!" exclaimed the men again.

"That will be all for today," announced Shenderovich, clearly afraid that an avalanche of unresolved state affairs would end up burying him alive. "You are free to go."

The courtiers rose from their places, bowing as they backed away, whispering amongst themselves and nodding their heads expressively. Jamal narrowed his eyes and thoughtfully regarded the new ruler and his vizier.

Shenderovich slapped the arms of his throne.

"We are leaving now," he said, drawing himself up to his full height, "for we can no longer ignore the need to fortify ourselves and rest from the burden of state affairs. Right, O Vizier of Mine?"

"Whatever you say, Misha," answered Givi resignedly.

"You may simply call me 'Master'," suggested Shenderovich.

And, distractedly stroking the decorated arms of the throne, he remarked, "I wonder what Lysyuk's up to these days?"

"**W**hat's the matter, O Duban?" asked Shenderovich, dismissing the dancers with a wave of his hand.

"It's about Masroor, O Leader," Duban moved backwards and bowed, before Shenderovich could wave his hand again.

"Take a seat! Relax, make yourself at home! We're all friends here."

Givi cast a sidelong glance at the fierce Mamelukes standing at the door with their yataghans at the ready, though he wasn't about to contradict him.

I wonder why Misha doesn't just send them away. We can't even have a proper chat with them standing over us. Look how they're rolling their eyes!

He was afraid of the Mamelukes even though he knew that in principle such timidity did not become a great man's great vizier. Especially as they were effectively his own Mamelukes. Or rather, Shenderovich's.

He was also afraid of the girls. The maidens were a bit too spirited, they winked at him and wiggled their backsides at him a little too intimately for his liking, which was making Givi feel incredibly awkward indeed. He had thought that the women in harems were supposed to at least know their place and respect their men.

"So what's up with Masroor?" asked Shenderovich distractedly. "Has he got sunburn? Are his bones aching from the ride?"

"Surely you jest, O Master!" said Duban, bewildered. "That man was born in the saddle…"

"Really?" asked Shenderovich.

"Figuratively speaking, of course. I mean that he is strong and sturdy and that such an insignificant journey for him is no ordeal in the slightest. However, he is exhausted beyond belief and is also emitting emanations, perceptible to the initiated, that bear witness to the influence of evil spirits... At first I even thought that some kind of vampire, maybe in the guise of a bat or some other even more abominable incarnation, was coming at night to drink his blood, but having inspected him I found no signs of extraction of this life-giving substance. Other signs are present, though, and these signs testify to the presence of another creature of the night, as terrible and destructive as a bloodsucking ghoul, if not more so... For bloodsucking ghouls are not the only embodiments of evil, not by a long shot!"

"What exactly do you mean, O Duban?" inquired Shenderovich, his curiosity aroused.

"Masroor is being eaten away by a succubus," explained the astrologer matter-of-factly.

"A succubus – that's…"

"Not a ghoul," answered Duban astutely, having noticed that contemporary demonology was not one of Shenderovich's strong points. "A succubus is a demon of the female variety, or capable of appearing as a female, voluptuous and nymphomaniac. In satiating its desires it feeds its own powers while depriving powerful men of theirs. And the consequences of such affairs are inevitably tragic."

"So it turns out," Shenderovich perked up, "that our valiant emir has fallen prey to a succubus?"

"Oh yes! And a particularly nasty one at that. I plunged him into a trance and asked a few appropriate questions, which enabled me to ascertain the reason for his suffering. I had no choice, because in a conscious state he would obviously not have opened up to me."

"Why not?" wondered Givi. "Is he embarrassed?"

"What has he got to be embarrassed about?" Duban was surprised. "It happens all the time! It could happen to anyone. No man would voluntarily turn down the opportunity to become intimately acquainted with a succubus, for in the loving arts they have no equals. Do you not wish to question him yourself, Master?"

"What for?" Shenderovich was surprised. "I thought that was your field of expertise!"

"I can establish the reason for his embarrassment," explained Duban. "However, I cannot eliminate it. The only one capable of banishing this succubus is you! After all the point of a king, O Crescent Moon, is to stand between his subjects and the forces of darkness."

Shenderovich, who evidently had rather different views on his royal responsibilities, asked sourly, "What are you suggesting? That I exercise my droit du seigneur, as it were? What, am I supposed to succubate the succubus, in order to dissipate its powers and cause it to dissolve into the darkness?"

"There is no man alive," said the astrologer firmly, "capable of conquering the succubus in bed! However, it is possible to conquer it by the strength of your spirit in the heart of its lair."

"By the strength of my spirit, you say?" Shenderovich was sceptical.

"Exactly, O Bridge of the Desert! Even though every fibre of your being may wish to take the alternative approach... In order to determine the whereabouts of its lair you need to talk to Masroor the Brave yourself before I wake him from his blessed sleep."

"Fine," sighed Shenderovich. "Come on then, let's go... I'll have a word with him. By the way, have you sorted out your stars and your spheres yet, O Duban? Because that quaking is getting stronger."

"The accuracy of my instruments has probably suffered from these oscillations," the astrologer admitted guiltily. "And the star-twin itself will not cease its perturbations, for it is turning on a single axis and this axis is in a very unstable position. However, it is clear beyond all doubt that you are indeed the King of Kings! You have confirmed the signs of the stars with your wisdom and your valour, and, most importantly of all, the Throne accepted you! The Fateful Throne of Iram! By the way, did you find a kind of lever under the left handrail?"

"What lever?" Shenderovich asked coldly.

"Ah! Yes, yes, indeed…"

Duban minced along behind Shenderovich, and six Mamelukes with their sparkling yataghans drawn led the way, throwing open the doors as they went. Givi glanced about with interest. He could hear laughter and snatches of musical chords being played. A boy dressed in nothing but a pair of shalwar ran past, holding before him a tray bearing various fruits, and a peacock with its tail fanned out strutted along behind him. One of the curtains was pulled back, and Givi felt upon him the gaze of a single beady black eye…

The whole palace seemed to be celebrating the ascension of a new ruler.

"Misha," whispered Givi, barely able to keep up with Shenderovich's lengthy stride. "What was that about a lever?"

"What lever?" asked Shenderovich in surprise. "There was no lever…. Alright?"

"Alright, Misha," Givi conceded despondently. "It's probably just some kind of mechanism… I knew it, that throne is just a theatrical prop! There's no way it could move by itself like that! If you activate it properly, it lifts you up…"

Shenderovich shrugged.

"I'm telling you, there wasn't any kind of lever there, O Vizier of Mine," he said frostily.

He made as if to walk on but Givi grabbed his sleeve.

"Misha, why are you talking to me like that? Stop it… That Duban, he probably organized some kind of intrigue… I wouldn't put it past any of them. Maybe he wants your help in getting rid of that Jamal? He was sitting there with such a sour look on his face! It would be easy enough for him to do – he's an astronomer, after all, a respected man! He said that the stars whispered to him, that they confided in him… He pointed at you! And you were loving it! Honestly though, Misha, you're not a king, are you? You're an engineer!"

Shenderovich looked at him coldly and pulled his arm free.

"I was an engineer in Odessa!" he said curtly. "And not a very good one either. But here I am a king! And a legitimate one, too. Anyway, how do you know, maybe I've always been a king! Maybe I was switched at birth!"

"Misha, just listen to yourself! Do you have any idea where we are? Where is this kingdom of yours? Which country are we in?"

"No idea... What difference does it make? I'll get them standing on their own feet! Transport networks, radio, television, proper toilets... I'll bring them civilisation! Set them up with some business contacts. We can get the tourist industry going! You heard what the man said, their rivals have got some sort of trade embargo going on. They've got a couple of nutters out there in the cliffs, howling and letting off all manner of pyrotechnics... The people are scared... It doesn't take much! You can see for yourself, the people here are wild, super-stitious..."

"Please hurry, O Master," exclaimed Duban, turning round. "Otherwise, the valorous Masroor will be plunged into a deep sleep and will be in no fit state to answer your questions..."

"Come on, O Vizier, get a move on," Shenderovich nudged Givi impatiently. "And do not obstruct me, for I am carrying out my royal duty..."

"Whatever you say, Misha," Givi answered sadly.

The windows of the small room in the living quarters of the king's guard were covered. Masroor had been brought here from the Throne Room and placed on a hard, narrow bed, where he lay with his eyes closed. However, Givi could see the emir's eyeballs rolling under their lids and it frightened him. Nearby a small basin containing a congealed red liquid stood alongside a blood-stained lancet.

"I let his blood," explained Duban, "for it was poisoned with venom from the voluptuous succubus."

"Ahh," Shenderovich was impressed. "He does look pretty rough."

"Because of the succubus," Duban lowered his voice and nodded suggestively. He leant over and whispered something to the prostrate emir, whose eyeballs began moving even more rapidly, though his eyes remained shut. Then, following the movement of the astronomer's hands, he sat up on the bed.

Now Givi was really frightened.

"Answer, O Masroor," ordered Duban sternly, "for your king and master is here!"

"Yes, O Predestined One," said Masroor in sepulchral tones.

"Eh?" Shenderovich looked at Duban uncertainly.

"Ask him about the succubus," whispered the astronomer.

"Tell me about the succubus, O Masroor the Seduced!" roared Shenderovich.

Masroor smiled blissfully without opening his eyes.

"Unearthly is the bliss she brings, for tireless is she in games of love and inexhaustible in caresses. Happy indeed is the man who finds himself in her embrace! Sleep in her arms brings dreams full of life whereas life without her is like sleep without dreams…"

"That does sound pretty special," remarked Shenderovich thoughtfully.

"Pah!" observed Duban . "Evil spirits are evil spirits!"

"Is she beautiful?" asked Shenderovich with curiosity.

"Unimaginably so," answered Masroor. "Let he who wishes to have some idea of her beauty take a vase of the purest silver, fill it with pomegranate seeds, drape a garland of roses around its neck, and place it so as to catch the interplay between light and shadow. That will only begin to convey her marvellous beauty."

"Mm-hmm," commented Shenderovich.

"Misha," Givi reminded him cautiously. "Don't let yourself be seduced."

Shenderovich waved him away without looking.

"Ask him where this spider spins her web," cawed Duban from behind Shenderovich's back.

"Where do you meet with her, O Masroor the Enamoured? Does she fly into your bed at night? Or what?"

Masroor's blissful expression changed to one of worry.

"I'm not telling you," he turned obstinate. "You want her for yourself, O Great One!"

"You will tell him!" Duban frantically gnashed his teeth.

"What would I want with your succubus, O Masroor the Suspicious," Shenderovich pacified him, "when I already have more concubines than I can count, all of whom are beautiful and skilled in the pleasures of love, which I have already been able to verify. I am concerned exclusively for your well-being, for you are weak from your nights of passion, though the time will soon come when I need you hale and hearty. Alright, let's start at the beginning, for I see that this interrogation needs to be carried out properly and skilfully. How did you meet her, O Masroor the Stubborn?"

Masroor gave another blissful smile at his memories.

"I was returning from the hammam," he disclosed, "from the bath-house attendants, from the barber and the bone-setter, from sweets and sherbet with ice, all clean, fragrant and feeling rather pleased with myself. However, as I walked past the deserted tower at the edge of the bazaar, I felt an irresistible force pulling me towards it and so, full of loving languor…"

"Ah!" Duban remarked under his breath. "I know the tower he means! It used to be a watchtower but the underground tremors caused it to lean to one side and it has stood empty ever since, for the predecessor of Masroor the Valorous led his troops out of there so that they should not perish with the next tremor…"

"That is indeed what happened," confirmed Masroor. "And

so there I was, walking past, when I heard a sort of silent call, sweet and irresistible, and my legs of their own accord took me to the top of the tower and she was waiting for me there with her arms open wide. And we plunged together into the depths of the pleasures of love, and the world ceased to exist, and we spent the evening and the night enjoying such delights that I am unable to describe, and nor should I, for it is exceptionally personal and secret…"

"I see!" said Shenderovich, intrigued.

"Pah!" commented Duban again. "That hammam is frequented by respectable men, his warriors among them. If that abominable succubus should attempt to entice them, to ensnare them in its web of voluptuousness…"

"Ask him how long he's been like this," Givi was equally intrigued and stood on tiptoes, peeping out from behind Shenderovich's broad back.

"Have you been like this long, O Masroor?" thundered Shenderovich.

"Not long," answered Masroor, with evident regret. "It is but three nights since I had my first taste of these incomparable delights."

"Hmm, interesting," said Shenderovich in the tone of a visiting professor.

Duban sighed and rubbed his hands together.

"Right, well that's all clear then," he concluded. "Now I will immerse him in a curative sleep to restore his strength, and tomorrow he should eat honey with pomegranate seeds and, if this succubus does not poison him further with its lustful venom, then he will probably make a full recovery, for we caught his illness just in time…"

The astrologer stepped forward and made another sudden movement with his open hands, this time away from him. Masroor obediently lay back down on the bed.

"Sleep, O Masroor," he said imperiously. "Sleep, until I awaken you tomorrow a cured man!"

He turned to Shenderovich.

"I must tell you though, O Master, if you do not destroy the succubus this will continue until the unfortunate Masroor withers away completely, together, I suspect, with several other distinguished inhabitants of the city of Iram – among them the merchants' doyen, the qadi, the wali, and various officers and commanders. They all visit this hammam and return through the square in the bazaar past this creature's refuge."

"I said I would take care of it, and so I will," Shenderovich said coldly.

"The sooner," sighed Duban, "the better. And, by the way," he lowered his voice, "I sincerely recommend, O Master, that you go there alone, dangerous though it is, for I do not know which inhabitant of Iram will become entangled in the web of this succubus next!"

"I'll take my vizier with me," agreed Shenderovich obligingly. "He's not from round here, so he'll be immune to her charms."

Givi was inclined to disagree. He could feel his heart sinking and a trembling deep in his soul, so agitated was he by Masroor's words.

But the succubus did sound quite attractive!

"**N**ot bad, my city, is it, eh?" said Shenderovich approvingly, eying his domains.

The palace stood at the highest point in the city and Iram unfolded before them as if cupped in the palm of a giant. The labyrinthine tangle of alleyways was illuminated by thousands of small lanterns and lampions flickering in the houses and on the flat roofs. The sound of laughter and distant voices came from balconies covered in vines, all but drowned out by the harmonious choir of cicadas, and from somewhere nearby came the jingling of a lute.

Givi looked round.

The stars were shimmering and twinkling in the sky as if reflecting the city lights, but in the distance a thick, black mist hung on the horizon like the dividing line between heaven and earth.

The air was warm and a warm breeze was blowing, but Givi suddenly felt a chill run down his spine.

"What's that over there?" he asked Duban.

"The Mountains of Darkness, of course," Duban answered ominously. In anticipation of the impending encounter with the succubus, he was not in the greatest of moods.

"And that over there?"

A single, solitary light burned at the edge of the sky.

"The dwelling-place of the eternal elder," answered Duban, with some reluctance.

"The what?"

"The holy man," explained Duban. "He has been resident there since time immemorial. Sometimes one of his people comes down from the mountains, but he himself never does."

"What does he look like?" asked Givi.

"No one has ever seen his face," Duban answered patiently. "He's a holy man! They do say, however, that he sometimes appears before people, but his appearance changes according to necessity and his mood. Many secrets are known to him, including, so they say, the secret of immortality…"

"Why has he not yet introduced himself to me?" pouted Shenderovich.

"I am surprised by that myself, O King," agreed Duban. "Even if he did not wish to appear himself he could have chosen another way to pay his respects. However, maybe everything that happens in the valley appears to him, from his heights, as merely a fleeting second…"

"Ahhh," breathed Shenderovich. "I get it… Perhaps I should send him my royal blessing. And gifts. Worthy gifts from my royal treasure-house, to delight his eye and relieve his loneliness…"

"If he should choose to accept them," said Duban dryly. "For hermits generally eschew all worldly goods."

The city gradually fell silent as it sank into sleep. The lights went out one after another. Market traders locked up their stalls on the square in the bazaar, which had been open late for the occasion, and the people of Iram headed home in order to continue making merry behind their carved shutters. In the guardroom near the palace walls the coarse voices of the guards alternated with the sound of weapons and the splash of wine flowing from pitchers.

"It is time, fellow travellers," said Shenderovich.

They made their way to the palace gates. This time the massive decorated gates were closed. Another guard was dozing by the wicket gate in the palace wall.

"Wake up, O Somnolent One!" Shenderovich ordered regally.

The guard leapt to his feet.

"By special command of the Ruler of Iram," cawed Duban, producing a warrant adorned with a wax seal.

"One moment, O Travellers," the guard did not recognise Shenderovich, whom he had seen before only briefly and in daylight. "I'll just let the asses through."

Shenderovich gnashed his teeth.

"Is he having a laugh?" he managed to hiss in a strangled voice.

"Not at all, O Master," replied Duban in a hurried whisper. "Right now, the middle of the night, is the time to bring the Nubian wild asses out from their stables, for these creatures cannot bear sunlight."

"So why bother keeping them?" asked Shenderovich in surprise.

"That I cannot tell you, O Support of Power, but such is the custom. Iram is the only place under the moon where these animals still exist. They are bred in stalls that never see daylight, but the poor creatures still need to stretch their legs occasionally! So they are brought out at night to graze on fresh grass and enjoy a little run around."

Shenderovich shrugged.

"An unusual national ass-et, as it were," he remarked. "But are they actually of any use to anyone?"

"By tradition, to you," Duban said sternly.

"What for?"

"It is a secret!"

A heart-rending bellow rang out behind Givi, punctuated by hiccups. Givi jumped and turned round. Dark silhouettes stretched past him. A driver sat on the leading ass but was letting the animals choose their own path and only whipped his animal from time to time for the sake of speed.

"But they're wearing blinkers!" said Givi in amazement.

"Of course they are," said Duban. "It is too light for them here. However, in conditions of total darkness they see all that is hidden from human eyes. They spend their days in stalls without even the tiniest chink in the walls, let alone windows!"

"But who clears up after them?" Givi was shocked. He shuddered as he imagined armies of blind slaves shovelling mountains of dung.

"Servants, and only the most trusted ones at that," explained Duban. "It is a hereditary duty. They clean their stalls out now, while the asses are out, for this is the only time that they are able to take light in with them."

The last ass passed Givi, gave an insolent hiccup and scattered pellets of dung over the cobbles.

"Now you may proceed," said the guard, fastidiously kicking the pellets away and drawing a hitherto hidden lamp out of the folds of his cloak. "Show me your warrant."

"Here?" Shenderovich jauntily threw the edge of his cloak over his shoulder. The cloak was modest yet tasteful, perfectly suited to a king travelling incognito...

"That's what he said," Duban answered gloomily.

The tower rose up above them like a dark chasm in the sky scattered with enormous stars.

Givi felt uneasy.

Of course, Misha looked like a man who was perfectly capable of dealing with a succubus, but then Misha looked like he was perfectly capable of most things... That was the problem, mused Givi sorrowfully, as he watched Shenderovich extracting the attributes from their kit bag with business-like efficiency.

"Get a move on, O Vizier of Mine!" hissed Shenderovich. "Don't just stand there like a pillar of salt!"

With a steady hand he shone the torch into the black opening. The light picked out the narrow, jagged steps of a staircase spiralling upwards like a shell. The stars glimmered in the narrow window opening now visible from within.

"Misha," said Givi despairingly. "Be careful!"

Shenderovich paused for a second. Then he took a crowbar out of their kit bag and weighed it up in his hand.

"You take the torch!" he ordered. "And I'll take this useful-looking attribute! Where are you shining that thing, O Dim-Witted One? Shine it down here by my feet, so I can see where I'm going! I'm not a Nubian ass!"

He moved decisively up the staircase, taking two steps at a time. Givi hurried after him, diligently lighting his way. Duban, casting a suspicious sidelong glance at the attribute in Shenderovich's powerful hand, brought up the rear.

The spiral staircase was narrow and steep. Givi reflected that, notwithstanding their valour, they'd managed to thoroughly exhaust themselves before they'd even met with the succubus face to face. Or whatever that creature would have instead of a face... I wonder if it's only the emir who has gone to her, or has anyone else? After pausing to catch their breath, they continued. The light from the lamp slid over dirty whitewashed walls and suddenly fell on a love poem, written in quaint ornamental script.

On my knees I begged my beloved – smile!
You are as lithe as a cypress tree and fragrant as musk!

Throw back your veil with the fragile petal of your hand,
I have come – lock the door, and bolt it well!
There is no one else here, the house yawns
                                        with emptiness,
Alone in this world I stand before you!

"Well, well!" said Givi admiringly. "Masroor wrote that? What a man will do for love!"

At the top of the tower there was a round balcony. The moon hung over Iram like a slice of ripe melon. The rooftops gleamed in its honeyed light, the tile-patterned walls gently shimmered ... On the distant horizon, the mountains loomed, silhouettes black on black, like a child's cardboard cut-out.

Givi switched the torch off.

An elusive charm emanated from Iram, from the white stones gleaming coolly in the night, from its hidden fountains and vine-covered terraces. The city of all cities, repository of dreams...

Just like Tbilisi, thought Givi.

He had first travelled to Tbilisi in his fifth year at school when his mother had sent him to spend the summer with Uncle Vano and Aunt Medea, and he had really liked the city.

"Yes, not at all bad, this city of mine," Shenderovich repeated approvingly.

"And the gratitude of your subjects will be eternal, O Master, if you vanquish this evil spirit that threatens it with innumerable woes," the astrologer reminded him.

"Ah yes," Shenderovich nodded indifferently. "The evil spirit... Come on then, shine that torch over here..."

Givi obediently switched the torch back on.

Someone down there, he thought, on a terrace or on the roof of a comfortable house, is probably quaking in their boots at the sight of a lonely light in the tower switching itself on and off.

The beam of light made a quick circuit of the room peering into all the corners.

"You see," Shenderovich remarked with disapproval, "we're dealing with a crafty piece of work here!"

"Maybe she's not here, Misha?" Givi suggested hopefully.

Shenderovich turned to Duban.

"Can't you sense the whereabouts of the succubus, O Astrologer?"

Duban stepped into the middle of the room and flung his arms out impressively then rotated about his own axis.

"I can feel the emanations most definitely and reliably," he confirmed. The astrologer filled his hooked nose with the stale air.

"This creature of the night makes use of perfumes and ointments... Jasmine, musk, orange flower... An exceedingly refined aroma, rather pleasant..."

Givi took in a lungful too, out of curiosity, but all he could smell was stale dust.

"So, where is it then?" inquired Shenderovich briskly.

Duban screwed up his eyes and remained motionless for a short time – only his head turned slowly from right to left, then he said:

"Over here!"

"Givi, where are you?" asked Shenderovich without turning round. "Shine that torch over there!"

"A secret door!" said Duban, clearly wise in such matters. "Look!"

The door was fitted into the wall so snugly that it was barely discernible.

Shenderovich ran up to it and drummed on it with his fists.

"Open up! Open up, sweetheart... Open up this instant, or you'll be in big trouble!"

"You seem," gloated Duban, "to have scared her off, O Passionate One!"

"She would have opened up for me," objected Shenderovich with dignity, "but you, O Fellow-Travellers of Mine, are enough to drive away even a succubus!"

He thought for a moment then waved his hand dismissively.

"Anyway, why are we wasting time trying to reason with it? I, King of Time, will break the door down!" And with these words he raised the crowbar. Givi dutifully shone the torch where required.

Shenderovich grunted as he put his full weight behind the crowbar and tried to break the invisible lock. The door creaked. The tower was ancient, after all.

Great, the whole thing's going to collapse on us, thought Givi, secretly terrified.

And, as if by way of response to his thoughts, the tower gave a lurch.

"Have you managed to make any sense of your stars yet, O Tardy One?" asked Shenderovich without turning round.

"No," Duban angrily replied. "When have I had the time? Instead of observing the secrets of the stars, which is best done by night, I find myself hunting a succubus. By your command, incidentally, O Lover of Risks!"

"Shouldn't we perhaps abandon these futile efforts and go down?" inquired Shenderovich, demonstrating magnificent composure. "This doomed tower seems to be in the process of collapsing… and taking the succubus with it, it would appear, seeing as it is too stupid to come out."

Through the door to the balcony, Givi could see stars slowly swimming: the top of the tower was tracing a smooth arc in the sky. Now I'm never going to see what this succubus looks like, thought Givi. Masroor knows, but I don't.

"I feel a bit sorry for her though, don't you, Misha?" he asked uncertainly.

"Ah, who cares," sighed Shenderovich.

"I do!" concluded Givi, his mind made up.

To his own surprise, he pushed Shenderovich aside and began to knock on the door.

"Hey," he yelled, "come out! You're going to die! We won't hurt you. We're good people!"

There was no sound from behind the door.

Oh, if the ruler of China could see your face!
He would bow before you, spilling gold at your feet!
Oh, if the padishah of India saw the silk of your hair,
He would prostrate himself in the dust, raze his temple
and palace to the ground.
What use to him is his palace, when your face there is
never seen?
What use to him are other gods, if you alone are both
his god and his queen?

Givi was really going for it.

A quiet sigh came from behind the door.

I am caught again in your lasso of love!
However I might try, I cannot escape it!"

"I don't believe it," Shenderovich was astonished. "He's reciting poetry!"

A piece of plaster fell from the ceiling. Givi hurriedly continued.

The shape of your body is carved on the tablet of my heart!
This image is all that I know!
For you are a poor teacher, my beloved!
Have mercy on this poor wretch that stands before you!

There was a quiet scraping sound from behind the door, like a bolt being tentatively drawn.

"Get ready, Misha, I've lured her out! As soon as she comes out, grab her!" Givi whispered urgently.

Shenderovich swore and pulled his cloak off.

The door opened the tiniest crack. A thin strip of light fell on the floor. Although a creature of the dark, the succubus obviously wasn't keen on spending all its time in it and had lit an oil lamp. A shadowy silhouette appeared in the doorway.

Givi had time to register only that the succubus was of average height and had curves in all the right places. His heart missed a beat. But Shenderovich remained unruffled and, indifferent to the emanations of the succubus, threw a cloak over it and grabbed the bundle around the waist.

The succubus kicked in self-defence.

"It's biting me!" Shenderovich was outraged.

"Hold on, Misha! Whatever you do, don't let go!"

"Her venomous teeth will poison your brain!" Duban cawed sinisterly.

But Shenderovich was already running down the stairs two at a time with the swaddled succubus in his arms.

The others ran after him, bumping into walls.

Pieces of plaster started to fall from above.

The tower listed to one side.

The succubus screamed.

They shot through the gates just in time to see the tower fall, as if in slow motion. Flocks of crows and bats erupted from the gaps, like billowing clouds of black smoke. Shenderovich observed the process from the sidelines, reproachfully shaking his head.

"Why did you not warn me, O Duban, that this hunt was such a dangerous business?"

The tower finally crashed to the ground, disintegrating into piles of rubble.

"You should consider yourself lucky, O Great One, for you are truly great," said Duban morosely.

"I am truly great," agreed Shenderovich. "So, let's see who we've got here then, shall we?"

Without letting go of the succubus he pulled back a corner of the cloak.

"I knew it," concluded Duban. "This creature has hair of an inhuman colour. Does hair really come in such a colour?"

"I'm afraid so," sighed Shenderovich. "Come on, Givi, shine that attribute over here!"

The light from the torch hit the succubus in the face. The succubus winced and screwed up its eyes.

"Alka!" exclaimed Givi.

Alka looked at him with her big blue eyes. Givi could see the light from the torch reflected in them.

"Who are you?" she asked.

"I'm Givi," Givi answered sadly. "You really don't remember me? Do you remember Misha?"

"Who's Misha?" Alka asked in surprise.

"He is," Givi explained, pointing at Shenderovich.

"Hello, Misha," Alka said politely, and there was something so irresistible in her voice that Givi's insides began trembling again of their own accord.

"Look, just pack it in, will you?" said Shenderovich roughly.

"Allochka, listen, can you remember sailing on the boat?"

"What boat?" Alka seemed genuinely nonplussed.

"Can you remember the captain?"

"Masroor?" Alka was obviously happy at the thought of him.

"No, the captain of the ferry. Yuri Nikolaevich…"

"She remembers Masroor," explained Givi, to no one in particular.

"Of course," said Alka coldly. "Masroor is a very nice man. But you, good gentlemen, I have never seen before in my life. And the same goes for that horrid old man over there. Was he on the ferry too?"

"This is all we need," snorted Duban, performing some complicated hand manoeuvres as if pushing something invisible away from him with his open palms.

Givi started tugging on Shenderovich's sleeves.

"Misha," he whispered, "she really doesn't remember!"

"You'll be telling me next that she's been put under a spell, O Incredulous One," said Shenderovich tersely, becoming increasingly irritated by the fact that he was unable to gain control of the situation. Alka was trying to work herself free of his grip but he kept holding her.

"I don't know," answered Givi uncertainly, "maybe she's under a spell. Or maybe she's just… adapted!"

"What do you mean by that?"

"Maybe this city of Iram alters everyone who strays into it to suit its own purposes, you know? For instance, you became the King of Time! And Alka became a succubus…"

"I," said Shenderovich coldly, "have always been a king!"

"I rest my case," said Givi.

"And what about you?" asked Shenderovich angrily. "What have you become then? The best accountant in the world, ever?"

Givi sighed.

"Have you always had this ability to combine words into radifs and ghazals, O Vizier?" asked Duban, feeling sorry for him. "And to tell such fine tales, which delight the ear and sate the mind?"

"Um, not really, no," Givi sighed again.

He had been aware for some time that whenever he attempted to externalise the strange images and convoluted fabrications that crowded his brain, they sounded pathetically banal. And he had learned to live with it.

"Right then," Shenderovich interrupted his reverie. "You'd be better off giving some thought as to what we are going to do with this succubus. Say we drag her back to the palace like this… and then what? She'll corrupt all the men!"

"Pah!" Duban exclaimed indignantly. "Have you taken leave of your senses, O Radiant One? What is there to think about? We should finish off this creature right here and right now, and be done with it once and for all!"

"Do you really imagine it is that easy to rid oneself of a succubus, O Decrepit Old Goat?" asked Alka, sinisterly parting her crimson lips. "Or has your innate stupidity convinced you that you are able to resist my charms?"

Duban started frantically waving his arms about again, and Givi noticed that his fingers were shaking.

"Misha, isolate her!" he cried.

Shenderovich, who had an impressively rapid response reflex, quickly threw the edge of his cloak over Alka's head.

Alka, thus isolated, squirmed and hissed like a cat.

"Let me go!" she called from under the cloak, which had the effect of somewhat diminishing the inviting overtones in her voice. "Let me go, O Mortal One, and you shall know unearthly delights!"

"No way!" yelled Shenderovich, thoroughly exhausted by the harem dancers. "In your dreams!"

He gave a troubled sigh.

"Well, what shall we do with her?"

"Maybe we could put her in a familiar environment?" Givi suggested timidly.

"Where are we going to find a familiar environment around here?"

"I don't know…"

"I'm the King of Time," lamented Shenderovich, as he wrestled with the swaddled, kicking Alka, "and I can't even sort out one stupid succubus! The shame of it!"

"Answer me, O Wise One!" called Givi meanwhile. "Am I correct in interpreting the following lines by Moshe Ibn Ezra from his famous poem *Necklace*:

The daughter of the vineyard has been given to us,
my friend, in joy,
So that with her help we might deal with the daughter
of the day!
And therefore in the never-ending sequence of days,
She will forever be extolled by us!

as a version of the old Russian proverb "morning is wiser than evening"? For, if I am not much mistaken, in Suleiman ibn

Daud's Song of Songs the brides who are ready to enter the conjugal bed turn to their husbands, comparing them to fox-cubs and themselves to the inhabitants of vineyards, or maybe fertile spirits, and…"

"What?" came Alka's indignant voice from under the cloak. "Where did you get such utter nonsense? The 'daughter of the vineyard' in Ibn Ezra's *Necklace* is quite clearly wine. Maybe such a vulgar translation offends your sensibilities, but wine in a poetic context frequently possesses the quality of saving man from the reversals of fortune and curing him of all ills. Incidentally, only a lazy person would fail to notice the same allusion in the *Song of Songs*, since anyone with an ounce of intelligence would perceive here the obvious parallel with Aesop's *The Fox and the Grapes*. This image may even have its origins in ancient Semitic tradition. As for the 'daughter of the day,' this image is a straightforward metaphor and means 'adversity,' particularly as a similar definition already encountered in verse twenty-six of the same section…"

"Absolutely," said Givi. "Let her go, Misha."

"Eh?" Shenderovich reluctantly liberated Alka's upper body from the confines of the cloak. "Are you sure?"

"We should not claim to be sure of anything in this world," said Givi, "but she does appear to have reverted to her true self."

"Just about," agreed Shenderovich. "Alka, are you alright?"

"How can I be alright?" snapped Alka smoothing her hair. "First, for some reason you stuffed me into a sack, then you started pestering me with all kinds of ridiculous questions…"

She looked round blinking in confusion.

"Good job, Givi," murmured Duban. "All the same, if I were you I would have slit her throat. Her character is exceedingly unstable."

"Don't worry," Givi answered sadly, "she's always like that."

"My point exactly," sighed Duban.

"Listen, Misha, so where are we?" Alka had finally noticed the ruins of the collapsed tower, the golden cupolas of Iram glittering in the starlight and the black silhouettes of the Mountains of Darkness, which were becoming impossible to ignore as the sky above them grew gradually lighter. "This is definitely not Istanbul!"

"Full marks for observation!" confirmed Shenderovich, smoothing out his cloak, which had been torn to shreds by Alka's resistance. "It's Iram. Does that word mean anything to you, Miss Know-It-All?"

"Of course," answered Alka, her earlier irritation returning. "It's a version of the 'heavenly city.' Sham Shaddad, the people's hangman, supposedly built it in the wilderness in imitation of paradise. Naturally, the Almighty didn't leave a stone standing – of Iram, I mean."

"The Almighty merely lifted it up in the palm of His hand and placed it into a contiguous vessel," spluttered an enraged Duban. "Why, O Woman, would he destroy something so beautiful created by the hands of man?"

"Well, he certainly put paid to Sodom and Gomorrah," remarked Alka.

"That was different," Duban interrupted her. "Those cities were awash with such debauchery that even the air above them had turned black! As for Iram, how can it perish when it is the very axis about which worlds turn? But what would you know about it, O Daughter of the Daughter of the Day!"

"Within the limits of biblical usage there is no such concept as Iram," Alka shrugged, "particularly not as an axis for the turning of worlds. Some additional sources have even claimed that Iram was destroyed by the djinns who rose up against the Lord. For this is just where they dug themselves in for their last battle…"

"Ah yes, I almost forgot!" Shenderovich clapped his forehead. "Djinns! Come on you lot, let's go! Djinns are the next item on our agenda."

"Mishka!" Alka exclaimed in surprise. "What's the matter with you, have you gone completely mad?"

"For your information, I am the King of Time," Shenderovich answered curtly. He thought for a moment, distractedly scanning the horizon. "However," he said, "the djinns can wait till tomorrow. It might not make a very favourable impression on the divan but I feel it is justified since Masroor is temporarily out of action."

"Is that a fact?" asked Alka coldly, then she turned to Givi, finally acknowledging his presence. "Ah, it's you! Hello! Have you got any idea what he's on about? He's talking complete and utter nonsense!"

"He really is the King," sighed Givi.

"Really?" Alka expressed surprise, again. "So what does that make me? The Queen of Sheba?"

"Up until today you were a succubus, O Loathsome One," sneered Duban.

"Great, another nutter," Alka noted phlegmatically.

They were approaching the palace gates. Daylight was almost fully upon them, and the clean morning colours danced on the green terraces that were staggered against the mountains as the long drawn-out cries of the water carriers resonated in the narrow alleyways...

"So anyway," wondered Shenderovich, "how did you get here, daughter of the day?"

"I wish I knew, Misha! I was just standing in the museum, when this man came up to me..."

"Handsome?" Givi was suddenly alert. "Dark skin? In a white suit?"

"Well, I wouldn't exactly have said handsome, but I suppose he wasn't bad-looking... Can you imagine, he recognized me straight away. He'd heard my lecture at Professor Zebbov's seminar and said that he was there working on a very interesting project but that several complications had arisen... He was reluctant to discuss the matter with his colleagues locally as he'd already had one theory pinched, but he really needed a second opinion. And then I showed up! What luck! And I thought, why not? I'm free until the evening, why not help him out if I can? Especially as he only lived round the corner from the museum… Anyway, we got to his place, he thrust some scrap of parchment at me and asked me to read it aloud, to check his interpretation, or so he said… It was in Aramaic… I started reading, and suddenly I noticed him doing something! He was fiddling about on the floor. I looked more closely, and he was drawing a pentagram. Around me. I started feeling really strange, Misha… I stopped reading, and he started flapping his hands at me – read, read, he said. I started reading again, and the pentagram burst into blue flames. Just like that!"

"And?"

"And that's it. I came to, looked around and saw you lot standing there… Bizarre, to say the least, don't you think? So anyway, what did you wrap me up in that cloth for, Misha?"

"To stop you catching a chill," Shenderovich answered vaguely.

Alka shrugged her white shoulders.

The sentry took the warrant, gave a deep bow and opened the gate.

"Cover her face, at least," muttered Duban.

Alka was looking in astonishment at the palace, which was sparkling in the first rays of the rising sun.

"Is this really all yours, Misha?" she asked incredulously.

"Yes, all mine…"

"But how…?"

"Hang on!" Shenderovich dismissed her question with a wave.

He slowed down and held up his hand, signalling the others to stop. Givi noticed that he was throwing anxious looks at Alka and muttering something to himself. Then he clapped his hands together. Two guards from the guardroom left their post and rushed to answer his summons.

"This woman," said Shenderovich, pointing at Alka, "is a former succubus, though she has now taken human form and is deprived of her powers thanks to my skill... So by the power vested in me as King of Time, I order you to take her to the women's quarters and be quick about it, and place her under lock and key, and do not appoint men or even eunuchs to look after her but only women, a dozen in number, and they should be older and less pretty than she – such women will not allow her to wrap them round her little finger, for they will take such a dislike to her that her succubus charms will be powerless to win them over!"

Alka jerked up her head.

"Misha," she asked in a calm voice. "Have you completely taken leave of your senses?"

Shenderovich shrugged.

"Sorry. It's just a temporary measure – I have to go and sort these djinns out, and Masroor is on his last legs. If you start succubating him again you'll finish him off, and then how will I manage without my commander-in-chief? Just hang in there till we get rid of the djinns, and when we come back I'll release you and you can do whatever you like! Within reason, of course... Now, get a move on, you children of the daughters of the vineyard! While she is her normal self, you have nothing to fear from her."

The guards cautiously approached from the sides and seized Alka by the arms.

"Misha!" Givi said quickly. "You're making a stupid mistake. Why are you doing that to her?"

"It's nothing personal," Shenderovich sighed, "just a political necessity." He clapped Givi on the shoulder with his powerful hand. "And in any case, it won't be for long. She can just hang out in there for a bit. OK, she might not be too happy about it but it's not going to kill her..."

As Alka was slowly propelled towards the women's quarters she glanced back over her shoulder and gave Shenderovich her most murderous look.

"I will of course do my best to forget this strange behaviour of yours," she informed him with a polite smile, "although I'm not sure I shall be able to."

"Yeah, whatever," Shenderovich waved dismissively.

"Misha," said Givi reproachfully. "What did you have to do that for? It wasn't very nice. Maybe you could install her in my harem instead? I could keep an eye on her! What do you think, eh, Misha?"

"Later, Givi my friend," Shenderovich waved aside his suggestion. "We'll sort it out later."

Alka turned round again and, looking at Givi this time, burst into loud, contemptuous laughter.

"You mean you've got a harem as well?" she asked at the top of her voice. "Ooh, you really did get lucky, didn't you! And so what do you do with this harem of yours? Or rather, what does it do with you?"

Givi stood with his shoulders hunched around his ears, feeling the colour of shame flood his face. Eventually he raised his eyes, only to meet with a sympathetic look from Duban.

"In order to release a succubus from its spell," the astronomer said quietly, "you need to love it sincerely and with all your heart. Its succubus nature will oblige it to love you in return. But once it is set free, it will be capable of loving, hating and scorning by its own will... And I'm afraid that is the sad truth, my vizier friend."

"Yes," agreed Givi, "it is a sad truth indeed."

"Your spirits are low, O Master," said the dancer named Zeinab. "How may I amuse you?"

Givi sighed.

He didn't mean to complain – it's rather nice having someone call you 'master.' And she was a pretty girl with a pretty name. He wondered what Alka was doing, in Misha's harem…

"Maybe I could dance for you the dance with the little bells?"

"Go ahead," Givi agreed despondently. "It's a nice dance…"

"Or I could sing you a song?"

"Go ahead…"

"Or play you a tune on the lute? Or both at the same time?"

"Both at the same time," Givi waved his hand.

"Incidentally," Zeinab shrugged her rounded shoulders, "whatever that sneaky witch Yasmin may say I can hit the high notes better than she can even in her dreams…"

"Which one is Yasmin?" Givi asked wearily. "The brunette?"

"You know," Zeinab wiggled her hips invitingly, "the one with the skinny backside."

Givi looked despondently at Zeinab. Local connoisseurs of female beauty favoured the fuller figure. Givi suspected that such standards translated into exceptionally strict criteria for the hiring of harem personnel, and Zeinab was evidently no exception to the rule.

"They don't call me Zeinab the Lutist for nothing, O Master," explained Zeinab, suggestively stroking the finger-board of her lute with her slender fingers.

"In fact, you know what I'd prefer," interrupted Givi, wincing from the shrill chords that were drilling into his head like toothache and feverishly running through the traditional pleasures of the harem, "I think I'd prefer you to tell me a tale."

"Oh!" Zeinab raised her tinted eyebrows. "I didn't think you were one of those!"

"What do you mean," Givi asked sternly, "one of 'those'?"

"Well, my grandmother told me that once upon a time there was a… um… rather a strange king, not in Iram or anything, but anyway he was crazy about these tales… Don't worry, Master, they teach us the art of story-telling too… They teach us all manner of pleasant arts… Amusement and enjoyment truly fit for a king… So, what should I tell you about, O Hankering One? About the hunchback and the dyer? Or Treacherous Delilah? Or maybe about King Solomon and his harem? It is your choice, Master, for one man's meat is another's poison…"

"Yes!" Givi cheered up. "The one about Solomon…"

"In that case lay yourself down, Master, close your eyes, and free your mind from all earthly cares. And I will tell you how once there lived in the land of Israel a king named Solomon…

A Tale of Greatness False and True, or How Wisdom is Powerless Against Cunning, as told by Zeinab the Lutist in the Heart of the World, Iram the Many-Columned…

Once upon a time in the land of Israel lived a king named Solomon. And he was the wisest man of all. He sat on his magnificent throne and passed judgements in accordance with his own wisdom and the principles of human justice. And his power was unprecedented. All other kings were in awe of him. Peoples and tribes paid tribute to him, and his enemies and detractors became his friends. He understood the language of birds and animals and creatures of the field – deer and gazelles were his messengers, snow leopards and panthers his sword-bearers. He ruled also over the djinns, with whose help he was able to fathom the depths of the oceans and the vaults of heaven, and his influence extended to the ends of the earth, beyond even the Mountains of Darkness…

And so Solomon decided to exalt the Lord and build a great temple, the House of the Lord, which would have arched windows and trees of pure gold, and pink marble, translucent in the sun, and Lebanese cedar, and jasper, and open halls and secret chambers…

And Solomon grew proud, for he commanded the spirits of the desert and the creatures of the waters, and the ants in the basement and the birds under the eaves, and the Leviathan playing in the seas ... And he decided to build a temple like no other. This temple was to be built from individual rough-hewn stones – neither hammer nor axe nor any other instrument would be heard during its construction. And then Solomon went to the vaults of his finest treasure-houses and ordered his Tablet of Stone to be brought forth from there. And this tablet was as old as the hills – some said that Shemhazai himself had created it for his descendants and others that it had been created by request and command of the archangel Raziel. And on this tablet was engraved all the wisdom of heaven and earth, and yet no one could read it but Solomon the great and the knowledgeable, for Solomon had command of all existing languages... And Solomon saw on the tablet the Shamir worm, which was capable of destroying stones and making them anew, possessing as it did the characteristics of an adze and a graver. Though the Shamir worm was no bigger than a grain of millet, even the toughest of substances yielded to its miraculous properties.

And Solomon said, "I have found what I sought."

And he fell to studying his Tablet of Stone once more and saw that the location of the Shamir worm was known only to Azazel, the prince of devils, and that by the command of the Lord Azazel was shut in a well, which was situated in the desert of Dudael, in the Mountains of Darkness, sealed with stones and plunged into darkness...

And then Solomon summoned Benaiah, son of Jehoiada, to his aid and gave him a chain forged by the spirits of the earth and himself put on his signet ring, which bore the inscription of Shem HaMeforash, considered by Jews to the be the name of the Lord, and also took a fleece and a wineskin full of wine and instructed the spirits of the air to carry all this to the ends of the earth, to the Mountains of Darkness, to the desert of Dudael. And they came to the desert of Dudael and the

Mountains of Darkness and they saw great pillars rising up in the darkness, and between the pillars stood an enormous black stone, which was bound in chains, and under this stone lay the jaws of a well. A writhing flame issued from the well, crimson and green, drawing a radiant veil over the mountains... But Solomon the wise and knowledgeable was not afraid, and he turned the ring with Shem HaMeforash and summoned the spirits of the earth once again, and they shook the earth and toppled the pillars. And Solomon summoned the water spirits, and they unleashed floods of water into the desert of Dudael, and the water poured into the well and extinguished the flame... And the radiance over the Mountains of Darkness was also extinguished, and the people, who saw all this, said, "Look, something strange is happening at the ends of the earth! It must be Azazel breaking free!" And Solomon summoned the spirits of the air, and they removed the chains and moved aside the stone, and the tossing and turning and moaning and groaning of Azazel in his cave could suddenly be heard by all... Then Solomon ordered Benaiah to lower the wineskin full of wine into the cave, and Azazel, tortured by his eternal hunger and his eternal thirst, drank it, became inebriated and fell asleep. And then Solomon again summoned the spirits of the air, the spirits of the water and the spirits of the earth, and all together (for alone they feared Azazel) they bound him with the chain of Power and pulled him to the surface. And thus Azazel appeared before Solomon.

And he awoke from his slumber and began to rage. For, although he had been freed from his cave, the chains of Power burned him more fiercely than the earthly fire, and most of all he was infuriated that he had been tricked by a man, son of man...

"Be calm!" said Solomon then. "The name of thy Master is upon thee! Thy Master is upon thee!"

And Azazel saw the ring with Shem HaMeforash and submitted to Solomon.

And Benaiah took him and led him. And Azazel, fettered

by the chain of Power, was nonetheless immense and fearsome – he brushed his shoulder against a palm tree, and the palm tree crashed to the ground. And when they approached the border of inhabited lands, Azazel brushed against a house and the house crashed to the ground.

"This will not do," said Solomon then. In the name of Shem HaMeforash, I order you to tame your flesh! Grow smaller!"

And Azazel submitted and tamed his flesh, and grew smaller, and became like the sons of men. But he nursed such a grudge against Solomon for this humiliation that he decided to use his cunning to break his bonds and free himself from the chains. And thus they entered the city of Jerusalem, and Azazel was full of forbidden knowledge and Solomon was proud to lead him. And on their way they met a blind man who had lost his way, and Azazel helped him to find his path. They met a drunkard reeling aimlessly, and Azazel put him on his path. They met a wedding procession, loud and merry, and Azazel wept. They passed a fortune teller, who was sitting on the ground performing his art, and Azazel laughed.

Solomon asked him, "Why did you help the blind man?"

"Because," answered Azazel, "the heavens know that he is a great and righteous man, and whosoever should afford him even temporary relief will himself receive relief, and no matter how slight this relief it will save his soul for all eternity."

And then Solomon asked him, "So why did you help the drunkard then?"

"Because," answered Azazel, "he is irremediably impious. So I afforded him a moment of pleasure, to allow him to ruin his sinful soul yet further."

And Solomon asked, "And why did you cry when you saw the wedding procession?"

"Because," answered Azazel, "the groom will not live more than thirty days after the wedding, and the bride will have thirteen years to wait until her husband's brother comes of age."

And Solomon asked, "Why did you laugh at the fortune-teller?"

"Because," answered Azazel, "a chest of the richest treasure lies buried under the exact spot where he sat. And he was telling fortunes, showing off, and yet he could not even tell what lay beneath him..."

"You are wise, Azazel, and cunning," said Solomon then. "However, no more wise and cunning than I. You are strong, but I am stronger."

Then Azazel pulled a reed from the earth, measured four cubits and threw the reed before Solomon. "There," he said, "this is all the space you will take up when you are dead. You wanted to subdue the whole world, but that was not enough for you – you thought to subdue me too!"

"I require nothing from you," said Solomon then, "but for one thing. I wish to build the House of the Lord and for this I have need of the Shamir worm."

"But I do not have the Shamir worm," said Azazel. "I do not have it, it belongs to the prince of the sea, who entrusts it to the mountain cock alone, and the cock has sworn to guard it well."

"And what use is the Shamir to the mountain cock?" asked Solomon.

"He uses it to build cities. He takes the Shamir in his beak to an uninhabited place in the wilderness and he places the Shamir on a cliff, which thereupon clefts in two. The cock throws tree seeds into the crevice, and olive trees grow, and figs, and Lebanese cedar, and people come and settle there. And a settlement soon becomes a city."

"Fine," said King Solomon then. "Then I entreat you by Shem HaMeforash, take me to the nest of this mountain cock."

And Solomon summoned skilled masters from the land of Egypt and ordered them to prepare a dome of opaque glass. And so strong was this dome that even a blow from a hammer could not shatter it. And when Azazel took him to the nest of the mountain cock, Solomon covered the nest with the dome and then he himself took shelter. The mountain cock flew home and found his nest covered. The mountain cock began to wail – oh, oh! He pecked at the dome with his beak, but the glass did not break. Then he took the Shamir worm and placed it upon the glass in order to break it. Solomon jumped out from his hiding-place and threw a clod of earth at the mountain cock. The cock took fright and dropped the Shamir, whereupon Solomon and Azazel picked it up and carried it away.

Thus, using his wits and his cunning and his might and on the advice of Azazel, Solomon took possession of the Shamir worm. And the Shamir quarried the stones for the building of Solomon's Temple, and Solomon kept him on Azazel's advice wrapped in wool in a lead container full of barley bran. And when the mountain cock realized that he had broken the oath he had made to the prince of the sea and could not return the Shamir worm, he hung himself.

And Solomon's Temple grew, with arched windows and trees of pure gold, and pink marble, translucent in the sun, and Lebanese cedar, and jasper, and open halls and secret chambers… And they say that not a single axe or spade or any other instrument for that matter was broken during its construction, for it was built without their use. And they say also that while this temple was being built no one in the land of the Jews fell ill or died. And they say also that light shone through the windows not from the outside but from within, and it lit up all of Israel, for this light was Divine…

And Solomon came to be known as the wisest man on earth, and he was served by the spirits of the sea and the fiery salamanders, and the powers of the earth and the Shamir worm, and even Azazel himself was counted amongst his helpers. And he understood and learned secrets of infinite profundity. His name sounded like thunder amongst rulers, as did his heroic deeds amongst the wise. And he was so just and pure that noblemen and earthly kings sent their sons and daughters to him as servants and maidservants…

And the most beautiful women in the world were

concubines in his harem. And the Queen of Sheba from the city of Kitor, where the trees were planted in the first days of creation and are irrigated by the waters of Eden, where the streets are littered with silver, came to honour him with all her treasures and her servants, and her maidservants of heavenly beauty. And the Pharaoh gave his daughter Bithia to be his wife, accompanied by an impressive dowry including a bed-curtain so covered with semi-precious stones that from the inside it resembled the night sky. And he sent also ninety virgins from the nation of Edom, black as the night, full-breasted and with pink palms, skilled in the art of singing, and ninety virgins from Ephesus, dusky as the twilight and supple as vines, high-breasted and with palms dyed with henna, skilled in the art of dance. And Solomon had ninety-nine wives in total and too many concubines to count, and they all glittered like stars in the sky and delighted with their songs and music and the pleasures of love, and Solomon ruled from his throne by day and by night indulged himself in his harem, and the days flew by like months and the months like years. But still Azazel harboured his desire for revenge, and finally he dreamt up a way to take vengeance on Solomon.

He appeared before Solomon (while he was building his temple, Solomon had kept him by his side) and said, "You are a wise king, and cunning, but you do not know everything. Would you like me to show you something you have never seen before?"

"Such a thing does not exist," answered Solomon.

"Ah, but it does!"

"Then show me!"

Azazel held out his hand towards the land of Tevel, and before Solomon appeared a man with two heads and two pairs of eyes. And Solomon was seized with fear, though he concealed it well and said, "Blessed is the Lord, King of the Universe, who has given me to live to this day! I have heard from Ahitophel that there are people living beneath us, though I did not believe it! For it is a journey of five hundred years to the centre of our world, and between this world and that five hundred more!"

"Be that as it may," said Azazel, "one of them stands before you now!"

Solomon began then to question the man.

"Who are your kith and kin?"

"I am from the family of Adam," answered the two-headed man, "descended from Cain!"

"Where do you live?"

"In the land of Tevel."

"Do you have a sun and a moon?"

"We do."

"Where does your sun rise and where does it set?"

"It rises in the West and sets in the East."

"How do you make your living there?"

"We sow and reap and tend our flocks."

"Do you pray?"

"Yes."

"What do you pray?"

"How numerous and blessed are your deeds, Lord! All that is wise is your work!"

"You are no different from us, it seems," said Solomon. "Except perhaps in appearance. And since that is the case I cannot keep you here by force. Would you like me to return you to your country?"

"I have no greater wish, Your Majesty!"

Solomon then summoned Azazel and said, "Take this man back."

"It is not within my powers to do so," answered Azazel, extremely content that the hour of his revenge was drawing near.

The two-headed man began to weep. Tears flowed from all four of his eyes.

Solomon then said to Benaiah, son of Jehoiada, "Such is always the way with Azazel. He is incapable of bringing anything that he starts to a satisfactory conclusion. Constancy is evidently not in the nature of demons. Go now, my friend, and make this unfortunate man comfortable and give him everything he needs, that he should not yearn for his lost homeland."

So Benaiah, son of Jehoiada, gave orders that the treasure-houses should be opened and the two-headed man given sixty silver sickles, and that he should be allocated a plot of land with vines and a well and an olive grove. The two-headed man pined for a while then settled on the land, built a house and tilled the soil, and became under the patronage of Solomon one of the richest men in the world. He felt at home there, and then he took himself a wife, for although he had two heads he honoured God and lived a moral life, and he had seven sons, and then suddenly he died.

And he left seven sons. Six of them were of normal appearance, but the seventh resembled his father, having two heads and two pairs of eyes. Seeing this, Azazel rubbed his hands with glee and sniggered, for the hour of his vengeance was drawing near.

And an argument arose between the heirs of the stranger from the land of Tevel. Six of them said, "We are seven brothers, therefore the inheritance should be divided into seven equal shares."

The seventh said, "We are not seven but eight, for heads and mouths are what count. And since it is thus, then I have the right to two shares of the inheritance!"

"Let Solomon himself be our judge," said the brothers.

So, they came to Solomon's palace and said, "Your Majesty, we are seven, and our two-headed brother holds that we are eight! How should we divide our inheritance?"

Solomon was presiding in the divan, and Azazel was with him.

"How should I judge them, O Subjects?" asked the King.

"We do not know," they answered, "and cannot tell. For this matter is beyond us."

They decided to put off their decision until the following morning.

That evening Benaiah, son of Jehoiada, appeared before Solomon. "It is an insidious affair thought up by Azazel," he said, "O King of Time! He is stirring up the people! He is going among the viziers talking of how Solomon boasts of his wisdom yet is not so wise, since he is not capable of judging such a simple matter. 'The King's supply of wisdom is spent. And without wisdom what kind of king is he? How will he now judge litigants? There is trouble in the city, for justice is no more!' What should we do, O King of Time?"

"Do not fret, tomorrow I shall give my answer," said Solomon. But his heart skipped a beat.

At the stroke of midnight he went to the temple, prostrated himself and appealed to the Lord, "Sovereign of the world! When you revealed yourself to me in Gavaon, did you not ask, 'What I shall give thee?' I did not ask then for silver or gold, only wisdom did I request, to judge my people fairly. Will you really now refuse me your gift? Will you really permit the triumph of iniquity?"

Thus he spoke, and then he heard the Voice of God, stronger than thunder and softer than a breath of air, "I will enlighten you. Go now, and as the sun rises, leave your palace and approach the first person you meet. Everything will be as I promised – I give you my word."

Solomon was delighted and went back into the palace and slept with a light heart. He rose at first light and went into the field. A light wind was blowing, the birds were singing, and there was not a soul to be seen. Solomon waited. He heard someone singing. The voice was so clear, like the warbling of a heavenly lark! He looked and saw a girl coming towards him along the path – a very young girl, not yet beautiful or shapely... She was dark and frail, like a wild flower. She was carrying a pitcher and singing a song. And that, thought Solomon, is the source of my wisdom?

However, what could he do? He went up to her and bowed, though he didn't introduce himself.

"How may I help you, O Girl?" he asked.

"I do not need your help," the girl replied, "for I have all that I need. I have sheep's cheese, olives and figs, the sky above me and the vines in the garden. Although there is one thing – perhaps you could push the stone from the well for me? For I have no water for my sheep."

Solomon pushed the stone from the well, she filled her pitcher and then Solomon spoke.

"I helped you, O Girl, so help me in return! Will you not help me solve a riddle?"

"My brothers say I am a fool," laughed the girl, "but tell me your riddle! Two heads are better than one!"

"Well, on the subject of heads…" said Solomon. "Once upon a time in the land of Tevel lived a man with two heads…"

And he told her the whole tale.

"Oh!" said the girl. "But it couldn't be simpler!"

"What do you find to be simple in this tale that confounded King Solomon himself, O Girl?" asked Solomon, somewhat irritated.

"I will tell you," said the girl.

And she told him how to solve the problem.

And Solomon understood that what the girl said was true and right.

And he felt a great joy and laughed, and said, "How can I reward you, O Maiden? Shall I shower you with gold or silver? Or with jewels? I will cover you with jewels from your head to your dusty little toes! I will fill the cellars of your house with foreign wines and fragrant resins, amber and frankincense, oil and myrrh."

The girl laughed.

"You must be King Solomon himself to promise me such riches! It is enough that you helped me fill this pitcher with water. Though if you like, you may help me to carry it home!"

And when morning broke it found Solomon the King of Time in the modest abode of the unknown girl. He bowed to her older brothers, who were preparing to drive the sheep to pasture, filled his flask, bade farewell to the wise girl and hurried back to the divan. He had time only to call, "What is your name, wisest of maidens?"

"My father and mother named me Sulamith," answered the girl. And with this answer Solomon went into the palace.

Hordes of people had already gathered in the divan. And the entire army, stirred up by Azazel, stood in the square with spears and shields shining in the sun, to hear how just their just king would turn out to be. And all the townspeople abandoned their affairs and gathered by the palace to hear the decision proclaimed by the heralds. And the noise was so great that a turbulent sea seemed to churn beneath the windows of Solomon's palace. And then Solomon entered the divan and went to his decorated throne, with its lion and its lamb and its eagle and its dove, and ordered water to be boiled and then poured, hot, into a narrow-necked pitcher with a curved spout.

Water was boiled, poured into a pitcher and brought to the divan.

Then Solomon again ordered the two-headed man and his one-headed brothers to be brought before him.

They were brought before him.

"Now," said Solomon, "we will perform an experiment. If one of this man's heads can perceive and feel what is happening to his other head, then he should be counted as one man. If not, then he is two separate individuals. And now pour water onto one of his heads!"

They took the pitcher and poured a little water onto the crown of the left head.

"Your Majesty! Your Majesty!" cried both heads at once. "We are in agony! We are dying!"

"He should be granted but one share of the inheritance," said King Solomon then, "by all that is just and fair, for he is but one and the same man."

And when the verdict was announced, the courtiers in the divan rejoiced and Solomon's army began to beat their spears on their shields, thus expressing their joy, and the people in the palace square cried, "Solomon, the King of All Peoples, is great indeed!"

And everyone was full of praise for King Solomon's wisdom.

Only Azazel did not rejoice.

"Someone must have told you the answer," he said.

"My Lord was with me," replied Solomon.

And at noon he gathered sumptuous gifts and five vehicles laden with oil and myrrh, and sixty silver sickles and five white oxen with golden horns, and he mounted his finest steed with its gold saddlecloth and silver harness and went at the head of the procession to the house of Sulamith's father and mother. And when Sulamith saw all of this she clasped her hands together and ran into the house in confusion. But the women of his retinue followed her inside and dressed her in the finest silks and anointed her with scented oils and braided her hair and brought her out and stood her before Solomon. And Solomon took her hand and presented her to the people. And she stood confused, radiant as a rose of Sharon, pure and fragrant as a lily of the valley... And Solomon seated her in a carriage under a scarlet canopy and ordered silver trumpets to sound and rose petals to be scattered before her, and thus she was conveyed to the palace, where she became the hundredth wife of King Solomon, the wisest and most beloved. And everyone was glad, and they celebrated for three days and three nights, and the square in front of the palace was strewn with grain and rose petals, and only Azazel did not rejoice.

And Solomon was so joyous and proud that in his joy he said to Azazel, "So, pray tell, how exactly are you stronger than men?"

And Azazel answered, "Release me from my chains and give me your ring, then I shall be able to show you how we are stronger than men."

So Solomon removed the chains from him and gave him his ring. And Azazel seized Solomon and swallowed him whole. And he came to rest with one wing touching earth and the other in heaven, and then he spat Solomon out and took him and threw him a distance of four hundred miles.

And Azazel said, "That is for the mountain cock!"

And Solomon disappeared, for Azazel had condemned him to wander the lands of man in the times of the Lord. And thus was Solomon punished for his arrogance, for contriving to build the Temple of the Lord without use of human hands but by employing the services of a demon, whom he subjugated with his cunning and deceit. Solomon was forced to wander without knowledge of time or place until he was reduced to the status of a child and comprehended true wisdom rather than false, until the whole world became a temple to him…

And what of Azazel? Azazel assumed the appearance of Solomon, but fearing to ascend the Throne, which would accept Solomon alone, he spent all his days and nights languishing in the harem. And, being a demon, he gratified the queens and concubines so skilfully that they merely marvelled and rejoiced that the King had finally come to prefer the pleasures of the harem to affairs of state. Only Sulamith the Wise withdrew to her chambers, claiming to be sick, for something about this self-proclaimed king seemed strange to her. However, for the time being she did not speak a word of her suspicions.

And what of Solomon? When he came to, he found himself in the land of Egypt, the land of his father-in-law the Pharaoh, and he resolved to go to court to ask for help. However the guard would not let him cross the threshold.

"I," said Solomon, "was King of all Israel and you good-for-nothings dare to refuse me an audience with my father-in-law?"

"King Solomon," they answered, "sits to this day on his throne in Jerusalem."

Then Solomon understood that Azazel had assumed his appearance and began to weep bitterly.

He wept for his forfeited kingdom and for his former power,

but most of all he wept because he missed the beautiful Sulamith, whom he had come to love more than life itself.

And he trudged about the earth and lamented, "What use are man's earthly labours? Is this to be my fate, after all my labours? I was King of all Israel, but today I am king of my staff alone!"

And King Solomon wandered across lands and among peoples until he lost count of them all. And he helped people with his wise counsel and consoled them with parables, and composed songs for weddings and laments for funerals, and his word was always appropriate and timely. And for this the people gave him alms and he lived on these alms alone, which is how he earned his nickname 'Koheleth,' meaning 'preacher.'

And Solomon came to possess great wisdom, greater than that of any other king. And that is what happened to King Solomon.

And what of Azazel?

Azazel continued to take his pleasure in the palace, drinking expensive wines and eating rich victuals, and he dissolved the divan and did not take counsel, and state affairs were abandoned and there were no more fair trials. And the people were troubled, for he had set two golden calves in Bethel and Dan and instead of converting his wives to the true faith he himself began to worship their idols, and he went to his wives and concubines at all hours of the day and night, and he did not observe the Sabbath or any other holy days, and the people began to worry and in the land of Israel there grew a great discord.

And then Sulamith the Wise summoned Benaiah, son of Jehoiada, and said to him, "I cannot help but wonder whether Solomon reigns truly over Israel these days. Does he sit upon the throne?"

"No," said Benaiah, "he does not sit upon the throne."

"Does he judge fairly?"

"No," said Benaiah, "he does not judge fairly."

"Does he observe the Sabbath?"

"No," said Benaiah, "he does not observe the Sabbath."

"Then it is not King Solomon," said Sulamith the Wise.

And Benaiah exclaimed in horror, "Who then is reigning in place of the King?"

"I do not know and cannot imagine," answered Sulamith, "for he has not come unto me since our wedding night. But I will ask the other queens and concubines, for it is time to shed some light on this dark matter."

And then Sulamith went to the wives and concubines, bringing them sweets and ointments, perfumed oils and adornments, and she said, "My heart is troubled, for it is already a year now since I have seen the King, my lord and master. What ails him? Has he taken ill?"

"No," answered the wives (and in the depths of their souls they were glad that Solomon had forgotten Sulamith the Wise and did not go to her any more), "our master is hale and hearty and comes to us every night and every day!"

"And on the Sabbath?" asked Sulamith the Wise.

"And on the Sabbath," answered the wives. "And he expends such efforts in bed as he has not expended since his youth, may God keep him so! And if he does not come unto you, then it is because he no longer loves you, for you are dark of face and slight of hips, and such a simple little thing!"

"Oh, oh!" said Sulamith the Wise then. "I see I deserve to have fallen out of favour with the king! But tell me, girls, has the king changed at all? Is his face full of joy? Does he look wise?"

"He looks good to us," answered the wives.

"Are his robes splendid? Are his silks luxurious?"

"As never before," answered the wives.

"And pray tell this simple girl, does he still wear the bracelet around his ankle that I gave him as a token of our love? For I wove it from my own braids!"

"We do not know and cannot tell," laughed the wives, "for he does not remove his shoes."

"What, not at all?" asked Sulamith.

"And what does it matter that he does not?" laughed the wives.

"Ah, I knew it!" said Sulamith the Wise, and she bowed and left.

And she sent again for Benaiah, son of Jehoiada, and said, "I have found out everything from those clucking hens. It is not King Solomon who reigns over Israel at this time, no, not at all, but the demon Azazel, since he does not remove his shoes when he goes to the women, firstly because demons are not like people and they do everything that is offensive to people and pervert customs and shake foundations, and secondly because he hides his feet, which despite his power to change his appearance are a characteristic beyond his control. I tell you, he has the hooves of a goat!"

"Oh, oh!" cried Benaiah then. "What shall we do?"

"Leave it to me," said Sulamith the Wise.

And so she summoned slave-girls and eunuchs, cooks and musicians, and ordered them to put on a feast and prepare all kinds of fish and fowl, everything that swims and flies and runs on four legs, and to bring the finest wines and to light fragrant censers, and she sent it all to the fake king and ordered a message to be relayed thus: your Sulamith pines for your caress, she wishes to arrange a feast so that you, O Luminary of the World, should be delighted and your spirits lifted. As the moon rises, pray show your servant the great favour of coming to her chambers, for she awaits you there...

And Azazel was delighted, for until this time Sulamith the Wise had kept herself from him. So he dressed himself in his most splendid royal attire and, as soon as the moon rose, proceeded joyfully and with pleasurable anticipation to the chambers of the wife of Solomon. And he beheld the scented smoke and radiant jewels, and Sulamith the Wise, in bright apparel and with jingling bracelets, received him with a bow at the entrance.

And Sulamith rested her eyes upon him and saw that he

did indeed resemble her beloved Solomon in every way, but for that he did not remove his shoes from his feet. But she hid her thoughts and led him to her chambers, and she smiled at him tenderly and seated him on cushions and sat down beside him.

And he leaned towards her, wishing to embrace her, but she moved away and said, "First delight yourself with wine and refresh yourself with apples, O Beloved of Mine, for you must be exhausted from love!" And she herself brought to him all manner of dishes, seasoned with fragrant herbs and intoxicating spices, and sweet wine and bitter beer, and Azazel drank and was sated and desired Sulamith more than before. But she again leaned away from his embraces and said, "Delight your ear with music and your eyes with dancing, my lord and master!" And she clapped her hands together and summoned the musicians and singers and dancers and they sang love songs, and their bracelets jingled and their bodies writhed, and the flame of desire within Azazel the Insidious burned brighter than ever before. And again he threw himself upon Sulamith the Wise, wishing to embrace her, but she sighed and moved away and began to weep bitter tears, saying, "You do not love me and I am nursing a grievance against you."

"What is the cause of your grievance?" asked Azazel.

"Many times have I implored you to place a ring on my finger, yet each time you turn away and leave, and not once have you granted me my wish!"

"I will do anything your heart desires!" exclaimed Azazel, who was by now burning with ardour.

"Then let me wear that ring," said Sulamith the Wise. "For I have sworn to myself that you will not lie with me until that ring is on my finger."

"You women are fools," said Azazel then, "for even when you have everything, you still want more!"

However, he removed the ring with Shem HaMeforash and placed it on Sulamith's finger.

And then Sulamith clapped her hands together and guards ran in and she pointed at Azazel and cried, "Seize him!"

"What are you doing, you madwoman?" exclaimed the demon. "I am Solomon, your beloved sovereign!"

"I do not know where my beloved sovereign is now and cannot tell," answered Sulamith. "However, you are not he but a vile demon. And already twelve moons have passed since you have begun to stir up trouble and dishonour the wives of Solomon, failing to observe the Sabbath and passing unfair judgments. And if you do not believe me, take off his shoes!"

And then Azazel cried out, "Return my ring, O Crafty Woman!"

However, the ring could not be taken by force but given up by goodwill alone, and when Sulamith heard this she laughed and said, "So this is all your demonic cunning is worth! How then are you greater than us? You thought to deceive a woman but were deceived by her instead! You will not have this ring, or the King's power or throne, and from this moment forth you will crawl in the dirt and be condemned to exist only in darkness, which is all that you deserve."

And they seized Azazel and dragged off his boots, and it was true – he had the hooves of a goat.

And the people cried, "Destroy him!"

But Azazel distracted them and disappeared while their eyes were averted, and from that day forth Solomon never saw him again, although they do say that he continues to wander the earth in various guises, passing unfair judgments and sowing discord and provoking the people.

And that is what happened to Azazel.

And the wise men of Israel, courtiers and judges, came to Sulamith and bowed before her and said, "You drove out the demon, the false king, now bring back our beloved king, the true king!"

"That is not within my powers," said Sulamith. "However, I believe that he will come back to us when the time is right, and we must bide our time and be prepared."

"What are you saying?" they exclaimed then. "You have

in your possession Shem HaMeforash, so order him to bring our King Solomon back to us."

"That will not be," answered Sulamith, "for it has been revealed to me that it is within the power of Solomon and his descendants alone to control Shem HaMeforash and give orders to him, and he is mine only for safe-keeping."

"Then give Shem HaMeforash to us," cried the high officials, "and we will decide what to do with him."

"That will not be," answered Sulamith, "for on taking him you will fall prey to temptation and will become no better than Azazel, the crafty, pleasure-seeking demon."

And the high officials left with nothing, for, as has already been said, Shem HaMeforash could not be taken by force but given up by goodwill alone. And Sulamith the Wise retired to her chambers and gave orders not to be disturbed until her master Solomon, the true king, should return.

And that is what happened to Sulamith the Wise.

And Solomon wandered the earth and consoled with his parables and aided with his counsel and chastised the impious and gladdened the wise, and he came to know many new lands and strange and wonderful customs. And he journeyed as far as the gates of Eden, whence flowed the river of life, and the Mountains of Darkness and the gates to the Underworld, and he heard the songs of angels and the gnashing of demons' teeth and saw salamanders cavorting in the fire and the Leviathan playing in the seas.

But he pined more and more for the land of Israel and for Sulamith the Wise, and when he woke up one day in a far-off land he looked at his staff and saw that it had begun to turn green and flower, like a rose-bush. "My time has come," said Solomon. And he bent his steps toward the land of Israel. But his path was so long that another twelve moons passed before he found himself at home. And when he arrived, he walked about the blessed dry red earth of Israel, saying, "I am your king, Solomon, I have returned from my exile!" And some believed him, though others did not.

As he walked past one house, the owner of the house – a rich man – came out to meet him, and he bowed and said, "Your Majesty the King! Deign to enter my abode and show me your charity today." And the man ordered Solomon to be taken to his upper chambers and that roast calf and other fine dishes be brought to the table, and when Solomon gladly sat down to eat he began to ask, "So is this how you ate when you were king?"

And Solomon began to weep and stood up and left, saying, "See how everyone now exults over me..." And weeping thus he passed a pauper's shack, and when the pauper saw him he ran out to meet him, saying, "Your Majesty the King! I beg you to do me the great honour of stepping into my humble abode!"

"Do you invite me in purely with the intention of mocking my misfortune?" asked Solomon.

"Your Majesty," answered the pauper, "I can offer you neither sumptuous victuals nor upper chambers, but all that I have I am ready to give to you." And he asked him into his shack and washed his feet and brought to the table all that he had in the house (wild garlic and bitter herbs), and while Solomon ate he consoled him. "You are blessed by the Almighty," said the pauper, "and he will return your kingdom to you, for as God punishes so he forgives. Exile cannot diminish the dignity of a king."

And Solomon was delighted and went to his palace and ordered his advisers to be summoned. But seeing his rags and his staff, the guards decided that he was a madman who had convinced himself he was king. Nonetheless, remembering the instructions of Benaiah, son of Jehoiada, they took him before the advisers in the divan, who did not recognize him and asked, "Who are you?"

"I am King Solomon, your master," he answered.

"This old man is completely mad," said the advisers.

And then Benaiah, son of Jehoiada, intervened and asked, "And do you know such-and-such?"

And Solomon was able to answer all their questions coherently and intelligently and struck his questioners with his great wisdom.

Then they asked him once more, "Who are you?"

"I told you, I am King Solomon, your master," answered Solomon again.

"This is most odd," said the wise elders, "for madmen do not usually display such single-minded lunacy. But, since you claim to be king, let us see if your Throne will accept you."

And they led Solomon to the throne room, and no sooner had he placed his foot on the first step than the sculptures were delighted and the lion and the lamb reached out their paws so that Solomon could lean on them and ascend the throne. And the silver turtle-dove flew down from on high and placed a crown on the king's head, and everyone exclaimed, "Indeed, our king has returned!"

And Benaiah, son of Jehoiada, exclaimed, "Indeed it is so!"

And trumpets sounded in the square, and Solomon arrayed himself in his king's attire and spent the whole day on his Throne and passed righteous and fair judgments. And he went to the temple and offered up a prayer to the Lord for his happy return, and the news spread throughout the land of Israel that King Solomon had returned, and his enemies were discomfited and his friends were glad. And Solomon called for Benaiah the Loyal and asked, "What has happened here in my absence?"

"You would have been absent for all eternity, O King of Time," answered Benaiah the Loyal, "were it not for your beloved wife Sulamith, for Azazel deceived everyone but her alone."

And then Solomon ordered Sulamith the Wise to be brought before him, and when she arrayed herself in her finest attire and appeared, escorted by her maidservants, and bowed before the king, Solomon exclaimed, "Here is my beloved!

My dove in the cliff's ravine, sheltered by the crag! Show me your face, let me hear your voice, for your voice is sweet and your face most pleasant. Oh, garden-dweller! My friends are listening for your voice, let me hear it!"

And Sulamith answered, "Here is my beloved! Sixty strong men about him, from among the strongest men of Israel! Behold, daughters of Zion, King Solomon in his crown! His lips are sweet and he is kindness itself! This is the man I love and my friend, daughters of Jerusalem!"

And everyone exclaimed, "He is here, the true king, and here is his true queen!"

And Solomon ran down from his throne and bowed before Sulamith, and she said, "Here is your signet ring, I have kept it safe for you! Place me like a stamp upon your heart and like a signet ring on your hand, for my love is as strong as death..."

So said Sulamith, and Solomon placed the ring on his finger and began to weep, and he led Sulamith to her chambers and lavished her with great honour and sent away his other foolish wives, for they were not able to tell true from false. And from that day forth Solomon and Sulamith lived together in peace and joy, until they were visited by the destroyer of delight and the divider of unions. And that is what happened to Solomon and Sulamith. However, they do say that whenever the hot wind blew from the desert Solomon grew anxious and disquietude entered his heart, and he secretly turned the ring and said Shem HaMeforash and travelled body and soul to strange realms, where he wandered under a strange sky and foreign stars, and taught the foolish and enlightened the wise and helped people with his counsel and consoled with his parables, for he understood that no land or time exists where man is without need of counsel and consolation, even five hundred years away... And they also say that his conscience gnawed at him on account of the poor mountain cock, innocently ruined by the incitement of Azazel, and that from that time on he loved all creatures of the fields and forests and found a common language with all the birds in the sky and all the animals in their lairs, and all the Lord's creatures served him, for the Lord's mercy is great and his goodness immeasurable. For the Lord knows that no man is without sin, though he may be wise, and no man is irreproachable, though he may be repentant, and if one man falls another will help him to his feet, and this is what distinguishes true people from demons and creatures of the night. Although they say that even creatures of the night know love and repentance, but that is another story, O Master!

Givi didn't like the wind. It was somehow irregular and was blowing with a blind constancy, as if a hidden mechanical fan were operating at the base of the cliffs.

The setting sun was painting the basalt a deep crimson hue, and the long shadows cast by the crags divided the ground up into boxes with slightly tapering sides, making it look like a giant chessboard. If there really are djinns here, thought Givi, then they have a distinctly warped sense of humour.

Shenderovich's main attack force stopped, throwing up a cloud of sand.

Prancing about on Al-Bagum and with his hand shielding his eyes, Shenderovich surveyed the surrounding countryside.

Enviously, Givi surveyed Shenderovich. Misha looked magnificent.

How does he manage to look so dashing, sighed Givi to himself. The way he's sitting up on his camel, he looks... like he was born in the saddle! And that short battle cloak lies so beautifully on his shoulders. And what a physique! The physique of a king!

Givi himself was fidgeting about on his mule – he hadn't dared risk climbing up onto a hot-blooded battle steed. Which, on the whole, was nothing to be proud of. Of the whole main attack force, the only person apart from Givi riding a mule was Duban. But it was alright for him as he was an old man. Masroor over there, who had made almost a complete recovery from the pernicious influence of the succubus, was prancing about on a stallion, would you believe it! With fire in its belly! And strong pasterns, and everything…

Maybe Misha had been right to isolate Alka. Misha knew what he was doing.

However, as Givi came to think of it, Masroor did look rather pale and worried. He was also surveying his surroundings, not quite so picturesquely as Shenderovich but still quite professionally. His stallion did several nervous pirouettes in place and then cantered up to Al-Bagum. Al-Bagum reacted by sticking out a contemptuous lip.

"Are you sure you know what you are doing, O Master?" Masroor inquired uneasily. "The sun is just on the point of setting!"

"Good!" answered Shenderovich cheerfully. "We'll lure them out, those vermin!"

"But they will be immeasurably stronger than us in the darkness!"

"Nobody," answered Shenderovich coldly, "can be stronger than the King of Time."

Givi sighed and turned to Duban.

"Are these djinns really afraid of sunlight?"

"Yes, O Vizier," Duban responded gloomily. He was not very enthusiastic about his role as scientific advisor and would have preferred to remain in the rearguard. "As soon as the first rays of the morning sun break through, the angels are permitted by the Almighty to fire their blazing arrows at the damned! That is why they take cover in the darkness of caves, from where they dare to attack passing caravans, for the sun does not penetrate into the heart of the Mountains of Darkness…"

"I see!" said Givi and, spurring his mule with his heels, he galloped up to Shenderovich.

Although to say he galloped is probably something of an exaggeration – it was more like a trot.

"Misha," he said, craning his neck to look Shenderovich in the eye, "are you sure you've picked the right time of day?"

Shenderovich shrugged his cloaked shoulders.

"You are trembling again, O Vizier of Mine," he said, sounding bored. "Relax! Just look at the army I've got! A thousand men have come out to fight a few pathetic djinns. Eagles! Lions! And not one of them, you will notice, is scared."

"But I'm not an eagle," said Givi pitifully.

Shenderovich shrugged again. The cloak draped around his regal figure caught in the wind, flapping its wings like a gigantic bird. Shenderovich ripped off the diamond clasp in irritation and threw the expensive silk under Al-Bagum's hooves.

The cliffs were deserted. Even the flies seemed to have forsaken them. The wind was howling monotonously through the crevices. The main attack force was frozen some distance behind Shenderovich in battle formation, headed by the enthusiastic emir.

Givi looked around. The army bristled with spears. The cavalry was prancing about, holding their hot-blooded steeds in check, the shields of the foot soldiers were shining brightly, and narrow banners were fluttering... It was all very impressive.

"Misha," Givi began warily, "uh... how are they all going to fit into the ravine? They won't be able to fully deploy!"

"Listen, my friend," Shenderovich said patronisingly, "if you don't know anything about the high art of war then you should keep your stupid questions to yourself! They're not going into the ravine, OK?"

He shielded his eyes once more with his royal hand and proudly surveyed the scene. The entrance to the ravine was a gaping black hole, like the neck of an enormous bottle. Everyone was waiting, full of silent respect.

"Right, then," Shenderovich finally concluded. "The King of Time will personally assume the hardest part of the task, for I myself will go deep into the cliffs. We'll try to lure these creatures out. If they are what you say, then the sunlight will be fatal to them. If they are creatures of flesh and blood, on the other hand, then the arrows of my brave men will be equally fatal. And that, Givi my friend, is the proposed tactical plan!"

"Well you'd better get on with it, Misha," said Givi despondently. "The sun's about to set…"

"I am getting on with it," Shenderovich shrugged, his eyes on the waiting army. "I just need some volunteers. Two dozen, at least, O Masroor!"

"I doubt you will get many volunteers, O Master," remarked Duban. "Who wants to be eaten alive by a djinn?"

"What's a volunteer," mused Shenderovich absent-mindedly, "but a man with another standing over him, armed with a bow and a strong arrow…"

Givi gave another involuntary shiver but then forced himself to straighten his shoulders and take a deep breath, filling his lungs. When Misha was in this kind of mood, it was better not to argue!

"It does not surprise me that you, O Leader of the Army, should be well versed in all the tricks of war," said Duban, warily. "However, allow me to point out that in Iram we are accustomed to treating evil spirits with respect. And, if I may be so bold as to assure you, we fear them no less than we fear strong arrows."

"Appeal to their sense of honour, Misha," Givi risked intervening.

"OK, fine!" Shenderovich waved his hand. "Tell your men, O Masroor, that anyone who follows me will be made commander of a battalion and will receive four slave-girls, two white slaves, twenty silver sickles and a horse from my stables, which he may choose himself."

"I hear and obey, O Father of the People," Masroor answered morosely. "However, allow me to point out…"

"And tell your commanders that they will be replaced by brave and worthy men! So go now and return with a detachment of courageous men. I wouldn't get too hung up on the exact number, though, for the paths through the cliffs are narrow…"

"I hear and obey," Masroor repeated, placing his hand to

his forehead. Then he swung his horse about and galloped towards the army of bristling spears.

Givi followed him longingly with his eyes. The emir's black-maned Arabian with its big lips and small head, its powerful pasterns and fiery eyes, gobbled up the desert with its gigantic stride. Givi dug his heels once more into his mule, which had bashfully turned away from the fissures in the cliffs and was attempting to put them altogether behind it and gallop back to where it had come from.

"Misha," Givi began again, "are you sure you haven't, uh, wrapped yourself too tightly in the, um…. cloak of conviction? We are talking about djinns, here, you know…"

"You think the King of Time is bothered about a few evil spirits?" Shenderovich waved his hand dismissively.

"But are you sure you're the King of Time?"

"Of course," said Shenderovich coldly.

"And do the djinns know that?"

Shenderovich's eyes flashed. Then he glanced back at Duban, beckoned Givi with his finger, leaned down from his saddle and began to speak quietly.

"Listen here, you romantic! You don't actually believe those fairy stories, do you? What djinns? It's just a couple of weirdos camped out in the cliffs, trying to scare people with their pyrotechnics. Remember that Sharrik-Tarrik chap? Well, some of his mates have just found themselves a comfortable hiding-place, that's all…"

"Nobody, Misha," Givi said firmly, "nobody in Iram has ever said that Sharr al-Tarik is a djinn! That he's a bastard, yes, and a villain. But a djinn? No. I assure you, they've got a pretty good idea round here of who's a djinn and who isn't."

"Listen," hissed Shenderovich through his clenched teeth, "can you remember what that bloke said about the ghouls? If you believe in them, they exist, and if you don't, they don't… A very sound approach by the way! You worry too much, Givi, that's your problem. Right, gather up the reins of your fate and let's go. Look, Masroor's already rounded up the volunteers! Strong men, horsemen of the night, sounding the reveille – that's just what we need! For there is no better weapon against evil spirits than cold steel in powerful hands... Come on, O Duban, move!"

"I would prefer to remain here," said Duban with as much dignity as he could muster.

"Do you dare to contradict me?" Shenderovich asked in surprise. "The King of Time? Have no fear, O Astronomer! Everything will be fine! We will lure them out and that will be an end to it!"

"Forgive me my impertinent words, O Master, but your humble servant ventures to express a doubt... Just one tiny doubt... From what I know of djinns, they are immeasurably stronger on their own territory and destroy anyone who dares to disturb them there."

"In that case," said Shenderovich with annoyance, "if they destroy the witnesses and appear only in the dark how do you know that they are actually djinns?"

"But who or what else could they be, O Master?" Duban asked in surprise.

Shenderovich signalled to Masroor who went to the head of the detachment, holding back his agitated stallion with a firm hand.

Givi cast a sidelong glance at the astrologer. He seemed to be scrutinising Shenderovich with detached academic interest. Ekh, thought Givi, he's desperate for him to slip up...

Shenderovich and the emir rode into the opening in the cliffs side by side. Givi followed them reluctantly, steering his mule so that its nose was almost touching Al-Bagum's backside. The setting sun still burned behind them, but the caravan path, winding and twisting its way into the ravine, vanished into darkness. Deep shadows dyed the narrow battle banner black.

Givi could hear behind him the muffled whispers of the archers and the lancers. They were not happy.

Something crunched underfoot. Givi squinted down carefully, fully expecting to see human bones worn white by the sand, but his mule had simply trodden on a decorated narrow-necked pitcher. A thick liquid with a sharp smell was trickling out of the pitcher. The mule sneezed, contemptuously wrinkling its lip.

"Ah-chooooo!!!" went the echo…

"In there," said Masroor, his voice hoarse with suppressed fear. "That's where the accursed are hiding!"

"Hmmm," muttered Shenderovich eyeing the naked, brooding cliffs. "I wonder what they eat in there? What do they live on?"

"Djinns?" Masroor asked in surprise. "What do they eat?"

"They must feed from the caravans… They eat people, right, Duban? Or not?"

Givi sniffed cautiously. He couldn't detect any trace of organic particles, which would inevitably have accompanied any human habitation. All he could smell, for some reason, was rusty metal. A hot wind was blowing from the crevice with immutable constancy, giving the impression that there was an enormous oven on full blast somewhere inside, with rusty griddles…

"An infuriated ifrit could eat a man whole," explained Duban. "However, more out of pleasure than of need. I imagine they feed on fine matter, like the flame coming out of the abyss…"

"There's an abyss here?" whispered Givi.

"Oh, yes," answered Duban, matter-of-factly. "Over there, behind the wall…"

"With flames coming out of it?"

"Oh, yes…" Duban's voice even bore traces of something like pride in such an impressive abyss.

"And what's inside?"

"It cannot be named."

"And is that where we are supposed to be going?"

The astronomer shot Givi a piercing look from under his shaggy eyebrows.

"If that was where we were supposed to be going," he said, "then were our King of Time as tall as a tower and as strong as a hundred ifrits I would almost certainly refuse to follow him, even if he threatened me with death for my insubordination. No, O Vizier, there are long, blind tunnels that lead to the very heart of the mountains. Although the caravan path does pass dark and dangerous places, it merely brushes against them..."

"Ahh," said Givi. Although Duban's words had been intended to calm him down they had had the opposite effect.

Al-Bagum suddenly snorted and shied backwards.

"Aha!" said Shenderovich.

A thick, violet shadow cut across their path so sharply that the path seemed to dissolve suddenly into an inky puddle. The cliffs closed up above their heads, forming a vault... Ahead there was nothing but impenetrable darkness, hinting at dark deeds and a dark and endless night...

Shenderovich raised himself slightly in his saddle, turning his royal head from side to side.

"Hey!" he cried, using his hands as a mouthpiece. "Come out whoever you are! Or I'm coming to get you!"

"Misha," ventured Givi. "Maybe you shouldn't shout at them like that? We're not dealing with a succubus now, and there are more of them!"

"How else are we going to get them to come out?" Shenderovich said haughtily. "Hey, you in there! You snakes! Your King is here!"

"HA-HA," came the resonant response from the darkness.

The troops behind Givi started whispering amongst themselves and the horses wheezed, flattened their ears, and rolled their eyes.

"Master," began the emir uncertainly.

"Everything is now in the hands of all-powerful fate," remarked Duban resignedly, apparently having lost the capacity for fear.

The troops started howling.

Several ghostly figures appeared out of the darkness.

At first Givi thought they were just violet spots, the kind you get in front of your eyes when you look into the dark for too long. Then, to his horror, the shapeless blotches became more defined – gigantic, swelling arms and legs and enormous heads – and a greenish, purplish, whitish light swirled inside the ghostly bodies, like a chemistry experiment in a glass beaker.

Al-Bagum, who was apparently quite sensitive to supernatural phenomena, began to bellow as if she had already been slain.

"Mish-a," whispered Givi.

"Shhh-a!" answered the cave.

"Bloody hell!" gasped Shenderovich.

The djinns were condensing before their very eyes. Their empty faces had fiery bubbles for eyes, their mouths opened, their monstrous hands grew fingers, then nails...

"Misha, do something!"

The receding clatter of hundreds of hooves rang out behind them... Givi couldn't begin to imagine by what miracle the riders had managed to turn their horses in the narrow ravine. Al-Bagum grunted and bumped blindly into the walls. Givi's mule was trying in vain to stand on its hind legs and Duban's mule hung its ears sorrowfully, clearly having resigned itself along with its master to the inevitable... Only Masroor was keeping his stallion in check with a firm hand, though flecks of foam were flying from its bit...

"Misha, you said they don't exist if you don't believe in them!"

"Well, I believe in them now!" yelled Shenderovich, turning Al-Bagum with a kick.

The cliffs flashed past as if they were being carried along on a flood tide. Givi was flying along, his shoulders hunched up around his ears. Behind him he could hear heavy steps and a low sighing.

Ahead, he caught fleeting glimpses of Shenderovich's manly back.

"Come on! Come on!" cried Shenderovich being jolted into the air by Al-Bagum's humps. "Come on! We need to get them outside…"

"Misha!" yelled Givi, "I'm begging you! Faster!"

"Just do something if you really are Zul-Qarnayn!" Masroor began to wail disrespectfully. "Or they'll devour us, bones and all!"

"The sun!" shouted Shenderovich as he was vigorously thrown back into the saddle. "The sun will destroy them! Right, astronomer?"

Silence.

"Where's Duban? Where's that bastard gone?"

"OOO-WOOO!!!" howled the djinns behind them, as a blast of burning air hit Givi's back.

A blurry white patch was barely visible up ahead. Sensing salvation, Al-Bagum had put on speed and was now tearing along at a full gallop, the sparks from her hooves blinding in the darkness. Givi's mule was following suit.

"Ahead, O Fearless Ones!" cried the emir, spurring on his stallion and waving his curved sabre.

Givi had the impression that he had drawn his sabre specifically with a view to settling his score with Shenderovich.

Bloody hell, he thought in despair, if the djinns don't get us this lot will…

The light of the setting sun was viscous like white honey… They burst out of the ravine, blinded by the whirling cloud of sand thrown up by the departing detachment of volunteers. The sudden threat of the sun's rays brought the djinns up short. Phosphorescing weakly, they clustered at the mouth of the cave.

"Well?" breathed the emir pressing himself to his horse's withers.

"Well what?" Shenderovich repeated warily.

"For some reason they don't seem to want to be destroyed!"

"Mmm," agreed Shenderovich. "They're not going anywhere, are they? Well, no big deal. At least they won't come any closer…"

He gestured majestically towards the sun.

"Are you absolutely sure about that?" asked the emir, caressing the hilt of his sabre. "And do you plan to detain them for long, O Tail of a Donkey?"

"Um…" Shenderovich hesitated, visibly deflating by the minute, like a balloon with a slow puncture.

The crimson disk of the sun was already bisected by the horizon. The combination of the cloudless sky and the clouds of sand raised by the fleeing army promised an exceptionally beautiful sunset.

"How dare you speak to the King like that, you cowardly jackal!" Givi erupted.

"If he really is the King…" remarked the emir.

"I wasn't aware," remarked Givi, "that you had any doubts on the subject, O Masroor!"

"Well, I wasn't aware that he was going to bury us up to our necks in calamity," answered the emir. He had a point. "But if I am to die at the hands of an ifrit, then I assure you that the one responsible for it will die by my hand first…"

Givi looked around. The djinns were swimming in mid-air in front of the black mouth of the cave, in complete defiance of the laws of gravity. It was actually rather beautiful.

"Look!" cried the emir. "Another one!"

Something was rising up out of the sand and taking human form right before their eyes. The emir's sabre flashed in his hand, sliced through the air with a whistle and flew towards it. It was deflected by a valiant warrior just in time – the falling sand had revealed the stars and moons of the astrologer's crumpled cloak.

"For heaven's sake," said the emir wearily. "May the

heavens deprive you of sleep and peace, O Duban! What were you doing hiding in the sand like that?"

"What do you think I was doing, O Masroor?" answered Duban, brushing himself down and spitting out sand. "That damned creature shot out from beneath me like a fatal arrow fired at its target! I see our position is rather lamentable, O Remaining Ones..."

Shenderovich let out a protracted sigh.

"Well, what would you do if you were in my shoes, O Duban?" he asked.

"I cannot answer that, for I am not in your shoes," answered the astronomer, "am I? Although right at this moment we are certainly in the same boat – the jaws of an ifrit do not distinguish between a fake king and a genuine astrologer."

"Misha, don't let him insult you like that. Do something!"

The sun was disappearing over the horizon, and Givi couldn't help thinking that it seemed to be doing so far more quickly than usual. It hovered over the edge of the earth, sprawled across the fiery anvil of the horizon, then contracted to a tiny blinding dot, which seemed to Givi to be mockingly winking goodbye.

"But what?" Shenderovich asked despairingly.

As the sun disappeared and the shadow from the cliff lengthened, the giant bubbles began to fill with independent phosphoric light. They emerged slowly and lazily from the darkness, as if testing the air. So that's what djinns look like, Givi thought despondently to himself as he watched their movements. I thought they would be different, somehow...

"Order them to leave! What are you waiting for?"

"Get out of here!" yelled Shenderovich, flapping his hands at them, as if trying to scare off a flock of tiresome birds. "Go on, pshht! Go away, you foul creatures!"

"OOO-WOOO!" answered the djinns.

"Not like that!" cried Givi, reining in his mule and turning on the spot. "You've got to do it properly. You're the King, aren't you? Stay still, you quivering creature!"

To his surprise his mule stopped short and blinked at him in astonishment.

"Hang on," muttered Givi as he turned the ring mechanically on his finger, "that's not the way to do it! Say... how did those damned Brothers get rid of the demon... Ah, I've got it! Now I say to you, go, and peace..."

"GO!" bellowed Shenderovich.

"...and peace be with you..."

"AND PEACE BE WITH YOU!"

"...in your domains and abodes – and may there be peace between you and me, until I summon you once more..."

"ONCE MORE!"

"...by word or desire!"

The djinns began to oscillate, looking even more like bubbles caught in the wind.

"DESIRE!"

"...for I am your King and Master from the beginning of time to this very day..."

"THIS VERY DAY!"

The last ray of sunlight burst into blinding green flames and then was gone. The shadows around the cliffs had spread and now covered the whole desert. A young star was burning in the sky.

The emir glanced at Shenderovich, who was caressing the handle of his sabre.

"Our fate is tragic indeed," grumbled Duban, blowing his nose on a fold of his cloak.

"No!" retorted Givi. "Look!"

The air bubbles rose into the sky, fell into line like a convoy of migratory geese and soared off into the distance.

"OOO-wooo!" rang the dying howl.

Blinking, Givi watched as the pale shining dots disappeared into the thick blue.

Somewhere in the distance, almost out of earshot, a rapturous answering roar went up from the fleeing army.

"It worked!" muttered Shenderovich in amazement, stroking Al-Bagum's neck as she calmed down.

"Such is the will of fate," Duban concluded philosophically.

The emir jumped down from his stallion and ran over to Al-Bagum, getting tangled up in the folds of his jubba.

"Forgive me, O King of Time," he said kneeling and holding his sabre out to Shenderovich. "Forgive a foolish man for doubting in you! Here is my life, and here is my head. If you wish, take them both right now!"

Shenderovich thought for a moment, absentmindedly looking at his hands.

"On your feet, O Masroor," he said eventually. "And let this sorry episode be a lesson to you. I – your King from the beginning of time to this very day – forgive you and entrust to you my army, whose behaviour also, incidentally, left something to be desired. I suggest that you explain to them in words they will understand that they must carry out their leader's orders to the letter, even at the cost of their own lives. Stand up, O Masroor the Loyal, my emir! Masroor the Loyal is how you shall henceforth be known, for as long as the sun shall rise in the east you will never again turn against your king!"

"I hear and obey, O Master," Masroor fervently exclaimed, kissing a fold of Shenderovich's robes.

"Great and magnanimous is the King of Time and Peoples," murmured Duban, tugging at his beard. "Not to mention powerful… Although I did not expect that his power would manifest itself so late in the day…"

"That was because, O Duban," Shenderovich said coldly, "I wanted to test your loyalty first. And I'm afraid to say that it has turned out to be cut from the flimsiest of cloth, which tears easily when put to the test. And now I command you, O Masroor, to catch up with those negligent subjects. Let them welcome their King in the appropriate manner, for driving out the spirits of air and fire has caused me to tire and I wish to fortify myself, to relax, and to refresh my limbs with aromatic water…"

"I hear and obey, O Sun-Like One!" answered Masroor.

Ekh, Misha managed to get out of that one alright, thought Givi. Now they will be at his beck and call. I wonder if it really was that stupid exorcism that scared those damned devils away… Or was it just time for their seasonal migration or something? Christ, when is this all going to end?

"Right then," Shenderovich surveyed the now-silent sands like an eagle. "Let's go."

Givi sighed. His mule was trembling quite violently beneath him but was gradually calming down. Enormous stars were spilling out into the sky.

He looked around. Even without djinns in them the Mountains of Darkness looked menacing, their thick blackness undiluted. They were not nice mountains. Givi's mouth fell open as a pillar of light shot up out of the distant cleft and danced in the hot air, then shrank back down and disappeared.

A split second later, the earth tremored.

"The King is resting!" came the stern rebuttal from one of the emir's private guards, who was standing stiffly by the patterned doors to the inner chambers, sabre at the ready. "The luminary of the universe gave orders not to be disturbed!"

"That doesn't apply to me," said Givi curtly, "for I am his vizier, the support to his throne. Go and report to him, O Negligent One, that there are three days' worth of orders and instructions awaiting the signature of his distinguished hand, and that if he doesn't start exercising his responsibilities soon the courts will be taken over by impious men and counsel given by the unjust… Look, just tell him that his friend Givi is pacing up and down outside like a wretched petitioner or some such…"

"I hear and obey, O Master of Mine," the guard answered uncertainly.

He signalled to his colleague and disappeared behind the curtain. Givi caught the sound of indistinct voices, female laughter and the discordant strumming of a lute.

He's got private rooms for this sort of thing, for goodness' sake, thought Givi with distaste. Why did he have to pick the throne room? They're not going to be too happy about that!

He shivered. And they call this the good life? His insides were all sticky from the sherbet and the Turkish delight, his robe stank from the aromatic smoke, and the thought of the lavish caresses of the harem beauties aroused in him nothing but weariness and a sluggish depression. Where on earth does Misha find the strength, he wondered.

The guard returned and gave a curt nod before resuming his stiff and motionless position by the door. Givi took this as permission to enter.

The throne room was illuminated with the same fragrant candelabras, and everything was saturated with their heavy, sticky scent. The throne was empty – Shenderovich was sitting on a mountain of cushions piled at its base. A cluster of beautiful houris with magnificent thighs had replaced the respectable, grey-bearded elders and were hovering around Shenderovich like a swarm of wasps – one of them was strumming on a lute, another had taken it upon herself to perform a belly dance while seated on the cushions, and the third was picking grapes from an impressive bunch and feeding them to Shenderovich one by one. Shenderovich himself was dressed in a satin robe and wide silk trousers, with a garland of roses wilting delicately on his head.

"Ah!" he murmured, spilling grape juice all over himself and making a sweeping gesture with his hand. "Come in, O Friend and Comrade-in-Arms!"

Givi approached him, feeling very small. He wished the ground would just open up and swallow him.

"Yes?" nodded Shenderovich indulgently.

"Misha... I need to talk to you..."

"So let's talk," Shenderovich consented magnanimously. "Sit down, have some grapes!"

"I'm alright, thanks, Misha."

"What do you mean, you're alright? Have some, go on! Your King invites you!"

Givi obediently picked a grape from the bunch.

"In private, Misha!"

"We are in private," said Shenderovich in surprise.

"I mean, can't you send these girls away..."

"The girls? Sure!"

Shenderovich waved his hand lazily, as if he were swatting a fly.

"Be gone," he said lazily. "Pshht!"

The girls rose silently from their comfortable perches and fluttered out the door.

"Well?" inquired Shenderovich, shifting his garland nonchalantly over one ear. "Cat got your tongue? I permit you to speak."

"Misha, now that you're the King..."

"I have always been the King," remarked Shenderovich in all seriousness. "Those that doubt me will be beaten and forced to crawl in the dust. On their bellies, I might add."

"Misha, while you're beating their bodies, watch out for the sting in their tails. This is the East. Insidiousness and intrigues... My point is that while you are in charge and that caravan path is clear, maybe we should think about getting a detachment kitted out so we can get out of here? Something doesn't feel right about this place, all this mysticism... I don't know what's going on but I don't like it."

"There's nothing going on," Shenderovich shrugged. "Everything's fine."

"How is it fine, Misha? Are you totally blind? There are djinns roaming about, Alka has turned into a succubus, and I'm sorry, but there isn't a single decent toilet in the whole place! What are we doing here, Misha? OK, so you've had something to eat, chilled out a bit, had your fun with the girls, but enough already! You're Misha, from Odessa! Iram, the Many-Columned – huh! What has Iram got that Odessa hasn't?"

Shenderovich scratched under the garland.

"I am sick and tired of telling you this, O Industrious One, but my patience knows no bounds so I will tell you once again. In Odessa, who am I? A mediocre engineer, an amateur shuttle trader. But who am I here? The King of Kings!"

"Misha, get a grip, for crying out loud! How can you be a king? How many kings do you know that deal in inflatable balloons?"

"I was a king in exile," Shenderovich was starting to get wound up. "I was in disguise, alright? A king in disguise! But you can't keep the royal essence hidden for long! The truth will out, know what I mean? And now here I am in all my glory, as formidable as an army marching into battle, trampling my enemies underfoot!"

I can't believe I'm hearing this, thought Givi in horror, feeling his limbs grow weak and relieved to be sitting on the cushions. He's completely insane!

"I was the one who caught the succubus that was making men's lives a misery…"

"Misha, don't be ridiculous, it was Alka! When are you going to let her out, by the way? You promised you would!"

"When I feel like it, that's when! The djinns were terrified of me! All it took was one word from me and they evaporated…"

"Misha, listen to me!"

"The throne," said Shenderovich, lifting up his hand dramatically. "That throne over there chooses those who are worthy and destroys those who are not! It lifted me up high, where I belong!"

"Misha, it's just a trick, a mechanical trick!"

"A trick?" Shenderovich seemed to swell up. "How dare you? You… well, go on then, you try it!"

"I will!"

"Ah, you'll never do it. You're too much of a wimp! Do you know what it does with impostors? It broke the Pharaoh's legs!"

"I don't give a damn about the Pharaoh!" yelled Givi, jumping to his feet. He felt empty and light, like one of Shenderovich's balloons, and to his own astonishment suddenly found himself approaching the silver steps that led upwards.

The beasts up the sides of the staircase glowered at him with their ruby eyes, but Givi was already beyond caring.

He seized the lion violently by the scruff of its neck as if he intended to lift the poor animal up by its mane and give it a good shake. The lion looked at him in astonishment and drew back slightly.

The lever, thought Givi feverishly, patting the beast behind its ears, there must be a spring or something somewhere here!

His hand slid over the smooth surface.

Was Duban lying? Either that or it was very cleverly concealed.

Givi looked up and happened to catch a reproachful look from the ox. Without thinking, he swung his free arm back and punched it right between the horns. A short bellow broke from its metallic throat, then the ox jerked up its head and moved backwards, clearing the path.

Givi stepped quickly up and fixed the next pair – the wolf and the lamb – with such a murderous glare that they quickly made way. The inflatable balloon floated inexorably up – Givi felt as if he were caught in a powerful current and was being carried, carried, carried up the steps.

He came to his senses only at the very top of the throne.

The turtle-dove flew down and laid a crown on his head, though it was a little too big and slipped down over his eyes.

Givi worked his head free of the crown and cautiously glanced around.

It was considerably higher than he had expected.

Way down below, amongst the scattered cushions, a tiny Shenderovich was looking up at him.

I wonder where that lever was then, thought Givi. Did I press it without even noticing? He licked his dry lips.

"You see, Misha," he called, as convincingly as he could. "It's just a secret mechanism! A trick!"

"Really!" responded Shenderovich from below. His voice was difficult to make out but sounded somehow completely different.

Artificial birdsong was coming from somewhere overhead.

Givi shook his head, trying to dislodge the stupid crown. Shenderovich slowly got to his feet. He still looked really small. For several moments he craned his neck, silently staring at Givi, then he clapped his hands.

The door flew open and several Mamelukes burst into the throne room, their torsos as naked as their unsheathed sabres.

"Seize him!" ordered Shenderovich.

Misha!" cried Givi again, and the silver canopy made his voice sound particularly resonant and impressive. "What are you doing, Misha? It's me, Givi!"

The Mamelukes shuffled about a bit uncertainly at the foot of the throne. Shenderovich shrugged.

"I'm sorry, my friend," he said, "but Iram only needs one king!"

"I don't want to be king of Iram! Misha, I just wanted to…"

"Seize him," Shenderovich waved his hand again. "The traitor!"

One of the Mamelukes, obviously the most courageous, stepped forward uncertainly, placing his foot on the first step of the throne.

There was a terrible, ear-splitting scraping sound.

Givi shivered under the canopy.

The lion on the first step reared up on its hind legs and growled, stretching its sharp-toothed silver jaws wide, and the ox waggled its backside obscenely and lashed out with its metal hoof, catching the Mameluke's knee-cap. He staggered from the step and fell to the ground, whimpering and clutching his shattered knee.

Bloody hell, thought Givi in horror, it's broken his leg! The remaining Mamelukes started howling and jumping up and down, their teeth and their sabres glittering, but they remained where they were.

"Misha!" Givi cried again from the top of the throne. "Call them off, will you?"

Shenderovich stood there frowning and plucking rose petals out of his hair.

"How did you manage to get up there?" he eventually asked, quite calmly.

"I have no idea! Call these thugs off, Misha!"

"OK!" Shenderovich clapped his hands and the Mamelukes regrouped with evident relief and fell into two ranks, standing stiffly along the sides of the throne.

Phew, thought Givi.

"Now come down," ordered Shenderovich.

"Misha, you're not mad at me?" Givi asked cautiously.

"No. Come down."

"They won't touch me?"

"They won't touch you. Just come down."

"And you won't touch me either?"

"No, as long as you tell me how you got up there in the first place."

Givi had no idea how he had got up there in the first place, but he instinctively nodded his assent.

"Uh…"

"Are you coming down?" cried Shenderovich, losing his patience. "Or do I have to come up there and drag you down those bloody steps myself?"

"OK, OK," Givi hurriedly replied and carefully started to climb down. The animals regarded him benevolently with their ruby eyes.

Shenderovich gradually grew larger, his eyes fixed on Givi. The descent altered Givi's entire perspective: the Mamelukes, so inoffensive from his lofty vantage point, now formed a sullen fence and were staring at him with their unblinking, bloodshot eyes. Givi's head didn't even reach the chin of the shortest of them. His heart sank and he hunched his shoulders up around his ears, but this didn't make him feel any better.

He stood on the lowest landing, looking around and blinking. Why had everything looked so wonderful from the top? And why did it all look so bleak from down here?

"Well?" asked Shenderovich, looming majestically in the gangway formed by the Mamelukes.

"Well what, Misha?" Givi answered sadly.

"What did you do to the throne? Is there really a lever?"

"What lever? I didn't find any lever. There's a lion!"

"Yes," Shenderovich said coldly, "I noticed."

He pulled thoughtfully at his lip.

"You know," he said eventually, "if you had even stumbled... But you didn't even stumble, did you?"

"I didn't stumble," Givi confirmed sadly.

"In that case I'm sorry, my friend!"

He clapped his hands again. The Mamelukes encircled Givi.

"Misha!" bleated Givi. "What are you doing, Misha? What will they say?"

"What will who say?" asked Shenderovich in surprise. "There's no one here!"

"These... Black..."

"They won't say anything," Shenderovich reassured him.

He clicked his fingers. The Mameluke closest to Givi opened his pink mouth wide and Givi saw the stump of his tongue pulsating behind his bared white teeth like a frog.

"They're illiterate too," Shenderovich nodded benevolently. "So what happens in this room stays in this room, Givi my friend."

Givi stood up straight and pulled his shoulders back as far as he could.

"This isn't right, Misha," he said reproachfully.

"As you yourself quite correctly pointed out, O Luckless Fellow-Traveller of Mine, this is the East. Insidiousness and intrigues. And I am the King of Kings! I am exempt from the generally accepted norms!"

He clapped his hands once more.

"Take him to the dungeon," said Shenderovich, as he turned indifferently away.

Givi sighed. His sigh rose towards the stone vaults and dissolved into the darkness.

To hell with Iram!

If truth be told, he had enjoyed his brief time on the throne. He could clearly remember the feeling – as if you were being lifted up by a powerful hand, and you were big and strong and everyone else was small and weak. It speaks to you, that throne. It tells of great deeds, powerful armies and mighty conflagrations, of falling cities and fluttering banners…

Givi could almost see where Shenderovich was coming from.

But the throne also spoke of wisdom and justice, of a faraway temple with columns soaring into the sky, of a temple with an amethyst floor, of a temple with a secret room where God dwells in the rays of an unbearable white fire, of a room hidden behind a curtain… The throne spoke quietly of flocks and rich pastures, of valleys full of light, of vineyards with wandering foxes, of goat's cheese and figs, and of women's laughter in the shade of the olive trees.

But Misha probably hadn't heard a word of it.

Givi shifted. He felt the urge to rattle his chains, but there weren't any – his legs were clamped in wooden stocks, though his hands were free. There was nothing to rattle in this dungeon.

Every palace, thought Givi, has a dungeon. Up above, it's full of light streaming through the high windows, and the radiance of gold and semi-precious stones, and courtiers robed in silk, and courage and valour and strength… But down below, only damp vaults dripping with water, and gloom, and decomposing straw…

Somebody coughed nearby. Givi looked around nervously.

He would have jumped out of his skin but the stocks prevented it.

"Man," said a rasping voice, "is like a palace. Within him lie secret rooms and dark cells and vaulted halls… Of course, occasionally you come across people who are more like temples… And if they have a secret room, then God dwells within it. But such blessed are few…"

"Uh…" Givi asked cautiously, "who are you?"

"A prisoner," came the voice out of the darkness.

"And have you been here long?"

Givi had the distinct impression that when he had been thrown into the cell it had been empty.

"What is time to one who loves? What is time to a learned man? I have always been here. And who are you?"

"An unfortunate man," said Givi with a sigh.

"Misfortune soon passes," remarked his companion.

"Mine doesn't," retorted Givi. "Things are always going wrong for me. There I was, living a modest life, not particularly comfortable or exciting but I didn't have any complaints… Because when I had nothing I had nothing to lose. But then I started living a life in the fast lane and in a short time I had lost my country, my beloved, and my friend."

"And was this life yours?" asked the stranger.

"No," Givi answered sorrowfully. "I'd just borrowed it. It belonged to some bloke called Yannis."

"However, what would be right for Yannis isn't right for you," concluded his companion. "So what is right for you, O Destitute One?"

"I just wanted to be like everyone else," Givi answered honestly. "Or maybe just a little bit better. I wanted to be able to enter through unknown doors without stooping. I wanted people to respect me. When I visited my friends, I wanted everyone to say 'Look, here's Givi! Great! It was no fun without him!'"

"Did you wish to be strong?" asked the voice.

"I would have liked not to be trampled on by those stronger than me."

"Rich?"

"I would have liked to be respected by those richer than me."

"Loved?"

"Yes," said Givi angrily. "And there's nothing wrong with that. Doesn't every man want to love and to be loved…"

"Well, maybe all is not lost," answered his invisible companion. "Now and then, such misfortunes are sent to try us, for He pines for our prayers. Your prayer must be particularly valuable to Him."

"My prayer rises up into the vaults of this cell," sighed Givi, "and stays there. It certainly doesn't reach God. How am I supposed to know where He is? Who He is?"

"God is what flows between your heart and its auricle, like the tears that flow from under your eyelids. He is everywhere."

"And what does one little Givi matter to him?"

"One Givi is everything to him. For you are the only Givi that he has. Take heart, O Fellow Prisoner. Wherever there are ruins, one may hope to find buried treasure. Why not look for God's treasure in your own ruined heart?"

"Because it's not there," said Givi. "There's nothing of value in my heart, otherwise my friend would have recognized it. And wouldn't have become my enemy. And as my enemy he should have met me man to man, one on one, instead of setting his silent warriors on me…"

"Maybe he was afraid of you?"

"I don't know," sighed Givi. "Maybe at first. A little bit. But now, almost certainly not."

"Well you, O Prisoner, have taken your first steps down

the path of righteousness. For you cannot attain perfection while your enemy still fears you."

"Your words are beautiful, O Invisible One in the Darkness. Maybe they are even truthful, for such beauty cannot be a lie! And what should I call you?"

"Call me Zahid, for I am an ascetic. Call me Abid, for I am a believer. Call me Arif, for I am a gnostic," answered the prisoner, somewhat evasively.

"I shall call you Murshid, O Teacher,"sighed Givi, "for you are one who sets others on the right path. But tell me how you came to be in this dungeon?"

"I was preaching in the squares of Iram," Murshid said angrily, "although it was not really my place to be preaching anything in public... However, I sent my disciples among the bazaars and caravanserais and went myself among the people, in order to awaken those who were walking in their sleep, to teach the credulous and strengthen the doubters. For there is a terrible danger threatening Iram, and not only Iram but all other worlds too, and this danger is growing day by day. I spoke of those who had lost patience and of those who had not yet found it. I spoke of those who were seeking strength and of those who were seeking wisdom. Of the just king and the unjust king."

"So you... were calling for the overthrow of the autocracy?"

"What a stupid thing to say, Givi! It is not possible to overthrow the autocracy. Kings can be absent for a certain time but they always return, for such is the order of things. I was calling for the accession of the true and necessary king. And as for whether or not the present king of Iram fits that description, that is another matter!"

"Yes," said Givi sadly. "Misha really has changed. However, my eyes must be clouded, O Wise One, for I see him still as he was before. He is a powerful man now, though, a hero..."

"Frankly, O Givi, if we had to rely on heroes to save the

world," said the voice in the darkness, "then the world would not last a single day."

"The world needs saving then, does it?" Givi asked politely.

"The world needs saving every hour of every day."

"Well, at least Misha is trying! He chased the djinns away, didn't he?"

"That is true," said Murshid thoughtfully. "The King banished the djinns with a single word. But did he do the right thing? Every act has a double meaning…"

"I think it was a good thing that he got rid of the djinns. They were obstructing the path of the caravans and killing travellers."

"Let us suppose though, O Givi, that someone more powerful even than the King of Iram himself had placed them there – for it is not only caravan paths that lie within the Mountains of Darkness! Maybe the djinns were a lesser evil holding in check a greater evil… and now the path to the greater evil is clear!"

"What evil?" Givi was suddenly interested. "I was there myself, I saw… O Murshid, something is happening there that is causing the earth to quake!"

"The quaking is not the evil," said the voice in the darkness. "It will be more terrible if the quaking stops. However, this will not happen for a long time, and right now we have more pressing concerns."

"You're right," Givi agreed morosely, "it's not my problem. I am doomed to vanish into the darkness, where there is no path."

"Have no fear, O Doubting One, for there is always a way out. You just need to put your faith in God's mercy. Even if He closes all paths and passages to you He will show you a hidden path that you alone shall know."

"Ekh!" said Givi. "No one has ever escaped from a prison through its walls…"

"Maybe, maybe not. God has forty-one attributes, of which twenty relate to necessity, twenty to impossibility and one to possibility. And if your destiny pleases the Almighty he will give you this last attribute readily!"

"I wouldn't mind getting my hands on it right here, right now..."

"Salvation is nigh," Murshid said sternly, "but bear in mind, O Givi, that salvation itself is an ordeal!"

"Better the ordeal of salvation than the ordeal of this dungeon," retorted Givi, perfectly reasonably.

"Maybe, maybe not." Murshid repeated enigmatically.

Givi wanted to say more, but his words were drowned out by the heavy scraping sound of bolts being drawn back.

Hmm, thought Givi, struck by his own indifference, I wonder whether they've come for me or for that poor devil... And if they've come for me, then what do they want with me?

A shy hope stirred in his soul: maybe Misha had changed his mind after all... But no, that was highly unlikely.

"What's happening, O Murshid?" he asked in a whisper.

"The last attribute," answered Murshid, also in a whisper. "Look!"

The flame from a torch began to jump up the walls, illuminating the corridor. Unaccustomed as he was to the light, Givi was temporarily blinded by it. He blinked, and once his eyes had adjusted to the light he could see that the door was ajar and the flame was seeping through the slight opening. He could also make out several dark silhouettes.

Misha, he thought, as his heart began to beat a little faster. Ekh, no, it's not Misha!

None of the new arrivals looked like Shenderovich – one was too short, and the others were too tall.

He squinted at them.

"Master," came a whistling whisper. "O Master of Mine! Are you here?"

Givi glanced back to where his cellmate sat in the darkness, thinking that this appeal was probably addressed to him, but there was not a sound from the corner.

"Master Givi! Answer me, O Hider in the Gloom!"

"I'm, uh... here," said Givi, his response somewhat less eager than might have been expected. "And who are you?"

"Vizier Jamal, your servant..."

"Oh!" Givi was delighted. "Did Misha send you to fetch me? Has he changed his mind then?"

Of course, Shenderovich had thrown him in here in the heat of the moment, which was completely out of order, but on the whole he wasn't a bad person – he just liked to do things in a big way. And now he's changed his mind... It's all that throne's fault...

Jamal sadly shook his splendid turban.

"If he had sent me to fetch you," he explained, "then it would have been with cold steel in my hand or with a poisoned chalice... You, Master, are like a thorn in his flesh!"

"So why have you come then?" wondered Givi, tucking his legs under himself in fear, at least as far as the stocks would allow.

"I have come exclusively at the command of my own heart," Jamal explained with dignity. "For it is not right for the just to suffer at the hands of the unjust."

"Um..." said Givi indecisively. "That's very kind of you. I accept your sympathy and all that..."

"I am offering you not sympathy but assistance," retorted Jamal. "Empty lamentations are of no use to anyone."

"Well..." Givi was in a difficult position now as he had never been overly fond of Jamal. "If you, my friend, would care to bring me some fried chicken, or maybe a bowl of rice..." He stopped short, remembering with alarm Jamal's comment about the poisoned chalice.

"Even the tastiest morsel consumed in prison will stick in your throat," said Jamal firmly. "And it does not befit a noble man to dine in such cheerless surroundings."

Givi sighed. Jamal evidently had no intention of feeding him. Even with poison. Still, he retorted sadly:

"A noble man can ennoble any surroundings. Even such as these."

"You are wise and great, O Master of Mine!" Jamal clasped his plump hands together. "However, permit me to escort you out in order to render you the homage you are due by rights."

"You mean," Givi asked cautiously, "that you're going to get me out of here?"

"Oh, yes! I will lead you into the light, O Friend and Master! I will shelter you from impious eyes! And the tyrant will not lay a finger on you!"

"What tyrant? Ah, you mean Misha! And, um... where will we go?"

"Permit the small man to worry about the great," said Jamal meekly. He was jangling something, probably a bunch of keys.

Givi hesitated. Now that his eyes had finally grown completely used to both the darkness and the light, the massive figures behind Jamal looked pretty menacing. They were probably bodyguards.

I bet he's going to strangle me, worried Givi. Maybe Misha has suddenly decided to exercise his royal rights and they've been instructed to do away with me on the quiet, or maybe he's here on his own initiative... Either he's ingratiating himself with his boss or he's just wicked by nature...

"There is no other way out, O Radiant One!" insisted Jamal. "The town criers are already walking the streets of Iram telling the people of your perfidy and duplicity. They say that they are already felling cedars in the Mountains of Darkness, so that your gallows should be worthy of you."

Givi was in an agony of torment: was he lying or not? Either way, he didn't see how he could refuse his offer of help. Not with those two lurking behind him.

"I will hide you in a safe place, O Master of Mine," Jamal continued to insist.

Givi thought about it. Maybe Misha would eventually come to his senses but it didn't look like that had happened just yet. Jamal didn't seem to be particularly fond of Shenderovich. And two minuses make a plus, don't they? Your enemy's enemy is your friend, Murshid would have said... Yes, but when did Misha become his enemy? Oh, thought Givi, where did it all go wrong? Everything was going so well. What should I do? Who can I trust?

He wanted to trust Shenderovich.

But Jamal was the one who had come to save him.

"Ekh!" Givi made up his mind. "OK! But I must ask you one thing, O Jamal! My conscience will not allow me to leave my fellow-prisoner to his woes. If you will free me, then free him too!"

"You mean," Jamal was suddenly right in front of him, "that there's somebody else in here with you?"

"Yes," agreed Givi. "An unfortunate sage thrown into this dungeon unjustly, who has relieved my hours of loneliness with his tales and exhortations! Will you help him, Jamal, as you are helping me?"

"I live to render assistance to the wise and to save the righteous!" Jamal fervently assured him.

"Then deliver him from his stocks and lead him into the light! And see that he goes safely."

"Your servant will ensure that the wise man forsakes this dungeon," agreed the vizier. He clapped his hands, and Givi hunched his shoulders up around his ears. Bitter experience had taught him that such a gesture rarely heralded good fortune.

Jamal's massive escorts took a step forward under the dismal vaults, blocking out what little light was able to force its way through the dungeon door. As softly as tigers they crept past Givi, who followed their movements with a wary eye.

They shuffled about by the wall for some time, making a jingling noise and rustling in the stale straw.

"So where is your cellmate, O Master of Mine?" asked

Jamal eventually, when the search threatened to drag on indefinitely.

Givi suddenly realized that he had not heard a single word out of his cellmate since the arrival of the vizier.

"He was here a minute ago, I swear!" he said in confusion. Jamal's cohorts jangled something against the wall. They could also be relied upon to keep the palace secrets for the simple reason that they were not physically capable of passing them on.

There's something dodgy going on here, thought Givi.

"Why don't you call to your friend?" Jamal asked in a sugary voice.

"Hey!" said Givi quietly. "Speak, O Venerable One!"

Silence.

One of the guards went up to Jamal and made a series of rapid hand gestures. Jamal shrugged.

"The darkness and despair must be playing tricks on you, O Master of Mine," he said eventually, "for there is no one in this foul dungeon but you."

"Eh?" Givi was surprised. "But he was here a minute ago! And I have to say, O Jamal, he spoke quite coherently and intelligently. Maybe he, um… left?"

"He could not have just left the dungeon, O Martyr," Jamal explained patiently. "Unless perhaps your cellmate was Sahib al-Zaman himself – the Lord of the Age, who is able to appear and disappear whenever the fancy takes him and who has mastered tay al-makan, or the folding of space, which is to say the ability to be simultaneously in two places at once, or so the legend goes. However, although you are indeed great, O Master of Mine, it is highly unlikely that Sahib al-Zaman himself would have descended into the darkness to share your lot… " He shuddered. "But who knows? Hurry and follow me, Master of Mine. I will lead you to safety."

"You can start by getting me out of these damn stocks," said Givi.

It was dark and quiet outside. He could smell bitter herbs, wilting roses and dust. Givi looked around. They were standing in a wasteland, picturesquely dotted here and there with ancient ruins. The green light played on the rounded cupola of the palace, which loomed up in the distance, its sharp towers bobbing coquettishly up and down in the hot, shimmering night air. Bats flitted past them, their wings slicing through the greenish sky.

"Huh?" asked Givi uncertainly.

"You are free, O Master of Mine," answered Jamal cheerfully.

"Um…" Givi didn't know what to say.

Freedom was undoubtedly a good thing, but Jamal's men were flanking him so closely that there was no possibility of escaping their persistent surveillance. Givi took a deep breath, puffed his chest out as far as he could and inquired, "And what are your long-term goals, O Vizier of Mine?"

"To guard and protect you, of course!" Jamal clasped his hands together. "Which I shall prove to you now, O Wise One, by my actions!"

He gave a short whistle and a man in a cloak appeared from behind the ruins, leading several strong mules by their reins.

"They will be looking for you, O Fugitive! And in order to frustrate their search, you must take refuge. We have a safe place for you to hide."

A safe place? Yeah right, thought Givi. Whatever that means.

"And also, O Master of Mine, forgive my importunity but it is vitally important to cover your eyes, for the location of the refuge where we intend to conceal you must remain a secret."

"Do you not trust me, O Jamal?" Givi demurred.

"I trust you more than myself in this delicate matter, O Master of Mine, however such is the requirement of the current occupant of the refuge."

"Ah! So it is already occupied?"

"Oh, yes! Someone has to keep the refuge in order until the arrival of its true master!"

Givi couldn't help feeling that the vizier's words lacked a certain logic: if he was the true master why did they need to blindfold him? However, Jamal's attendants were already moving earnestly towards him so he considered it best not to argue. Anyway, he thought as a thick strip of cloth was placed over his eyes, if Jamal had wanted to kill him he could have done it ages ago. All the same, he ventured to ask:

"These aren't by any chance Nubian asses, are they, O Jamal?"

"Oh, no," Jamal shook his turban. "How could they be? The Nubian asses live in the stables of the sovereign of Iram and are guarded more closely even than the royal treasure-houses! These are mules, Givi, just mules, from my own modest stable."

Givi cheered up a bit – for some reason anything to do with the Nubian asses unsettled him. He stretched out his hands to touch the animals and felt himself gripped under the arms and lifted up into the air. He was clumsily deposited into the saddle and his mule set off behind its compatriots, its hairy legs delicately picking out the path. Givi desperately strained to catch every sound, trying feverishly to work out whether he had escaped danger or was heading towards it.

Initially, he felt a gentle swaying as they crossed ruts and hummocks, then they passed out of the wasteland and Givi realized that they were heading up into the mountain. They were travelling in complete silence. From time to time, obviously thinking to reassure him, either Jamal himself or one of his fellow-travellers gave him a friendly pat on the shoulder, which only made him shrink even further down into his saddle.

The wind fanning his face grew cooler, the animals' hooves rang out and the shingle dislodged by them continued to resound for some time as it rolled down the stony slopes. Then a hush fell, and Givi felt a light drizzle on his face. I would've been better off staying where I was, he mused despondently as he rocked in his saddle. Misha would have changed his mind sooner or later. But here I am, being thrown around like a sack of potatoes…

A bird whistled sharply and was answered by another, and after a while Givi realised that his fellow-travellers were exchanging signals with someone in the darkness.

He heard the quiet creaking sound of gates being opened, and his mule clattered across a paved courtyard. Then it stopped and Givi felt someone touch him lightly on the shoulder.

"You may dismount, O Master," Jamal's voice rang out.

Givi clambered down from his saddle and, stumbling slightly, allowed himself to be guided by an unseen hand.

"Lower your head, O Newcomer," said Jamal.

Givi obediently ducked and continued walking, then stopped and stood in his stooped position until Jamal spoke again.

"You may stand up now and reclaim your sight, O Joy of the World."

Givi pulled off the irritating blindfold and screwed up his eyes as he took in his surroundings. He was in an enormous room decorated with carpets and curtains. The first rays of dawn were visible through the narrow windows cut into the heart of the cliff, though they had not yet managed to drown out the light from the torches that burned along the walls. A low bed covered with snow-leopard pelts sprawled along one wall, and a curved pitcher stood on a beautiful carved table.

Jamal bowed before Givi and remained thus inclined.

"Make yourself comfortable, Master," he said. "Eat, drink and rest your weary limbs. The slaves and slave-girls await your command…"

Well, well, thought Givi. If this is a prison, then it certainly comes with all mod cons!

"Are you the owner of this outstanding abode, O Jamal?" he asked, by way of conversation.

"Oh, no!" Jamal shook his turban. "I am merely your obedient servant!"

"Then who is?"

Jamal placed a chubby finger to his lips.

"All will be revealed when the time is right," he said. "For now, I strongly advise you to rest and recover your strength!"

"Yes," said Givi, who was starving, "but…"

"A valiant man such as our guest will not permit himself to eat or drink until he knows the truth, is that not so, my friend?" said a quiet voice.

Givi jumped. Just a few moments ago he and Jamal had been alone in the room but now they had been joined by a majestic old man in snow-white robes, who had appeared from out of nowhere. His black eyes were piercing and stern.

Jamal bowed even lower, though it was scarcely possible.

"The Mahdi," he whispered.

The Mahdi put his finger to his lips.

"You may simply call me Imam," he said softly. And let us dispense with all unnecessary eulogies… Now leave us, O Jamal. I wish to speak with my guest."

His upper body at right angles to the floor, Jamal backed towards the door.

Sheikhs, imams, thought Givi forlornly. There seem to be a lot of them about! Or maybe they're all the same… In any case he also bowed, although not too low. He didn't want to let the old man out of his sight…

"So, Givi," said the old man, sitting down on the cushions and gesturing to Givi to follow suit. "Welcome home!"

"This isn't my home," retorted Givi with as much dignity as he could muster. "I am merely a chance guest here."

"But you are obviously the kind of guest who owns the place from the moment he arrives. Everything here belongs to you! Including this modest dwelling…"

He moved his hand again and it seemed to Givi as though the flame from the candelabras burned a little brighter, causing the gold carving on the dishes and the patterned hem of the silk curtains to glow.

"And these men, who are ready to throw themselves into battle on your command…"

The voices coming through the window hummed rhythmically, like waves breaking on the shore, and were accompanied by the sound of spears striking the cobbles.

"I have been preparing them in secret, O Givi, for I foresaw that the hour would come when you would have need of them. There they stand, awaiting the command to return Iram to you!"

"You cannot have something returned to you that never belonged to you in the first place!" objected Givi, who was prone to hasty displays of decency. "Iram belongs to Misha… I mean, Zul-Qarnayn…"

"Ah!" the old man waved dismissively. "Maybe that was a mistake. Yes, I admit, at first someone thought that he was the one. But you were always at his side, were you not? It is you, not him! You are King of Iram by rights, you possess the Word and the Throne, you are the chosen one, you are the only one."

"But Misha…"

"What about Misha? He's an impostor, lifted to the Throne by a fortuitous twist of fate! Did he tell you about the lever? Or did he prefer to keep that to himself?"

"There was no lever, O Imam!" Givi answered with dignity. "I couldn't find it, anyway."

"Of course you couldn't! That is because you have no need of it, O Givi! You ascended the Throne by yourself, without any contrivance, did you not?"

"Well, yes," Givi reluctantly admitted. "But so did Misha! And he said that he couldn't find the lever either!"

"Of course he said that," agreed the Imam. "What else could he have said?"

"But Misha is King!" Givi stubbornly insisted. "Even the magi predicted it!"

"Ah!" the Imam waved his hand. "Those poor wretches! Well, they merely misread the celestial signs, believing an unworthy man to be worthy. You have always been at your friend's side, have you not?"

"I suppose so... But what about the demon? The green one? The demon pointed at him!"

"The demon, my friend, pointed at you. They asked him, is he the one? And of course he answered in the affirmative, for you were there..."

"But..." Givi said uncertainly, "how do you know all this?"

"I know everything, my friend, even what those pitiable amateurs failed to comprehend. Only a true master is able to recognize you, O Givi, for your essence does not reveal itself to foolish eyes!"

"Yes, but Misha..."

"Is unworthy!" the Imam shook his head reproachfully. "Without you, O Givi, he would not be where he is today!"

"But he banished the djinns!" bleated Givi, basking in the glow of praise and feeling loathsome and delighted in equal measure.

"The djinns?" the Imam shrugged. "You gave orders and they obeyed. That Misha of yours just echoed you, howling and spinning around like an over-the-top fakir. You are the King! You are the master of the spirits, you are the source of all knowledge, you are the wisest of the wise, you know all the Names and all languages, you are the buttress that supports Iram, tamer of the Throne! So do you really expect me to sit by and watch while an unworthy man triumphs over a worthy man?"

Reality, which was strange enough already, seemed to be bifurcating. "Look," Givi exclaimed in despair, "I'm not a king! I just want to go home!"

"You are modest and have no desire for profit. However your heart is that of a great king and it will heed the call of Iram, for Iram is in grave danger. And this danger is ten times greater than before now that the Throne is occupied by an imposter."

"You mean Misha?"

"Of course! Do the towers of Iram not collapse under his feet? If he were the true king, I assure you that peace and splendour would immediately have prevailed in Iram! I beg you, O Givi, stop him, for he will be the final undoing of Iram!"

"Um…" Givi hesitated.

As far as he could remember, only one tower had collapsed under Misha's feet, and it had been old and rickety to begin with. And it was true that Iram was experiencing a few earthquakes, but they had been happening for ages… Givi hadn't noticed any other significant changes.

"So Iram's in grave danger, then?" he asked out of interest. "What kind?"

"Is it not enough for you that an impostor has usurped the Throne? Is it not enough for you that he has incarcerated all those who were close to him, the only ones who knew his true identity? Where is your other fellow-traveller, she of the beautiful face and slender figure?"

Frowning, Givi remained silent.

"And where would you be, had not my loyal servant saved you and led you out of that dungeon? Rotting in the darkness? OK, look… I should not be telling you this, Givi, but I will. The ancient books say that if an unworthy man takes the Throne, Iram will perish. The Throne will not allow itself to be taken unlawfully. The Mountains of Darkness will quake, pillars of fire will shoot up into the air, and everything on earth will be turned upside down…"

The old man's words were accompanied by mournful gestures, and Givi felt obliged to pass comment.

"That sounds terrible!" he sympathized.

"A whole world centres around Iram, and this world will shatter! Abundant light will spill from the cracks into other worlds, which will not be able to withstand the pressure! All worlds will disappear! Light will drain out of the universe, and it will be swallowed by darkness…"

"What a nightmare!"

"Is it not your duty to prevent this, O Givi?"

"Fine," said Givi uncertainly, "but after I save Iram can I go home?"

"Home?" asked the old man in surprise. "You are home, Master."

"No, my real home… back to where we came from?"

"I do not understand why you wish to return," the old man shrugged, "however yes, when the perturbation of matter around Iram has been silenced it goes without saying that you will be free to return home… That is, if you still want to, of course."

Givi hesitated again. Something was bothering him about all of this, but he couldn't for the life of him work out what it was.

"And what will happen to Misha?"

"If you were to defeat the unworthy one who threw you into the dungeon, it would only be right and proper to render him the same treatment."

"But I don't want to throw Misha into the dungeon! He's not that bad really."

"He is a despot! Cunning and insidious!"

"Misha's not a despot! I think Iram has just brought out the worst in him. And if you send him home too he'll be back to his old self in no time…"

"I do not think that he will give in to you without a fight, O Givi," said the old man.

"I'm not going to fight Misha," Givi said sulkily.

"You will have no choice. The well-being of Iram requires sacrifices, Master. You will save many people this way. I understand that he was your friend, but what is the well-being of one man compared to the lives of many?"

"Let me think about it, O Imam," said Givi, still sulky. "Don't rush me."

"All of my time is yours, O Master," assented the old man, placing his hands together in submission. "However, do not think about it for too long, for who knows what else this unworthy man is capable of?"

Givi thought about it.

"And what do you get out of this, O Imam?" he asked eventually.

"Nothing," said the old man with dignity. "I have all that I require and more. I have retreated from the world into these cliffs and am in no hurry to return to it. The well-being of Iram is all that matters to me. Along with your well-being, of course, O Givi!"

"I don't need anything either," muttered Givi.

"Really?" the Imam was surprised. "Just think what it would mean to occupy the place that is rightfully yours! Have you never felt that you deserve better? Have you never felt like an uninvited guest at a party? Have you never wished to say to people, 'Here I am, look at me! This is who I really am, sparkling like a rare jewel, and this pitiful exterior is but an outward appearance, a deception! So welcome me with the joy and respect that I deserve!'?"

"I suppose so," Givi admitted reluctantly, "but not here, not in Iram. Iram is just... Everyone tells you what you want to hear. But when I go home..."

"Home?" the old man raised his eyebrows. "But what is waiting for you there, O Ruler of Worlds? Your ledgers? The daily grind? Insignificant people, who trample upon your greatness as an ignoramus tramples roughly upon a valuable carpet? Darkness and cold? I have heard that beyond the sphere of this world there are countries where crystals of frozen water fall from the sky! Where nights as long as eternity give way to days as fleeting as life itself! Where women do not know how to gratify their men and go out with their brazen faces on show! Is your world not like that too, O Newcomer? And why do you have need of a world such as that?"

"It's the only one I have," said Givi. "If such a world exists, then someone has to love it. Otherwise, why would it exist?"

"Alright," the Imam shrugged, "alright! You will go home in splendour and magnificence! I give you my word, O Givi. But not before you save Iram! That is an honest exchange, is it not?"

Givi grew thoughtful.

"Everyone here is always talking about honesty," he said eventually, "but they keep telling lies. However... you can prove the purity of your intentions, O Imam. For you yourself have reminded me of a certain prisoner, my fair fellow-traveller, whom Mi... the usurper imprisoned."

The old man was visibly taken aback, though he tried to hide it.

"Maybe, O Friend of Mine, she is happy where she is?" he suggested cautiously.

"I don't care, O Imam," answered Givi sternly. "Show her to me, safe and unharmed, and maybe I will believe you! I swear by the heavens above!"

"I understand, O Givi... You fear that she will be the first victim of this feud. Well, alright then! I will deliver her here and keep her in safety. And no one, no one, O Givi, will be able to make use of her against her will! You do not plan to make use of her, do you?"

"No," sighed Givi. "What do you take me for?"

"But I warn you, O Givi, that this woman is dangerous, for her tongue is as sharp as a razor and her wits no less so. Furthermore, she has blonde hair, which is testimony to an imbalance of the humours. But if anyone is capable of resisting her charms, however strong they might be, I think it is you!"

Givi grew thoughtful again.

"And do you, O Imam, promise to bring her here without using undue force? Without harming a single hair on her head?"

"I am a slave of Iram and therefore your slave too, O Givi," the old man bowed his head, "and I shall order your servant Jamal to deliver this woman to you. Perhaps he is already on his way, for he needs to be back at the palace before dawn in order to further your cause!"

Givi had no idea how Jamal intended to further his cause in the palace. By spying, probably...

"Well, alright then," Givi assented. "Let him further my cause, for diligence is one of the finest qualities of a good servant. I, O Imam, shall wait until this woman is brought before me, safe and unharmed. And I require her henceforth to accompany me everywhere and at all times, for the fact that you have suggested that Misha is capable of using her as a weapon makes me suspect that you have similar intentions..."

"Your mistrust wounds my heart, O Givi," sighed the old man. "But I live to carry out your commands! And my greatest joy and only aim is to lead you from the darkness into the light. By the way, O Wearer of the Crown, Jamal told me that you had an imaginary cellmate to share your confinement."

"Oh, that was just confused daydreams," Givi made a dismissive gesture.

"Ah, I see... Fine! Then allow your servant to withdraw in order to issue the appropriate instructions..."

The Imam sighed again. At that exact moment there was a distant boom and a slight tremor shook the floor beneath Givi's feet.

"Did you hear that?" the old man raised his hand.

"I did," agreed Givi. "About a four or five on the Richter scale, I'd say. But what's Misha got to do with it? If I, your guest and master, have understood correctly, Iram has been suffering earthquakes for centuries..."

"They will get worse," the old man said ominously.

"Alright," answered Givi, sitting down on the cushions and folding his arms. Then let's see what we can do about it. And send someone to me, so that I may wash my hands and finally get to eat something..."

"I hear and obey, O Master of Mine," said the old man with dignity.

He looked at Givi and shook his head sadly.

"I have waited so many years for you, O Master!" he said. "I have been saving my strength! I have been nurturing my wisdom! I have been seeking your radiance far and wide! So why do you still doubt me? Do you really think that I am not capable of distinguishing a diamond among shards of glass? Do you really suppose that I will let you now reject something that is rightfully yours purely out of a misplaced sense of modesty?"

No, I don't suppose he will, thought Givi despondently. What do they need these Kings of Time for anyway? He had no idea whether Misha really believed any of it, but Givi personally felt like a total impostor and was waiting, with indifferent horror, for the deception to be revealed at any moment.

"I said, O Imam," he muttered, "I will think about it. Such matters cannot be hurried! Now go and let me be alone!"

"Of course, O Master," said the old man with restraint, though his voice betrayed suppressed resentment.

He folded his hands together, bowed and left.

Givi fidgeted on the cushions, settling himself more comfortably. To keep himself entertained, he started scrutinizing the ceiling, which was covered with fantastical tiled patterns. The patterns helped to ease his sense of melancholy.

So, I'm the King then, thought Givi. Not Misha – me! What a pity Misha doesn't know it… Never mind, he soon will! Ekh! He didn't want to fight. He wanted to eat. Misha just wasn't the kind of person you started a fight with. And anyway Misha had Masroor, who after that disgraceful episode with the djinns was ready to follow his master through fire and water. Misha also had his loyal mute Mamelukes. And regiments with banners. And a white battle camel. And, at the end of the day, he had the Nubian asses!

Givi got up from the cushions, went over to the high window and stood on tiptoes. When it became apparent that the combination of the height of the window and his own modest stature prevented him from even reaching the sill he came back and, huffing and puffing, dragged the little table over, then clambered up onto it and looked outside.

The castle was hanging over an abyss.

Or rather it towered above the abyss on a flat cliff ledge, which reminded Givi of a ship's deck. The nose of the deck jutted out in front and formed a kind of courtyard before the castle. The courtyard was shrouded in morning mist, but he could still make out the troops forming themselves into squares in a menacing silence.

Givi was terrified.

Are they, he panicked, my men? My army? Will they do anything I order them to? Will they attack Misha? Why were they so ready to turn against Misha?

The eternal elder, he remembered! The only one who did not recognize Misha as the sovereign of Iram! The holy man sheltering in the hills!

He had something against Misha right from the start.

Whereas for some reason he seemed to take to me!

Givi started back from the window in fright: as if they had sensed his presence the troops had simultaneously begun to bang the shafts of their spears rhythmically against the stone.

ℌe couldn't swallow the pilaf. Maybe I'm just sick of Eastern food, thought Givi glumly. What I really fancy is a bowl of borshch. And some black bread with drippings. Just then, Givi heard footsteps from behind the door curtain and quickly wiped his hands on the florid cloth, then sat up straighter on the cushions.

Two powerful, surly slaves carried in a colourful sack, the neck of which was bound neatly with a golden ribbon, which was tied coquettishly in a bow. The sack was jerking and wriggling, and every now and then it convulsed so violently that it folded completely in two.

The slaves lay the sack at Givi's feet and quickly retreated with a bow. One of them, Givi noticed, had a black eye.

The sack continued to jerk.

"You jackal, Mishka!" grumbled the sack. "Friend of a Baghdad thief! You'll regret this! I'll show you! Untie this sack, you seed of a scorpion!"

Givi bent down, pulled one end of the ribbon and quickly jumped aside.

"Allochka," Givi said nervously, "calm down!"

"Oh!" Alka jumped to her feet and shook herself down. "It's you!"

"I'm afraid so, Allochka," Givi answered sadly.

Alka furiously pushed a lock of blonde hair back from her forehead.

"Not you as well," she sighed. "It's bad enough that Misha's completely lost his mind!"

"You think he's lost his mind, then?" asked Givi, seeking confirmation.

"Too right! He locked me up in that bloody harem, appointed a load of shrews to look after me... Honestly, you should have seen them... They kept singing to me, can you imagine? And playing on their stupid lutes! He looked in once, explained to me in no uncertain terms that he was the King, and then buggered off again! He stationed a load of eunuchs at the door – they wouldn't let me leave, and they wouldn't let Masroor in. The King does not permit it, they said! The King! And who do you think they were talking about? That wannabe Sindbad!"

"Hang on a minute, let me explain..."

"Then, as if that weren't enough, they shoved me in that sack and dragged me all the way here! I think that ass has broken my back... I'm covered in bruises! Look, here! And here!"

Givi took a couple more steps back.

"I was the one who gave the order for you to be brought here," he admitted, desperately attempting to straighten his shoulders.

"You gave the *order*?" Alka expressed surprise, then added very coldly, "So, you're a king as well, are you?"

"Apparently so," Givi explained vaguely.

He looked around. The room seemed empty, but you never could tell... He had learned by now that everybody here possessed the unpleasant ability to appear wherever and whenever they chose.

"Allochka," he said, "you know, there's something really strange going on here... Misha threw me into the dungeon because apparently I'm the King as well, and then this lot helped me escape..."

"That's typical of Misha," agreed Alka in the same cold voice.

"And now they want me to take the throne over from Misha, because nothing good appears to be coming from his reign, quite the contrary, in fact..."

"Well, Misha is certainly a bit of a slacker," agreed Alka, "but he's not completely stupid... Maybe he's been doing his deals again and inadvertently bankrupted the state?"

"That's not the problem, Allochka... The thing is, they're saying he's an impostor because the earth keeps quaking... Oh, there it goes again..."

"Hm, very interesting," said Alka thoughtfully, twirling a lock of hair around her finger. "So, is this your fortress then?"

She cast a benevolent eye around the room then absent-mindedly picked up a fig and began to nibble on it.

"It would appear so," said Givi despondently. "It used to belong to that Imam of theirs but now it's mine."

Alka flopped down onto the cushions.

"And who's the Imam then?"

"I don't know... The Imam just... is. But then, who knows? You know, Allochka, they all keep changing their appearance..."

"So it seems," Alka agreed thoughtfully. "You've changed too."

Givi straightened his shoulders.

"You look terrible. Really stressed out..."

Givi's spirits fell. Then he pulled himself together.

"But I'm the King, Allochka. The leader of the army."

"That's what Misha said too," agreed Alka. "Maybe you both ought to work out who you really are? Otherwise, you know, this imbalance will lead to no good."

"We are in the process of working it out," Givi snapped.

Then he added thoughtfully:

"Tell me, though… Do you like it here?"

Alka shrugged.

"It was pretty boring in the harem. But on the whole, it's quite a laugh, isn't it?"

Givi peered at Alka, trying to perceive in her fine features the depraved and irresistible allure of the succubus and at the same time hoping not to. Alka fidgeted about on the cushions.

"You're beautiful," said Givi.

Alka gave another slight shrug.

"That's very kind of you, of course," she agreed indifferently, "but I'm afraid you're not really my type. You're too nice, Givi…"

"For your information, I am the King!" Givi reminded her in an aggrieved tone.

"Of course you are," said Alka reassuringly, "I can see that for myself. So what are you going to do now? As the 'alternative' King?"

Givi thought for a moment.

"Well, first we need to start negotiating. I'll send a delegation to Misha. To avoid unnecessary bloodshed."

"Hmm," mused Alka, "that's not very king-like, is it? You should ride out at the head of your army. Is that who's making all that noise, by the way? Your army?"

"It is, Allochka."

"You should gather them all outside the palace walls and ride out on a white horse. Issue an ultimatum. Make him abdicate. Being the King of Iram has already messed with his head quite enough."

"And if he says no?"

Alka thought some more.

"Set the djinns on him," she said.

Givi stared at her.

"They follow your orders, don't they? That's what I heard."

"Allochka," sighed Givi. "Djinns are a very unreliable substance. In actual fact, I don't know whose orders they follow. And I don't particularly want to find out. Especially as," he lowered his voice, "I haven't got the faintest idea how to summon them."

"Just try it!"

"But it's dangerous, Allochka."

"But that way you'd be able to sort all this out without sending men into battle. The djinns can just storm the palace, remove Misha, bring you in... And then you'll put me on the Throne..."

"What?" Givi stared at her.

"You'll put me on the Throne," Alka repeated authoritatively. "I'm sorry Givi, but you as leader would be like a mouse pretending to be a lion. I'm much better suited to the job. Particularly as I have a fairly good understanding of the Eastern mentality. I think the Throne will accept me."

"The Throne will not accept you, Allochka. They don't like blondes around here."

"The army would support me."

"Masroor has sworn eternal allegiance to Misha. As far as I understand it, Allochka, he is prepared to lay down his life for him!"

"We'll see about that..."

Huh, Givi thought feverishly, this serves me right! Who does she think she is, the Queen of Sheba?

I need to get out of here as soon as possible! This city is full of lunatics!

"I need to think about it, Allochka," he said in despair. "In theory, of course, it shouldn't be a problem..."

Alka stroked his cheek with her cool hand.

"I'll make it worth your while, O Givi," she said suggestively.

Givi's mouth went dry.

She's bluffing, said a nasty little voice inside him. I've already been on the receiving end of one display of royal benevolence, courtesy of Misha. She'll throw me back into that cell again, where the straw's still warm from my last sojourn.

"I'll repay your favour…"

"Repay me, then!" Givi croaked. "Right now!"

Alka cast a thoughtful, appraising glance over him.

"Payment on delivery, O Hasty One," she remarked.

"No!" Givi protested. "Now. Call it a deposit!"

Alka looked him up and down once more, causing him to shiver involuntarily. Then she uncovered her head.

She went up to Givi. Right up close to him.

Givi's head started to spin.

I wonder, he thought, trembling and on fire, whether she is a succubus right now… Or not? If she is a succubus, then I'm going to feel terrible… afterwards… And if not, what am I so afraid of? It's only Alka! Alka, here, in my arms!

Alka put her hands on his shoulders. She pressed her body against his. Her eyes were right in front of his, enormous and limpid. And her body was soft and warm.

He felt dizzy and mechanically fumbled for a cushion with his foot as he felt his legs start to give way.

"Oh, Givi," said Alka.

"Ekh," said Givi.

It felt a bit weird. But it was nice all the same.

He put his arms around her, desperately attempting to appear confident and manly.

She'll probably say "Oh, Masroor!" in a minute, Givi thought glumly.

"Oh, Givi!" repeated Alka.

"Master!" came a voice from behind the curtain. "Master!"

Perfect timing, thought Givi. Why can't they have normal doors around here? With bolts!

"Just a minute!" he yelped guiltily, straightening up his clothes.

"Master! O Master of the World!"

"Ekh!" said Givi.

Alka slipped smoothly out from his embrace like a silvery fish. He stood in the middle of the room, trying to calm his rapidly beating heart and looking into the formidable eyes of the Imam.

"Well, what is it?" he asked wearily.

The Imam cast a sidelong glance at Alka.

Alka insouciantly straightened her clothes.

"They are attacking, O Master! He has sent his army!"

"Who has?" asked Givi in confusion.

"Zul-Qarnayn, the unworthy one. He is heading this way at the head of thousands of men... He has obviously decided to strike the first blow. Your army awaits your command, O Master."

Givi's confusion grew.

"Maybe we should try to wear them out," he asked, shrivelling under Alka's contemptuous glance, "by assuming all-round defence positions?"

"This fortress is known as the Eagle's Nest," said the Imam, "and for good reason. It is virtually unassailable and is capable of withstanding a long siege. However, the army of Zul-Qarnayn is exceptionally great in number and very well trained. And if they block us in, then there will be no way out."

From behind, Givi sensed Alka observing the exchange with detached curiosity.

"What do you suggest I do, O Imam?" he asked eventually.

"You need to ride out at the head of your army, O Givi! Meet your fate head on like a man, and not like a rat caught in a trap!"

Givi was now too confused to speak.

"I have entrusted you with my life and the life of my men,

O Master," the Imam reminded him sternly. "I followed you, the chosen one, the blessed one! Did I pick the wrong man?"

"Misha wouldn't do anything stupid," Givi said uncertainly, "would he? What does he think I've done?"

His words were drowned out by the rumble of the army on the square in front of the fortress.

"Right now he would gladly believe that you are possessed of fangs and claws," said the Imam, "and that you have been hiding your true nature behind a mask of modesty and friendliness in order to stab him in the back the moment he turns away!"

"But it's not like that," bleated Givi, "I've always been…"

"You have always been a deadly threat to him, O Givi!"

Evidently tired of holding her tongue, Alka suddenly exclaimed in her musical voice,

"You just don't get it, do you? Mishka's army is idling."

"But he vanquished the djinns!"

"That wasn't him, it was you," the Imam reminded him.

"Whatever. So I vanquished them! Why doesn't Misha lead his army through the mountains… To the city of Baghdad, maybe?"

"And he will lead them still," answered Alka. "He'll deal with you first, then they'll be off. He's Alexander the Great now!"

"What? Who?" asked Givi.

"Did you not know, O Master?" the Imam was surprised. "Only the direct descendant of Enoch can occupy the Throne of Iram, and his descendant is Iskander – in other words Shah-Marsboun, the Guardian-King, sovereign of all inhabited lands, master of the universe, the Two-Horned One, Zul-Qarnayn!"

"I'm sorry, but how can that Greek be the direct descendant of Enoch? He's… Greek!"

"By Abraham's line, of course," answered the Imam. "For Iskander is the son of Philip, and Philip is the son of Madrab, son of Hermes, and so on and so forth, right up to the son of Esau, son of Isaac, son of Abraham. Every child in Iram knows that."

"Yes, yes, of course," Givi wearily shook his head. "Of course, Misha is Mikhail Abramovich… on his father's side. But he's dead. Alexander the Great, I mean. Not Misha. He's still very much alive and kicking."

"Iskander will return!" exclaimed the old man. "He will return when the need arises."

"So he's kind of a past *and* future king," explained Alka.

"So who am I then?" howled Givi.

"One of you most definitely is the King," agreed the Imam.

"Yes, but which one?"

"You, O Givi! Of course it is you! That impostor tricked his way onto the Throne!"

"Am I Iskander too then?" Givi asked forlornly.

"There can be only one Iskander! And it is you, O Givi! And that is the irrefutable truth. The Throne is able to tell which of you is the true king – that is its sole purpose! According to legend, Iskander the Great will return to Iram when Iram is in grave danger."

"What danger?"

In the distance, there was a noise like thunder. Givi stood on tiptoes and craned his neck to look out of the narrow window. All he could see was the stone verge of the cliff, which seemed to be swaying – one minute it was there and the next it was not. A wave of noxious smoke hit him in the face, and he started coughing and wiping his streaming eyes. They could hear shouting coming from somewhere below.

"That danger," the Imam said gloomily.

"Shit!" Alka sneezed too and covered her head with her veil. "He's got catapults out there!" she said, her voice muffled. "Looks like his engineering degree has finally come in handy! He's going to start bombarding us with that…what's it called… Greek fire! Givi, we don't stand a chance!"

Givi stood up. Dove-coloured puffs of smoke swam around the room, the flames of the candelabras flickered and went out, and the carpets curled up like autumn leaves.

"Fine," he said in a solemn, manly voice. "Just tell me what needs to be done."

The army swept down the mountain like a flash flood, skirting round the larger obstacles in its path and sweeping away the smaller ones.

And then all of a sudden there they were: two armies facing each other across a trampled plain, under a white sky scattered with lazy white clouds. The earth beneath their feet shuddered, though it was not clear whether from the heavy tread of the battle camels or from a force within.

A narrow black banner fluttered above Givi's head.

A narrow black banner fluttered above Shenderovich's head.

Well, thought Givi, I'm feeling pretty mighty. Here I am, on this hot-blooded battle steed (which is trying to sneak out from under me.) It's a bit of a distraction, but not too much because my thoughts are on a higher plane. I have a firm hand on the reins (damn, am I supposed to operate them with this finger… or that one?), the brilliance of the swords and spears are flashing like lightning behind me (because the sun is shining right into my eyes – I believe this is what is known in military parlance as an unfavourable position), I am defending my very own stronghold (and incidentally where has that bloody Imam got to?), and within its strong walls shines the face of a woman I have saved from a tyrant (who is probably more than capable of sorting out any tyrant with her own bare hands.) If I should be lost in action, then she will, um… happily return to him, I suppose. Ekh, I've got nothing to worry about – I am strong and wise (yeah, right!), I am a military commander, tactician and strategist, and I am waging war against Alexander the Great himself (who is about to beat the living daylights out of me…) No, this isn't doing much for my morale… OK, try again…

I am the King, and thousands of men stand behind me ready to throw themselves into battle at my command.

And over there thousands stand behind Misha ready to throw themselves into battle at his command.

Misha seemed to have a few thousand more.

Furthermore, there were catapults surrounding the unassailable walls of the fortress together with some mysterious contraptions that Givi took to be battering rams. Behind the frighteningly perfect rows of silent troops loomed an enormous tower-like structure, which appeared to be on wheels.

If that Imam wanted me to win, thought Givi despondently, why didn't he give us any equipment? He's the eternal elder, right? You'd have thought that in all those years he could have dreamed up something pretty special.

The sun was in his eyes, and there was nothing he could do about it.

Givi saw himself as simultaneously very big and very small.

Big, because his arms and legs seemed to exist independently and he had absolutely no control over them as he shamelessly bobbed up and down in full view of the enemy army like a floating duck at a fairground shooting range. Small, for the very same reason.

In the distance, motionless as a statue, Shenderovich towered up on his white camel. He looked magnificent.

Behind Givi, the troops were getting restless. Givi was very aware that he was as vulnerable from behind as he was in front. He was basically one big weak spot.

There's no way I'm going to be able to beat him, he thought. That bastard is a natural military commander. He'll squash me like a fly! No, he won't: I'm the natural commander, the exorcist of djinns!

So they keep saying, anyway.

Just then Alka, in the process of tying a silk sash around him with her soft hands, said briskly, "Don't forget, my Givi, you have a secret weapon, which is yours alone!"

If I really am the one and only King, Givi thought feverishly, which is on the whole fairly unlikely, then I suppose there's no reason why I shouldn't summon those ifrits... that would really give him something to worry about!

But what if I'm not the King? What if he really is the King after all?

Shit, they've really set me up here!

What the hell, I've got no choice!

Now, what did I say to them last time? That they should go until I summoned them once more or something?

In the distance, Shenderovich brandished his sabre and shouted something...

He thinks he's Lawrence of Arabia, Givi thought sadly.

Givi stood up in his stirrups and saw that the army of Iram had broken away from its positions and was advancing swiftly towards them in a cloud of dust. "Hey!" he cried in desperation. "Wherever you are! I invoke, I mean, swear by the Lord of Babylon, or whoever it is – pah! –I swear on my own life... oh, whatever! I released you and now I summon you once more... I am your master and I command you to come to my aid, across time and space, and banish this accursed army!"

The thunder of hooves drew closer. A wall of dust rushed towards them.

"If possible, without any human casualties," he added hopelessly.

Givi's stallion was pirouetting on the spot and flecks of foam were falling onto its bit as his wild gesticulations inadvertently tightened the reins. The ring had turned round so that the stamp was pressing into his palm and was now cutting into his finger.

Ekh, thought Givi, we need to apply a spot of aerial pressure... This is definitely a set-up. There's no way I'll be able to get those damn djinns out during the day... It's way too bright for them. Ekh, I suppose the main thing is to summon them and then they can work out for themselves what to do next. Hmm, I wonder if djinns have any technological gadgetry at their disposal?

"Misha!" he yelled, desperately attempting to remain in the saddle. "Misha! This is crazy! It's me! It's Givi! And Alka's here too!"

Givi tried to free his hand from the reins to point at the castle rising up against the radiant sky but he got a bit tangled up and only succeeded in making his stallion jerk its head up, which meant that he couldn't see anything at all.

Al-Bagum bellowed.

The sky suddenly opened up.

Enormous black dragonflies poured forth one after another, whirring so loudly that they completely drowned out Al-Bagum's bellowing. Givi's stallion grunted and shied sideways. Givi flew through the air in a perfect trajectory, landed in the sand and remained there, looking up at the sky.

Wow, thought Givi, I guess that answers my question about technological gadgetry!

Something broke from under the belly of the first dragonfly and whistled through the air, leaving a dove-coloured trail. It embedded itself in Shenderovich's siege tower, which immediately caught fire. The second flaming missile hit a catapult as it was about to release its load. Something soared over Givi's head and exploded in mid-air scattering green sparks.

By now the whirring of the dragonflies had escalated to a roar. Givi was so deafened by their ear-splitting howls that everything suddenly seemed ominously silent.

He crawled away behind a fallen fragment of the cliff and covered his head with his hands. Riderless horses covered him in scorching dust as they rushed past with their eyes open wide, their ears back and flecks of foam flying from their bared jaws.

He cautiously raised his head. Shenderovich had somehow managed to stay mounted on Al-Bagum and was waving his hands about. He seemed to be yelling something, but whatever it was he probably couldn't even hear it himself.

Givi looked around.

His own army had been forced back into the gorge – his men had abandoned their horses and were clambering up the walls like flies desperately seeking shelter within the castle walls. Givi thought he saw a white-robed figure flash like a spark on top of the castle wall and then just as quickly disappear.

The Imam, he thought, admiring his warriors!

The dragonflies were flying lower now. Their propellers were stirring up clouds of sand but Givi could still make out the pale-blue six-pointed stars painted on their smooth sides. The dark belly of the dragonfly nearest to Givi opened up and released a rope-ladder, which promptly unravelled.

A succession of identical dashing young men in tough boots spilled out onto the sand, bending their knees as they efficiently took the impact in a practised manoeuvre.

The rotation of the propellers gradually grew slower, quieter…

Givi got up and slowly scrambled up onto the stone.

He couldn't see a single horse. Or a single rider.

One of the new arrivals ran up to Givi. He seemed a little older than the others and was wearing his beret at a jaunty angle over one ear and a large machine gun across his strong chest. Givi instinctively tensed his legs, ready to jump out of the way quickly just in case, but Action Man stopped and raised his hand to his beret in a salute.

"Captain Yannis Shapiro reporting. Sub-unit Alpha at your command, Commander," he said.

"Yannis?" asked Givi in the silence that had fallen. "Excellent…"

The flat area on the roof of the palace seemed to have been designed specifically for the landing of the airborne forces. Helicopters came in one after another, each disgorging its cargo of men. Givi's helicopter was last.

Givi stood on the flat roof and looked around.

Iram shone before him covered with sun-baked dust and

washed by the hot wind from the desert, her multicoloured tiles shimmering and reflecting the tiles of the roof.

Givi sighed.

His men hadn't lost any time in lowering ropes down the walls and were now crawling down them like flies and climbing in through the narrow windows. Shards of multicoloured glass fell to the ground, shattered by strong elbows.

"So beautiful," muttered Givi. "Ekh! Such a waste."

Yannis placed his strong hand on Givi's shoulder.

"Peace to the huts, war to the palaces, eh, Commander?"

"I guess so," Givi answered sorrowfully.

From somewhere below came a burst of machine-gun fire, followed by the regrettable sound of flying tiles.

"Your lads aren't going to wreak havoc inside, are they?" worried Givi.

"It's just a show of force, that's all," Yannis looked at the illuminated dial on his wrist. "Sorted. Now we can go in."

"Down the ropes?" Alka inquired enthusiastically.

"No," answered Yannis, with obvious regret. "The lads will just sort out things in there then they'll let us in. What's that tower over there, Commander?"

"An observatory, sort of," Givi answered vaguely. "The local astronomer was based there."

"Aha!" Yannis unhooked the walkie-talkie hanging from his belt. "That's our way in! Is it linked to the main building?"

"I think so," nodded Givi, relieved that they were not going to have to start abseiling.

"Beseder!" Yannis issued a short command into the mouthpiece. "Right then, Commander, in we go!"

"We should talk to the people, calm them down," said Givi, anxiously.

"Later, Commander!" Yannis waved his hand. "You can go out onto the balcony early tomorrow morning and make a speech... We'll give you a megaphone! Come on, let's go and see where your Alexander of Macedonia has got to..."

"What... haven't they found him yet?" Givi inquired nervously.

"Not yet," Yannis shrugged. "But don't worry, Commander, we'll find him! He can run but he can't hide!"

Alka went up to the edge of the roof and cautiously leaned over. The wind from the helicopter's propellers whipped up her hair, making her look like a model in a fashion shoot. Alka tried to restrain her clothing, pulling it more tightly about herself with deft hands, which had the effect of accentuating her smooth curves in the searchlights.

"What a stunner," Yannis sighed in admiration, absent-mindedly releasing the safety-catch on his machine gun.

"We have to find Misha," insisted Alka, equally absent-mindedly smoothing the creases in the fine fabric wrapped around her. "Otherwise I don't fancy his chances."

"We'll find him," promised Yannis.

"Just bear in mind that he's probably going to be quite a handful. I just know what that King of the Universe is like... Whenever things aren't going his way, he can get a bit aggressive."

"We'll make sure he behaves himself," Yannis reassured her.

"But I'm the King of the Universe!" Givi muttered plaintively to himself. Nobody heard him.

The carved door of the observatory shattered with the first blow. A narrow spiral staircase was visible inside the building, its base hidden in the darkness. Yannis strode noisily towards it closely followed by Alka, who kept leaning into his powerful shoulder. Givi followed behind, clenching his jaw.

"All clear?" asked Yannis, kicking the astrolabe away with the toe of his boot.

"Seems so, Commander, yes," cried a paratrooper from below. "Although we did find this one!"

The torchlight picked out a gaunt figure in a shapeless dark robe embroidered with astrological symbols.

"Ah!" Givi exclaimed delightedly. "It's Duban, the astronomer!"

"Is that you, O Givi?" Duban inquired morosely. "Are you in charge of this horde of demons?"

"I'm afraid so," Givi admitted reluctantly. "But they're well-behaved demons, O Duban! They do as they're told."

"Well, tell them to go away then! Their appearance has brought innumerable misfortunes upon Iram!"

"Alright, old chap, calm down. No need to make such a song and dance about it… They're nice lads really. They're just stoking things up, making a bit of noise!"

"I am not your old chap, O Marid, Master of Marids!" Duban hissed through clenched teeth. "And speaking of misfortunes, I must tell you that your former friend and the former ruler…"

The floor beneath Givi's feet suddenly tipped up at an angle. Cracks snaked up the walls of the tower.

Duban grabbed the collar of Givi's jubba to stop himself from falling.

"Whoa!" exclaimed Yannis.

"…your former friend is reading! He's reading the book of Raziel!" cried Duban, gripping Givi so tightly that he ripped the fabric of his robe. "He is the genuine King! He will attain immeasurable power!"

"Don't worry about it," Givi reassured him. "So, he's reading a book! So what? Where did he get it from, by the way?"

"You yourselves brought it to Iram!" cried Duban.

There was another earthquake. In the distance, where the Mountains of Darkness loomed on the horizon, a pillar of fire shot up into the pale sky.

"Interesting," Yannis said nonchalantly. "What's that over there then? A bombing range?"

"Wait a minute!" cried Givi, attempting to extricate himself from the astronomer's tenacious grip. "What was that?"

Duban finally released his hold on Givi's torn collar, turned and rushed down the staircase. Givi bolted after him.

Yannis stood there for a moment, looking puzzled and shouting after them:

"Hey! We need to go up! Up! It's going to collapse!"

Then he capitulated and ran down too.

The room was empty. The floor was covered in fragments of glazed tiles. The palace seemed to be completely deserted.

"What? I can't hear you," Givi tried to make himself heard above the rumbling noise which seemed to be coming from everywhere at once and was getting louder. "Where's Misha? Where's everybody else?"

Duban waved his hand dismissively.

"They have all fled! Did you expect them to stay here awaiting certain death?"

"I don't believe it!" yelled Givi. "Misha would never run away!"

"Of course not," Duban made a wry face. "He's the King! And that's why when your marids defeated his army he returned to the palace and immediately sent for his emir and his vizier... And asked for a few loyal men..."

"Which loyal men?" Givi interrupted him. "Jamal?"

"Well, yes," Duban admitted with some reluctance – he and the vizier had not seen eye to eye for some time. "When everyone else abandoned him, Jamal stayed true and to my astonishment proved to be both loyal and trustworthy..."

"That..." Givi choked, "that..."

"And Jamal came to me and asked if there was any way to conquer these marids, and I said that there was not, unless the legend about the return of the King of Time should turn out to be true after all and the book of Raziel should reappear together with its owner! And then Jamal mentioned a certain attribute that had been retrieved from the brigands' camp by the valorous Masroor... And I looked at this attribute and saw that it was indeed the book of Raziel!"

"Raziel?" repeated Givi. "Which Raziel? You mean the archangel? Shemhazai's friend?"

"I find it very strange that you should be so well-informed on this subject, O Master of Marids," commented Duban.

"But where did the book come from?" Givi started shaking his head. The floor beneath him was lurching like the deck of a boat, forcing him to stand with his legs permanently bent. "We didn't bring any books!"

"It's not actually a book at all," Alka's clear, musical voice suddenly broke in. "It's a stone slab with writing on it. It was in the museum in Istanbul, next to the sarcophagus. There's even an image of it on the sarcophagus. But I don't understand, how did it get here?"

"The real king is able to summon it," explained Duban, "and vice versa – the book can summon real kings, the descendants of Enoch."

"I'm the King!" said Givi forlornly. "Mother always said that we Georgians were the descendants of Alexander the Great! He left us his harem, you know, in the Caucasus!"

"He left a harem in every godforsaken backwater, apparently," the astronomer shrugged. "So I don't know about your ancestry but what I do know for certain is that Iskander the Great ordered the eyes of the Nubian asses to be bound tightly, took the stone tablet, gathered his most loyal and trustworthy servants and headed into the heart of the mountains. For the path is now clear and safe!"

"You need to make a decision, Commander," said Yannis, impatiently. "My helicopter is waiting in the inner courtyard… We should get everyone together before it's too late."

"Fine," sighed Givi. "So, where exactly did they go, O Duban?"

"I told you, into the heart of the Mountains of Darkness, to the Black Stone! For he has learned that by placing this tablet on the Black Stone and reading the incantations engraved upon it he will be granted greater power than the world has ever known."

"So Misha can read the incantations then, can he?"

"He can," Duban confirmed morosely. "He's the King!"

"And what will happen?"

"He will truly be the King of Time," said Duban, morosely. "There will be no stopping him."

"Fine," Givi said wearily. "So he's going to be more powerful than anyone has ever been before. Then I have one question for you, O Duban. If as you say, Iskander the Great has been dragging this tablet with him since the beginning of time, then why didn't he read it as soon as he got to Iram?"

"You can't read it just like that," explained Duban. "It has to be read in the right place at the right time."

"So he could have taken it straight to the Black Stone. I thought he wanted to rule the world! Isn't that why he came to Iram in the first place? For the power?"

"Commander, we really ought to be going…"

"That was his plan, O Curious one," sighed Duban. "He even brought the Nubian asses to Iram for that very purpose…"

"Not the Nubian asses again!" groaned Givi.

"But they are essential!" Duban interjected. "For, as you know, the sun does not shine in the Mountains of Darkness and this – the most terrible place in the world – is where the tablet must be placed. Nevertheless, the Two-Horned One possessed great courage and was prepared to embark on this heroic undertaking! But then he met an untimely end…"

"I seem to remember," Alka said dispassionately, "that he was poisoned."

"Exactly! A foul and loathsome old man, calling himself his mentor…"

"Aristotle," prompted Alka.

"You are correct, O Woman. That accursed Aristotle sent him poison disguised as water from the spring of life."

"Good for him," commented Givi.

BOOM!

Through a gap in the palace walls, they saw a second pillar of fire and smoke shoot up in the distance out of the abyss. It swung back and forth over the mountains, like a giant hand groping blindly in the sky.

"Alright," sighed Givi. "Yannis!"

"Yes, Commander!"

"We'll have to make do without Nubian asses! Rouse the troops! Let's go and see what's happening with that abyss. And seeing as you know the area, O Duban, you're coming with me…"

"Have you completely lost your mind, O Givi?" Duban rebelled. "There is no way I am voluntarily crawling into the belly of that evil spirit!"

"You won't be doing it voluntarily," Givi retorted dryly.

"It's just mechanics, old chap," explained Yannis kindly. "Propellers, a winch… Haven't you ever seen a helicopter before?"

"God has spared me until now," answered Duban as he backed away.

Givi sighed again. The palace walls answered him with a heavy sigh of their own. Cracks ran along the azure wall.

"Right!" he said. "By the power vested in me, I hereby terminate all futile discussions and declare it time for decisive action. Alka!" he ordered, "get into that helicopter! Quickly, before everything starts collapsing around us! Get a move on, O Astrologer, or are you really going to allow yourself to be shown up by a woman?"

"That's not a woman," Duban reasoned, "it's divine retribution!"

"I said get in, O Garrulous One!"

The helicopter was bellowing in the inner courtyard like an angry Nubian ass. There were a few paratroopers milling about and one sitting in the open doorway with his legs dangling over the side. Yannis was yelling something into his walkie-talkie as he ran. Givi bundled Duban in and jumped in behind him, just in time to look back and see the elegant tower of the observatory slowly keel over and collapse in on itself.

The helicopter began its descent. Suddenly, the pilot turned to Givi in confusion.

"What's that, Commander?" he yelled above the noise of the motors. The cliffs had suddenly opened up like a giant flower unfurling its petals.

Even in the blinding searchlights they could see the pillars of flame shooting out of the stony depths into the black sky. The earth was shaking so much that the outlines of the mountains appeared smudged.

"I don't know!" Givi yelled back. His teeth were chattering, though it wasn't clear whether it was from the vibrations of the machine or his nerves. "But that's where we're going!"

"It's too dangerous, Commander!"

"Land, I said!"

The helicopter hovered over a relatively flat section and landed reluctantly. Givi climbed out. It wasn't as dark as he had expected. There was a weak luminescence flickering all around, and the air was pulsating as if a giant fiery heart were beating somewhere nearby.

"Well, well!" Yannis squatted down, one hand holding his beret and the other absentmindedly stroking the machine-gun hanging across his chest. "What have they got here, Commander? A secret base?"

"Worse!" cried Givi, looking all around. "It's a… um, what is it exactly, O Duban?"

"I don't know!" cried Duban as he pressed himself up against the body of the helicopter, which at that point in time clearly represented the lesser of two evils. "It is a forbidden place! It cannot be named! No one has entered it since the time of Iskander!"

"And where's Misha?"

"In there!" Duban opened his eyes wide in terror.

"And where's the stone?"

"In there!"

"But how did he get in there?" asked Givi in desperation.

"There is a tunnel that passes beneath the cliffs. The air is stagnant and the darkness eternal but it is possible to pass through it... You could even take an animal in there although it would have to be a..."

"I know, I know – a Nubian ass!"

"Commander, is he testing a secret weapon or something, your Misha?"

"Sort of," Givi answered vaguely.

Yannis anxiously checked the dial on one of his bits of equipment and shook his head in bewilderment.

"All clear, though... I don't understand!"

"It's not a bomb," explained Givi. "It's..." he hesitated.

A wave rolled towards them as if they were on the surface of the sea. It tossed the helicopter into the air, threw it down again at their feet and continued on its way, irritably scattering boulders and shrugging off crags. A low, even rumble rolled after the wave.

"...something very strange," Givi concluded vaguely.

Yannis issued some final instructions to the pilot.

A second wave, lower than the first, rolled towards them. They seem to be radiating out like rings from a central source, thought Givi.

"That's where we need to go, right Duban?" he turned to the astronomer.

"In there? Beware, mortals! The heart of darkness conceals a heart of fire!" wailed Duban in a sepulchral voice.

"So, two hearts, then," Yannis summed up in a business-like manner. He looked at Givi, shook his head strangely and then beckoned him with a tanned finger.

Givi went over to him, swaggering like a bowlegged sailor on a stormy deck.

"The old man's lying," said Yannis, lowering his voice. "He knows something!"

"Really?" Givi exclaimed. "What is there to know? We're up to our necks in it here, that much is perfectly obvious!"

A strange little ball flew towards them and landed at Givi's feet. Givi recoiled. He was prevented from moving any further by something wrapping itself around his knees with a prehensile grip.

"Forgive me! Forgive me, O Master!"

"Get this idiot off me!" Givi howled as he tried to shake the vizier off his leg.

Yannis bent down, took Jamal by the scruff of the neck and lifted him up into the air. Jamal's short little legs dangled – he looked pathetic and also rather tragic.

"What was that you were saying to the Commander, you civilian rat?" asked Yannis coldly.

"It's all a trick!" wailed Jamal, wriggling and spinning around. "He tricked me!"

"He tricked you? And you tricked me, you lying jackal, you piece of camel dung, you double-crossing agent provocateur! Who are you working for?"

Givi's face looked like thunder and his piercing glare drilled into the vizier.

Yannis gave him a shake for good measure.

"For Iram," said Jamal with surprising dignity for someone dangling in mid-air. "I sought strength and power not for myself but for the Eternal City!"

"Alright," sighed Givi. "The purest of motives. Let him go, Yannis!"

Yannis released his hold and the vizier fell to the ground.

"I didn't do anything wrong!" he repeated in despair. "I was doing it for Iram! And he tricked me!"

"Who tricked you?" Givi stepped back cautiously because Jamal was doing his best to grab hold of his ankle again. "Misha?"

"No! Not Misha!" Jamal began to shake his head and its swiftly unravelling turban in vexation. "He tricked him too! He tricked everyone! Me! Iskander! You, my friend!"

He sobbed and wiped his nose on the sleeve of his kaftan.

"Another one has turned up, he said. Though we did not expect this we might be able to profit from his appearance too. For there will be discord between them, he said! Neither will be willing to concede the Throne of Iram, and one of them will go to the Mountains of Darkness in search of Power... And the one who receives the Power will give it to Iram – that's what he said... And this Power will be the greatest and most majestic power ever known to man. And in this way the Two-Horned One will do what he was unable to do the first time he appeared, for this is how it is meant to be!"

"Excellent," nodded Givi. "And who, may I ask, had such splendid things to say?"

"Commander!" yelled Yannis who had clambered up onto the nearest rock and was surveying the surrounding scene. "Come and see what's happening!"

Givi leapt up onto the rock. His legs automatically found their way to the top.

Pillars of fire were shooting into the black sky from the yawning abyss. Something was moaning and shifting in the depths of the chasm – a choir of barely articulate voices, a whisper that dislodged stones from the slopes, a scraping that made the hair on the backs of their necks stand on end. The edges of the abyss were shaking, and the writhing jets of fire were coming from every part of it at once. Strange shapes materialised in the darkness – monstrous winged figures emerged and receded, misshapen and illogical like hastily assembled puppets, with two heads, four arms, crescent-shaped horns... They possessed an ancient power, intangible and insane, the ungovernable strength of primitive elements. And in the midst of all this fluctuating fiery chaos gaped a precise triangular void – the celestial stone, black as the chasms of the icy alien wastelands from which it had fallen to earth, swallowing up light and fire and sprawling motionlessly, flat as a table.

The ill-starred Tablet was shining on top of it.

The altar of the unfortunate Brothers was but a pitiful

parody of the genuine article. The Tablet towered above the black stone emitting a faint luminescence. The writings crawled over and around it writhing and contorting like fiery scorpions.

"The Tablet of Union!" said Givi in a broken voice. "So that's it! That's what started this whole thing!"

"Look, it's Mishka! Oh my god!" Alka was craning her neck and hopping up and down, desperate to catch even the tiniest glimpse of what was going on.

Shenderovich towered above the stone, holding his arms out in front of him. He seemed to have grown so tall that his head was touching the black sky. Fiery reflections danced on his face.

"Tsorer! Netzach! Malchut! Or-Gayashor!"

"That's it!" came Duban's voice from behind Givi. "At last I understand! That's why he came to Iram! It is just as well that Aristotle stopped him! He hasn't managed to release them yet. But it looks like he's just about to!"

"What?"

"Stop him!" cried Duban. "Can't you see what he's doing?"

"What? What is he doing?"

"He's releasing Yajuj and Majuj! They're down there in the abyss! And he's letting them out!"

"Yajuj and Majuj?"

"He's releasing Gog and Magog," Alka explained matter-of-factly. "Legend has it that they're shut up behind a stone wall and every night they try to dig their way out underground... They have been obstructed to date by Allah, but now Allah is being obstructed by Misha. So now they will emerge!"

"And will rush headlong from every height" wailed Duban in a sepulchral voice. "And it will be the beginning of the end of everything ... They appear only when the end of the world is nigh, for they are loathsome and powerful and will spread only misery! Stop him, O Givi! I beg of you!"

"SHIMUSH-ACHORAIM!"

"This looks bad, Commander," commented Yannis. "Shimush-Achoraim is bad. Now, if he'd shouted Shimu-Panim-el-Panim, that would have been a different matter…"

"Stop him, O Givi!!!"

"OK!" Givi gritted his teeth. "Anything to shut you all up!"

He threw his arms out in front of him and screwed up his eyes. Even through his closed eyelids he saw a white flame escape from the tips of his fingers and form a crackling ball spraying sparks, which launched itself towards Shenderovich.

It didn't reach its target.

Shenderovich turned round, lifted his hand, and a ball of darkness escaped from his palm and flew towards the ball of light. The two whirling balls collided above the gorge and exploded, showering everyone with prickly sparks. The air smelt of ozone and, bizarrely, rusty metal. Givi waved his arms to shake off the last of the sparks, ran along under cover of the overhanging crag and jumped from the cliff. He didn't have such a good view from there but the Tablet, gradually gathering strength, was by now shining so brightly that it would have been impossible to miss.

He held his breath and aimed his fingers.

"Do not disturb my master, you accursed sorcerer!"

Givi turned round. Masroor stood menacingly before him, his white kufi dyed crimson by the underground fire, his curved sword gleaming like lightning, his fiery glare gleaming even more so…

"Leave it, O Masroor," Givi said coldly. "This does not concern you. Step aside and let the mighty do battle."

A second ball of darkness flew over the gorge and exploded on contact with the nearest cliff. Givi only just managed to dodge out of the way. Drops of molten basalt flew in all directions.

"His army of good-for-nothings deserted him," exclaimed the emir. "The cowards fled! But he will gather a new army, an invincible army, and his loyal Masroor will head it! I abandoned my master once – I will not abandon him again! And we will defeat the impious!"

"Head it? But they don't have heads, O Masroor," retorted Givi. "Do worms have heads? For they are shapeless and blind like worms, and just as greedy! They cannot be controlled!"

"That's what you think," Masroor answered contemptuously, with a flash of his sabre.

Givi hunched his shoulders defensively but the emir suddenly froze – his gleaming arc was prematurely curtailed and he looked at Givi with such bewilderment and reproach that Givi was quite embarrassed. Blood trickled from his mouth, his knees buckled and he slowly keeled over.

"Oh, Masroor!" Alka ran to the emir, picking up her skirts, and fell to her knees beside him holding his head in her hands. "Yannis, you son of a bitch!"

"Forgive me, my little bird," Yannis answered sorrowfully, "but he's looking out for his commander and I'm looking out for mine... Shame, he was a brave fellow..."

"The bravest," sobbed Alka, wiping her eyes on a silk sleeve.

"Ekh!" said Givi, who was also rather moved.

"Leave him, Commander," Yannis said briskly. "Hit him with that bio-field of yours..."

Something rose up above the edge of the fissure. A shapeless, many-fingered hand reached out and seized the nearest cliff, clawing deep furrows in it before darting back again.

Givi clenched his teeth and waved his arms. Another ball of white fire rolled towards Shenderovich.

Shenderovich waved his hand in response, but the tongue of darkness that burst from his hand this time was weak and translucent – all of his energy was being drained by the Tablet.

Givi's white ball hit a gigantic figure clambering out of the abyss. The figure was engulfed in a blinding white fire and let out a monstrous howl, causing cracks to run up the nearest cliff, before collapsing back down.

Givi raised his hand again.

"Look, Commander," exclaimed Yannis. "Look, there's another one!"

Givi looked up. On the summit of a distant cliff stood the figure of a man dressed all in white. Slowly and solemnly he opened his arms wide. The abyss responded by sending forth tongues of flame, which painted his white robes scarlet.

"It's him!" cried Jamal. "He has come!"

"Who?!" Givi shouted over the rumble coming from the earth. "Who? Who is it?"

Their new guest was inhumanly enormous – even from a distance he towered over the crags.

"Him! The Imam! The old-man-on-the-hill! The eternal elder!"

"How eternal, I wonder?" mused Yannis, raising his machine-gun.

The former elder exuded such palpable power that Givi instinctively bowed.

"Will he be able to stop Misha, O Jamal?"

"Stop him?" Jamal was surprised. "Why would he stop him? He is the one who has made this all happen, for he has been promising Iskander the Power since the beginning of time."

"He promised me the Throne," muttered Givi.

"He promised it to the Two-Horned One too," said Jamal. "He promised him the Throne and power over the whole world."

"Kill it!" shouted Duban at Givi's side in such a shrill voice that Givi jumped. "It's evil! It's deadly!"

"It doesn't feel right shooting an old man," muttered Yannis as he adjusted the barrel of his gun.

"It's not even human! You know, I didn't think he seemed particularly learned for a spiritual elder!"

"Look! Look!"

The figure of the elder grew even taller. His white robes flew open and enormous rainbow-coloured wings burst from within them, marked with eyes, charred at the tips and illuminated by the dancing crimson reflections of the fire shooting up from the abyss.

"Azazel!" gasped Givi. "It's him! Get him, Yannis! Kill him!"

"What, with a machine-gun?" Yannis was sceptical.

The bullets sprayed like a fan. The monstrous wings shook, turned pale for a second, then burned more brightly than before.

A chorus of inhuman voices howled from the abyss, and Givi thought he could detect frenzied and malicious exultation. It was the sort of noise a group of prisoners awaiting their execution might make on seeing the locks smashed from their cells.

"Stop him!" Duban was clutching at Givi's robes in horror. "He has come before the end of the world and he himself will bring about this end!"

"How can I stop him? He's an archangel!"

"He was an archangel! Now he's a demon!"

"What's the difference?! I've never in my life done battle with either!"

"Yes, but there is no one else to ask," Duban answered sadly.

The Tablet shone atop the Black Stone like a burning bubble of freshly blown glass. No other pedestal would have been able to support it, but the Black Stone stood unwavering, swallowing up both light and darkness...

Azazel's wings pulsated and glimmered above it like a pair of charred rainbows.

"He's trying to distract us," realized Givi. "Don't look at him! Misha... we have to stop Misha!"

Shenderovich was still yelling, hoarsely and incomprehensibly. Even from where they stood they could see how monstrously distorted his face had become.

"Misha!" roared Givi. "It's not you! It's Azazel! He can't release them himself! He needs a human! A descendant of Enoch!"

Shenderovich turned towards him, gave a strange smile and lifted his hand again, echoing Azazel's gesture.

"Givi, stay strong!" exclaimed Alka, glowing with a terrible succubus beauty. "Remember who you are and whose ring you are wearing!"

Givi looked down. The ring on his finger was burning with a pure white fire.

"Hang on!" Givi grabbed hold of the ring. "What did you say just now, Yannis? Shimu-Panim-el-Panim? Right! I, the wise one, the powerful one, master of the djinns... I, King Givi? No, I, Builder of the Throne, order you, Azazel, to return to the darkness whence... Oh, just go back where you came from! SHIMU-PANIM-EL-PANIM!"

A gust of cool wind rushed over the earth, sweeping away the tongues of flame.

The rumble from the abyss grew louder and turned into a howl. Now it contained notes of fear.

Azazel's wings flushed dark and folded like a tent. Stars were visible through the anthracite membranes.

"The star-twin!" whispered Duban.

Givi stood with his knees bent, reeling from the exertion, with white lightning still crackling from his fingertips. The cliff below him was caving in.

"Wow, Commander!" shouted Yannis enthusiastically. "You did it! That was at least an eight on the Richter scale!

The Tablet was swelling up and rocking backwards and forwards on its stone pedestal. The fiery letters were swarming all over it, round and round. Shenderovich was still waving his arms about as if in a trance, jumping up and down.

"Shoot, Yannis!" grunted Givi. "I can't hold him! Shoot!"

"I already did! The bullets aren't touching him!"

"Aim for the Tablet!"

"I've only got one grenade left, Commander," warned Yannis.

"Misha! Get down! Shit! Fire! I'm sorry, Misha!"

Yannis narrowed his eyes and pressed the trigger.

The fiery bubble shook, swayed and exploded, scattering crimson balls of light all around. A desperate cry escaped from the abyss and rose to a plaintive, piercing scream before dying away altogether.

Azazel fell from the cliff like a black comet and plummeted through the tongues of fire into the jaws of the earth, which closed up over him.

Somewhere in the distance, the Nubian asses bellowed in despair.

The earth gave a heavy sigh like a somnolent beast and shuddered as it grew calmer, calmer, calmer… then there was silence.

Givi made his way back down to the cliff, utterly spent.

"Are you alright, Master?" Jamal asked anxiously.

"I am now," answered Givi sadly. "I'm absolutely fine. Get out of my sight though, Jamal, I can't bear to look at you."

Duban got to his feet, shaking out his cloak.

"The Tablet of Raziel has left this world," he announced.

"Yep," agreed Givi, "and so has Azazel."

"Well, I doubt we've seen the last of Azazel," sighed Duban, "but the Tablet has gone for good… All that knowledge! All that power!"

"What knowledge?" Givi waved his hand dismissively. "And as for its power… well, it's just as well it's gone as there would have been no way of controlling it…"

"I am sure you would have found a way, O Master," the indefatigable Jamal flattered him.

Ekh, thought Givi, there's a real courtier for you. He's been well trained!

"Maybe he didn't read it properly?" Duban would not let it lie. "Maybe it was the wrong king reading it? Or maybe he should have read it differently?"

"It wouldn't have made any difference, O Duban!

However he'd read it, Yajuj and Majuj would still have been released. And the End of the World."

"But Raziel... he's supposed to protect the weak! I cannot believe he would have written something like that."

"Do you really not get it, Duban?" said Givi wearily. "Raziel didn't write it. Azazel did. He wrote the Tablet and it survived the Flood. And he wrote it specifically so that Yajuj and Majuj should be released by the hands of the sons of Adam. Because it was not within his power to release them himself."

"But why?" Yannis was surprised. "I know he's a bit of a bastard but what did he need that Yajuj and Majuj for? You saw what they were like! If they had crawled out of there it would have been game over! They would have destroyed all of mankind!"

"He didn't care about mankind! All he cared about was them! He was doing it for them and them alone!"

"But what would they have done for him?"

"They are his children," sighed Givi. "That's what this whole thing has been about..."

"His direct descendants," nodded Duban. "And there are more of them, too. They are innumerable, ungovernable, locked up by God in inescapable darkness, in a dungeon, where pillars of dark fire are destined to fall for all eternity, where He decided they should remain until the Day of Judgement and the end of their guilt, in the Year of the Secret. However, neither they nor their father had the patience or strength to wait until the end of time."

You see, thought Givi as he watched the rows of workers bustling about industriously in the ruins of the former palace, we'll manage just fine without the Shamir worm.

"Are you sure you don't want any ivory, O Master?" Jamal asked nervously.

"Look," said Givi angrily, "for the last time, no ivory! It's completely unethical. You can count the number of elephants left in the world on one hand!"

"So?" Jamal expressed surprise. "That's what makes it so valuable!"

"I said no! And no gold doors either! It's just too over the top."

"But it's so beautiful," Jamal replied defensively. "And so regal!"

"True value has no need for rich trappings, O Jamal!"

"Really?"

"Yes! For its brilliance can be seen all around and is immediately recognized by learned men! The main thing you need to worry about is making sure that the walls are earthquake-proof. Those last reinforcements were useless! Most of building materials were looted."

"But there won't be any more earthquakes!" said Jamal with absolute confidence.

"Well, just in case. Jamal!"

"Yes, Master?"

"I have spoken!"

"Your wish is my…"

"That'll do! Duban, keep an eye on him, would you? Give me the final accounts! Right, now they balance."

Givi dipped his quill into the inkwell solicitously placed before him by Jamal and paused.

The accounts were finally in order, but how should he sign them?

In the end, he carefully wrote:

'G. Mesopotamishvili, Chief Accountant'

Then, in brackets, he added 'Leader of Numbers.' Then he sighed quietly.

He felt like an imposter.

"And?" Jamal urged him on.

Givi thought for a moment. Shrugged. Then thought a little more.

"And nothing. Summon my people, O Jamal! They've had their celebrations, and now it's time to call it a day. We're leaving."

"What do you mean you're leaving, Master?" exclaimed Jamal in horror. "How can you leave now, when everything has been resolved? When the Throne rises above a peaceful Iram and the people are ready to kiss the ground beneath your feet! When power and glory are about to descend from the heavens to crown you with roses?"

"Now is exactly the right time for us to leave," confirmed Givi, "before Misha comes to his senses. Otherwise I dread to think what he might get up to next! You two were outstanding deputies, and now that Iram is delivered from evil…"

"Perhaps I could cope," admitted Jamal, pursing his lips.

"I'll keep an eye on him," confirmed Duban.

Both deputies froze, each drilling the other with a look of pure hatred.

Yes, thought Givi, it looks like everything is going to be well and truly under control. As long as they don't poison one another… They did seem to have managed fine up until we got here though. And from now on their lives are going to be busy and exciting and full of meaning and purpose…

"Then gather everyone, O Jamal! And let the silver trumpets ring out across the whole of Iram, for tonight her people can sleep soundly in their beds. The dark forces are vanquished, the abyss in the Mountains of Darkness is no more, and the end of the world has been postponed indefinitely! So, having executed his mission with honour, their King and Master is heading back to his former domains! If they wish they may scatter our path to the helicopter with rose petals, as a farewell gesture!"

"That thing is the devil's machine," muttered Duban, who had been roaming about the building site all day, not letting go of his astrolabe. "Pah! I wonder, incidentally, where it gets its lifting force. It's not from the propeller, is it?"

"I'll leave you to think about it," said Givi. "And you might also want to think about the fact that steam takes up a greater volume than water... about saltpeter and sulphur... about the curative properties of mould... and what else? Oh, and I sincerely suggest you remember, O Duban, that there is such a thing as a safety-valve!"

"Ekh," sighed Duban, "if only that Tablet really had held all the knowledge in the world! If it had, furthermore, it would not have been coveted with such ardour or had battles fought over it, for it would have been of no interest to anyone! People constantly strive for power and might but set shamefully little store by knowledge!"

"Some say, wrongly I might add, that in actual fact all the knowledge in the world was engraved upon it," remarked Givi. "From which it follows that knowledge is power!"

Duban grew pensive.

"I might write that down!" he said. "It would be a sin not to bequeath such a wise expression to your descendants."

"As you wish," said Givi feeling like something of a plagiarist. "Actually, my advice to you would be to take up your quill, O Astrologer, and record this entire tale for posterity, because otherwise your descendants will almost certainly get the story wrong! Like with that Alexander... I can't believe they mistook a future annihilator for the saviour of the world!"

"The world is still standing," confirmed Duban, "and all thanks to you, O Givi."

"Well," Givi felt a bit embarrassed, "sort of. I can't help thinking, though, that higher forces have been on our side from the very beginning. Who knows, maybe even Raziel himself?"

"Raziel would not have helped just anyone," Duban said sternly. "From which it follows that you, O Givi, are the chosen one after all!"

"Maybe I am, then," agreed Givi. "Cheer up, O Duban! For this story has a happy ending!"

"This one does, yes," the astrologer reluctantly agreed,

"which is a rare thing these days. However, my sorrow is great, for the Throne of Iram will remain empty, ancient legends have been overturned, and you, O Givi, are leaving for lands unknown."

"I am leaving," confirmed Givi, "by desire and with pleasure, though not without sadness."

"But how will you get home, O Givi? For if this world is connected to yours, then I know not where or when."

"The ring brought me here," said Givi, "and the ring will take me back! And, um, Jamal…"

"Your wish is my command, O Master!" Jamal bowed joyously, his whole body radiating his desire to obey.

"Make sure that Misha doesn't take any more than he can carry. I know what he's like!"

> They say that Alexander of Macedonia did indeed make it to the Edge of the World. He conquered the impassable Mountains of Darkness with their abundance of gloomy gorges and deep abysses, which had never before been seen by mortal eyes. Alexander was able to pass through them with the help of the Nubian asses, which are accustomed to the dark and are therefore able to find secret paths. And Alexander armed himself with balls of string, tying the ends at the entrance to the gorges in order to find his path back without hindrance. They say that he did this on the advice of his teacher Aristotle, to whom all the secrets of the world were known.
>
> And so the king overcame the mountains accompanied by a few loyal and daring men. They passed through the dark gorges, wriggling like worms into the heart of the stone. And as dawn began to break in the distance Alexander said to himself that a wonderful reward must await him at the end of such an arduous path – the most beautiful world imaginable would surely appear before him.
>
> However, to his astonishment, he saw nothing but desert – a cheerless plain under a scorching sun. The only movement came from the wind blowing sand from the brown hills.

And then Alexander said:

I thought that having overcome this arduous path my reward would be great, yet all that I have received for my troubles is another path, more arduous than the first!

And Aristotle, who was traveling with him, said: Such is always the way.

And in the distance, under the scorching sun, Alexander saw more mountains rising up at the ends of the earth and he went towards them through the desert and said to himself that he would know neither sleep nor peace until he saw where the World ended.

For he was King!

And day and night he traveled with a few loyal men, under the scorching sun and the enormous stars, and starlit salt lay on the edge of his sword. And finally he reached those faraway mountains, and they rose up before him like a wall, and there was no way into them – no passage, no path, no ravine…

And then Alexander said:

There must be a way through for the King!

And then Aristotle said to him:

Not if you have reached the Edge of the World.

And Alexander stood at the foot of these mountains and decided to dine, but they had exhausted all their supplies while wandering in the desert and all they had left was a single salted fish. And he took that salted fish and turned and saw a spring gushing from the mountains. And that spring smelled delightfully sweet. And so Alexander decided to season the fish with this sweetness and dipped it into the water, whereupon the fish flipped its tail, leapt out of his hands and swam away.

And Alexander exclaimed:

It is a miracle!

And Aristotle said:

There is nothing miraculous about it – it is the river of life, which flows from Paradise itself.

And then Alexander said:

Then I shall have neither sleep nor peace until I reach the gates of Paradise!

And Aristotle said:

Perhaps you will reach them but there your journey will end. For they are closed to beings of flesh and blood. Personally, I prefer to remain here, for it makes good sense from a philosophical point of view.

And to this Alexander said:

I am the King!

And the mountains parted for him, and he followed the stream back to its source and found himself in a wonderful place. A wonderful fragrance was emanating from the gates that stood across this place, and birdsong, and the earth all around the fence was strewn with the petals of wonderful flowers, which fell every night and grew every morning anew. And Alexander knocked on the gates and said:

Open!

And the gates opened and someone wearing a halo came out, and he was majestic and awesome, and he said:

Who knocks at these gates and disturbs the righteous?

And Alexander said:

I am the King! And who are you?

I am the guardian of this place, came the response, and as for kings, well we have as many of them here as there are grains of sand in the desert!

But I am a great king, said Alexander. I am famed far and wide! I am the conqueror of the world, the ruler of the universe!

The universe is ruled not by kings but by wise and righteous men, the Guardian replied. Why are you here when your teacher and adviser remained at the boundary of this world?

And Alexander said:

Wise men consider me to be the descendant of Abraham himself, for Greeks and Jews share common ancestry and furthermore I am Alexander, son of Philip, son of Madrab, son of Hermes, son of the son of Esau, son of Isaac, son of Abraham! That is who I am!

And the Guardian said to him:

We have the sons of Esau here, and the sons of Jacob, and Isaac himself, and Abraham too is here! So it matters not that you are his descendant, for there are too many descendants of Abraham in the world to count. Which is precisely what the Lord promised him! So leave this place, my friend, and do not disturb your forefather. As if there weren't enough of you here already!

And he was about to slam the doors when Alexander exclaimed:

Stop! No one will believe that I have spoken with the Guardian of the Gates himself! Pray give me something as a souvenir!

Fine, said the Guardian, take this and do not turn back until you reach an inhabited place!

And he gave him something and then the gates slammed shut and Alexander found himself alone in the desert.

And he turned back but he lost his way. And he stumbled through the desert unable to find his way and suffering from hunger and thirst. And he thought he may as well see what the Guardian of the Gates gave him before he died, for it was sure to be a great treasure to delight the eyes. And he was about to unwrap the present when he saw an old man in white clothes.

And the old man asked him:

What are you doing here in this wilderness?

And Alexander said:

I come from the very Gates of Paradise!

You have found something to boast about indeed, said the old man, for you are not going there but coming back.

I order you to take me to an inhabited place, said Alexander. For I am the King and my word must be obeyed.

You may be a king in your own kingdom, answered the old man, but this is my kingdom and I do not take orders from anyone. To me you are just a man in the desert tormented by hunger and thirst, and all your power is at my mercy.

In that case I ask you to take me, said Alexander, bowing his head.

Since you ask, then I will gladly take you, said the old man.

And he took Alexander by the hand and led him out of that fateful place and said:

"And now we go our separate ways!"

"Wait," cried Alexander. "Tell me your name that I may know whom to thank! And tell me also, O Wise One, what is this thing that I was given? And can I take it back to my kingdom? Will it do me harm or good?"

"It will do you neither," answered the traveller, "for your kingdom is full of such things. For what you have wrapped up there is a human skull!"

"Just what I needed!" exclaimed Alexander. And he was about to throw this gift away but the old man said to him:

"But when you come to the inhabited place take some scales and place this skull on one side of the scales and on the other side place all the gold and silver that you once had."

"And what then?" asked Alexander.

"You will see," said the old man. "And now farewell, for I have my business and you have yours. My name is Saint Hizr, protector of travellers."

And he disappeared.

And Alexander returned to his camp and told Aristotle what had happened and showed him the skull and said:

"What a tale that Saint Hizr told, may he be blessed for all eternity!"

"Before you draw conclusions you should carry out the experiment," Aristotle said to him. "For that is the scientific method, which I follow rigorously."

And he took that skull and placed it on the scales, and Alexander took a handful of copper coins and placed them on the other side. And the scales remained motionless. And he took a handful of silver and threw it onto the other side. And the scales did not move. And he took a handful of gold and threw it on the other side.

And he said:

"Bring all the gold that there is in our camp!"

And they brought him all the gold, and all the silver, and all the valuables and they threw them onto the scales, and on the other side lay the human skull.

And the skull tipped the scales.

"**S**o tell me," said Givi wearily, "what did you have to bring her for?"

"I've become rather attached to her," explained Shenderovich proudly. "A man can form emotional attachments, can't he?"

"To a camel?"

"For a start, she's not just any camel, she's a she-camel," Shenderovich was offended. "And secondly, she is of the finest breed! Was I supposed to leave her in Iram? They would have worn her out!"

"Worn her out, indeed!"

Givi cast a sidelong glance at Al-Bagum, who was digging her heels in as eight stevedores did their best to drag her down the gangplank. Al-Bagum cast a sidelong glance back at him and spat on the ground. Shenderovich stood with his hands in his pockets anxiously supervising the proceedings.

"I'll have a word with customs, make it worth their while," he muttered under his breath, "and the veterinary authorities… No big deal, it'll be fine! I'll hire her out for breeding! Or not – maybe I'll rent her to the Sheherazade café as part of their entourage! I can see it now, along the low road from Arcadia to Shevchenko Park, in a harness… They'll be queuing round the block! Ten bucks a time!"

"Misha, give it a rest!"

"What? I think it's a great idea. You can come in with me on it, if you like. Hey, what's that? I don't remember that being there when we left. Why did they have to go and put up a bloody great pyramid like that?"

"It's a hotel," explained a stevedore wiping his bald patch with his sleeve and simultaneously dodging one of Al-Bagum's massive hooves. "It went up virtually overnight. And right here in the port! I don't know how he managed to get away with it…"

"I don't suppose he wants a camel?" Shenderovich became animated. "A bit of authentic exoticism?"

"What would he want with your camel?" the stevedore shrugged. "They say he's got a whole zoo in there. With a crocodile and all! And an orangery, and a casino with a fountain…"

"Sounds like quite a player," said Shenderovich with respect. "What's his name?"

"Lysyuk, or something," the stevedore shrugged.

Shenderovich blanched.

Givi tactfully turned away.

"Mishenka," a voice rang out. "Mishenka! Look who it is! Yannis! My little Yannis!"

"Varvara Timofeevna!" Givi greeted her enthusiastically. "I didn't expect to see you here! What are you doing here?"

"I'm meeting Yurochka! He's a navigator now – after you disappeared they demoted him temporarily, but he's still a valued member of the crew! Allochka, how well you look! And we were so worried, so worried! We feared that you had been kidnapped and taken off to a harem."

"She was kidnapped," sighed Givi. "And you're not looking so bad yourself, Varvara Timofeevna!"

It was true, Varvara Timofeevna had blossomed like a late summer rose – she was wearing patent leather sandals and a striking blouse, and her plump shapely legs were wrapped in an alluringly figure-hugging skirt. The delicate strap of a little handbag was thrown over her shoulder, her plump cheeks glowed with dimples and her eyes were shining beneath their carefully made-up lashes.

"Oh don't, Yannis dear," she sighed. "I've had a terrible

time of it of late. You see, I buried my poor mother just recently – straight after I left, would you believe it, she went and died! God rest her soul… Yurochka has been such a support to me, such a support! We sold Mother's house and bought a little apartment in a good part of town, you know Mishenka, on Sadovaya. It needed a bit of work but Yurochka did it all himself, he can do anything with his hands… But just lately he's been having a bit of trouble with his heart…"

She broke off suddenly, raised her head and listened.

"Va-arvara," came the cry from somewhere above them. "Va-arvara, my love!"

"Oh!" Varvara was delighted. "There's Yurochka now! I'm coming! I'm coming!"

She blew a kiss to the travellers and, heels clacking, ran along the wooden walkway to where a small colourful boat was moored.

"Like mother, like daughter," Givi reflected.

"You reckon?" asked Shenderovich.

"Time will tell," answered Givi.

He looked around sadly. No one was there to meet them. Al-Bagum had finally deigned to step onto solid ground and was now standing and looking round contemptuously. The wind was whipping the white horses from the crests of the waves and flinging them at Al-Bagum who curled her lip in displeasure. Seagulls were squawking over the pier.

Ekh, thought Givi, so the miracles are over! Someone needed us so badly that they were prepared to spy on us, to hunt us down! Azazel… Just think, Azazel himself! He travelled through space and time, tracked down Misha and led him to the Black Stone! I wonder who it was sitting with me in that dungeon then… Raziel? Or maybe Shemhazai himself? Either way, no one will ever believe me. And then there's the ring! I wonder who gave it to me that?

"Young man," said a voice. "Could I borrow you for a moment?"

Givi looked round. A sad-looking old Jew was sitting on a battered suitcase. The suitcase had been tied around the middle with a linen cord for safety.

"Are you talking to me?" asked Givi.

"Yes, you. Would you be so kind as to give me a hand with this suitcase?"

"Where do you want it?" asked Givi obediently.

"The exit, of course," said the old man in surprise. "Or rather, the entrance. Customs is over there, isn't it?"

"I think so," agreed Givi wearily.

It felt quite strange to be back on dry land again… he was finding it hard to keep his balance. He glanced at Shenderovich, who was fully occupied with Al-Bagum. Tufts of fur were bristling on her flanks where she'd started moulting from the stress.

"God bless you and keep you healthy," murmured the old man as he skipped along after Givi. "You are so strong! And polite! Such a rare thing these days, a polite young man!"

Givi straightened his shoulders.

"Everyone's always rushing everywhere," chattered the old man as they walked. "And for what? They should sit and relax a bit! But no, rush, rush, rush! What are they all chasing after?"

"Happiness, probably," said Givi.

"Happiness, young man, is not a function of location," retorted the old man. "And I should know. Just here, please."

Givi put the suitcase down carefully.

"What is the point of wasting all that energy?" murmured the old man. "You always end up right back where you started. See, like you did! With that young man and the girl, if I am not mistaken?"

He looked Alka's slender figure pointedly up and down. She was saying something to Shenderovich and stamping her foot.

"She is beautiful," he said respectfully. "And as formidable as an army marching into battle! Are you sure that you two are suited?"

"I'm starting to wonder," Givi answered wistfully.

"Alas! The world is full of great mysteries and revelations but man allows his head to be turned from them all by one slender hand! Well, good luck!"

Givi held out his hand and the old man seized it in a bird-like claw covered in brown age spots.

"The ring, if you don't mind," said the old man.

Givi looked at him in astonishment. The old man was wearing old-fashioned sandals with holes in them and trousers that ballooned at the knees.

"You won't need it any more, I promise you," said the old man.

"I believe you!" Givi concurred.

"So you may give it back!"

Givi pulled the signet ring from his finger. It slipped off easily, as if it had suddenly grown.

"Wonderful," cooed the old man as he placed the ring on his own gout-ridden finger. "Now it's time I was going… And, by the way, Alexander of Macedonia wasn't the only one with an impressive harem. He himself was descended from someone, I assure you."

"We are all descended from someone," agreed Givi.

"Each and every one of us," nodded the old man. "But we cannot all count amongst our ancestors King Solomon, possessor of the ring, commander of the djinns. Anyway, I really must be going, young man."

He nodded to him, straightened his shapeless hat, effortlessly picked up his suitcase and headed into the belly of the customs building where a tower of possessions sat waiting, including a small cage with rusty bars. The cage contained a multicoloured bird, which was cleaning its feathers with its beak. The old man took the cage in one hand and the suitcase in the other and bustled off somewhere.

Givi stood watching him go, his mouth agape.

"Hey, my friend, what's up?" Shenderovich's voice rang out behind him.

"Nothing," said Givi.

"Let's go, we're all sorted. Turns out one of my old classmates works in there! They're letting her through without quarantine. Can you imagine what all the neighbours are going to say when I turn up on a white camel, eh?"

"I think I've got a fairly good idea," said Givi.

"He says that that scumbag Lysyuk was banged up, can you believe it? And it wasn't a short sentence either… But then they let him out! He bribed his way out, or something… Anyway, now he's back to his old tricks, wheeling and dealing – unbelievable! But I'll have the last laugh! You know," Shenderovich leaned towards Givi and whispered in his ear, "that bloke in customs says that the latest thing is samurai swords … Fake ones, obviously… Basically, any kind of martial arts gear. Shaolin bamboo staffs, that kind of thing… So all we need to do is buy up a load off our mates in China, then he can sell them on for us! Eh, what do you say?"

"I say no way," said Givi firmly.

"I'll find a way to buy that hotel off him," Shenderovich muttered through clenched teeth.

"You're the King!" Givi reminded him. "What about all those beautiful things you brought back from Iram?"

"They're not enough. I've got all that money to pay back before they come looking for me! Stupid mangy camel… just getting her here cost a fortune! And that Vitka, the bastard, he could have let me off a bit for old times' sake … And second-class tickets, those fake passports… It all adds up! Anyway, my friend, let's go! Shenderovich would never dream of abandoning his fellow throne-mate at the port! I'll give you a lift. Come on, my beauty!"

Alka looked up, but Shenderovich was talking to Al-Bagum.

"You mean we're going by camel?" asked Givi with horror.

"What, you want me to take her in a taxi?" Shenderovich was outraged. "She'll never fit!"

"No," said Givi. "I've got to call in at the office. I need to send a telegram to Mother. Otherwise she'll worry. She was almost hysterical when I called from Tel Aviv!"

"Well come round this evening, then!" Shenderovich declared happily. "Number ten Kanatnaya. Just ask for Shenderovich, someone will point you in the right direction. Everyone knows Shenderovich!"

"I'm sure they do," said Givi. "Goodbye, Misha."

"See you later, then."

"See you later," agreed Givi. "Goodbye, Alla."

Alka held out her cool white hand.

"You're leaving, then," she mused.

"That's up to my boss," Givi answered cautiously.

"You know," said Alka, appraising him pensively, "I had an idea... There's not much keeping me here in Odessa. I've had a good time here but that's about it. It's just a bit too, you know, provincial... I mean, it's nice enough, but there's no work. And I need to write my dissertation."

"Yes, that's a thought," Givi said cautiously.

"So I was thinking, maybe I could come to St. Petersburg with you? You could introduce me to your Mum..."

Givi pictured Alka clapping his flabbergasted mother cordially on the shoulder and grimaced.

"To be honest, I've had enough of this heat," Alka was saying as she gently took his arm and turned to face the cool sea breeze. "And you've got a good school of Semitology up there, run by the son of Professor Zebbov! Where do you live, in a communal apartment?"

"Yep," said Givi.

"And where does your Mum live?"

"She lives in a communal apartment too. A different one though, with her sister."

"And how many rooms have they got?"

"Two."

"So, we can move in with her and her sister can have your room. What's her name, by the way?"

"Natella," said Givi gloomily.

"We'll get Aunt Natella settled, I'll sell my place down here, or maybe not... I'll hang on to it and we can come down here for the summer... And rent it out during the winter... And your Mum can live with us, it's not right for an elderly lady to be on her own. You'll see, it'll all work out just fine!"

"Ekh!" said Givi.

"Hey, you two, are you coming?" Shenderovich sat proudly erect on Al-Bagum. "See that bloke over there? I bet him a hundred bucks that I'll ride her down the Odessa Steps! You can be my witnesses!"

"Yeah, because you're as mighty as the Battleship Potemkin, aren't you," scoffed Alka. "The Emir of Bukhara!"

"A hundred bucks! Givi, did you hear me! He shook on it!"

"Yes," said Givi, "I heard you alright."

AFTERWORD

When I was looking for ideas for a new novel, my good friend (and specialist in all things Jewish) Leonid Dreyer suggested I write a contemporary version of Sindbad the Sailor – as he put it, 'the original shuttle trader.' For anyone unfamiliar with the realities of contemporary Russian life, let me explain: a 'shuttle trader' is someone who picks up stock abroad, usually in China or Turkey, brings it home, sells it and uses the proceeds to go back for more. In the post-Soviet era, a fair number of people made a living out of this kind of trading. "And," added Leonid, "you should write it in the style of *The Arabian Nights*."

The first task was to create my leading men. As I spent many happy years living in Odessa, it was an easy decision to make my main character a native of that city, with a typically Odessan personality: enthusiastic and full of the joys of life, though tragically hapless... but his energy and zest for life would be so great that they would render his haplessness somehow irrelevant, at least to the reader. The straight man in this double act would also be no stranger to misfortune, but I wanted him to be kind, modest and sincere.

Once I'd decided on my main characters the mysterious process of plot development began, almost of its own accord. For instance, the Odessan immediately acquired the name Shenderovich. Shender (Sender) is the Jewish form of Alexander. Thus, by extension Shenderovich means 'descended from Alexander,' which of course turns out to have great bearing on events. I must admit, I honestly couldn't tell you why the other half of this double act ended up being Georgian, and specifically a Georgian from St. Petersburg. I suppose St. Petersburg (Leningrad) has always had a kind of special relationship with Odessa... But why is he Georgian? I have no idea! The Georgian names most familiar to Russians are Givi, Giya and Goga, so once his cultural identity was decided Givi virtually named himself. And this name turned out to be uncannily appropriate, as my subsequent research revealed that the giant descendants of the fallen angel Shemhazai (Hiwa and Hiya) were also known as Givi and Giya. Such incredible coincidences make you feel that some things are just meant to be. Thus, the novel acquired its working title *Givi and Shenderovich*, under which title it was published in Russian. I didn't think twice about where to send my hapless heroes – across the Black Sea and the Bosphorus to Istanbul, following the route favoured by every 'shuttle trader' from Odessa before them – and I knew I wanted them trading in something ephemeral like inflatable balloons... But what next? What escapades and encounters were to be had? I cast my net wide and read voraciously, devouring in the course of my research over fifty different titles, some more specialist than others: from the ancient Apocrypha to contemporary guidebooks, I left no stone unturned. One area that my research led me to was the practice of magic. 'Master' Therion and Frater Perdurabo, whom Givi and Shenderovich meet at the very start of their adventures, are an overt parody on the English occultist Aleister Crowley and the pomposity, arrogance and crudeness of his particular variety of magical practice. However, as I immersed myself in Crowley's biography I became increasingly aware that the fate of every famous magus seemed to follow the same very simple path – first estrangement from family and friends, then connections in high society and the promise of power and glory, then exposure, dungeon, poverty and ultimately ignoble death. Why shouldn't I take this observation a step further and suggest that all famous magi were in actual fact one and the same individual? Master Therion presents this idea to the reader by recounting his former incarnations, each of which had ended identically – in complete failure.

It was through the works of Aleister Crowley that I learnt about Iram, the eastern Atlantis – a forbidden city, destroyed by djinni when its inhabitants came too close to understanding the mysteries of life. My studies of Arabic mythology introduced me to The People in the Well and Yajuj and Majuj (Gog and Magog), and within the Aggadic texts of the Talmud I discovered the reasons for the Flood and learnt about King Solomon's Throne and the Book (Tablet) of Raziel, where all earthly knowledge was supposedly recorded. I also learnt that the Hellenic, Muslim and Jewish worlds are linked by one immensely powerful individual – Alexander of Macedonia.

At this point I knew I had all the material I needed to write my novel.

My Iram became the City of Cities, the City at the Centre of the World, where even the slightest event could have far-reaching consequences (hence the English title); this Iram is isolated from the outside world due to the proximity of a great abyss wherein the terrible Gog and Magog are awaiting their freedom and the end of the world. The Tablet of Raziel became the Stele, a kind of 'instruction manual' that could be used to release them. Legend has it that Alexander attempted to protect the world from Gog and Magog by imprisoning them in the abyss, but my Alexander attempts instead to use the Stele to release them, hoping thereby to create an invincible army. I couldn't help feeling that this would be more in keeping with the behaviour of a tyrannical conqueror.

The essence of the novel is the eternal confrontation between two kings – one a creator (Solomon, whose legend is universally respected) and the other a destroyer (Alexander). My heroes are simply their latest incarnations, which is of course where the name Shenderovich ('descendant of Alexander') turns out to be particularly opportune. The novel explores the intoxicating and corrupting effects of power, but it is also about how the ordinary dreams of an ordinary man can act as a powerful antidote to dangerous temptations.

In order to avoid overwhelming the reader with the diversity of Eastern mythology – from Jerusalem to Istanbul – I have chosen to present this content in the form of inserted novellas, which (I hope) serve to illustrate the narrative. These novellas are my personal interpretation and stylisation of Aggadic, Sufic and other parables and legends.

When the legends and traditions of the Hellenic, Jewish and Arab worlds are woven together, they combine to form an integral picture of the world revolving around the two kings, Solomon and Alexander. This cosmogony is home to a Throne and an Abyss, to fallen angels and their monstrous descendents, to the mystical Book of Raziel and even to a herd of Nubian asses... Only Christianity is notable by its absence: the invented world proved to be too hermetic and the boundaries of cyclical time too rigidly observed (whereas I believe that one of the fundamental elements of Christianity, by contrast, is its openness), although some allusion is made to the notion of redemption by the enigmatic Sheikh (actually Solomon, travelling through time and space). This singular cosmogony was created for a reason and exists nowhere outside the pages of this novel, of course... but that was all I wished for, and I could not hope for more.

Maria Galina